LAGUNA

A Novel

by

Michael Putegnat

Laguna
Published by Synergy Books
2100 Kramer Lane, Suite 300
Austin, Texas 78758

For more information about our books, please write to us or call 512.478.2028, or visit our website at www.bookpros.com.

Printed in China. All rights reserved. No part of this book may be reproduced in any form or by any electronic or mechanical means including information storage and retrieval systems without permission in writing from the copyright holder, except by a reviewer, who may quote brief passages in review.

This book is a work of fiction. Names, characters, places, and incidents either are the product of the author's imagination or are used fictitiously. Any resemblance to actual persons, living or dead, events, organizations, or locales is entirely coincidental.

ISBN-13: 978-1-933538-19-8 (hc)
ISBN-10: 1-933538-19-8 (hc)

Copyright© 2006 by Michael Putegnat

Publisher's Cataloging-in-Publication (Provided by Quality Books, Inc.)

    Putegnat, Michael.
      Laguna : a novel / by Michael Putegnat.
      p. cm.
      LCCN 2005934047
      ISBN 1-933538-19-8 (hc)
      ISBN 1-933538-21-X (pbk)

      1. Family--Fiction. 2. Texas, South--Fiction.
      3. Mystery fiction.   I. Title.

PS3616.U L34 2006   813'.6
                                QBI05-700371

10 9 8 7 6 5 4 3 2 1

For my father and mother.

Chapter 1

A SNOWY EGRET WADED through the tidal pools hunting for stranded minnows. Easy pickings. In the blink of its eye, a swoosh, a squeal, a spray of blood and feathers, and the egret felt the Peregrine Falcon's cold, stiletto-like talons tearing through its flesh.

One moment predator, another moment prey, Octavio Paredes thought as he watched the falcon carry away the bird. He cast his fishing line where moments ago he had seen the water ripple, and considered the nature of justice.

His hands were the texture of well-tanned leather and his face marked with deep lines that came from a lifetime of squinting against the persistent Texas sun. A steady easterly breeze carried the scent of salt grass as it swept across the barrier island and onto the long shallow bay called the Laguna Madre. A wind other than southeast made Octavio uneasy and he warily scanned the horizon for any hint of trouble. It was November 2, and the weather was about to change.

Winter came to the Texas coast with a vengeance. Great blue northers, as the locals called them, charged in like an invading army, instantly turning warm peace and calm into torrential rains hurled by howling winds, punctuated by exploding thunder and blinding bolts of lightning.

The sun had just set and he felt oddly unsettled as he stared across the Laguna to the gray silhouette of the gangly legged water tower, which is all anyone can see of Port Mansfield from a distance. The falcon perched on a nearby channel marker, pulling strands of flesh with its hooked beak, watching Octavio as Octavio watched him.

A century and a half ago, most of the land from where he sat in his second-hand fishing skiff to one hundred miles inland, belonged to his family. That was before the *Anglos* came. It was their land now, he told himself with a slight shrug, and anyway, it was a long time ago.

When it was dark, and no one could see where he was going, he would pull in his line and coax his old Evinrude to cough then purr its way across the Laguna to his favorite secret spot by the old rotted pilings of the dilapidated Magne Ranch Landing, about four miles north. When he was a boy of fifteen some sixty years ago, he used to go with his father who worked as a vaquero on the Magne Ranch. They herded the cattle to the dock and loaded them on the barges. There must have been thousands of head in those days. The docks had been washed out in a hurricane a few years back and never repaired. There was no point. Cattle were not shipping out like that any more. That was then.

For now, he'd wait just a little longer until it was a bit darker. He would fish all Friday night as he often did. By the time he got back to the house late Saturday morning, Anajita would already be gone, out junk collecting with Ocky. He'd make himself some *huevos rancheros*, read the paper and take a nap until she came home in the early afternoon.

When the sun set, the sky was washed with broad wild strokes of orange, red and purple against swatches of sky in blues and greens. It was so still that the only ripples were those that trailed behind Octavio's skiff as it glided across the sky reflected in the Laguna. A full moon loomed just below the deep purple eastern horizon.

At the same time, a mile west, Jason Grider, hands in the pockets of his khakis, leaned against a white-washed 4x4 column on the porch of the Port Office, staring out to the distant barrier island. His brother, Jack, would have said it was hard to tell Jason from the column, given that both were long and lanky and tended to stay in the same place. A perennial tan didn't fully hide the peaches and cream complexion that made him look younger than his forty-one years, an impression helped by his sandy colored hair that he kept short cropped, but not mowed.

He could see a piece of the eastern horizon beginning to glow. In a moment the moon would breach the horizon and send its rays dancing on the water until it painted a golden path from the heavens to Port Mansfield, the kind angels might use on occasion. The air had gone dead still. It smelled like a wet dog, Jason thought, but one you cared about. He was lost in a dreamy gaze and time passed over him unnoticed, as it often did for the few souls who passed small and quiet lives in the sleepy backwaters of the southern Texas Gulf coast.

Jason was startled by something sounding like a muffled pop. He instinctively turned to his left, northward, where a few sailboats were berthed in the marina. He wondered if it was a loose halyard slapping its metal mast. In a storm they sounded like off-key wind chimes, but there was no wind now. Then he raised his eyes to the northern horizon and out into what was now pitch blackness. He cocked his head and held his breath to be completely quiet.

Nothing.

Then, in the bubbles of a distant thunderhead he saw the flash of rose and yellow veins.

Jason was Sergeant of the Watch at the Port Mansfield Port Office police station and the Sergeant of the Watch was also the night janitor. He liked the night shift; it suited him. He could get the place cleaned up in an hour or less and have the night to listen to those wee hour radio talk shows, the ones with the psychics and people who'd been abducted by aliens: crazies, he called them.

The norther would be there in a matter of hours, making another dull Friday night in Port Mansfield. The locals would be hunkered down for the storm passage and there would be no out of town visitors to stop by the office seeking directions. Another night of nothing.

It wasn't that Port Mansfield was hard to find. There were only two kinds of folks on the forty-mile road that ran from the interstate: those who sought its dead end on purpose and those who were lost. Sometimes a little of both.

From spring to late summer sports fishermen would come from towns inland to try their luck in the shallow Laguna Madre, behind the protection of the long and narrow Padre Island. There were a few town people, and lately, some older folks were discovering the cheap land and quiet. These made enough trade for a small general store and a restaurant, and not much more.

Twenty-five years ago, there had been visions of a port for shipments of cattle and produce from the vast ranchlands that stretched inland for millions of acres. But like the post war National Geographic Magazines, with pictures of cowboys herding cattle and young lasses posing with giant grapefruit, those plans were finally stacked away and forgotten.

Port Mansfield, without ever having any, had seen its better days. Jason liked that just fine.

But he'd had a bad feeling since August. Strangers were showing up more often, wearing suits and carrying briefcases. They weren't interested in the fishing, and they sure as hell weren't lost.

Maybe it was the change in the weather, the coming winter prying open the death grip of the merciless Texas summer, Jason wasn't sure, but something odd was going on and he didn't like it.

Chapter 2

TUESDAY, THREE DAYS earlier, John Magne IV, sat in his grandfather's chair, staring out of the huge picture window. His late wife, Francie, had tried on at least three occasions to have the old ox-blood red leather redone, but John resisted. The worn and wrinkled texture and the smell of it, was like an old, favorite saddle. It was a long relationship where one grows into the other.

She'd tried to convince John to refinish the desk too. The leather inset on the top had lost most of its tooling on the near edge and there were places where the rosewood was worn into by that odd Magne way of constantly swinging a crossed leg like the pendulum of a hall clock. To John, the dents and dings were verbs in a venerable ancestral saga. The Magnes tended to think like that.

Francie was gone, but not the chair, not the desk.

In his outer office, Patricia Wilson, his secretary of fifteen years, cradled the phone in the crook of her neck, wondering if she ought to disturb him with the call. For a moment she stared at his portrait across the room above the fireplace. Francie had commissioned it. How much, at sixty-three, John Magne looked like a maturing John Wayne, she thought. Both had a kind of rustic elegance.

"Mr. Magne?" the voice poured out of the intercom box.

"Yes, Pat," John Magne responded, swinging his chair around to the desk.

"Congressman Monde on line two."

"Thanks, Pat, I'll take it." He pressed the button, "Lencho, good of you to return my call."

"I called as soon as I saw the message, John. Always good to talk to you. What can I do for you?"

"Lencho, Gabriela and I want to take you and Eva to dinner next Monday night when we're in D.C. Can you make it?"

"Mario told me you were coming, John, and we're all clear for Monday. Say around eight?"

"Perfect, Lencho, we'll pick you guys up at the house."

"Fine."

"See you then, bye," John returned the receiver to the cradle and stared at it for a moment.

"Pat," he called out.

"Yes, Mr. Magne," she responded from the office doorway.

"Pat, call Quinkaid's and make reservations for four on Monday night at, say, nine. If they give you any trouble, ask for Benjamin and tell him it's me. He'll take care of you."

"Yes, sir," she said, jotting on her note pad.

"Oh, and Pat....Send Mrs. Monde some of those long stemmed pink roses…She likes those…For, say, Friday. Got that?"

"Yes, sir, flowers Friday, Quinkaid's Monday, November 5," she said as she scurried out of the room.

John Magne leaned back into his chair and swung it slowly around so he could see out of the floor-to-ceiling glass wall that framed a nearly endless vista of his ranchlands. His father had this scene laid out to replicate the savannahs of the Argentine property the family had acquired during the twenties. It was compensation from Presidente Albrego, who owed John's grandfather a favor for the U.S.'s help taking down the Machado government and bringing him to power. It was the way the Magnes did business. They made the world to their image and liking.

Stands of oaks, stretching long arms and gnarly fingers with whole handfuls of deep green leaves, cordoned the edge of the grassy plain. While most hunters settled for glass eyed stuffed heads staring from their perches on paneled walls, John Magne preferred the real and living thing. Before him grazed Nilgai, a few Zebras and even a pair of giraffes he had brought in from Africa. The view from his office could just as easily have been from a camp in the Congo as it could Argentina, yet it was Texas.

On a knoll that rose barely above the coastal plain, the original ranch house, begun by his great grandfather as modest shelter for his family, had been added to and modified to meet practical needs.

Then, Magne's grandfather built the new main house, or, as it came to be called, *Casa Blanca,* directly in front of the old one, bringing in architects from California and craftsmen from New England. What emerged was a grand mansion based upon Southwestern, Spanish, and Italian architectural styles. Whitewashed brick and plaster walls began at the ground and rose twelve steps to the entry level of the house where an arched arcade wrapped around the structure. The house then rose two more stories and was capped with a red tile roof. In the center of the front of *Casa Blanca,* a tower rose another two stories above the roof line.

It was from this vantage the Magne men gathered on New Year's Eve to drink whisky and cast grand plans as they surveyed their world. It was the Kingdom of Magne, built by all means and passed down through the generations.

The scale of the house made it the largest element of the landscape, easily dwarfing cowering oak and mesquite trees and thickets that were held at a distance from the outer perimeter of the grounds. Washingtonian palm trees stood tall around the perimeter of the house like sentinels. The mansion amazed and intimidated those locals who were fortunate enough to penetrate the nine miles into the ranch to ever see it.

Above the massive fireplace in the library of the Main House, a huge carved black marble falcon was poised to pounce on its prey. Its talons grasped a long scroll inscribed with the Magne family motto: *Porro, omni modo*, "Forward, by all means."

"By all means." It took that kind of persistence and sacrifice to build and hold this ranch of just under 1,000,000 acres on the land that once upon a time even God forgot, bounded by the Gulf of Mexico to the east, Mexico to the west and south and the Nueces River to the north. Farms in the U.S. averaged 500 acres. The Magne Ranch was bigger than Rhode Island. Texas may have joined the Union in 1845, but the Magnes always thought of their land as a separate country: independent and self-reliant.

As he gazed across the stretching sea of grass, shadows of drifting clouds dappled the light in countless hues of yellow and gold. He was the fourth John Magne to rule over these lands. He rested his chin in hand, furrowed his brow and worried that he'd be the last.

Chapter 3

TUESDAY EVENING, JASON'S older brother, Jack, wallowed in his scruffy robe and his duct tape-patched Barcalounger, waiting for relief that only came with brief dozing.

It had been a month since he slammed the door and stormed out of the office. "It," was his famous last word, but it was the penultimate one that sealed the deal. Now poverty competed head to head with his depression. In another month, he'd be practically homeless, he thought. But that was self-pity and melodrama and he knew it, which made him feel worse.

It wasn't the usual swoon into his periodic depressions; it was the freefall into the abyss. Again, that dismal inventory of stupid things said, done, missed…again that gut wrenching guilt. If somehow he could just turn it off.

Drink, drugs, death: the unhappy trinity of options. But none of these held much allure. Too much alcohol made him nauseous, drugs meant needles and he had always been afraid of those and death was just too much of a commitment.

He pressed the remote: talking head, smoldering car frame, wailing mother. Deja vu. He drifted into a daze, mesmerized by the patterns on the screen.

The sudden ring of the phone startled him. He didn't want to talk to anyone, but it persisted.

"Damn it," he shouted into the mouthpiece.

"Jack?" It was his sister, Joan.

"Yeah."

"What are you doing home on a Tuesday?"

"What do you want?"

"Your office said you didn't work there anymore. What happened?"

"Quit."

"Quit? Why?" she asked, surprised.

"I couldn't stand it anymore, that's why."

There was a pause, then, "Are you all right, Jack?"

"Oh, I'm fine."

"You don't sound fine. You sound sick or something."

"I'm fine, I'm fine," he protested weakly.

After a pause, "I'm coming over," she said with concern in her voice.

"No, don't, uh, I'm just about to go out."

"I don't believe you. You're lying."

"No, I'm not, honestly, I'm going to an interview and running late. I'll call you tomorrow," he said quickly and hung up.

It would take an hour for him to calm down. He flicked the TV on again. He must have dozed, because when he blinked his eyes open again, he wasn't sure if it was day or night. The room was dark before, but now the walls flickered in a soft green light. Gradually the sound of the TV seeped into his consciousness, a meaningless garble of voices and music. He fumbled for the remote and switched it off and the room went completely dark and silent. All he could hear was the distant bark of someone's dog. He drifted back into sleep.

The banging in his head grew louder until it woke him.

"Jack!" a voice was insisting from the front door.

"Jack, open up, it's Joan!"

"Dammit!"

More banging on the door. She wasn't going away. He swung his legs around and put his feet on the floor. He tried to collect himself enough to get up but when he did, his head felt light and faint. He stumbled toward the door and opened it.

"What!" he growled.

She pushed past him and into the room. "Interview, my ass," she shouted. "You haven't moved from here in a month. What the hell is going on?"

He gave out a low groan and staggered back to his Barcalounger. "Leave me alone," he protested.

"Leave you alone," she echoed with a disapproving tone. "To do what exactly?"

"Oh, for Christ's sake, Joan," he answered as he flopped down into the chair.

"This place looks like a garbage dump," she said, surveying the strewn trash: pizza boxes, beer cans, magazines. "What's going on with you?" she demanded.

"Nothing," he replied. "I'm just resting between things."

"Resting. Right. And just how long do you intend to be 'resting'?"

"It's no skin off your nose, Joan, so why do you even bother me?"

She looked around the room for a clear place to sit down. She swept some newspapers off an ottoman and sat, then looked straight at him.

"Jack, you can't go on like this."

He stared straight ahead in a stupor.

Joan felt a sinking in her chest to see her older brother in such a state. He was supposed to be the successful one, the one everybody admired and wanted to be with, the hope of the whole family. If he crashed, what did it say about them, she thought. She looked down at the floor and a long time passed between them.

"I'm going to fix something for us to eat," she said at last, rising to her feet.

"I'm not hungry," he said.

"Well, I am," she declared as she walked toward the kitchenette next to the room. She opened the refrigerator to find a lone carton of vintage milk, a rotten apple and some dried out slices of cheese. "This all you got?" she asked.

"No," he sneered, "I keep the meat in the bathroom."

"You are a mess, brother," she said.

"Tell me," he agreed.

"Well, get dressed, we'll go get a Subway."

"I don't want to go anywhere. What the hell time is it, anyway?"

She looked over to an old mantle clock. The pendulum was dead still. "Well, looks to me to be about November. You're going to get up, put on some pants, a T-shirt, some loafers and we're going to get a sandwich or I'm going to drag your ass out to the car just like that," she threatened.

He sighed deeply. "Ok, ok, hold your horses." He slowly rose, weaved a little and made his way to his bedroom.

Joan idly scanned the walls of the room as she waited. There were no pictures hanging, but on the floor below, frames leaned against the wall. She couldn't tell if he was putting them up or taking them down, but knowing him as well as she did, she suspected he hadn't decided. There were seven pictures like that, all of them sailboats.

On a shelf were a few frames with pictures of people she didn't know, except the one of Jack with his friend Saul in their graduation robes at Harvard in '95. Her brother hadn't seemed to change a bit in the six years since: still the stormy eyes, furrowed brow, tussled brown hair; but now there was early salty grey around the edges. He wasn't as tall as their brother Jason but he was nearly as thin. In fact, the way Jack stood, leaning a bit to the right, his head up and alert, he reminded her of a Great Blue Heron. And that long distance gaze. He seemed perpetually lost in thought.

She realized how little she really knew about her brother's

life. What she did know were essentially "resume" facts. He went to work computer programming the day after he graduated from Texas A&M in '80, a fact he liked to boast about. "Next day," he'd say. "Not even a weekend off." He was like that, always deep in his work, and usually alone in it.

Three years later he joined a small trucking company. She didn't know what it was he did there, but she recalled it had something to do with accounting. Anyway, somehow he ended up running the place then bought out the owner. A few years later, after buying up some other small companies and organizing them under some sort of software system he'd developed, he sold the whole thing to a big national company who wanted to get hold of the systems and get rid of Jack, who was becoming a real threat. He never talked much about it. He must have gotten some money because he bought a boat, took a year off and traveled around, if modestly. Then, six years ago, he went back to grad school, mostly working out of Woods Hole, at the neck of Cape Cod, and got his masters in marine biology. That's how he connected with U.S. Fish & Wildlife Department, doing systems analysis in a field office just outside Weslaco, Texas.

Jack came back into the room now dressed.

"Well, if we're going to do this thing, let's do it," he said.

Chapter 4

"SOPHIA LOUISE POOLE," she read the picture caption out loud to herself as she smoothed the dog-eared page 54 of the 1943 Port Isabel High School yearbook. No one ever called her Sophia, though. For as long as she could remember, her father called her "Sophie L," which he pronounced as one word: "Sophiel". Somehow that became "Sophie" among her friends and it stuck.

She sighed to see the fresh, innocent, yet unfamiliar face smiling back at her, barely eighteen at the time. She remembered thinking of her grandmother as old and how it seemed to young people that old people had always been that way. They were born old and young people were born young. Of course she got it now. But knowing and getting it are not the same thing. Her high school annual photograph still mystified her.

She looked up to the picture of her mother above the hallway table just in front of her. The way the light came through the window in the autumn lit her face, and that reflection is what she saw in the glass covering her mother's image, but as she focused she could see more of her mother's face bleeding through. She was struck with how alike they looked once, but how much younger her mother looked to her now. She had died at sixty-five. Sophie was ten years older than that now.

She looked back down to the annual and scanned the

pictures of her classmates. The pictures were arranged alphabetically, so all the Ps were together, leaving the false impression that this was a group of close friends forever captured here as they usually assembled. Most of the other Ps were nothing much to her, but there were a few special friends.

Amelia Perez, one of her dearest and most treasured friends, married a Pan Am pilot a few years after graduation and moved away. She never heard from her again. She wondered how her life had turned out.

Ester Ponder and Sophie had been girl scouts together and had been tent mates at summer camp twice. They would spend hours dreaming about who they'd marry and how many children they would have. Ester was sweet and delicate, very beautiful. It broke Sophie's heart when she heard that Ester had been killed in a skiing accident while she was away at college. The two of them had grown up in a place where it never snowed. It seemed ironic to Sophie that a girl who grew up with sand between her toes would die in snow. It said a lot about the surprises life could bring, she thought.

Then there was Roquelle Paredes, "Rocky." They were inseparable. Nearly everyday, Rocky and Sophie would walk home from school together, and on most days did their homework on the front porch of the Poole's house. Sophie's mother would bring out chocolate chip cookies and tall glasses of cold milk. They'd study some, chat some more and would carry on until Sophie's father came home from the furniture store. Rocky would go home then.

Sometimes Sophie would go to Rocky's house for a birthday party or to work on some school project. She was never allowed to sleep over.

Sophie's finger traced a line across the page of the annual to Rocky's picture and paused to look at it. Then she slid it over one to Rocky's twin brother. He was cute and funny. And maybe only Rocky knew that Sophie had always loved him. She knew it from the first time she had seen him when they were in the first grade. Octavio.

Then there was that night when they were both sophomores. She could still recall the bitter taste in her mouth from her streaming tears and saliva, thickened by her crying. Octavio had asked Sophie to the Halloween Dance at the high school gym. Her mother's best efforts to intervene on her behalf did nothing to assuage her father's fury over it. Those were different times, she remembered. She couldn't understand any of it then. Octavio never again asked her out and she found herself avoiding him thereafter. She never again went to Rocky's house.

She closed the yearbook and placed it back in the hallway table drawer. It was no longer fun to look at it.

On her way to the kitchen to make some tea, Sophie only unconsciously glanced at the three picture frames on the old grand piano in the living room. There her mother and father posed in separate photographs with identical frames, arranged so that they were slightly turned towards one another.

A newer frame held a picture of her only daughter, Angela, who lived in Boston and worked across the river at M.I.T. This was her human family, she would often joke to visitors. "My real family is over there," as she pointed to a wall of shelves loaded with photographs of what looked like scores of animals.

Each frame was either silver or bronze, complete with engraved nameplates for each. Noble, Amadeus, Romulus, Nordyke, and George were a few of them. Dogs, cats, a raccoon, and even an opossum. On another set of shelves across the room were hundreds of books on animals, from zoological texts to novels. Her favorite had always been *The Call of the Wild*.

On the wall in the entry hall was an arrangement of photographs of the Laguna Madre and South Padre Island beach. One featured a woman standing with Sophie, both wearing broad brimmed straw hats and smiling from ear to ear. Below it read the inscription, "To Sophie, my hero!" And signed, "The Turtle Lady."

Over the hall console hung a picture of Sophie standing ankle deep in a backwash of the Laguna with a grizzly faced man who wore a broad and easy smile. In one hand he held a notebook of some kind and with the other a long handled net. They wore matching straw hats and looked as if caught in the middle of a pleasant, busy chat. Sophie remembered the day as if it was yesterday, but it was twenty years of yesterdays. She smiled at the fellow.

"John," she said softly with a sigh.

Chapter 5

AT SUBWAY, THEY picked a booth where the windows formed a corner. It was middle afternoon and the lunch crowd was gone. Jack ate hungrily, barely looking up.

"So why'd you quit?" Joan asked.

"I don't know," he said slowly, "I guess I just tired of the BS."

"There's always BS, brother; what exactly triggered it?"

"It wasn't one thing. It was building. They're all a bunch of gutless phonies. They wear colon wall for contacts."

"I worry about you, Jack," she admitted.

"Why?"

"You get depressed and I just worry about you."

"Joan, I'm not clinical. I just get down once in a while, that's all. Who doesn't? For me, when I get into one of these, I can fight it or I can just go with it. Wallow a while. It passes just the same."

"What's the cause of this one, then?"

"I don't know. Maybe I'm just antsy again. You know I can't do the same thing very long, never have," he said. "And when I get to the end of them, well, I get unhappy and then angry at myself for not being satisfied, then I get blue."

"So you quit because you were tired of it."

"I've been tired of that job for two years. It just took me

two years to get tired enough to quit. It's not just the job or the people there. It's me. I just can't be satisfied with anything very long."

"You've always been that way, Jack. Always trying new stuff and leaving things undone," she said.

"It's just that I get hooked on something and I can't get enough of it, then after a while the newness fades and I can't drop it fast enough. I worry sometimes that I am never going to be able to relax at one thing."

"It's because you are so smart, you know. You'll never be satisfied with one thing," she said.

"Yeah, well if that's so, it's a curse," he complained. "Sometimes I think how it would be nice to come home from a regular job, like *Father Knows Best*, be greeted at the door by my beautiful wife and brilliant kids, eat dinner together, help with the homework, watch the Tonight Show and drift off to sleep in her arms after screwing her brains out," he said wistfully.

"You?" Joan hooted, "That's not you and never could be."

"I know, but I do dream about it."

"No, brother, you are a confirmed bachelor. You couldn't even share a life with a pet. Hell, for a while I was sure you were gay, at least until you married Maxie."

"Maxie," he said pensively.

"Ever hear from her?" she asked.

"Not since Christmas two years ago. She moved to Seattle. Got a job there at the TV station."

"I liked her," Joan said, "just not with you." After a pause, Joan asked, "You aren't gay, are you?"

"No, not gay," he paused, "but I do like gay people," he added. "They're so…cheerful."

"Funny," she mocked him. "Whatever happened to that girl from last summer?"

"It didn't work out. She wanted to have a husband and I wanted to have the virgin whore."

"Of course, the perfect woman."

"Any way, that's history," he said.

"You're already sounding much better."

"Oh, I'm ok. I was coming out of it already. I can tell because I hit bottom before I bounce. Fact is, the whole thing is so predictable that I stopped even worrying about it. I just go with the flow, wallow a while, then, hell, I get tired of that too."

"So what's next?" she asked.

"Well, that's a good question," he answered. "I just don't know. I'm broke, so it can't be anything fancy."

"Broke? How can you be broke? What happened to all the money you got for the company?" she blurted.

"I hate accounting," he explained to her expectant face.

"What do you mean?"

"It just sort of went."

"Went?" she repeated.

"Went."

"So, basically, you are broke," she summed up.

"Not completely, but basically."

"What are you going to do now?"

"I think you've asked that already."

"Yeah, but I didn't get much of an answer."

"I've got a few ideas. I've still got the Beneteau, so I thought I'd live on it for a while, until I get something going. Slip rent is cheap."

"Oh, yeah, the sailboat," she remembered. "So, you still have that."

"Yep, and it's in good shape, too. Heck, I've been wanting to get back out on the water for months, so this'll work out okay," he said with the first hint of enthusiasm she'd seen today.

"What about you, Joan? How are you doing?" he asked, both genuinely interested and feeling guilty for not asking sooner.

"Oh, same ole' same ole'," she said.

"Any interesting prospects?" he asked.

"Not really. I don't know if I'm up for the maintenance any more. I kind of like my freedom."

"Body clock not ticking so loud?"

"Guess not. Funny how that sort of passed. I mean, I was so ready to have a kid and all that, but now, well, now I wonder if I really want all the hassle," she said.

"Figures," he mused.

"What do you mean, 'figures'?" she challenged.

"Well, you are one of us, after all. None of us, not you, not me, nor Jason have been much for marrying. I figured if you got past thirty-five you'd probably cool on the idea."

"Guess you were right. I like dating occasionally, though. It is kind of nice to have a 'regular' to cozy up to, but I'm finding I really enjoy my solitude at home. Can't say I really want to bring anybody home."

"And kids?" he asked.

"I've got thirty kids all day in the classroom," she explained. "That'll do it."

"Destined for loneliness," Jack announced.

"Guess so," she agreed. "Sweet, crowded loneliness."

Chapter 6

VOICES IN THE OUTER office brought John Magne IV back from his thoughts about his ancestors and he looked up in time to see Clinton strutting through his office door. His second son had the unmistakable bow-legged walk of a man who'd spent a lot of hours in the saddle, but with a gait that testified to purpose.

He was the spitting image of his grandfather, John Magne III, about five foot eight, ruddy complexion, solid, square and muscular, and the only true rancher of the two sons. Yet Clinton, more than John Jr., reminded Magne of Francie: same muted red hair, same bright blue eyes, but mostly it was the smile, impishly turned up at the corners.

She was dead nearly ten years now. It had been hard on the boys losing their mother to cancer so young. Magne knew they would never accept anyone else as their mother and Gabriela had never tried to assume that role. She was his wife now, not their mother, and that understanding made her acceptance much easier when their father married her last year.

"Dad!" he exclaimed enthusiastically, as he always did.

"Clint!" John responded in kind, as he nearly always did.

Clint smiled as he pulled off his hat long enough to wipe the sweat from his forehead with his sleeve. "She calved!"

"Fantastic! No trouble?"

"Well, it looked like it hurt a bit," drawled Clint in his dry humor, "but she's fine and the calf looks pretty good…wobbly, but good."

"Isn't she the first in the States?" asked John.

"Think so; think there was a zoo that tried it a couple of times, but no go."

"Damned good, Clint, what you've been able to do with the game is unbelievable. You ought to get a message to Fredrickson. He'll be anxious to know."

"Yep, but I'm calling Dr. Perceval first. Aggie's always come first, Dad."

"The Corp," he exclaimed. "Hey, Clint, seen Junior?"

"Not since yesterday afternoon. Passed him on the beach road. Gotta get back to the action," Clint called over his shoulder as he left the office.

The idea of importing wild game and breeding them for the ranch was Clint's. It was a way that Clint was unlike his grandfather, a true naturalist. But Magne could see the potential in it. Already their nescient herds of exotic game--Axis deer, Nilgai, and black buck antelope--were doing well. The ranch was already thick with the indigenous deer, quail, dove, feral hogs, javalina, turkey and several species of duck, but these were the game for hunters of more modest incomes.

The exotic species were the province of the truly rich. If it worked, in a few years they would have enough of a population to charter hunts for African game right there in Texas. The amount of money well-healed arm-chair adventurers would be willing to pay was serious. It was a vanity business. They could land their private jets on the ranch's long runway any Saturday morning, bag a gazelle by mid afternoon, pose for the requisite pictures, have cocktails under the *palapa* and still be home in time to watch the late news. John smiled to himself as he thought that the one most valuable person to the Orvis catalog crowd was a taxidermist who could hide the rope burns.

Promising as it was, it could do nothing for the problems facing the Magne Ranch now.

In his great-grandfather's day, before the scourge of mesquite scrub, the ranchlands were a sea of grasses that could sustain a head of cattle on fifteen acres of land. But cattle brought the beans that led to the virulent spread of the brush. In the beginning, the Magnes hired armies of Mexican workers to clear the land by hand, but in the fifties they had devised a method using pairs of bulldozers with root plows dragging 100,000 pound chains, clearing nearly four acres an hour.

When water was the problem, they drilled 300' to 400' wells and found clean, clear artesian well water.

When the more common breeds of Herefords, Angus and Brahmans struggled in the Texas heat, the Magnes bred their own varieties. It was his grandfather, John Magne II, an amateur geneticist, that in 1921 culminated years of careful breeding to produce a calf that was the beginning of the first truly American breed, the Santa Maria. It was hardy, resistant to common stress diseases, more drought tolerant, and put on weight quickly and easily, even on the harsh South Texas plains.

The Magne Dynasty was a story of challenges and survival, of perseverance against all threats and dangers. And these seemed to come in never-ending waves.

Then came the Mad Cow scare and it ruined the cattle business. Not one of his herd had any sign of bovine spongiform encephalopathy, but Europe, Canada, Mexico, and Japan had shut down all imports from the U.S. and prices had plummeted. Worse, he had doubled his bet on those prices in the commodities and options markets. The Magne Ranch was land rich but cash poor. He had relied on working capital loans for a couple of years and those notes were coming due.

Before he died, his father made him swear that Magne land would never be sold. Never. And he promised. But the reality was the banks could take it.

He could never let that happen.

And he wouldn't. He had a plan, simple and effective.

In some ways it was the culmination of a century and a half of Magne breeding and hard work, and the powerful drive to survive. All around the edges of the Magne Ranch, pockets of natural gas had been found and it was being extracted for huge royalties to the mineral rights owners. Families with mere fractions of percentage points were drawing staggering monthly checks from the oil companies.

The Magnes owned all their own mineral rights. So all they had to do was prove there was gas under the ranch then enter into lease agreements with an oil company. Better yet, Magne could form his own oil company and sell the gas directly into the market. It would mean hundreds of millions of dollars over generations. Never would a Magne ever have to worry about money again.

But the path from here to there was strewn with obstacles. He needed capital to drill for the gas and build the infrastructure to transport it into the market. An investment bank could be hired to create an IPO, an initial public offering, to sell shares in the new oil company. He needed approvals and permits from the state and federal government, and for that he would call in the mountains of political chips he had carefully sown over the years. But he needed help figuring out how to get all this done. All he needed to solve that was to hire the experts who knew how.

It may not have been what his father would have done, but it was the family's best chance, Magne knew, and he would do what ever it took to fulfill the Magne destiny.

Chapter 7

THERE WAS THE SOUND of clicking at a slow but deliberate cadence. "There you are!" Sophie declared. "I wondered where you'd gone off to. Hungry yet?"

A face, that looked to be made of melting brown wax and planted with two glass eyes, turned up to her. The lower jaw dropped to reveal a long pink tongue that immediately fell to one side of the broad and wrinkly bloodhound's mouth. He panted in approval, lifting one eyebrow, then the other.

"Geez, Louise, Hannibal, you look like you've been on a four day drunk," Sophie said to him as she moved sideways to the refrigerator. She pulled out a Ziploc freezer bag of a meat and gravy mix and dropped it into a pot of water and turned up the gas.

"I really wish you'd give up meat altogether, Hannibal, but I know you won't, you old scoundrel. But I guess it's okay if that's what you'd eat out in the wild," she reasoned. For herself she pierced some sweet potatoes and popped them in the microwave then retrieved a Tupperware tub of left-over Black Bean Chili to heat next. Over the years she had learned that with some onions, tomato paste, and hot pepper sauce, she could fairly imitate the heft and texture of the meat version of the same foods.

She ate alone at the kitchen table, her eyes fixed on the article pinned in the center of the corkboard by the kitchen door.

She had cut it out of *The Herald* features section nearly a year ago. The article was about the Magne Ranch, where rare game animals were being imported from Africa to be bred and raised for wild game hunts.

Prominent in the middle of the full-page story was a photograph of the most elegant gazelle she had ever seen. It stood bold, dignified, defiant. Yet the eyes, those huge eyes, revealed to her a certain sadness. The eyes mesmerized her. They seemed to stare at her personally, pleading. Every night since she pinned up the article, she sat at the kitchen table staring at the photo while she ate. Occasionally, Hannibal would turn his head when he heard her speak, thinking she was calling to him.

Eventually she gathered up her dishes and washed them, dried them and put them back in their proper places in the china cabinet. The kitchen was spotless by the time she made her way to her bedroom to change into a nightgown and her flannel robe.

Hannibal finished off his dinner and took up his usual place on the floor by the hearth in the living room, waiting for her to come sit on the green leather sofa. It was a ritual. He'd watch her read her book and after a little while, her head would loll and then roll forward until her chin rested on her chest. Her breathing would slow and take on a rhythm and then he too would drift off to sleep.

It was well after midnight when Hannibal's head suddenly jerked up. He struggled to shake off his grogginess and he rose cautiously to his feet. His eyes were glued to the kitchen door at the back of the house. He held his breath in anticipation.

There came the sound of scuffling from beyond the door. Hannibal huffed in a muted effort to bark, the hair on the back of his neck rising. Then there was the slow squeaking of the outer screen door's hinges. The door handle slowly twisted left then right. After a long pause, the screen door snapped lightly on the door frame, followed by the sound of footsteps moving away.

Hannibal remained at attention, his head turning slowly as if following some invisible figure across the front of the house. A shadow danced across the curtains, weaving in and out with the furls of the fabric. A pin-hole beam of light flowed from the street lamp through the peep hole in the solid wood front door. Then the beam instantly blackened. Hannibal began to huff again, trying to bark. He could see the doorknob as if it were magnified ten times. It began to turn. There was a click and the door began to open slowly.

Hannibal was frozen in fear, incapable of defending his master. A trickle of urine began to form a pool under him. Suddenly he was blinded by the light and yelped in terror.

Chapter 8

"HANNIBAL?" ANGELA ASKED. "Is that you?" With the light on she could see her mother sleeping on the sofa and put her finger to her mouth. "Shush, Hannibal, don't wake up mom, now." She stepped outside the front door to retrieve her suitcase and managed to move it inside the entry way with some extra effort. She closed the door.

She surveyed the room as she pulled off her coat and hung it on the hall tree. Nothing had changed since she'd been there last Christmas, nearly a year ago.

"Angela, honey, is that you?" Sophie stirred from her sleep.

"Yes, Mom, I'm home. I didn't mean to wake you."

"Well I was wondering what happened to you?"

"The planes were running late, Mom. I thought flying midweek would be easier but there was terrible weather in Boston. Logan was closed for two hours."

Sophie rose and steadied herself then put her arms around her daughter. "I'm just so glad you made it, honey."

"Me, too."

"Have you eaten?" Sophie immediately asked, automatically adopting her mother persona.

"I'm fine, Mom. You go back to bed. I can find a snack in the kitchen."

"Oh, I'm not sleepy. I was waiting for you. Let me have a

look at you, hon," she said putting on her bifocals and tilting her head back to get a clear picture of her. Angela had been a pudgy child, but when she hit her growth spurt in the sixth grade, all that changed. Sophie found it impossible to keep her in clothes that fit. But Angela never cared much about fashion. She could be found most days with her blond hair gathered haphazardly into a pony tail and wearing a pair of baggy khakis and a T-shirt, usually with some sort of political statement blazoned across it. As she matured to womanhood, her face grew thinner, her chest filled out and, more and more, her green eyes reminded Sophie of Angela's father.

Sophie had raised Angela alone. She'd told Angela her only lie: that her father had died before she was born, that it happened in Mexico and that he was buried there in an unmarked grave.

"Angela, I just don't know why some fellow hasn't snapped you up already. You are the prettiest thing."

"Oh, Mom. I'm too busy for all that. I've got my work."

"Well, you can't warm your cockles on a cold night with books, Angela, dear."

"You can if you burn the books, Mom," Angela retorted teasing her.

"Then you'll go and get your cockles burned, too," Sophie joined in as she followed Angela to the kitchen.

"Mom. There is one thing I've always wanted to ask you…"

"What's that hon?"

"What exactly are cockles?"

Sophie laughed like a young girl and said, "Well now, dearie, one thing's for sure, when you finally find yourself wanting come cockles, they get as rare as hen's teeth."

"And I suppose that's a crack about my turning forty last year," Angela said, opening the refrigerator and acting hurt.

"Oh, child, you're just a baby yet, I wouldn't worry about that. You're getting just about right to settle down. I was only a little younger than you are now when I had you, remember?"

"I'm not worried at all, Mom. I'm pretty happy with things to tell the truth," retrieving a banana from the bowl in the counter. "Amesha and I have talked about it until I am blue in the face. We like our choices. We're doing important work."

"Amesha make it to New York all right then?"

"All set and rarin' to go," Angela replied.

"Well, you know that I'm happy if you're happy, honey. You know that, don't you?"

Angela looked into her mother's beaming face and saw how pleased she was that she had come home. "I do know that, Mom." She kissed her cheek. "Now go to bed!"

"But I want to catch up," Sophie pleaded.

"Me too, but I've been fighting off groping security cops, double-belt seat partners, and puking infants for the last twelve hours. All I want to do is shower and crash. What's say we catch up tomorrow?"

"Ok. But you promise?" Sophie acquiesced.

"G'night, Mom."

Chapter 9

JACK SLEPT SOUNDLY and when he awoke Thursday morning, he felt a surge of energy. His dark clouds were clearing. He immediately went about cleaning up the house and putting his keep-ables into boxes he'd saved and stored in the garage from when he moved in. So much useless stuff, he thought, where does it come from?

He would have no room for it on *Wist*. Even with all its nooks and crannies, his 39' Beneteau sailboat could fill up pretty quickly. But what to do with the surplus? He wanted to be out in a week, or at least before another rent payment, so he decided to have a garage sale instead.

Sorting through his unopened mail and bank statements, he'd found an IRA money market account he'd forgotten that had a balance of some five grand. With his checking account, that made almost eleven thousand dollars in all and that, plus whatever he could clear on the garage sale, would take some of the pressure off.

He set the date for the coming Saturday. That would give him two days to get ready. Putting the ad in the *Morning Star* was easy. All he had to do was enter the text online at their website and pay with his credit card. The ad would run Friday and Saturday morning. Now, all he needed were some supplies.

Jack drove his Jeep to Target to buy materials for price tagging and a poster-board size sign to put on the mailbox. He'd had the Jeep since his days at Texas A&M. It was still painted Aggie maroon. He stood in the school supply aisle, staring at the colored markers, mesmerized by the array of choices.

"Those are edible," chirped a soprano female voice from behind him.

"Pardon?" he said instinctively.

"Those are eat-able. You can eat them," she explained. "But I wouldn't. Who knows what's really in those things, I mean, I don't think you should cook with them or anything, but I think they mean kids can put them in their mouth and not get sick." She paused for a response.

"Oh," delivered in a tone of useful discovery, is all Jack could think to retort. Her bright red, tight, cleavage screaming halter top distracted him, but he averted his eyes to not be so obvious. When his eyes finally found hers, she was smiling and he visibly blushed.

"I meant the colors, mister," she said laughing. He liked the lilt in her laugh and the lines that spread from the corners of her green eyes. She continued on down the aisle and he felt compelled to watch her until she was gone.

In the parking lot, loading the two large bags on the floor of the back seat of the Jeep, Jack heard a faint, high-pitched trilling sound. He looked around but saw nothing in the parking lot. When he came round to climb into the driver's seat he spotted a small wicker Easter basket in the tall grass by the curb. He didn't remember seeing it when he parked. Again he heard the sound and it seemed to be coming from the basket.

Carefully he peered into it and saw a lone kitten, crying plaintively. He looked around for the owner, but there were no cars or people nearby. He paused for a moment staring at the basket and the cat, then he climbed into the Jeep, backed up and began the drive to his house.

At the first stoplight, he found his thoughts wandering back to the kitten, but he dismissed it. At the second light, he noticed the gathering clouds and realized he'd need to get home quickly or risk being doused in his open air Jeep. Then he thought about the cat again.

For reasons completely beyond his understanding, and against his better judgment, he found himself making a U-turn and heading back to the parking lot. There, where he had first seen it, was the basket, taking the first pelts of rain that were starting to fall. He looked down at the cat and could see the raindrops confused him. He reached down, gently picked it up and, holding it at arm's-length, studied it. It was barely large enough to fit in the palm of his hand. Its stomach was disproportionately large. He was a cute fellow, for sure, but it was none of his business. Out of the corner of his eye he could see a Peregrine Falcon sitting on a telephone pole, disapproving of this intervention into what he was intending to be dinner.

Jack knew the kitten would be taken if he put the animal back into the basket. But, he thought, survival of the fittest…it was the way the world works. Who was he to intervene? He paused in indecision. He put the cat back into the basket. Then he picked up the basket and put it on the passenger seat of the Jeep. In minutes he was racing toward the house in hopes of beating the rain.

Both of them were soaking wet by the time he pushed the door open with his shoulder and put the basket on the kitchen table. He fetched a towel from the bathroom and dried his own hair and face first, then went to work drying off the cat as best he could.

It was a pitiful looking creature, ordinary gray and white and short-haired, yet but for what Jack had heard in the parking lot earlier, the kitten made not a sound. Jack seemed to see in its eyes a genuine appreciation, which he thought was pretty silly of him. It was just a cat.

"So what were you doing out there, little fellow?" he was

surprised to hear himself saying out loud, as he continued to carefully dry the pencil-thin legs of the little creature. "You were like Moses found floating in a basket on the Nile," he said idly, gently kneading his ears. "Moses, that's who you are, Moses." He thought for a while, stroking the cat.

"If you're looking for the Promised Land, little fellow, you are pretty well screwed."

Chapter 10

FRIDAY'S WERE WHEN John Magne reviewed the cash flow reports and projections. In the last few years this had become a drudgery of robbing Pedro to pay Paulo, trying to keep the horde of Magne Ranch creditors a little edgy maybe, but not angry. Instead, it was he who was both.

"Mr. Magne?" the intercom intruded.

"Yes, Pat."

"Mr. Stubb is here."

"Hold there a minute, Pat; tell him to meet me at the Rover. I'll be out in just a minute." Magne would have a shot of Glenfiddich first. He needed it. He despised Stubb and all those like him, but it is the price he had to pay. In this case, close to a million dollars for Stubb's expertise in organizing and managing the effort, from finding the gas to floating an initial stock offering. It was small potatoes compared to the potential income, *ad infinitum*. A delicious way to say forever.

Stubb and his kind were maggots. They cleaned up after mortal messes, but none too prettily as they went about it. Magne had weighed the options. His first duty was to the family, and that meant the Magne Ranch. He pulled his Stetson from the hall tree, grabbed his dark glasses and headed for the Rover, passing his secretary at her desk.

"I'm headed over to the test site, the one by the old docks, with Stubb. See if you can track down Junior. I'll be on my cell."

"Yes, sir."

Magne found Stubb standing in front of the Rover, with his elbows akimbo, legs spread, facing out to the expanse of ranchland that ran all the way to the Laguna. Short, blanche white and overweight, with wispy-thin blond hair, Stubb had a delicate, urban pallor about him, emphasized by large black-framed plastic glasses which he continually pushed back up his nose with his middle finger. In the middle of the Magne ranch, he looked like a squat-necked mannequin dressed in a safari outfit, two sizes too large, too pressed and too perfect.

"Well, Stubb, looks like you're pretending to be a rancher," Magne startled him.

"Oh, no, not me, I'm an oil patch boy," Stubb chortled, "but I could get used to it."

"Well, don't get too comfortable. This'll all be done by spring I hope."

"Spring. Yep, or sooner," Stubb said under his breath as he climbed into the passenger seat of the Rover.

"What about the geologist reports?" Magne asked as they pulled away from *Casa Blanca*, the main house.

"They're coming along. I talked to Philips yesterday and he said he just needs a few more soundings to wrap things up. No problems."

"And are they looking favorable?"

"Oh, yes. Great, in fact. You're going to be an even richer man, Mr. Magne."

Magne wasn't going to share the truth of his situation with the likes of Festor Stubb. The Rover wound through the low, tangled brush, giving way to the salt flats that ran to the Laguna. His grandfather had long complained that it was the most useless land on the planet. But his father thought it was the most beautiful. When Magne was a boy, his father would bring him along for long collecting hikes, often wading knee deep into the Laguna, inspecting grasses, animals, and nests. He was an amateur naturalist, but many marine biologists interested in the fauna and flora of the area eagerly sought his specimens. It had not changed in a thousand years, his father often told him, and if they were good stewards, it shouldn't for a thousand more.

As they drove along, a pink cloud of Roseate Spoonbills drifted up into the teal sky. Two years ago Magne had seen what he was sure was a Whooping Crane. They wintered just a little north of the ranch, in the Aransas Wildlife Refuge. A loner must have wandered down a bit. And there were the usual residents: piping plovers, pelicans, ospreys, falcons, and the scores of other birds that migrated south through the Rio Grande Valley.

There were times, Magne remembered, many times, when in the evening as the sun sank into the mesquite silhouettes inland, this place took on the color of a blush wine while everything aloft and afoot was illuminated against the darkening eastern sky. At those times he would stop and just take it in and a feeling of great awe and pride would wash over him, clearing away all his worries and leaving a smell of dewy saltgrass. He'd often thought he'd wear it if they ever bottled it.

"There. There it is," Stubb said, pointing ahead and to the right, and dispersing the sweet aromas of Magne's reverie. Magne recognized Junior's Ford F250. His older son was leaning on the passenger side door, the heel of his right boot hooked on the running board. He had adopted a James Dean kind of slouch during his teenage years, what John knew was a kind of defiance that he hoped he would grow out of. He hadn't, and what was a youthful affectation then, was in a grown man of thirty-two years, annoying to his father.

Magne pulled up to the small shack and got out. It stood out like a pimple on a virgin's ass, he thought.

"Hey, Dad," Junior called out.

"Hey back," he replied, "I was looking for you."

"'S up?"

"Just wanted you to meet us out here, but, hey, here you are!"

"It's all magic, Dad," Junior joked.

Stubb came around to the front of the Rover and walked around to the back of the shack where a metal plate covered the coring hole.

"I always thought you had to have a big rig to drill a test hole," said John.

"That was the old days, Mr. Magne. Nowadays, in this kind of soil, mostly sand, we do a core sampling instead," Stubb explained.

"Sort of like they drill holes for pilings, you mean?"

"No, sir, more like bringing up a column of mud to study." Stubb felt himself fighting the urge to chuckle out loud.

"So the geologists show up Monday, then," Magne said.

"Yes, they'll be doing sonar soundings to map the underground, looking for layers and pockets."

"How's that work?" Magne asked.

"Different structures echo different sounds. Gas pockets have a certain signature," Stubb replied, then turning back to Magne said, "and they ought to have a report next Wednesday."

"Then what?"

"Well, then we get the report to New York and Fenre Pease Investment Bank takes it from there. I've already got the investment memo done and they're doing their due diligence on it. The lab test is the final piece. In a month or so, they'll put the IPO, that's the first stock put up for sale, they'll put it out on the street and you, sir, will be laughing all the way to the bank."

Magne felt uncomfortable with Stubb's growing familiarity. He just nodded. He reminded himself why he needed him. When he was done, he'd discard him like a used cardboard box and until then he'd have to hold his nose. He turned and looked across the Laguna toward Port Mansfield.

"Hey, Junior, Gabriela's expecting you for Sunday dinner. What'll I tell her?" Magne asked making his way back to the Rover. "Let's get back," he said to Stubb.

"What's she fixin'?" Junior asked.

"A whole lot of ass whupin' if you ain't there," Magne shot back.

"I'm there, I'm there."

As they drove back to the main house Stubb said, "Junior's a good boy, Mr. Magne."

"Thanks, Stubb, he owes that to Francie, his mom."

"I mean, he's been a big help to me on this project, picking people up at the airport, showing us around, taking care of stuff," Stubb complimented.

"I'm glad he's taking an interest in something," Magne said. "He was never much of a student in College Station, more a magnet for trouble. It was a bitch getting him graduated. Junior was happy to be a student. He just didn't much care for being a scholar."

"I hear ya," Stubb chortled. "It took me a while to get serious in college."

"Where'd you go to school, Stubb?"

"Me? Tech. Lubbock," Stubb replied.

"Major?"

"Accounting, but I minored in Engineering, mostly petroleum."

"How old are you now?"

"Forty-three."

"So you graduated in, what, '83? '84?"

"Eighty-five, actually," Stubb corrected.

"We kicked Red Raider butt pretty regularly back then," Magne teased.

"Yes, sir. The Aggies were pretty tough."

"So, what's your story?"

"Sorry?"

"What have you been doing all this time? Your career…"

"Oh, well, I grew up in Midland and after I graduated, I took a job with Halleborne, down in Brazil, working on one of their government contracts," Stubb explained.

"Doing what?"

"I was an office accountant, or, as we called ourselves, 'Cost Magicians'."

"Cost Magicians?"

"Yeah," Stubb giggled, "those government contracts were cost plus, so we were busy inventing costs. Got pretty good at it, too. But then I got hired at one of the 'Big Eight' firms--well, it's like 'Big Four' now--doing audits for oil company clients."

"So, how'd you get into this line of work you're doing now?"

"I got tired of living offshore and came back home to take a job with the I.R.S…"

"The IRS?" Magne exclaimed, surprised.

"Yep, the Treasury. I was an investigator after a while, tracking down tax shelters mostly. But then I figured that these tax shelters were a gold mine. Hardly any of the agents understood them and whole bunches of them were slipping under the statute of limitations before any action could be taken; so I thought, why not put together bullet-proof shelters for investors, using all I know about how they're investigated?"

"Sort of the fox in the hen house."

"Right. Except the more I put together these tax shelters, the more I was finding good deals and that the money was more in the investments than in the tax credits," Stubb lied, "and with my oil patch background, naturally I tended toward oil and gas deals."

"So what you do is put the deal together," Magne led him.

"Exactly. My job is to collect all the information you need for an investment memo: the facts, arrange for the tests, put together the documentation--all the 'due diligence' stuff…in a form that investment bankers like, then get all that to the IPO types, usually in New York, and they hammer it into something that passes Security and Exchange Commission sniff tests, get it farmed out to the different brokerage houses, and when it goes public, they collect up the loot and get it distributed to the offering group…in this case, you."

"Lot's of work," Magne responded.

"Lot's," Stubb agreed. Then after a pause, "I wonder if I could ask you a question, Mr. Magne?"

"Sure."

"How'd you come to contact me?" Stubb asked curiously.

"Amberson is our family's accounting firm. Your name came up during a strategy discussion. Frasier Hemphill gave me your name and number, and I figured that anything recommended by Amberson has to be up and up," Magne explained.

"Fraiser, right. I haven't talked to him in years. He was in Houston when I was in Sao Paulo." Stubb wasn't going to explain that Frasier would be getting his usual gratuity once the deal turned golden. This adulation of big accounting firms was a source of constant amazement and steady money to Stubb. He wouldn't complain. After all, "hypocrisy was vice's tribute to virtue," he'd read somewhere, and in a world where what appeared to be true was as good as true, there was plenty of opportunity for the morally ambivalent.

"And now I wonder if I could ask you a question?" Magne inquired.

"Shoot."

"Festor. Where'd you get a name like that?"

"Oh, that's not my given name. I'm actually Earl. I got 'Festor' as a nickname from my mother, but she never told me why. I think I might have had a relative by that name once. I think his name was Fes Parker, or was that a movie star? I really don't know."

The Land Rover drove up to the motor court in front of

Casa Blanca, Magne pulled the door lever without pushing the door open, then turned to Stubb and said, "Well, I guess we'll know more on Wednesday." It was clear the meeting was over. "Yes, sir. I'll call you as soon as I have the word. Oh, Mr. Magne, we're going to need to draw another hundred on Monday. We've got fees to pay, and I'm due a progress payment."

"A hundred," Magne echoed, wondering if he had the one hundred thousand left in his accounts. He knew he had to keep Stubb working. It was a race against shrinking cash and time. He knew he had to find a way. "We'll mail you a check on Monday, then," he said, hoping Stubb wouldn't ask for a direct draft. He slammed the door and dashed for his office to cut off any such suggestion. "Have a good weekend," he hollered.

Chapter 11

THE ROLLING THUNDER and wind-blown branches tapping the windowpanes woke Jack around 5:00 A.M. Saturday morning. The back screen door was loose and slammed intermittently to no particular rhythm. The norther had blown in.

He couldn't get back to sleep. That, and he was sore from spending all day Friday and most of the night organizing and pricing his items. First thing was to put on the coffee.

He stood, surveying the array of items in his living room. Toolboxes with prodigal parts, orphaned tools that weren't the prodigals, the odd appliance, lamp, exercise devices and like implements of torture. Then there were the books and magazines, mostly novels, but a lot of technical books, a few old bound reports he'd done, piles of *Sailing*, *Cruising World*, and dog-eared *Practical Sailors*.

Atop one pile perched the greatest threat to his cherished confidence in rational thought: a fondue pot. He scratched his head. What state of mind would compel anyone to buy a fondue pot, he wondered. What need or urgency was satisfied by it? How did that seem like a reasonable thing to do at the time? What in retrospect often seemed nuts, he realized, nearly always made sense at the time. How can you know which is which?

It amazed and disturbed him that he had accumulated so much now irrelevant junk. The he who he was that once needed these things, seemed odd and unfamiliar now. Lately, he had become so tired of dragging so much ballast around from place to place that he found himself pausing before buying something until he could figure out how he would be rid of it.

The perfect product was the trash bag, he thought. It went from store shelf to home to trash can almost immediately. It was used and gone. It had no sentimentality about it. It had perfect utility and left no tracks. He should be more like that. A trash bag.

His acquisitive phase was fading. Thoreau was making more and more sense. A 10' by 10' house on a remote pond, or an uninhabited island like Crusoe found--these would be perfect. Life would unfold one hour at a time, full of serendipity, surprise, yet all in slow motion. The issues of weather, insects and feeding could be quietly measured out and processed in geologic time. No complications, no disappointments. No people.

His eye caught the yellow corner of it sticking out beneath a stack of old reports: the lynch pin, the reason he was doing all this. He should have left well enough alone, he thought. Who the hell cares? But he knew it wasn't in his nature, even though he also knew it wasn't in his best interests to succumb once again to that nature. A yellow cover and twenty-five pages of nothing important. Twenty-five pages of trouble. Nature, his and God's, that was the problem.

It was an ordinary assignment. Gene Bardino called him into the regional office and said that some big-wigs wanted notes on the environmental impact of gas wells on the Laguna Madre. Nothing fancy. A memo. No problem.

Jack knew this was not exotic data. There had been scores of studies done over the years investigating the impact of dredging channels, the Intracoastal Waterway, marinas and the like. And a few more on the consequences of sedimentation on the fine grasses where Texas' shrimp matured.

Alexanders, an oil industry newsletter, reported on concerns that the warm hyper-saline waters of the Laguna were critical habitat to several species of endangered and exotic birds, among them the piping plover and reddish egret. The National Park Service was studying the impact of gas drilling on Padre Island, but weren't expected to decide on permitting for a couple of years. And, of course, environmental groups like the Sierra Club had chimed in as well.

As it turned out, there had been some work done by the Environmental Protection Agency on gas and oil well exploration some years back, somewhere, so it would be a simple matter of digging those out and doing some light-fingered reconnaissance.

Moses, jumping up on his lap, startled him. He'd almost forgotten the new resident. "It's a good thing I can't get a label to stick to you, Mose, or you'd be sold too," he said to the cat as he scratched him behind his furry ears.

Coffee was becoming an imperative, but he was still in his boxers and T-shirt when there was a rapping on the door.

Chapter 12

"HAVE A GREAT WEEKEND," Magne had hollered at Festor Stubb Friday afternoon, but he had no idea just exactly what Stubb had planned.

The sun was just peeking over the horizon by the time Stubb had reached Corpus Christi. He was exhausted and dirty but with Junior's help they had gotten it all done, although much later than he had planned. He had expected to be home by now, but in every plan there are complications. He'd be back in Houston in a few hours.

Junior was a little flustered by the pressure of it all, but Stubb knew his long experience in his art gave him a measure of confidence that made the going easier and the outcome more predictable. Still, the night had its surprises, but nothing he couldn't handle. He wondered what that old man in the boat had been up to.

The long drive began to calm him down. He had always honored the principle that a good businessman did his homework and left as little as possible to chance. He was a professional. He didn't believe in taking chances.

At first it was a stifled giggle, but before long he was laughing out loud. "I'm a frigging genius!" he yelled at one point, banging the steering wheel with his palms.

He knew that there were all kinds of ingeniousness. No, he

didn't have the technical or engineering knowledge that some had, but he did have the imagination and the connections to figure things out and get things done.

All that hard work, all the thinking, was about to pay off.

Chapter 13

"HELLO?" A VOICE CALLED impatiently from the porch, followed by more aggressive rapping.

"Yes?" Jack answered as he pulled the door open about six inches.

"You the garage sale?" a short but broad black woman of about fifty asked.

"What?"

"The garage sale, is that you?" she repeated insistently.

"Uh, well, yes, I'm having a garage sale today. What the hell time is it?"

"Time to get yo ass moving, mista, 'cuz Anahida is on the trail," the woman barked like a drill sergeant.

"Ma'am, it can't even be seven o'clock, what the hell you doing here so early?"

"I gotta lot a ground to cover, mista, and I mean to get an early start. And the early bird, well, she has the worms," she blustered.

"Jesus Christ," was all he could manage.

"You got some coffee in there? I smell some coffee. I could use some of that," she proposed. For some reason he pulled the door open and stood aside as she barged on in, headed for the kitchen.

"Where you keep dem cups, honey?" she asked even as she

opened one cabinet after another in a search of the premises.

"The one on the right of the fridge, yeah, that one," he offered as he pulled out a chair from the dinette table in the middle of the kitchen.

"A'hm Anahida," she introduced as she picked two cups from the middle shelf and headed for the Mr. Coffee carafe across the counter. "Who you?"

"Jack. Jack Grider," he answered watching her put a cup in front of him, then sitting down in the chair across.

"Well, well, mista Jack-Jack, don't you have a bunch of stuff here," she remarked as her eyes surveyed the jetsam. "I'm a professional, you know, I buy this stuff for a livin', such as it is."

"Pardon?"

"It's a bidnis. I goes about takin' in dem garage sales and then I takes 'em all to the flea market in Brownsville and sells them."

"There's money in that?"

"A little," she said, "an' it beats workin'."

"Sounds like a lot of work to me."

"Well, mista Jack-Jack, there's work and then there is *work*," she explained.

"What do you mean?"

"Well, when you have ta be under somebody else's thumb and gotta be here or gotta be there, and you can't even go to the bat'room when ya feels like it, well, that's no better 'n being a cotton-pickin' nigger," she said with fire in her eye. "Ah don't have to put up with no crap from nobody. I does my bidnis when I wanna do it and all ah make ah keeps for myself," and then quickly added, "An' my man, too, naturally." She took another sip of her coffee.

He found himself gaping at her and looked down to his coffee cup to avert his eyes. In a few sentences she had summed up his entire life philosophy about work more eloquently than he'd managed in a decade of trying. He watched her sip her coffee, inventorying the room in her head. He could hear the wheels turning.

"Whatchu want for all dis here junk," she asked in a business-like tone.

"What, all of it?" Jack stuttered, surprised.

"All of it. Lock, stock and barrel; the whole enchilada," she sang.

"Enchilada," Jack repeated in feigned surprise. "I didn't know black folks ate enchiladas."

"Honey, I'd eat the eye raht outta yo head for the raht price," she laughed. "My man's a Mexican," she continued, "…'fact, he's what fust called me '*Anajita*', don't ya know, writin' a 'j' 'nstead a 'h', which I don' git at all… an' I had a learn all about enchiladas, tamales, tacos, you name it, to make him happy and that was worth the trouble. An' look at me," she teased, "you gotta know I can eat me a bunch o' dem bur-ritos." When she laughed her whole ample body jiggled like it was used to having a very good time. She made Jack smile. "Now tell me, honey, what's it gonna take to send you back to bed for all Saturday mornin' and forgettin' all about dis here garage sale?"

It was an intriguing idea, Jack realized. If he could get all his junk converted to a few bucks and not have to put up with a parade of gawkers and the stint of forced good behavior, it might be worth a lesser take. "Well, Anajita," Jack began, using the correct form, "….that's right, isn't it?"

"Anahida," she corrected, forcing a hard 'h' and emphasizing a sharp 'd', "that's right."

"Well, Anajita, I haven't given much thought to a total price for the whole thing. I wouldn't know how much to ask."

"Of course you do mista Jack," she boomed, "you know 'xactly how much."

"How's that?" he asked mystified.

"Well, now," she began after a sigh, "jus' why you sellin' all this stuff?"

"Why am I selling this stuff?"

"Mista Jack, are you addled or somethin' lahk 'at?"

"Addled?"

"Addled! Slow! A few bricks short of a load…"

"Oh, oh," Jack caught on, "why no, I'm not like that."

"Well, you is the dummes' white man I've eva seen. You can't answer the simplist quesh'n."

"Oh, no, I'm sorry, I just don't see the point of your question," he explained.

"Jus' humor me," she insisted.

"Fine, fine."

"Well?"

"Oh, uh, well I'm moving and I won't have room for all this stuff where I'm going so I thought I'd be better off selling it than putting it in one of those storage places, you know, the one's where they rent you a closet or store room by the month."

"How much dat storage place cost?" she asked.

"Hmm, I guess about a hundred a month," he replied.

"An' how long you gonna rent that place?"

"Well, I don't know, maybe a year, maybe more."

"So you figures that yo gonna pay out 'bout $1,000 good money to put this stuff in a storage, maybe $2,000 if'n you forget all 'bout it. Then when yo' gets tired of payin' that rent you gotta either get it out or sell it, raht?"

"I guess that's probably how it'll play out," he realized.

"So's if ah was to just put this ole junk in my pickup truck and hauls it away this mornin' you'd be better off by more than $1,000, won't you, mista Jack?"

"Well," he stalled as he tried to reconcile in his own mind how she wasn't exactly right, and if she was, what he'd respond to do better than the nothing she seemed to be offering. "Well, I'm not going to give this away, Anajita…"

"Anahida," she corrected.

"Whatever…, by your own logic I'd be better off selling

this stuff all day for anything at all and putting the rest on the curb for the trash man."

"Well, yo' isn't the dummes' white man afterall," she smiled, then added, "maybe the third or fourth dummes', but not the dummes'!" She laughed out loud and jiggled, and it was so infectious that Jack found himself laughing out loud too.

"Lis'n here, honey, I'm gonna do yo' a great big favor. Ahm gonna give you $500 cash money for everythin' you got over there in that room," she said pointing to the collected items he'd set aside to sell. "That's more than fair and Anahida is an upraht Christian woman."

Jack was more taken by Anajita than her pitch. He realized he liked her and it was that more than anything else that persuaded him. But his head still swam a bit as it tried to convert itself from thinking about the items he was selling, as elements of the transaction, to her thinking, which was that this was a transaction about relief. "You drive a hard bargain, Anajita…,"

"Anahida," she corrected again.

"Anahida," he said as he pensively tapped his finger on his upper lip. Then he looked into her eyes and nodded, "Ok, Anahida, you've got a deal if you can get all this stuff out of here and into your pick-up by noon today."

"Ooh, honey, that's no problem," as she rose up from the chair and pried open her carpetbag of a purse and pulled out a manila file folder and counted out five crisp one hundred dollar bills. "And don't you worry none about that." She flipped open her cell phone and speed dialed a number. "Ocky? Dat yo', honey? Honey, you needs to git on ova ta 1628 Huisache Street, overn' Weslaco an pick up a load from a mista Jack," she instructed. "Jack," she repeated in a shout. "Now, yo's got ta do dis raht now, honey," she admonished. "Now did yo' get that numba? 1628 Huisache. Yeah, Weslaco. Fahne. Movin' on." She turned to Jack and explained, "That's mah boy, Ocky, well axially, 'Octavio', lahk his daddy, buts ah calls 'm Ocky."

"So, you don't pick up the loot in your pick up?" asked Jack.

"Oh, no, mista Jack. I'm the brains behind this bidnis. Ah lets otha's do the heavy lift'n," then she paused before saying, "Well, it's been a real pleasure, mista Jack, and thanks for the coffee; you've been real nahce."

"It's been a pleasure to meet you, Anajita…"

"Anahida."

"A real pleasure to do business with you. By the way, what's your full name?" he asked.

"Now mista Jack, you ain't one of them In-ternal Rev-noo 'gents, is you?" she asked as if half joking.

"Now Anahida, you act like you might be skipping a few taxes there," Jack teased.

"Skippin'? Well, I don' know nothin' about no skippin'. You take a look at a big woman lahk me and tell me ah's been skippin'," she teased back.

"Good point," he laughed, nodding in understanding of her want for anonymity.

At that moment, Moses walked into the kitchen from the bedroom.

"Oh, my God!" she shrieked, "what is that varmint?"

"Varmint! That's just a cat," Jack reassured her as he reached down and picked up Moses.

"Ah knows a cat from a rat, mista Jack, but that's a poor excuse for a cat."

"Well, he is a bit raggedy. I just found him a few days ago. He's a rescue."

She took a long look at the cat, then at Jack, in his disheveled state and asked, "Who rescued who?"

Jack cocked his head.

"You take care, honey," she said as she walked through the door to her car.

"You too," he called back absentmindedly. He wondered who did rescue whom, as he plopped into his Barcalounger.

He fell asleep, waiting for Ocky to come pick up the stuff.

Chapter 14

CALVIN RICHTER SQUINTED to focus as his right eye caught a glimpse of girl running frantically past the window of the restaurant. New York City is a place where anything can happen, and Calvin didn't want to miss anything if it did. From his table right next to the door, he watched her continue down Park Avenue. She was shouting something. He rose to lean out the door to get a better view and saw a man suddenly catch a piece of paper that was flying past him. The woman ran up to him. He smiled. They talked a few moments. He handed her the paper. Calvin returned to his one-chair table and his lunch: deli-sliced honey ham on rye with Durkee's.

Same exact sandwich, same deli, same table, every weekday and most Saturdays, for the last three years. Normally, he'd be reading his *Barrons*, occasionally putting down his sandwich, pulling his highlighter from his coat pocket, and coloring a line from an article, or a bond in the listings. But today was Saturday so he would read through the classifieds in the *New York Times*, especially the ads for "previously owned" Porsches. One day, he thought, one day.

He saw himself riding along the Parkway on a summer weekend up through Connecticut. The top is down and the tree canopy that reaches across the highway and touches fingers, rushes by in a blur, as if he were barreling down a tunnel of green, the wind blowing on his face and his thinning blonde hair dancing on his head. The dashboard is reflected in his Costa del Mars and under them stretches a pencil line of a smile, turned impishly up at the corners. All is right with the world.

"You leaving?" a voice rudely interrupted.

"Pardon?" he blurted to no one in particular, briefly disoriented.

"You leaving?" the words repeated, only now associated with a small woman under the mound of an aged overcoat that had jutting from it two spindly arms with hands of gnarly fingers on each, one hand holding a paper plate precariously, and the other tenuously grasping a huge plastic tumbler of tea.

"Ah, sure, sure," he said awkwardly as he retreated in self-defense.

When he was in his last year at the B School in Cambridge, the conventional wisdom was that rising stars had the same imperative as sharks: move or die. Three years in a job was the max. He was in the sixth year of the same job title, V.P., Research - Gas and Oil, at three different banks. Yet he hadn't moved out of his office even once. Same office, same desk, same water stain on the ceiling tile, the one that was four rows from the door, and two from the window.

The merger mania that swept the banking industry in the '90s had shaken things up quarterly. They called them "Velcroes": The loud ripping sound that you could feel deep inside your gut was the old sign being torn off and the new one being applied. The only thing that really changed was the name of the bank.

That made him nervous some of the time. Most of the time, he was just bored. This week, at least, he worked for Fenre Pease.

But, if things worked out as planned, all that was about to change.

His cell phone chirped. "Richter, here," he answered.

"It's on," the voice announced.

"Stubb," Richter boomed, "you are one wonderful sonuvabitch!"

"Yeah, but I want to be one rich sonuvabitch," Stubb returned.

"When's the test?"

"Monday."

"You set?"

"Set and then some. I've got some 'divine intervention' at work," Stubb explained.

"Gotcha; I hear that," Richter said, then added, "But are you sure about this? Are you sure this is going to work?"

"Trust me, Calvin, I know what I'm doing. By Wednesday morning the lab will confirm that Tract 52 of the Espiritu Sancti Grant, Share 25 is the new center of the natural gas universe," Stubb chuckled.

"The what?"

"The Magne Ranch!"

"Right," confirmed Richter, feigning that he understood all along. He had learned to be good at that.

"And how 'bout your end, Calvin; are you ready up there?"

"Covered. The minute the lab report is released we are supposed to meet upstairs with the legal eagles. Counsel is supposed to issue its recommendation. It'll be a 'go.'"

"Are you sure?"

"Fes, you do your job and I'll do mine," Richter replied testily.

"Okay, okay," Stubb smoothed. "I was just being interested."

"I'm interested enough for the both of us."

Stubb made a muted laughing sound and said, "I hear that. Gotta go."

Calvin Richter folded his cell phone and held it to his chin briefly before returning it to his inside coat pocket. This deal had to go. The Magne Gas Field Project was how he was going to break out of the stranglehold over his career. A public offering for a new company that had proven gas reserves was going to make a huge hit. The investment banking fees for Fenre Pease, his own small equity position's capital gains for his 401K, and the serious enhancement of his reputation on the street. These would all be measured in tens of millions of dollars. Calvin Richter was about to become somebody--all because of an accident.

Amazing, the workings of fate, Calvin thought. If he'd not been coming out of the Mall in Poughkeepsie at the moment he did, if he'd not seen the khaki colored Ford Escape rental car back into his Mercedes, he'd never have met Sam Kiel. And if he'd never met Sam, he'd never have gone to that party at the Renaissance Hotel. And if he'd not done that, he'd never have met Festor Stubb. Without Festor, Calvin Richter would have never had this shot.

Fate, Calvin thought, and justice.

Chapter 15

WHEN HE HEARD THE tapping on the door, Jack pulled himself up and went to the front window and peered out through the blinds. There was a red Jeep parked in front. There wasn't any way to get all this stuff into a little Jeep, he thought, as he opened the door.

"Well, looky here, if it isn't the edible color guy," purred a familiar voice. He blinked in surprise at the image through the screen door.

"What?" he responded, bewildered.

"At the Target," she explained, sensing his confusion, "you know, the other day, you were looking at the colors…"

"Oh, right, the markers. You're the girl, I mean, the lady there…"

"Yep, that's me," she filled in. There was an awkward pause as they stared at one another.

"So…" prompted Jack.

"I'm here for the garage sale. This is the address, right?" she asked, suggesting a fear she'd gotten it wrong.

"The garage sale!" Jack blurted. "Yes, yes, this is it," he said, opening the door to let her in, then suddenly realizing that he'd sold it all to Anajita. "Oh," he said, almost to himself. "The thing is," he said slowly, "the thing is…"

She walked past him and into the foyer.

"Well, what *is* the thing?" she interrupted playfully.

"The thing is, that it's all sold."

"Sold," she exclaimed, surprised.

"Sold," he repeated.

"It's not even nine o'clock!" she insisted.

"Not even eight-thirty," he corrected.

"What was it, a midnight sale?" she said sarcastically, strolling over to the stacks in the living room.

"Wha…, no, no," he stammered, "it's just that a lady came by before dawn and bought the whole thing."

"Honestly?"

"Honestly."

"Hmm," she said looking to her left and right, then idly inspecting a lamp that she held up to eye level, turning it this way then that.

"It isn't anything you'd want," he offered in consolation.

"How would you know that?"

He struggled for an answer. "I'm psychic?" he suggested, weakly.

"Hmm. Honestly?"

"Well, almost, I am possibly psychotic," he teased, but sounding serious.

"Now *THAT*, I could believe," she played, adding, "So, you're funny."

"Honestly?" Jack replied.

She stifled an out loud laugh, but failed, as she fanned the pages of an old book. "Even the books…they're sold too? I like old ones, the way they look and smell." She raised the book to her nose and sniffed. "And there's lot's of stuff you can use again," she said, studying a three-ring binder, flipping it over and sideways, testing if the official looking yellow front cover insert could be slid out. "Like this binder. They cost almost four bucks new, you know. Mind if I take it?"

"Sorry, can't do it. I promised…"

"Ethics," she muttered, "and who's that?" she suddenly insisted, pointing by lifting her chin in the direction of the cat.

"Well, that little fellow," Jack explained, "I found him. In fact, I found him on the same day we ran into each other at Target," he added, suddenly realizing the coincidence.

"No foolin'?" she said, now dropping to her knees and gently tugging at the cat's ears. The cat immediately responded to her warmly.

"Yeah. I don't know why I brought him home, really."

She looked up at Jack with a serious curiosity and asked, "So, are you going to keep him?"

"Keep him?" Jack said realizing he hadn't actually given that much thought. "I've never really had a pet."

"Why not?" she asked.

"I guess it was my father more than anything else. He wouldn't let my brother or sister or me have pets. He said we had no time for them. We needed to be studying."

"Fun guy," she observed sarcastically.

"Yeah, a barrel of laughs," he added realizing there was more that could be said that wouldn't be.

"Well, yo' daddy ain't here now," she said, affecting a gang member accent.

"Good point."

"Does he have a name, this cat?"

"Moses."

"Moses, hmmm," she said starting to smile. She looked over to the kitchenette and saw the food and water bowls on the floor and the litter box in the corner by the back door. "Looks to me like you've already decided."

Jack followed her eyes to the items and admitted, "Yeah, I guess I have."

"Ya like him?" she asked directly as she rose to her full height.

"You know," Jack found himself saying even as he felt silly doing so, "I think I do."

"So this stuff is already sold, then," she changed the subject.

"'Fraid, so."

"And I guess I'm too early for the next garage sale…"

"About five years."

"Hmm," she said and paused. "Well it was nice not buying anything from you," she said backing and starting to turn.

"Nice not selling you anything," he replied, following her to the door.

"Oh," she suddenly stopped and turned.

"Yes?"

"What's your name?" she asked.

"Jack."

"Angela."

"Nice meeting you, Angela."

"You too," she said, then turned and walked through the door.

Jack paused and regarded her retreating form with some satisfaction. She was pretty and there was something about her manner that attracted him. He closed the door once she was into her red Jeep. As he turned to head for the kitchen, a shrill squealing sound virtually blanked out all conscious thought for a split second.

"Oh, Moses," he apologized profusely, "I didn't mean to step on your tail!" He reached down to pick up and comfort the cat, who responded by arching his head back and offering his chin for some scratching. "Well, I guess you're not too bothered," Jack said, feeling relieved.

It had been a busy morning already and it wasn't even nine o'clock. He was too awake now to nap, so he dressed and started to survey his kept items to determine what he'd need to package them for transport to the sailboat. He sat down at his lap-top and began to key in a list of items, with a column specifying the location on the boat where they'd be stored. He had created a numbering system for each possible locker, bay, nook and cranny.

A diagram of the boat hull, both top down and in cross-section, was tacked to the wall to the right of his desk, identifying each space with the respective number. He thought how his sister would laugh at him to see this. It was so his nature, she'd say. And it was. "A place for everything and everything in its place," his father used to say.

Moses startled, crouched and looked towards the door. Jack wondered what he heard, then understood when there was a tapping on the screen door. He felt a sudden surge of excitement as he rushed to open it.

"This 1628 Huisache?" a young man asked efficiently, reading off a clip board, pulling a pencil from behind his ear.

"Yes."

"I'm here to pick up the stuff."

"Are you…"

"Ocky, yes, sir."

"Come on in," Jack said, pulling the door all the way open. "It's over there. All the stuff in that room, except for the rug."

"You sure about the rug…" Ocky inquired in an almost admonishing tone. My mom didn't say nothin' about no rug."

Jack looked at the young man, thinking about how to interpret the confusion of double negatives and quickly grew tired of thinking. "Never mind about the rug; take the rug," he surrendered impatiently.

"And what about that cat," Ocky pressed, pointing with the pencil at Moses, who was now ensconced on a stack of books in the middle of the room.

"Not the frigging cat!" Jack shouted, surprising even himself with the vehemence of his protest.

"No cat, no cat, fine. Ain't no use for it. And if it is a 'friggin' cat', you ought to get it fixed," Ocky quickly retreated, sensing the discovery of Jack's definite boundary. Ocky was a sophomore at the community college, a straight-A student. He knew how far to push the bumpkin act and when to let it go. "You need to sign this here sheet. I'll fill in the stuff once I've got it on the truck."

Jack wondered at the function of such a form but it was entirely irrelevant to him, so he quickly obliged.

"Know if that Jeep's for sale, mister?" Ocky asked feigning no serious interest.

"Geez, you're like a plague of locusts, I swear. I'm just selling this stuff in the living room. Not even the dust under it, not the floor, not the land under that…" Jack said with an edge.

"Ok, ok!" Ocky said defensively, "Just askin' 'cuz I've had my feelers out for a red Jeep."

"Maroon," Jack corrected, handing back the pencil to Ocky.

"Whatever," Ocky replied, sliding the pencil over his ear.

In a half hour, the room was cleared to the wood floor. Jack stood at the doorway between the kitchen and the empty room, coffee in hand. It felt amazingly larger, all of a sudden, and relieved. Being rid of the ancillary accumulations of day to day life was a wonderful feeling. It seemed to open things up for new opportunities, he thought, and erased old mistakes.

He drained the last drops from the cup and started toward the sink to wash it out. Half way there he stopped abruptly. He turned to the trash can, stepped on the pedal to open the lid, then with a flourish, dropped the cup into the gaping trash bag and dropped the lid. "Yes!" he said agreeably, dusting his hands as he walked toward the bedroom. Moses scampered after him.

Chapter 16

"PORT MANSFIELD POLICE," Jason announced into the phone.

"Have you seen mah husband?" the female voice insisted.

"Who is this?" Jason asked.

"Have you seen mah husband?" she insisted again.

"Ma'am, I don't know who your husband is unless you tell me," Jason explained, exasperated.

"'Tavio Paredes, that's who," she replied in a mixture of anger and angst.

"Tavio Paredes?"

"Yes, that's who, have you seen him?"

"No ma'am. Was he due to come by the office?" Jason asked.

"Ah don't know 'bout that, but 'Tavio, he went fishin' last night and he ain't come back." Her tone was clearly worried now.

"Well, I've not seen anything of him. Have you called over to The Palmetto? Think he might have gone over there for a few beers, maybe?" Jason offered.

"'Tavio don't drink beer or nothin' else," she spat impatiently.

"Have you tried any of his fishing buddies?"

"He don't go fishin' for a hobby, mista. He fishes for a livin'.

It ain't no social thing," she explained indignantly.

"I'm just trying to help, Mrs. Paredes," he tried to calm her down. "Let me check around the marina here and see if he's here or if anybody else may have seen him. Can I have a number to call you back?" He took her number and put the phone down and picked up his VHF radio mike. "Elroy?"

There was a long pause. Elroy was the Texas Parks and Wildlife game warden who patrolled the waters near Port Mansfield.

"Elroy, here," a voice crackled.

"Elroy, Jason. Do you know a Tavio Paredes, a fisherman?"

"Jason? What're you doing up? Thought you were off at noon?" Elroy wondered.

"I'm going. Just got this call on the way out from some lady looking for her husband…Tavio Paredes, know him?"

"'Tavio? Sure. An older guy. Has one of those john boats. Painted blue, I think. Why?"

"His wife just called in and said he didn't come in this morning."

"That's not exactly an emergency," Elroy said drolly.

"Probably not, but just thought I'd check around."

"No sign of him, but I'll keep an eye open and tell him to call home if I see him."

"Thanks." Jason thought a moment. He picked up a Daily Activity Sheet and wrote down, "Saturday, 1300 hrs." and content of the call. "Uh, what's your name again?" he asked the clerk across the room.

"Phyllis?" she responded but in the form of a question.

"Phyllis?" he replied also in a question, confused.

"Yes, sir," she answered.

"I'm headed out, but I just made a note here about a call…somebody looking for a fisherman who didn't come in this morning. You might get a call later."

"Wha'…Ok," she responded absently, riveted while whiting out a typing error on a report.

Jason looked at her hunched over and meticulously painting out a letter. "Phyllis," he said in a soft voice.

"Uh, yes," she said without looking up or pausing.

"What are you doing?"

"Typing," she said as she stopped, the brush poised mid-air above the paper, and looked up at Jason through her coke bottle bifocals. Her eyes looked like two blue tropical fish swimming in a bowl.

"That's a typewriter, Phyllis," he gently revealed.

"I know," she confirmed.

"It's an historical display, not for doing reports."

"Oh," she said looking back down to the aqua Smith Corona and pushing her lenses back up to her face with the back of her hand, still holding the white-out brush and inadvertently painting the few strands of her hair with it.

"Use the computer over on that desk," he said while pointing to the counter.

"Oh," she said with a productive sniffle. She stalled.

"Well?" Jason asked impatiently.

"Well," she drawled finally, "the thing is…well, I don't know anything about computers. They didn't say anything about using computers at the unemployment office. I'm not high tech." She paused to see if there was an impact to be had from this confession.

Jason stared at her for a moment. For an instant he began to think about the nature of the Port's policy regarding "non-professional" office help, then the educational state of the workforce, implications, then… He stopped himself mid-thought. It was a half hour past his shift. She worked for the Port, not him. "Good night," he called over his shoulder as he walked out into the afternoon light.

"'Night," she responded, staring at the typewriter.

Chapter 17

THE ANNUAL PORT ISABEL Historical Society Awards Lunch was the one event each year that sent local members to Dillard's in Brownsville to look for a new outfit. Sophie reflected the casual lifestyle of the town and would not otherwise bother, but this occasion was different.

This year Sophie was on the decorations committee and had worked late into Friday night, setting the tables and making the floral centerpieces at the old Port Isabel Yacht Club. Decades earlier the Yacht Club had been *the* hotel and restaurant, an important destination for landlubbers and sailors alike. The old marina was now converted into a boatyard, but the buildings still stood on a knoll, in a cluster of tall Washingtonian palm trees, overlooking the docks.

The guest of honor for this year was John Magne IV, whose family had owned several large tracts of land nearby and some of the old buildings on the main street, just opposite the light house. The old Magne mansion still stood on the east side of town, overlooking the Laguna Madre.

Before John was fifteen years old, his mother and father would bring the whole family to stay at the place during most summers. During the other times of the year, his father often stayed at the house when he had business in the area, while the family was back on the ranch.

The local historical society had approached Magne earlier in the year, suggesting that he donate the house to the society, who would then restore it to its original splendor and use it to house the historical museum. Today's award was in appreciation for the donation, and Magne and his wife Gabriela were present to receive it.

The attendees gathered on the front porch for wine and cheese and chatted while they waited for Magne to arrive. Sophie moved from group to group, exchanging pleasantries and at one point found herself standing aside with Eva Luz.

"Eva, dear, how are you?" Sophie asked in that southern friendliness that actually expects a qualitative reply.

"Oh, Sophie!" she answered, as they kissed each other on opposite cheeks.

"Isn't this wonderful," Sophie gushed. "Finally, we're going to have our own museum."

"It's just so hard to believe. I know how you have always loved that house, Sophie."

"Well, it's part of our heritage, Eva, and we have to do what we can to preserve it," Sophie said in an officious tone.

"So true. I just know it is going to be fabulous when you and the committee are done with it."

"We have high expectations," Sophie said.

"Mr. Magne has been so generous, hasn't he?" Eva cooed.

"The Magne's have always been good to Port Isabel," Sophie agreed.

"Yes," Eva said, as if she knew more than she was saying.

"How is Ted doing?" Sophie changed the subject.

"Wonderful," she gushed. "In fact, he'll be here today for the award presentation."

"Wonderful," Sophie echoed, wondering why Marco Luz would be attending when he had never attended any society event before.

"Can I tell you a secret?" Eva whispered importantly, leaning into Sophie.

"A secret? Of course."

"My Marco is going to run for Congress," she said in a hushed but excited tone.

"Really?" Sophie blurted. "What district?"

"This one, silly."

"Why, that really is a surprise, Eva. What about Lencho Monde?"

Eva looked at Sophie and smiled knowingly.

At that moment, there was a build of chatter that announced the arrival of John and Gabriela Magne. Sophie invited everyone back into the dining room and led the Magnes up to the head table. As the attendees filed in and took their chairs, Sophie recognized Marco Luz sitting with his mother on the far right of the room.

After the lunch and Magne's acceptance of the award, people came up to shake hands, thank him and pose for pictures.

"Doris," Sophie said to the society historian, "I want you to get a picture of Mr. and Mrs. Magne here." John Magne stood stiffly next to Gabriela, who after a instant's delay, took his arm and turned, smiling to the camera with dark brown eyes that seemed fixed on something far away. She wore her lustrous black hair drawn up in a perfect bun, which emphasized her long aristocratic neck. As she stood next to her husband, her head tilted slightly away from him, her poise was dignified, her manner reserved and cool, but gracious. It was as if Gabriela had a touch of royalty in her, Sophie thought.

"Now, Mr. Magne, would you mind posing with some of our guests? You don't mind, do you, Mrs. Magne?" she said winking at Gabriela, who smiled back. Sophie then arranged different groups to pose with Magne.

"Eva," she called out, "bring that boy of yours over here so we can have a picture." Then she arranged them by placing John Magne between them. "Now how about a picture with just Eva and Mr. Magne, and then Marco and Mr. Magne?" When the last photos were taken, Sophie said, "Doris, let me have that film and I'll get it processed. I'll want the pictures right away for the next newsletter."

Sophie stood at the top of the stairs at the front of the Yacht Club with the rest of the officers of the society, waving as the Magnes drove away. One more task in the long plan completed, she thought.

Chapter 18

JASON WAS BACK AT the Port Office for the Sunday afternoon shift.

"Jason? Are you there?" a voice crackled over the VHF radio at the Port Office.

Jason pushed the mike button to reply. "Yeah. Elroy, is that you?"

"Figured you weren't at Mass," Elroy joked. "I think I've found something."

"What's up?"

"I've found a boat. I think it could be Paredes's."

"Where 'bouts?"

"I'm across the Laguna, on the back side of Padre. It looks like it was stranded after that high tide we had when the norther passed."

"Any sign of the old man?"

"No, but there is something strange about it."

"What's that?"

"Well, it's all normal-looking. You know, everything's all organized, neat and pretty clean, at least for a fishing boat. There's some bait on the sole, a loose weight, some spots of fish blood, the usual. Nothing really out of the ordinary."

"So why do you call it strange?"

"For one thing, there's a pole all rigged. Looks like it just dragged along as the boat drifted. The tackle box is open, sitting on the sole of the boat. It looks like everything is all set to fish, except for one thing."

"And that is…"

"There's no fisherman."

"Any signs he was there, like footprints in the shallows around the boat?"

"No, but that doesn't mean he didn't get picked up by another boat."

"The motor," Jason nudged.

"What about it?"

"Did you try it?"

"No, but that's a good idea. Let me give it a shot and call you back."

"I'll be here." Jason put the mike back onto its hook on the radio transmitter. Motors broke down all the time and fishermen regularly rescued other fishermen. The old man could be anywhere with some drinking buddy or working his way back home. Or he could be stranded on Padre Island. It was sixty miles up the island to Corpus and nothing between there and the Mansfield jetty except the occasional four-wheeler, but it was nearly three miles from the back of the island to the beach where they would likely go. An old man out there very long could get into some trouble.

"Jason." The mayor interrupted his line of thought.

"Yes, Mayor," Jason said as the mayor entered the front door. "What can I do for you, sir?"

"I want to call a meeting for next Friday. Could you get an agenda posted?"

"Sure. Do you have one made out yet?"

"It's a Special Meeting, so you only have one agenda item, none of the usual reports and stuff. Get a pen and write this down," he said, pausing for Jason to be ready.

"Ok, shoot," Jason said.

"Put 'discussion and possible action regarding certain exploration opportunities in the Laguna Madre,'" the mayor dictated.

"Explorations?" Jason asked.

"Yes, just put that for now," the Mayor ordered.

"Ok, got it," Jason said, "I'll get it posted on the board in the morning. Oh, Mayor, what time?"

"Make it 4:30 P.M."

"Got it, thanks."

"Thanks, Jason," the mayor said as he left.

Jason knew it was begrudgingly that the aldermen and the mayor held their required monthly meetings. This Special Meeting thing was entirely new. Something was cooking. His thoughts were interrupted by static, then a click on the VHF radio.

"Jason," he could hear Elroy calling.

"Jason, here. Whatcha got, Elroy?"

"Hear that?"

"What?"

"That," Elroy said as an outboard motor purr grew louder and louder, as if the radio mike were being brought closer to it. "Do you hear it?" Elroy yelled over it.

"It works, then?"

"Started on the first pull. I checked the fuel line for kinks, took a look at the filter and tank. All clean. There's no way this motor conked out on him."

"What do you think?" Jason asked.

"Seems pretty weird to me," Elroy replied.

"Give me a description of that boat so I can see if it matches the old man's,"

"It's a shallow sport, blue hull, sort of off-white deck. The outboard is an old Evinrude."

"Any state registration numbers?"

"Yeah, hold on. Uh, here: TX 43688821. Got that?"

"TX 43688821," Jason repeated.

"Right. Anything else you want me to do here?" Elroy asked.

"Take a look around. See if you can find any tracks north of the boat. Maybe it drifted loose when he got off, maybe to un-snag a line or something. Then bring in that boat."

"Will do," Elroy signed off.

Jason thought he ought to call Mrs. Paredes to see if all he had to report was a found boat, when a large black woman marched through the door and up to the counter.

"Mah name is Anahida Paredes and ahm lookin' for my husband, 'Tavio," she declared with a clear sense of urgency.

"Mrs. Paredes," Jason answered, "I was just about to call you. We found a boat. Can you describe his?"

A look of fear came across her face, which she fought back to answer. "It's one of those flat bottomed boats," she said imprecisely.

"What color, ma'am?"

"I think it was blue colored."

"What about the motor. Do you know what that was?"

"I don't know much about motor boats," she confessed, then added, "But I do know he spent a whole lot of money gettin' it fixed up."

"I don't suppose you know the state registration number…"

"No sir, ahm not sure what that is," she said in a subdued tone.

"We're going to bring in that boat we found, Mrs. Paredes, and I hope you'll come in and see if it's your husband's. Meantime, we are looking for him but he's probably either on another boat on the way back in or somewhere on the island. We're going to keep looking. Do you have a cell phone number I can call to reach you?"

Anajita was folded in and seemed smaller as she took a piece of paper from her purse and wrote down her cell number with a shaking hand. She handed it to Jason and looked at him through gathering pools, "You'se have to find my 'Tavio," she pleaded. "Ah din't make him no samiches, not even no coffee, so he ain't got nothin' and he's gonna be real hungry. Ah was bein' such a bitch to him 'cuz I din't want him going out wit' that there norther comin', but he jus' won't listen to me sometimes."

"We're doing everything we can, Mrs. Paredes, but you don't need to be getting all worked up. I'm sure he's fine and will be home sometime today, if he isn't there already. Go on home and wait there. If he comes in, please call me right away," Jason instructed.

He watched Anajita Paredes turn and walk slowly to the door. She paused before she went out, as if about to say something, then went on. Jason reached under the counter and pulled up the binder with important local phone numbers, ran his finger down the page with the U's and found the number and dialed it.

"U.S. Coast Guard," a young man answered.

"I've got a report of a missing fisherman," Jason began.

Chapter 19

"SMART MOVE, THERE brother," Clinton greeted Junior from the comfortable slouch in a canvas folding chair upwind from the smoking mesquite logs. Junior pulled a wooden Adirondack up closer and sat down, stretching his long legs out and crossing them at his brown cowhide boots.

"Just good politics, little brother. You see, I figure if I come to every other one of these Sunday dinners, I get two things done at once," Junior explained.

"How's that?"

"Well, when I don't show they're pissed and wonder where I am and when I do they're glad to see me. Either way, I'm the center of attention," Junior half-joked.

"Figures. You've always got an angle," Clinton laughed. They both gazed into the red embers of the cooking fire, taking in the sweet scents of a South Texas twilight, mesquite, *pan de campo* and a heavy green damp that arose from the undergrowth of the chaparral surrounding the camp site.

As children they had helped out on the late autumn cattle round-ups. At first they were officially assigned to Juanito, the camp cook. He had them kneading out pillows of flour, baking powder, salt, sugar, corn oil and some milk into fat balls of dough. Then they rolled them out into round loaves, pounded them flat with their little fists, and put them into Dutch oven covered pans that were buried in the mesquite embers. Junior sometimes liked to add lots of sugar and when he did, Juanito called them *pacharelas* and baked them separately in butter instead of Crisco. Later they took turns perching on their father's lap as he sat above a gate at the separating chute, working the lever to decide which cattle went to market and which would be turned out to pasture. To Junior, he seemed to have the power over life and death.

As the boys grew older they joined on horseback. It was tough and dirty work, but as their grandfather often said, it would make men of them.

The boys competed rigorously for their father's approval. Try as he did, Junior was never the cowboy that his younger brother Clint was. He bristled still as he remembered his father's constant stream of corrections and admonitions, but mostly when his father would compare him unfavorably to Clint. But Junior excelled as a competition marksman and his proudest moment came the day he won the state championship. It was then that his father gave him his great-grandfather's Merkel, perhaps one of the rarest and finest game rifles ever made. He treasured it over all other things.

Clint was not happy when the herding was turned over to helicopters later, when they were teenagers, but Junior was relieved.

The familiar white Land Rover appeared around a clump of huisache trees and pulled up to the camp.

"So there's the Prodigal Son," Gabriela chided, opening the passenger side door.

"Hi, Gabriela," Junior replied perfunctorily.

"Good thing you're here, Junior boy. I was going to go out and round you up like one of Clint's wild animals," she warned good naturedly.

"Don't I know it, and probably branded me too," Junior admitted.

John Magne came around the front of the Rover, "Whoa, look what the horse drug in," he exclaimed in a faux surprise.

"Hi, Dad," Junior said, extending his hand to shake his father's.

"Hey, Clint!" John greeted his second son.

"Hey, Dad!" Clint answered.

"Get me a chair, there, Junior," Magne ordered, while Clint dragged another Adirondack over for Gabriela.

"Beautiful evening," Magne observed as they all turned to watch a spectacular skyscape of orange-glowing clouds. The air was chilly but not cold. The fire radiated a toasty warmth on the faces that were now turning golden in the yellowing, dusky light.

"It's hard to get tired of this," Clint spoke slowly and softly.

"It would be perfect," Junior said, "if we could set up a big ole' TV out here."

"Oh, Junior," Gabriela admonished, "you don't mean that."

"What are we drinking?" Junior asked, then turned to the camp wagon and shouted, "Juanito!"

"I wish you wouldn't do that," Gabriela said in a loud whisper.

"Juanito!" Junior called out impatiently.

"Si, Junior," replied a deep, nasal voice that didn't seem to come from the old, bent-over man that emerged from the shadows.

"Corona, no, tres," Junior ordered.

"Si, señor," the old man replied, turning back to the wagon.

"Junior!" Gabriela said sharply.

"What?" he replied testily.

"You shouldn't speak to Juanito in that tone of voice. He's your elder," she admonished.

"Oh, for Godsake, Gabriela," his father interrupted. "Let the boy alone."

"Just the same," she said, "it's not respectful."

"Oh, here we go…" Junior said growing angry.

"Cool it, Junior," Clint whispered to his brother.

Junior went quiet and an awkward silence amplified the sounds of crackling fire. He did not care that his father married Gabriela last year. She wasn't his mother; she was just his father's wife, a glorified gold-digger. What annoyed him was her superior attitude, like she was better than them.

Gabriela bristled at the tone Magne used with her and it angered her that he would let Junior speak disrespectfully to her at times, especially when he was drinking.

It was the way about the Magnes that she particularly hated, and she suspected it was well ingrained in their genes, at least that was what she had always been told. By her own witness she could see they were rough and uncultured, in many ways, even though generations of wealth and opportunity should have smoothed the edges more, she thought. Sometimes the arrogance was insufferable, but she could tolerate it, in the balance. She had bigger plans for the Magnes that would refine the ranch. And she was infinitely patient, a trait well ingrained in her family background.

"Tres Coronas!" Juanito announced coming up to the Magnes. Junior snatched the three bottles from him abruptly. Everyone pretended not to notice.

"Juanito," Gabriela asked politely, "could you please bring out some more for Clint and me and a nice Glynnie for Mr. Magne?"

"Si, Señora," he replied and headed back to the wagon.

"What's the deal with that gas thing you've got going, Dad?" Clint asked, hoping to relieve the tension.

"Far as I can tell, ok," Magne explained. "They've got some sort of test working tomorrow and I guess we'll know after that."

"I've been wondering, though," Clint said, sounding worried.

"What about?" Magne asked.

"Well, all the commotion. You know, when they have all these trucks and pipes and barges and all, won't that make a lot of mess and noise?"

"At first, maybe, but all that'll die down pretty quick, I think," Magne reassured him.

"I mean, well, why didn't granddad get into all that oil drilling back then when all the other ranchers were trying it?" Clint probed.

"He didn't like the idea of a lot of strangers having free run of the range, Clint, and I can't say that I blamed him," Magne responded frankly.

"And aren't we going to have all that with this gas drilling?" Clint challenged.

Junior snickered and drained a bottle of beer, immediately twisting the top off the next.

"Not the way I've got this thing figured out," Magne explained. "You see, when they did those oil deals the ranchers made leases with the oil companies, giving them the right to access the drill and well head sites. That's not what we're doing. We're forming our own drilling company, with some of those fellows in New York--banker types…for their investment money, but we are the ones who run it here. Everybody on Magne land will work for us. So there won't be any strangers wandering around."

"And that's gonna mean millions," Junior interrupted enthusiastically. Gabriela squirmed as Junior's slurring grew more obvious.

"Well, let's hope," Magne said cautiously.

"Why," asked Clint, "what could happen?"

"They could find no gas, Clint, that's what," Magne explained.

"Fat chance," Junior blurted.

"Well, we'll see, Junior," Magne admonished.

"Mr. Stubb said we were going to make millions and millions," Junior said, "and he ought to know."

"Maybe so, but I'm not counting the chickens," Magne said.

"Well, I hope they don't find any," Clinton declared.

"You're a damned fool, brother," Junior said in a loud, angry voice.

"I know that granddad wouldn't like it," Clint argued.

"He was just an old time tree hugger," Junior said.

"Now, Junior," Gabriela intervened.

"Well he was. Always putting up butterfly cases, planting those dumb monte plants. Hell, they already grew wild everywhere!"

"Your grandfather was a naturalist," Magne insisted. "He was a scientist nearly."

"And he would never have gone for this gas thing," Clint chimed in.

"Maybe not," Magne argued, "but times have changed and we need to keep up with them…if we want to keep this ranch."

Silence underscored the seriousness in Magne's tone and it was the tone that all the family members knew meant that the topic was closed.

"Gabriela and I are heading up to Washington tomorrow for a few days," Magne said, changing the subject. "Any of you boys want to come along?"

"Not me!" both Clint and Junior shouted nearly in unison.

"All right then, I'll expect you boys to behave while we're gone," he admonished.

"We're not kids anymore, you know Dad," Clint teased him.

"I hope not," Magne said, then turning to Gabriela, "Now, let's eat."

Chapter 20

"WALTER, THIS IS JOHN MAGNE. We're going to need another couple of hundred thousand draw on our line of credit tomorrow. Could you see that the money is moved over to the Magne Ranch operating account?"

"Mr. Magne, hello," Walter Preston replied, shell shocked by Monday's first phone call and the instant jump into business.

"Can you get that done for me Walter? I'm on the way to Washington and I won't have time to deal with this," Magne bulldozed in a rapid, commanding tone.

"Did you say two hundred thousand, Mr. Magne?"

"Yes, that's right."

"Mr. Magne, I've called your office and spoken with Pat several times over the last two weeks…"

"Yes, yes, she told me. Walter, I've been real preoccupied this month and just haven't had time to get back to you."

"I understand, sir, but we do need to meet as soon as possible. Your line of credit has been exhausted, Mr. Magne."

"Walter, Walter," Magne derided him, "we've been down this road before. All I need is a little cash to cover operating expenses. It's only temporary."

"I understand, Mr. Magne, but we have to comply with regulations."

"Oh, for Christ's sake. I'm your biggest customer. You know we're good for it. Can't you just cooperate with me on this?"

"We appreciate your business, of course, Mr. Magne. It is very important to us and we want to be of whatever service we can, but…"

"Look, Walter, I've got to get moving here. Just get me a couple of hundred today and I promise: next week, you and I'll sit down and iron out any problems. We'll talk about anything you want."

Preston paused to think. It was the commitment to meet that he needed more than anything else right now. The Magnes had the bank in a difficult position. If the bank pressed so hard as to annoy John Magne, he could move his accounts and stall repaying on the line of credit for months, even a year, putting the bank into a serious liquidity crunch. But if the bank didn't press for payment, and the present trend continued, the bank would get further and further into trouble if the Magnes didn't settle the loans before the next bank examination. Preston knew he had no choice.

"I'll talk to the loan committee, Mr. Magne. I'm sure they'll approve another extension. But I cannot promise that they'll continue to do this. We must meet and work out a new plan, sir."

"You're a peach, Walter. Take care of this and we'll get together next week up at the ranch, promise."

"Should I call Pat to arrange a date and time?" Preston pushed back.

"Yeah, sure, call Pat," Magne replied before he hung up.

Preston was angry for allowing himself to be pushed around by Magne yet again. He was the president of a bank. Customers shouldn't treat him as if he had to apologize for trying to collect on a loan. That wasn't how it was supposed to be.

He sighed as he admitted to himself the truth of the world. The rules were different for the very rich and powerful.

Chapter 21

"MR. STUBB, PLEASE," the voice asked though the phone.

"Stubb, here."

"Mr. Stubb? Victor Sprague, Stembark Testing. I've got a note here to call you once we completed the tests at Magne Ranch 100."

"Yes?"

"We just finished taking the last soundings and are going to drive back to the lab in Houston. Just wanted you to know."

"Great, thanks, Victor was it?"

"Victor Sprague."

"Thanks, Victor. So, I understand the results will be out Wednesday?"

"Not my department, Mr. Stubb. You've got me there. We just do the tests, but I guess a couple of days is right."

"Fair enough. Thanks for reporting, Victor."

"No problem."

Festor folded his cell phone and turned to the calendar above his desk. If everything went as planned... his thoughts were interrupted by his cell phone ringing.

"Hello?"

"Festor?"

"Yeah."

"They're just leaving the test site."

"Yeah, I know. They just called me. How'd it go?"

"Far as I can tell, nothing unexpected."

"So they did the soundings at the old dock site…"

"Yeah, that's what I saw."

"Anywhere else?"

"Not as far as I can tell, Fes. They spent the whole time around the shed."

"You're sure."

"Yeah, I'm sure. I've been watching through the scope on my rifle."

"You did what I told you to, right?" Stubb asked urgently.

"Yeah, yeah, don't worry."

"I'm serious, Junior, you don't want any connection," Stubb warned.

"Fes, relax. It's ok."

"Any news on the *other thing*?" Stubb asked, intentionally vague.

"I haven't heard anything about it, at least so far."

"Where are you now?"

"I'm still here in the stand. I'm set up with the scope. I thought I'd stay until I was sure they weren't coming back for something."

"Good idea. See anything else?"

"Just a lot of birds."

"Anybody out there? Any boats?"

"Nothing. Just me 'n the birds."

"Good work, Junior," Stubb congratulated him. "You can take the rest of your life off!" He folded his phone and put it on the desk, stood up, uncapped a dry-erase marker, and drew a check-mark next to item twenty-nine with a flourish. He sat back down and elevated his feet to the lip of his desk, leaned back in his leather desk chair and surveyed a chart that arrayed an 8' by 4' melamine white board. "Another work of art," he said out loud to himself, smiling broadly.

Above and to the right of his corner-facing computer desk, ran three rows of shelves. The top one was a nearly matching set of like booklets, labeled as far back as fifteen years. These were the artifacts of a lifetime of deals. He called the shelf the "Grave Yard." He thought about how they were his version of the presidential library.

The second shelf was a series of binders holding all eight thousand pages of the *U.S. Federal Income Tax Code* and another companion set of interpretations and accounting standards. This he called the "Cornu Copia," the fertile fields that he cultivated for virtually free tax money, generously fertilized by the most plentiful of organic chemicals: greed and hope.

After about twenty pages or so, he had at an early age learned that the federal income tax code was a book of invoices, bills of lading for the delivery of political favors to some loyal, meaning "generous," group or friends of a few hundred legislators. In the midst of this intended tangle of conflicting and obfuscating regulation was a virtual universe teeming with opportunity and ripe for the brazen and clever. There was a reason they called it the tax "code."

Defending against literally millions of aggressive and ever drilling, never sleeping tax termites was an under-funded, under-trained, under-staffed bureaucracy which was just as bewildered by the law as the hapless citizens who honestly tried to comply. In the end, the harvest of this transaction between the powerful and the rich was that the only fools paying taxes according to Hoyle, were the middle class, who for their efforts, reaped a persistent, gnawing fear and guilt.

Stubb watched his father work himself to death, trying to provide for his family of four, only to lose his business, retirement savings and his home to an I.R.S. claim for back taxes. He remembered how they hounded him at home, at his shop, humiliating him by seizing his bank account then posting an official sign on the pad-locked door of the business his father built over thirty years.

Festor recalled with a shudder the sound of his mother's voice that Christmas Eve fifteen years ago. His father was found at his mechanic's shop. He'd run a hose from the exhaust of his pick up to the passenger side window, then duct taped it sealed. A policeman, who was called to the scene, later told him that there was a tape playing in an endless loop when he found the body, sitting in the driver's seat, wearing a white shirt, tie, and a sports jacket. It was a Glenn Campbell song, "Wichita Lineman." The funeral home said they could never fully get the grease and oil from under his fingernails, but that they could hide it.

The letter that came to his mom a year later drew different responses from his mother and himself. She collapsed into his sister's arms, sobbing. He read it and found himself laughing out loud. It was a notice written as a form letter. It referred to a date about four months before his father's suicide. It reported that the case against him was dropped because they had inadvertently pursued the wrong tax id number. They offered a perfunctory apology. They said that he should ignore all previous notices and that he could apply for a return of his property by filling out and submitting an enclosed form. The form, it happens, was not enclosed. Festor kept the letter, framed it, and hung it on the wall by his office door.

The third and lowest shelf was what he called, "The Field of Dreams," after the Costner movie. "I build it; they come," Festor knew. He could build the deal and the greedy would come to it like moths to a candle, bright, aromatic and irresistible.

His was the simplest and surest of alluring scents: money. For some of his marks, it was taxes avoided, for others, the promise of fabulous profits, and still others, rocketing investments. John Magne was something of a variation on the theme, but the object was the same. Festor's plan for Magne was to offer shares in a gas exploration and distribution company. Its inside track would be leases with the Magne Ranch for access to the heretofore undiscovered gas field under the coastal wetlands on the east edge of the ranch.

It answered all of Magne's preferences. It provided a quick surge of substantial money and yet gave up none of his land. As the controlling force in the new company, he wouldn't even have to put up with outsiders on site. It was the best of all worlds. And it explained in a nutshell how a person like Festor Stubb could ever get access to, much less a deal with the likes of John Magne.

For Festor Stubb, John Magne was the perfect mark. He at first worried, then wondered how Magne could park all common sense, even a lifetime of intuition, but he really already knew. It was the same with all his marks. Sweet greed. The smell of money perfumed away all the stench of rot that hung heavy in the air. He had to admit he almost enjoyed doing people like John Magne as much as taking the money. The arrogance was infuriating. People like Magne, powerful and wealthy, saw themselves as a privileged race. Magne, Stubb thought, made in the image and likeness of a god.

For most con men, making off with the loot was the measure of success. For Festor Stubb, that was amateur play. For him the art in these schemes was coming off as one of the duped, always escaping scot-free and a lot richer. He was a true artist. The landscape was strewn with the carcasses of his deals.

Stubb liked to amuse himself recalling the observation made by Sam Kiel, "Festor Stubb: A just man. Just within the law, just out of sight, and just plain genius.'"

He was especially going to enjoy doing John Magne, that arrogant, self-righteous, spoiled bastard.

The key to selling the I.P.O. was proof that there was gas under the ranch. As clever and compelling as Festor was, he couldn't make that so. But that was no impediment. Stubb knew that it wasn't the presence of gas that counted. It was the presence of the proof, and he was an efficient person, if nothing else. It might take God to make the gas, he joked to himself, but only a mere mortal to make the test.

The test was done. The field men for Stembark had taken care of that. But what they didn't know or think to question was the order that came down from the Dallas office, specifying the specific site of the test. Festor knew that these were randomly selected by the geologists. Some random selections, Festor knew, were more random than others. Randomness was too important a concept to be left to mere chance. And then there was *Repete* to deal with the rest of it.

Number twenty-nine was done, on schedule, on budget. Number thirty, the test results, come Wednesday. Two more days.

Chapter 22

MAGNE REQUIRED THAT Gabriela accompany him on his frequent trips to Washington. Being from an old and wealthy Santander family that settled and thrived in Mexico in the eighteenth century, she exuded a European class and sophistication that he could not. She was beautiful and charming, with a slightly mysterious quality about her that enthralled all the men and most of the women she met. He appreciated that she took such a strong interest in the Magne Ranch affairs and was a true asset to him in dealing with the recently pressing problems.

"Mr. Magne," Benjamin exclaimed at first sight of one of his most generous patrons, who at that instant entered Quinkaid's vestibule with Congressman Monde and their wives.

"Ben," Magne responded more quietly.

"So good to see you again, sir, and you too, Congressman," said the matre'd.

"Hope you've got my table, Ben," Magne replied

"Of course, Mr. Magne, please follow me," he beckoned, clearing a path through the groups and couples who had long been waiting for their tables. The Magne party wound through the restaurant, past the main dining room into an elaborately paneled hallway, then to a private room with a single table, magnificently arrayed with silver, crystal ware, hand painted china and decorated with flower arrangements. A fire was crackling in a carved stone hearth. A waiter, standing at attention just inside the door, bowed slightly to the group as they entered and then immediately moved to pull out the chairs for the women, seating them each in turn as the men took up chairs so that they sat next to one another, across the broad table from the women.

"Ladies and gentlemen," Benjamin announced in a formal fashion, "this is Phillippe, and he will be your lead server this evening."

"Hello, Phillippe," said Gabriela Magne.

"Thanks, Ben," Magne said.

With the drinks order taken, and but for the occasional discreet interventions to provide the various courses and orders for refills, the group were left to themselves. Benjamin had long learned that Mr. Magne preferred privacy with his meals at Quinkaid's and he knew how to clear the room but for the essentials so that Mr. Magne could conduct his business and entertain as quietly as possible.

Dinner arrived in courses to complement the conversation. The wives talked about their days and the men talked about themselves.

"Gabriela, why don't you little girls go powder your noses, or whatever it is you do in those restrooms? Lencho and I have to talk," Magne announced suddenly. A vein on Eva Monde's neck suddenly bulged and she glared at her husband. Gabriela ushered her toward the door.

When the wives had gone, Magne offered the congressman a cigar to go with his cognac.

"Lencho, I want to thank you and Eva for joining us tonight," Magne began.

"John, you know it is always a pleasure to be with you and Gabriela. We owe a lot to the both of you."

"Nonsense, Lencho, we feel honored to do our part."

"Well, you've always done more than that. I don't know how I'll ever be able to repay you for convincing Ted Luz not to run against me in the last primary. I don't mind telling you I was pretty worried after the new district boundaries were drawn and found most of my district in Marco's neighborhood."

"It would have been pretty tough, Lencho, that's sure. He's awfully popular," Magne agreed.

"But when he announced his support for me, well, I don't mind telling you, that was a huge relief." The congressman turned facing Magne directly to say, "Entre nos otros, John, exactly how did you wave him off?"

Magne looked at him, then lifted his napkin off his lap and spoke as he carefully folded it on the table before him, carefully ironing in each crease with his large forefinger. "Lencho, in this world there is a close connection between ambition and pride." He looked into the congressman's eyes and intoned, "And in most cases one has a way of tangling up the other. Let's just say that Marco had a choice to make and I helped him make it." He winked mischievously and the line of a smile drew across his face, "at least for now."

They both laughed out loud and the congressman lifted his snifter in a toast and said, "To tangled ambitions!"

"Hear, hear," Magne replied as they clinked their glasses then drained their cognacs.

The congressman seemed to pause in pensiveness for a moment.

"What's up there, Lencho?" Magne asked, sensing the moment.

"What about next time, John, and the next threat?"

"Lencho, you can always count on me to be there to help," Magne reassured him.

"I know I can, John, and you know how much I appreciate it.

"Think nothing of it."

"That, John," the congressman pledged good-naturedly, "will never happen. I've counted on you, and you, John, know you can always count on me."

Magne rose from his chair, pulled the congressman up with

him and gave him a firm hug, just as the wives re-entered the room.

"I just don't know about these boys, Eva," Gabriela said in a mocked seriousness.

"Me neither," giggled Eva, joining in the joke.

"Honestly," Gabriela continued, "I'm not so sure that John would rather spend the night with Lencho than me!"

Magne backed off awkwardly, clearly embarrassed by the comment. "That's a damned fool thing to say, Gabriela."

"Why, John Magne, you know it's still early for us younger folks," Gabriela teased in reference to the twenty-year difference in their ages.

"Young folks!" Magne blared back. "Come on, Lencho, what's say we teach these teenagers a lesson or two about endurance."

"I'm game," asserted Eva.

"'Atta girl," Gabriela egged on.

"I don't know," Lencho demurred, "it's late and I've got a committee meeting in the morning…"

"E.P.A. budget?" Magne inquired as if idly.

"Yeah, and oversight," Lencho answered, not unaware of Magne's strikingly specific knowledge.

"Come on!" Gabriela pleaded.

"What are we going to do with these little ladies?" Magne shrugged at Lencho.

"All right, but just a short one at the Ritz, that's it," Lencho acquiesced.

"Party pooper," accused Gabriela good-naturedly.

"It's the Ritz, then!" Eva announced.

"Let's go," Magne declared and started for the door, the women in tow.

"What about the ticket?" Lencho asked.

"Never mind that, Lencho, they know me," Magne explained.

As they stood while the valet called in their limo, Magne

turned to Lencho and leaned in close to his face. "Lencho, about that little problem I mentioned, the one with Fish & Wildlife for my little project on the ranch…"

"What problem is that, John?" Lencho responded, with an impish smile.

Magne read his eyes and smiled back. "Exactly!" he said, passing a knowing wink to Gabriela, who smiled back in approval.

Chapter 23

THREE THOUSAND MILES away, Jason walked into Ma Jolie's in Weslaco, Texas, and paused in the vestibule, surveying the sea of heads in search of his brother, Jack.

"Over here," he heard a familiar voice call out, and following the sound of it, saw a hand waving back in forth from a booth in the rear. He waved back to signal he got the message.

"Jack!" he yelled as he met his brother about half way to the booth.

"Jason, you crazy son of a bitch," Jack said as he hugged his brother.

"Well, if I'm a son of a bitch, you know that you are a son of a bitch," Jason called back.

"Come on, sit down and tell me what the hell's going on before I have to beat the crap out of you for insulting my mother," Jack played. "Man, how long has it been, two months since I saw you?"

"It has to be at least that. What was it, Mom's birthday?"

"Probably, hell I don't remember. But whenever it was, it was your fault."

"So what else is new?" Jason registered his fake complaint, then continued. "So what's up with you, bro? Why the sudden call to drag my ass across the Valley to Weslaco to have dinner with you?"

"Well, I figured I owed you a good dinner in our finest restaurant…while I still could. So, to the important stuff, you getting any?"

"Any what? I live in a penal colony," Jason declared.

"Penal colony. Actually that sounds pretty busy."

"Funny, but once the summer goes, Mansfield dries up. It's just the townies and the hard core fishermen."

"All right, enough of this. Let's get some beer and nachos," Jack announced as he waved down a passing waitress. "Hey," Jack blurted, "guess what? I'm moving my stuff down to the boat."

"Mansfield?" Jason said in surprise, "Why?"

"I'm giving up the rent house. Gonna lighten up, so I thought I'd gunkhole down in your neck of the woods for a few days."

"Then what?" Jason asked.

"Well, not sure yet, but I'm thinking of getting all the rigging and gear checked out on the sailboat and then heading up the coast to, say, Galveston, maybe even Mobile."

"What brings this on all of a sudden?" Jason asked, surprised.

"I don't know. I guess it's just time. I guess Joan told you I wasn't working for Fish & Wildlife any more, so I think it may be a good time to move along to something new."

"What about that Texas A&M marine biology school up in Galveston? Have you thought about maybe trying to hire on there?" Jason suggested.

"That is something to check out, who knows."

"You ought to give Don Welts a call. He's a full-blown prof there now, you know."

"I'll think about it."

"I did talk to Joan on Friday," Jason admitted. "She thinks you are depressed. I told her you were just sadly cynical."

"There's a difference?"

"Enough of one. So, are you?"

"No, not really. I've just been stuck in a rut, trying to figure what to do with my life. And I am basically lazy, which might look like depression to the untrained eye," Jack smirked.

"She didn't tell me what the deal was with that government job. What happened there? You get canned?"

"I guess I sort of canned myself," Jack said. "You know how I am. I'm not the thirty-year and a gold watch type…do they still give out gold watches…?"

"Did they ever?"

"…well, I was getting to the end of my rope anyway. I think the report fiasco was just a catalyst."

"Report fiasco?" Jason quizzed Jack. "What was that all about?"

"Damnedest thing, Jason," Jack said, leaning closer to his brother and speaking earnestly. "I'm given this assignment to put together a report on some environmental impact crap on the Laguna Madre. Well, hell, this isn't like anything new. I mean, there have been bunches of these things done, or at least I figured there must have been over the years. So I figured I'd just collect them all up and sort of summarize them for this memo I was supposed to write. Well, I go looking for this stuff, first over at EPA, then U.S. Fish & Wildlife, then even the stacks at the two university flagships."

"So what did you find?" Jason asked.

"Well, that's the thing. Nothing, or almost nothing. Oh, there were a few pieces I found on Google, but the big deal hard copies I expected to find were non-existent."

"Had you ever seen them before?"

"No, not really. I just thought they must have been done. So I ask around and just about everybody I talk to seems to think the same thing….that studies have been done, but no one could produce one."

"That's weird," Jason commented.

"Well, yes and no. Just because we think that somebody did these studies sometime ago doesn't mean that they did. It may be that all this national, hell, *inter*national, focus on environmental impact has just sort of passed the Valley by."

"That wouldn't be the first time, brother."

"And that's exactly what I figured. Apparently, while everyone else was all in a tizzy about this stuff, the sleepy ole' Rio Grande Valley was snoozing away."

"Still, Jack, it seems that some grad student has pumped out a thesis or at least a paper on it."

"My thinking too, but a search of the schools turned up nothing."

"So how does all this lead to you moving on to a sailboat?" Jason zeroed to the point.

"Well, I am a good and reliable bureaucrat. I was able to find enough stuff to cobble together something of a quick memo as I was asked to do…and, after all, I do have some credentials here, so I did some of my own prognosticating…nothing too exotic or that wandered too far from common sense."

"What did you finally conclude in it?"

"It was pretty easy to support that the impact of drill mud and the brackish water that comes up with it, plus all the trucks coming and going, would play hell on the breeding grounds in the Laguna and be a hell of a disturbance to the shrimp, fish and birdlife, so I did what all good bureaucrats do."

"And need I ask what that is?"

"No, but I'll tell you anyway. I concluded that what was needed was a more thorough analysis: a bigger, broader and substantiated report."

"Perfect," Jason exclaimed. "Another government study called for by another government study!"

"What would they do without us?" Jack declared triumphantly.

"Reach a conclusion," Jason laughed. "So, how could this get you anything less than a promotion?"

"That's the thing," Jack said, puzzled. "I figured that I'd either get an "Atta boy,' or an assignment, or a kick in the head…"

"And…"

"Well, I got absolutely nothing."

"Nothing?"

"*Nada!*"

"So, what do you figure? Another report buried under the rubble of other reports?"

"Ars gratia artis? Well, reports gratia reports!" Jack said, only half amused now.

"That was the straw, then?" Jason asked, not seeing the point.

"It was more the needle."

"The needle that broke the camel's back?" Jason teased.

"No, it was more like fitting the friggin' camel through the needle's eye."

"I don't get it," Jason said, still confused.

"Me neither," Jack laughed, "Now, here come the nachos!"

Chapter 24

"SECRETARY RODE!" MONDE called across the Congressional hearing room as the Secretary of the Interior was rising from the table where the testimony notes and reports were being collected and boxed by his staff.

"Yes, Congressman," Rode replied, momentarily wondering if the committee hearing was suddenly being reconvened.

"Would you have time for a quick bite in the Dining Room?"

Rode looked at Cindy, his legislative liaison, who returned a pained expression, then a nod. "Of course, Congressman, it would be a pleasure. We can walk down together."

"Excellent," Monde replied, then turned to his chief of staff to say, "Go ahead back to the office, Mario. I should be done in an hour." He handed him his brief case.

As they wound through the back labyrinthine passages of the U.S. Capitol, the two men exchanged the usual pleasantries and perfunctory inquiries into the state of their respective families. Normally, it would be about spouses and children, but Bill Rode had neither, which left Monde the only option of asking about his Golden Retriever. Rode was known for his dog, Skipper, and the fact that they were constant companions. From the first day he arrived at Interior, he brought the retriever to sit with him in his office. The dog was elderly and contented himself with lying quietly by the unused hearth. When meetings made it inconvenient to bring the dog with him, a staff member looked after Skipper at the office.

It was mid-afternoon on a Tuesday in November, so the tourist season was done and the House Dining Room at the Capitol was unusually empty. When they were situated at Congressman Monde's usual table and had placed their lunch order, they turned to business.

"Bill," Monde came quickly to the point, "I know how hard you have been working to streamline the Department of the Interior. Word is getting around about how you have been real tough on waste and regulation. I want you to know how much I appreciate your making it a priority to see government becomes more 'user friendly'."

"Why, thank you, Congressman. And I appreciate your support on the committee. You know we can't make much progress without the willingness of members like yourself to stand up for what's best, even when there are a whole lot of interests that would feel a lot better if things stayed exactly as they have been."

"If only people knew how tough that is," Monde concurred. "Tough, like the good people of my district," he continued. "You know my district is the second poorest in the country. Our per capita is about half the national average. Somehow these citizens have managed to cut out a thin slice of the American Dream in spite of it."

"It is remarkable, Congressman."

"My job is to try to level the playing field for my district, Bill. We've been left out in the cold for too long. We're the Appalachia of the 21st century. The government needs to be more proactive toward South Texas. We need to have a chance to catch up."

"I couldn't agree with you more, Congressman. As you know, in the last several years Interior has been aggressive in buying up habitat and protecting the last of the native brush and fauna down there. We've bought or gotten conservancy groups to buy thousands of acres around the Laguna Atascosa Refuge, thanks to your help getting funding for much of that, and we've continued to add to the Padre Island National Sea Shore area. What we're building towards is a preserve that will have tremendous long term economic impact on the area through nature tourism, fishing and hunting, and all that goes with it."

"I think you folks are doing a fantastic job, Bill. And that focus on economic development is exactly how we have to think if we want to bring the Valley up with the rest of the country."

"Thank you, Congressman. We're going to continue to need your support going forward."

"I think we need to help each other, Bill. We're a team, working in the best interests of our people. You can count on my support for that and I know I can count on yours."

"That's very good to hear, sir."

The waiter brought the two lunches and set them down. The two men immediately dove into them.

"You know, Bill, one thing I have really appreciated about your approach to your department is the sense of balance between *environmental* issues and *economic* issues," Monde commented, pausing to draw quote marks in the air with his fingers. "You've always seemed to see that there is value in preserving and promoting each with respect to the other. I don't mind telling you that is a huge improvement over your predecessor's way, even though that was when my party was in charge down there."

"Again, thank you, sir. We're just trying to apply common sense."

"We have just such a case in my district now, for example," Monde began. Rode could feel it coming. "You know how hard we've been hit by the Mad Cow embargoes. Cattle ranchers in my district, well the whole state really, have had a hard time of it and, frankly, I am worried about them, Bill. We need some help."

"What do you have in mind?" Rode asked.

"It would be very important to my district for your department to help us push aside any pointless obstacles that might interfere with important economic development opportunities for our people."

"You can be sure, Congressman, that we aren't too fond of 'pointless obstacles' either." Rode knew he was about to step into a minefield, forewarned by his legislative liaison, who had been approached earlier by Monde's chief of staff. The proverbial "trial balloon." But he was going to make Monde work for it.

"Of course you aren't, Bill," the congressman smoothed over any ruffled feather. "I didn't mean to suggest you are. In fact, I know that is exactly what you've been working on at Interior. It's just that we've got one of those cases working here that I think is exactly what's wrong with how government works."

"Which case are you referring to, Congressman?"

"The Magne gas exploration issue."

"I'm not familiar with that matter," Rode lied.

"Let me tell you about it, Bill," Monde proceeded, knowing by heart, after twenty years, the steps of this traditional dance. He would tell the tale the bureaucrat would pretend not to know anything about. He would ask the bureaucrat to "look into it." The bureaucrat would promise to. He would mark up another "action" taken to report to his donor/constituent/lobbyist. The bureaucrat would mark another kilogram on the weight the issue ought to be given. Sometimes these were just *pro forma*, so the congressman could say he tried. Those were 2s. Sometimes they were the real thing: 7s. Time would pass, and either it went away or it didn't. There were more bars to the waltz yet to play.

"Thank you for alerting me to this, Congressman," Rode replied after hearing the long narrative delivered by Monde, "I'll look into it."

"I'd appreciate that, Bill," Monde thanked him.

"No problem, Congressman," Rode replied as they both rose from their chairs to go.

"One thing, though, Bill," Monde added suddenly.

"Yes, sir?"

"Could you get back to me on this tomorrow?"

"Tomorrow?" Rode said surprised.

"Yes."

He paused briefly in thought then replied, "Sure, Congressman, I'll get someone on my staff to contact your chief tomorrow afternoon," he proposed. It was looking like a 7 he thought.

Monde stopped and turned to Rode, looking him straight in the eye, "I'd really like to hear from you, Bill, directly."

"Of course, sir, I'll call you tomorrow," Rode said definitely.

"Thank you so much, Bill. Please let me know if there is anything I can do for you. You're doing such great work at Interior. You deserve our whole-hearted support."

They parted on a handshake and walked off in different directions, almost simultaneously pulling out their cell phones and flipping them open.

"Mario," Monde started, "call Magne and tell him we'll have a report for him tomorrow night."

"Cindy," Rode barked into the phone the instant she answered, "just finished with Monde."

"And..."

"We've got a 9."

"Damn!"

Chapter 25

STUBB WAS JUST SHORT of five and a half feet tall and fifty pounds overweight. The pale, colorless skin of his face flowed like tallow from under his wispy thin blonde hair over the collar of his white short-sleeved shirt and oozed an oily stain on the over-fat knot of his K-Mart tie. The only color above his black trousers, black socks and black shoes were huge black plastic eyeglass frames holding lenses that made his eyes appear like a snake's peering through the wrong end of a telescope.

Nearly every Wednesday morning when he wasn't traveling and away from Houston, Festor Stubb parked his car in front of Neiman's at the Galleria and walked through the women's perfume and lingerie departments on his way to the Krispy Kreme in the middle of the mall. But first he'd pick up a grande latté at the Starbucks. Then he'd sit at a small café table next to the rail on one of the mezzanine crosswalks that overlooked the ice rink. Wednesday mornings were when the girls from the nearby high school would practice their skating.

He would bring a copy of the Wall Street Journal and place it before him so he wouldn't appear to be loitering and leering. He had learned to be more cautious since he was approached by a police officer after a mother complained about him at the North Star Mall a year earlier.

His cell phone beeped.

"Hello," he answered.

"Festor?" Richter asked.

"Yep, that you Calvin?"

"Yes. Listen, have you gotten anything from the lab on that Magne test yet?"

"No, but it's only ten o'clock. I didn't expect to hear anything until about noon. Why, have you?"

"Me? No, there's no way they'd know to call me. But I really do need to get that report up here for my meeting with the lawyers tomorrow. I mean, it's the main point of the meeting."

"Don't, worry Calvin, you'll have it. Let me get on the horn and find out where it's at and I'll call you back."

"Great."

Stubb squinted at his PDA as he used his stylus to scroll through phone numbers. He found the one he needed and dialed it.

"Yes," the voice said curtly.

"Bob?"

"Yes, this is Bob Philips, who is this?"

"Festor."

"Oh, Festor, uh, Mr. Stubb," the voice said hesitantly, then there was an audible but unintelligible series of words that seemed to be spoken to someone else with the mouthpiece slightly covered.

"Mr. Stubb, sorry, I was just finishing a meeting," he explained, then said away from the phone, "I'll call you later, Wade...could you get the door? Thanks." There was a pause, then, "Festor?"

"Yep, what's with the 'Mr. Stubb' bullshit?"

"Had some people here in the office, you understand. How are you doin'?"

"You tell me."

"What do you mean?"

"The Magne test, Bob, what do you think I mean?" Stubb asked impatiently.

"Oh, the Magne test. I haven't seen that on my desk yet, Festor. Did we promise that today?"

"What's with you, Bob? You know goddamn well it's due out today. What's this bullshit all about?"

"Now, Festor, don't get excited. We've got procedures here, you know. We have to follow form."

"Cut the crap, Bob. When am I going to have that report?"

"Well, the lab has to give us a print out of their results and conclusions, then we've got to put that into our firm's format on a Word doc, and when it's printed it has to be reviewed then signed by a partner."

"So what time today am I going to see this thing? You know it has to be in New York by tomorrow morning."

"Tomorrow?" Bob half said, half asked.

"Listen here, Philips," Stubb spoke deliberately through gritted teeth "Don't start screwing with me on this. Don't give me any of this 'procedures' crap. I want that report Fed Exed to New York tonight and a copy to me this afternoon or I'll get on Southwest and be in your office by three o'clock, do you hear me?" he shouted.

There was a silent pause on the other end of the line. A cautious voice said, "Yes. I hear you, Festor."

"Good," Stubb said in a feigned delight. "You know, Bob, I sometimes wonder if you appreciate all the little favors I've done for you over these last few years…"

"Festor, not on the phone," Bob interrupted in a hushed but urgent tone.

"What's the matter, Bob?" Stubb asked, mocking. "Afraid someone might be listening in? Afraid that they might not like to hear about how accommodating you've been in our nation's search for new energy sources?"

"Enough, Stubb, or I'll hang up," Bob threatened.

"Oh, I wouldn't do that, Bobby boy. Just be a good ole boy

and do what you've been paid to do. Get that 'glowing' report signed, sealed and delivered by Fed Ex time tonight and all will be wonderful. You'll go home to your big ass house on Turtle Creek, kiss the wife, play with your three little kids….they still at St. Ignatius? And everybody will live happily ever after," Stubb sang, sending a chill deep down Bob Philips's spine.

There was another silent pause.

"The report will be sent out this afternoon," Bob said weakly.

"Wonderful. You're a wonderful fellow, Bob, and Stembark is a wonderful firm. I'll send you all a fruit basket for Christmas," Stubb said sarcastically then instantly hung up.

He took his stylus and brought up on his PDA a numbered list with the heading, "Magne Project." He scrolled down to a row with the entry, "30. Gas reserves proof test results." He touched the box to the left and a small "x" appeared. He smiled, picked up his phone and dialed.

Chapter 26

A MAROON JEEP PULLED up to the Mansfield Port Office just as Jason was coming out the front door.

"Hola, Bro!" Jason shouted when he saw Jack.

"Where you going?" Jack asked, climbing out of the Jeep.

"Just about to take a walk down to the marina to look at a john boat we found adrift in the Laguna near the island, want to come along?"

"Sure. I have no life."

"Let's go," Jason said as they began toward the docks together. "So what brings you out here anyway?"

"I'm moving all my stuff on the boat," Jack explained.

"That's a pain in the ass."

"And the back," Jack added, rubbing the small of his back with his right hand. "But it's amazing just how much stuff you can stow away in all the cubby holes and hatches on that thing. I've actually already lost stuff on it, which reminds me, I've got to stick with my floor plan," he added to himself.

"So, when you moving in?"

"This is it. I'm in. Here until I leave, at least."

"Have you decided where you're going yet?" Jason asked.

"Not for sure. I'll spend a few days looking over the charts and checking weather before I settle on a target," Jack said.

"In the meantime, maybe you and I can hang out and chew the fat a little."

"Mmm, fat. Sounds real appetizing," Jack retorted just as they made the ramp to the dock area.

"There it is," Jason said as he headed for slip seven.

Jack noticed that as Jason approached the boat, his head cocked to one side. He'd never seen his brother the cop at work and it was intriguing to see the sudden change come over him as he moved along side the boat, intent in the study of it. Jack stood back, not to interfere.

After several minutes, Jason carefully stepped into the boat and began to look through an ice chest on board. It was empty. He picked up a fishing pole that was lying on the sole and worked the reel handle. He looked down the rod and with his fingers felt each of the rings the fishing line guided through. In the bow of the boat was a pile of yellow nylon rope in a jumble. Jason moved it around and exposed a mushroom type anchor beneath it and a crumpled Tecate beer can. There was dead bait floating in the little water that stood in the lowest part of the boat. Jason sat down in the back bench as if he were set to work the outboard motor. He looked closely at the motor tiller, then the motor itself. He pulled the prop out of the water by tilting the motor forward and then dropped it back in. Finally, he climbed back on to the dock.

"What's all this?" Jack asked curiously.

"Not sure. One of the Texas Parks guys found it nudged up against the island on Sunday."

"Nobody around?"

"No, looks to be just a boat adrift somehow."

"So, what do you think?"

"Well, could be it just got loose from one of those stilt houses up the Intracoastal Waterway during the norther and blown down until it snagged on the island, but I don't know."

"What's bothering you on it?"

"Well, for one thing, when they found it there it had a pole rigged, that one there, I think, and the line was out. Looks like someone was fishing and I don't think anybody would have a boat tied up to his dock with a fishing line all rigged and out."

"No, I see your point. But why not just look up the state registration number," Jack suggested, raising his chin in the direction of the digits on the port bow.

Jason looked at his brother in feigned amazement and said, "You see! That's why you went to college!"

"All right, all right, so what's wrong with the idea?"

"Nothing, except that once you get south of the Cactus Curtain, most all the normal rules just don't apply--you know that. More than half the cars don't have insurance, hell, even the Immigration Service backs its ass up to Sarita, a hundred miles from the Rio Grande, to make a border it can really hold."

"You've got a point," Jack nodded in recognition. "The numbers are bogus."

"Ours are a clever people, brother Jack. The law says you're supposed to register your boat and when you do you get the number stickers to put on the bow. That can cost real money and it's a hassle. But, you can buy stick-on numbers at Home Depot for a few cents."

"Ah, true, but you've got to respect the efficiency of it," Jack said.

"In the end, all the boats have numbers." Jason looked down a moment. "I'm an officer of the law," Jason observed seriously, "but I've got to tell you that it's damned hard sometimes to enforce laws on good people down here that were clearly written for people somewhere else, in a different world. This isn't Dallas or Austin. People here are just too poor on the average."

Jack looked at his brother and smiled. "You're starting to sound like a friggin' Communist." Jason took the cue to get back on the subject.

"I was feeling sure it was the boat belonging to a local fisherman who was reported missing on Saturday, but when I had the wife take a look at it she wasn't sure it was her husband's boat. She wasn't sure it wasn't it either. She'd never been on it. And there wasn't anything else that she recognized, no clothes or gear, or anything like that. Still in all, you've got to think: missing fisherman, found boat, hell, what are the chances?"

Jason got down and studied the port side gunwale near the center bench. "Hm," he said to himself.

"What?"

"Well, there looks like there's some dried blood in this oar lock hole. Take a look," Jason said as he pointed and directed Jack to the spot.

Jack looked closely at it. "Well, it isn't brown enough to be old, if it's blood."

Jason pulled out a pocket knife and asked Jack, "You got any paper on you?"

"Paper?"

"Yeah, anything I can scrape a little of this into."

Jack produced a note pad he used for making and marking off his list of things to do. "How about a page from this?"

"Yeah, that's good," Jason said taking the page and carefully folding it into an impromptu envelope. He carefully worked the material off his blade, into the envelope and closed the top. As he got back up on the dock he said, "Well, this won't do for real evidence but it's enough to see if I'd be making a fool of myself."

"Barney Fife."

"Exactly: Mayberry." Jason said. "I don't want to hear the Sheriff making fun of me for starting everyone out on a wild goose chase."

"By the way," Jack asked, "can I see the bullet they let you keep in your shirt pocket?"

"Very funny, but if I show you where I do keep it we'll have the whole damned town talking."

Jack laughed. They started back up to the Port Office.

"So, Jason, is every day as exciting as this?"

Jason smiled at his brother's ribbing. They hadn't always been close. In high school they had been fierce competitors. Even though Jason was two years younger, he was a better athlete and played on the varsity football squad along with Jack. But Jack was the scholar of the two, pulling nearly straight-A's and graduating class Salutatorian. Jason couldn't seem to get himself indoors if there was sunlight still to be playing in. While Jack would sleep to the last possible second and still make the bell at school, Jason would rise before dawn to get in an early morning hunt. And after the football season, he headed out to go fishing as soon as the last class ended. But different as they were, they had grown closer since the death of their father ten years ago.

As they reached to Port Office Jack asked, "So, brother, what are you doing later?"

"I've got the graveyard again. But I'm not working tomorrow night."

"Well, why don't you come by the boat Thursday night and we'll fix up something to eat, drink a little beer…"

"Sounds great," Jason said.

"I've got to run to Raymondville to get some things, but I'll be back by five. Come on over anytime after that and I'll be there."

"Take it easy. See you tomorrow," Jason called over his shoulder as he bounded up the steps and into the Port Office.

Chapter 27

"MR. MAGNE'S OFFICE, Pat Wilson speaking," a female voice answered.

"Pat, this is Festor Stubb, calling for Mr. Magne," he said in an ebullient voice.

"Yes, Mr. Stubb," she said formally. "One moment please."

"Mr. Magne?" she said into the intercom. "Mr. Stubb on line two. Will you take the call?"

"Yes, Pat, I'll take it," Magne replied as he reached over and punched the blinking button. "Stubb," he said into the phone.

"Mr. Magne, I just called to give you a report on the test results," Stubb began.

"So, how'd they turn out?" Magne asked, concealing any sign of his anxiety.

"Well, sir, just as I told you. The Magne Ranch is sitting on one hell of a pocket of the sweetest natural gas in Texas," Stubb said enthusiastically.

"Goddamn, that's great news," Magne shouted in obvious glee.

"Yes, sir, your family is going to be set for generations."

"I can't tell you how relieved I am to hear this, Festor. This is incredible news," Magne cried. Stubb noted that it was the first time that Magne had called him by his first name.

"Well, I'm glad to help," Stubb said ingratiatingly.

"And so you have….so when can I get a copy of this report?"

"In a day or so I'll get one to you, Mr. Magne. Right now we're focused on getting all the paperwork ready in New York for a meeting tomorrow with the investment bank lawyers."

"Oh, right," Magne said. "We still have to do all that."

"Yes, sir, there's a whole lot left to do, but you leave all that up to me. I'll take care of everything. That's what you're paying me for."

"Well, you certainly have earned your fees today. I'm sending you a bottle of Dom Perignon!" Magne said.

"Thank you, sir, I appreciate that. I'll keep you up to date as things get along."

"Fine, thanks," Magne said then hung up.

Magne sat for a few minutes staring at the phone. It was as if a great weight had been lifted off his shoulders. He suddenly felt light and euphoric. He jumped to his feet and ran out to Pat's office.

"Pat, Pat!" he exclaimed.

"Yes, Mr. Magne," she replied wondering if there was an emergency.

"Find Gabriela and Clint and Junior. Get them over to *Casa Blanca* right away. I've got some good news."

"They found the gas?" Pat asked.

"Yes. It's official," he shouted in glee.

"Oh, Mr. Magne, that's wonderful," she said as she rushed to the phone on her desk to summon the family members.

Magne seemed to fly back to his office. He stood at the picture window overlooking the ranchlands that stretched away to a distant tree line. He put his hands in his pockets and his form was a dark grey silhouette against the bright light flowing in. The crisis was finally coming to an end. At last he could stop worrying and return to that carefree feeling he enjoyed all his life up to three years ago. That wonderfully warm and secure feeling of being very, very rich.

When Stubb folded his phone and began to gather up his PDA, the newspaper and notepad to leave, he smiled to himself. Magne had called him "Festor." The plan was unfolding perfectly.

Just then, three ninth grade girls hurried past his table and bounded down the stairs toward the ice rink. They were evidently late. Stubb eyes followed them until they went out of sight into the girls changing room.

Chapter 28

AS HE ENTERED THE door, Jason immediately saw Anajita Paredes sitting in a chair, a large purse in her lap, and her eyes fixed expectantly on him.

"Mrs. Paredes," Jason greeted her in a soft voice.

"Officer," she said forcefully, but then followed in a weaker voice, "have you heard nothin' about mah husban'?" Her eyes pleaded and filled with tears. Jason came across the room and sat down next to her. She turned her body to face him directly.

"No, ma'am, I'm afraid not," Jason said.

"It's been nearly four days now," she said half incredulously, half despaired.

"I know, and we're still looking. The Coast Guard is searching the Laguna, the channel and even out in the Gulf. We're doing everything we can," he offered in ineffective reassurance.

"Wull, maybe it's a good thing, they haven't found him then, right?" she urged plaintively.

Jason looked into her pained face and knew what the both of them knew, that none of this was good news, but he said, "I guess so."

Anajita looked down to the floor in front of her. She didn't know what to do next. She didn't know where to go. She couldn't find in herself any reason to do anything. All energy was drained out of her. She began to sob quietly. Jason put his hand on hers.

He was near tears himself, he felt so sorry for her.

"Mrs. Paredes, let me drive you home. You ought to get some rest," Jason offered after a few minutes.

"Thank you, officer, but no. Ah knows I can't sit here all blubberin' up the place. You all have work to do. Ahm gonna go but ah wants to walk back home. You see," she said earnestly, looking into Jason's eyes, "if ah takes mah time and walks home I can jus' a little longer hold out a hope that whens I come up to that old house, that silly old man will be there awaitin' for me on the porch, all smilin' and grinin'. Oh, I'd give anything for that to be, anything to see that wrinkly, smilin' old face…" She gasped one more time, fighting back her urge to cry. Then she opened her purse and pulled out a folded tissue, meticulously unfolded it, and pressed it against one eye, then another. She carefully put it back into her purse and slowly snapped it closed. She raised her shoulders back and with some struggle rose to her feet. She turned to Jason and put a hand on his cheek and forced a smile for him. Then she walked out the door into the sunlight.

Jason sat for a few moments. He was collecting himself and organizing his thoughts. He sprang to his feet and walked quickly to the counter, calling out, "Phyllis, have we gotten a call back from the goddamn sheriff?"

"No, sir," she replied, "not yet."

CHAPTER 29

IT WAS THURSDAY, 10:40 A.M. eastern and fine beads of sweat were forming on Calvin Richter's upper lip. His shirt collar felt tight and damp. He could feel his stomach muscles tighten as he sat at his desk, staring at the clock to the right of his computer screen. He knew the Fed Ex's didn't show up at the mail center until about ten thirty, then they had to be sorted before the mailroom could get them on the carts and the deliveries dispatched to all fifteen floors of the Fenre Pease headquarters building. New York might be the center of the financial universe, the Olympus of money, but it still moved on the backs of dishwashers, store clerks, and even blue-frocked mailroom boys.

So close, he thought, so close. He had already put together the Power Point presentation, and Stubb had provided the memo on the particulars, the packet of background materials on the Magne operation, pro-forma financials, all the usual due-diligence needed to feed the Investment Memorandum.

It was paying off, those expensive years at the "B-School" at Harvard, on which he was still making payments. And those thousands of hours of editing paperwork of other deals by other dealers who made the money. The hundreds of beers in Wall Street watering holes, listening to the tales of countless big hits that were the stuff of lore among the hungry minor sharks that circled in the water.

Calvin remembered the mesmerized stares of the other young bucks as they hung on every word of some deal that had launched someone just like them into stardom. They had the faces of religious followers: awed, bathed in a yellow light, eyes full of hope and faith. He knew that feeling. He was one of them.

He imagined himself standing at the end of the bar, all eyes on him as he took his turn as the ascendant oracle. He could hear a voice proposing a toast of praise and congratulations, the chorus of "hear, hear," the clinking of glasses. Even in this reverie he found himself smiling.

The sudden tap-tap and swung open door startled him.

"Fed Ex," announced his secretary as she brought in a large white square of cardboard emblazoned with the familiar label. He seized it from her and tore it open.

The cover read, "Magne Project Field Report."

He leafed through the table of contents, scanning down for the Executive Summary, found it, and turned to the first page. He had to slow himself down as he read it. He was comprehending none of the words. He began again, forcing calm deliberation. There, in the fourth paragraph, the operative term: "positive."

There was no time to lose. It was nearly eleven. He had three hours to get everything ready and get himself upstairs to the counsels' floor. He started to use his phone to call back his secretary, then instead just shouted out her name.

"Doris!"

"Yes, Mr. Richter," she said opening the door.

"Doris, we've got three hours to get a whole lot done. Looks like there are five originals here. I need twenty copies, color, bound just like the originals, and boxed, back here in an hour and a half latest. Can you do that?"

"I've got a luncheon but I can cancel," she said, hoping for a reprieve.

"Great, thanks. Do that and get these back here by one at the latest."

"Yes, sir."

He swung around to his keyboard and brought up the Power Point. He took the first page of the Executive Summary and placed it face down on his desktop copier/printer/scanner. He scanned the page, captured it, and pasted it into a blank slide already prepared in the presentation. On screen, he drew a circle around the key paragraph.

"Got it," he said to himself as he played the keyboard and the mouse like a concert pianist, whipping images and text from place to place, slide to slide, in this, his magnum opus.

He was in his element. He could feel the surge of adrenaline coursing through his veins, the bristling sinew. Now the dash to the finish line.

At fifteen minutes before two, he was ready. He sat panting as if he'd just run a wind sprint. He sat square at his desk, both feet planted firmly on the floor. His shoulders were back and his spine straight. He looked forward with the intensity of a tiger frozen in the instant before it would spring on an unsuspecting prey. His muscles twitched in anticipation.

At five minutes before two, he rose. He took his laptop in one hand, slipped the box of books under his arm and marched to the elevator like a general marching to the battlefield. When the elevator door opened he took two steps in and did a military about face. The doors opened at the twenty-third floor. He strode out and past the receptionist to Conference Room C, entering in a flourish and moving directly to the end with the projector connections.

"Good afternoon," he said perfunctorily to the staff milling near the refreshments bar. The lawyers had not yet arrived. He put down his laptop and aligned the infrared window with the sensor next to the projector, switched both on and turned to watch the screen gradually come to life. He opened the box and removed the report copies, stacking them to his right as the first of the lawyers began to enter the conference room and detour to the coffee dispenser. In a few minutes nearly all were present and sitting, facing Calvin. The center chair on Calvin's right was conspicuously vacant. At five minutes after two, a tall, slim, very well groomed man with graying, nearly white hair came into the room and paused at the doorway. Everyone in the room stood. He proceeded to the empty chair and sat down. Everyone then sat. The man looked at Calvin and nodded for him to begin.

"Good afternoon," Calvin said in a cheery opening, which was answered with nods from some, while others seemed absorbed with printed materials they had brought with them. One by one he unfolded the facts of the Magne Project, beginning first with background on the principals, the nature of the investment and an overview of the financial projections. He had included pictures of the Magne Ranch, a map of Texas to show its location, and other eye candy.

Calvin had long learned that in the droll business of number crunching, the addition of photographs seemed to attract the attention of even the most jaded of the audience. It was as if their lives, leached out a day at a time in the gray and texture-less confines of the monoliths and concrete valleys of Manhattan, were rendered in the dull grainy green of old black and white television images. The hardness in their faces softened at the first sight of the world beyond, where there were such exotic things as horizons, skies and animals without bars in front of them. Calvin could see it now, working its magic.

As the colorful images gave way to the spreadsheets of numbers, the gleam in their eyes began to fade like dying embers. By the time he was done, their pupils were fully dilated and glazed over. And the dull murmur of Calvin's voice in their heads suddenly became distinct at the words, "Any questions?"

"Nice work, Richter," came a low, sonorous voice, dripping with feigned sincerity. It is what was said by the senior member of any such gathering to confirm the pecking order. He was the one deigned to give approval. Nothing could begin until that part of the ceremony was completed. One new staff member spoke up in agreement but immediately looked down to his notepad when eyes of disapproval chased him back down to his warren. The senior attorney turned his head to the other, younger lawyers and nodded a signal that it was now all right to begin. They in turn nodded back. It was the way of the brood, the lion and its cubs.

"Mr. Richter," the first one began, "Can I have the proformas in Excel?" he asked, as was usual. Anything to save work. Getting all the numbers in a computer file meant less hassle. Less work to get his hoop jumped through.

"Yes, sure," Calvin replied, "Just give me a card with your email address and I'll get it to you right after."

"You mentioned that the field report on the reserves was done. Can we have a copy?" asked one young female associate.

"They're right here," Calvin answered taking the pile of copies, dividing it in half, and passing it down both sides of the table at once. "You'll find what you're looking for in here."

"And the results were…?" she prompted him.

"Positive. The reserves estimate is substantial. Almost three times the threshold values we had set for the viability of the project. Of course, these are usually far too conservative, as you know is the practice of these engineering firms. Most fields prove to be far larger over time."

"Good," she said.

"This looks pretty good," the senior attorney said as he thumbed through the memo Calvin had provided a few days earlier. "You seem to have all the bases covered pretty well. Anybody else?" he asked to his posse.

There was that plateau of silence that preceded the ending ceremonies of these kinds of meetings and Calvin began the liturgy of the closing.

"Oh, there is one thing," the young female lawyer said raising her hand nervously. She must have been a new associate or perhaps an intern from one of the Ivy League schools, Calvin figured.

"Yes?" Richter asked.

"The environmentals," she began. "Are there any environmental issues that are involved?"

"Environmentals?" Richter echoed back.

"Yes, you know, like impact studies, state or federal approvals," she elaborated.

Richter felt a flash of heat suddenly sting his body, and he sensed the instantaneous release of a torrent of sweat. He smiled broadly in a superior manner and grandly swept his right hand up and to his right, in a gesticulation of dismissal and confidence. "Of course, Miss…" he struggled.

"Spentas, Amesha Spentas," she filled in.

"Miss Spentas," he replied in a patronizing tone with an over-emphasis on the words. "All the, ah, 'environmental issues' are settled. No need to worry about that." Richter searched the eyes of the others as he smiled at them reassuringly.

The young lawyer looked down. The senior lawyer inverted his mouth and narrowed his eyes. It was his demeanor whenever he heard the words, "no need to worry about that." His patrician ways were part theater, sure, but also the mantle of decades of legal experience. He had developed the intuition to know that those were the most worrisome words of all.

Richter could see the cloud forming. "State and federal agencies have been involved from the start and all the permits have been arranged, Miss Spentas," he quickly intervened, now in a more respectful and interested tone. "It is an excellent question. Naturally we have been alert to this aspect of it, as one must in all mining and recovery programs."

"Excellent," Miss Spentas replied, new but very aware of the protocol of such confrontational moments and equally interested in diffusing any unpleasantness. Then she pressed courteously, "Can we get copies of those materials, Mr. Richter?"

"Of course," Richter pronounced magnanimously. "I'll see that all those are sent to you right away."

The senior member seemed to nod in approval and all the room seemed awash in relief.

"Anything else?" the senior lawyer asked again, this time eliciting nothing, and after a sufficient interval, turned to Richter and thanked him for the presentation and directed his staff to proceed with the work in drafting the investment memo. At that he rose and immediately all the junior members rose and stood while he left the room. Then they followed closely behind, junior counsel, then the associates, and then the staff, in the order of their rank.

Richter was left in the room alone. He was suddenly aware that his knees were tired and he sat down, staring straight ahead across the empty table. He'd done it. *Alia jacta est*, as Caesar said, crossing the Rubicon. "The die was cast."

Chapter 30

"HOW'D IT GO?" Stubb asked Richter as he juggled his cell phone while turning onto the Southwest Freeway heading to the north side of Houston.

"Good, good, the presentation went fine, and they ordered the investment memo to proceed."

"Excellent! That is good news, Calvin…man, you sound whipped."

"I think I'm just tired out. The tension of the build up, now the post partum, I guess," Richter said, adding, "Oh, and one of the lawyers asked about environmentals on the project and I said we had the permits and approvals and that it was all taken care of. That's right isn't it?"

"Absolutely. Remember Sam Kiel?"

"Sam, sure."

"Well, Sam ran the traps on getting all that paperwork pushed through the agencies in Austin and Magne worked the feds in D.C."

"So that's all done."

"Yeah, but don't think it was easy. Magne had to do a lot of consultant hiring and palm greasing, but it turns out the son of a bitch sure knew what he was doing. The guy's connected; I'll say that for him."

"Man, that's a great. Hey, I've got to get copies of all those permits and approvals…whatever you've got…to pass on to one of the lawyers. She's going to be waiting for them."

"No problem. Let me put together a set of everything and get it up to you. When do you need it?"

"Well, early next week will probably be ok."

"No problem. I'll get on it right away. Great job, by the way, on the presentation. I'll bet you blew them away."

"Thanks, Festor, I feel pretty good about it."

"You ought to feel like a Donald Trump, Calvin. This deal is about to happen and all of us are going to get well on it, that's a promise."

"Man, I'm counting on it."

As Stubb folded his phone, he gracefully slid across to the right lane of the freeway, then wove back between two slower cars, the motion felt like an intricate ballet.

The deal was like that. A dance featuring all kinds of different artists, each performing his part and together making a single elegant thing happen. He was the choreographer. Even he had to admit he didn't have the figure for a dancer. Then he laughed out loud to himself at the thought of all the players on the stage at once, leaping and splitting and turning pirouettes, all to virtual music, music that they thought they were hearing but in fact was no music at all. Just noise.

How funny it seemed to him that real people could be convinced that noise was music and not only that, they liked it. But that was the way of the world. There were flute players and lemmings. Mostly lemmings.

But he was a financial type, and all these other details were not his forte. It bothered him a little that he had to deal with them at all, but this environmental stuff was off his radar screen. Frankly, he'd forgotten all about it until Richter brought it up. Thanks to pros like Sam, he didn't have to worry about every detail. Still he needed to bird-dog the stuff for Richter.

He had to get some gas, so he swept down off the expressway, down a ramp and into a 7-Eleven. Unleaded for the Hummer and cheese smothered nachos and a Coke for himself. He found a booth in the corner and sat down to dial Sam Kiel.

Chapter 31

"HEY," SAM SORTED through the bag of different colored phones and answered the red one, the Magne project.

"Hey, yourself," Stubb bantered.

"'S up?"

"Remember the permit push you did for me on that Magne deal?"

"That's that ranch in Texas, right?"

"Yeah."

"Sure, I remember it."

"Where are we with all that?"

"Let me see," Sam paused to think. "Oh, yeah, hell, that was only a couple of months ago. My mind is going to shit. Yeah, well we've got all the state approvals worked out. We don't need any permit until you're actually going to do something, but I've got letters from the Railroad Commission and Texas Parks & Wildlife that pretty much lay out the process and what to do to comply…"

"But did you get approvals?" Stubb interrupted.

"It's not like that, Festor. You get approvals for particular actions, not on concepts. What I got was the reassurance that as long as we didn't have any opposition or objection due to sensitive environmental impact issues, it was all pretty ordinary. Sort of like getting a building permit for a house."

"What do they mean by 'sensitive'?"

"You know, like Snail Darters, Whooping Cranes or some other exotic, endangered species kinds of things."

"That it?"

"Well, you can't be dumping junk all over the place either. You have to have a plan for protecting the environment while your project proceeds."

"And was there any kind of endangered stuff to worry about?"

"Well, that's the funny part. On private land like that ranch, the only people who'd know about any would be the owners and you know how that works…"

"What do you mean?"

"Well," Sam said, chortling, "if there are any, they aren't endangered very long. They're extinct-a-fied!"

"Oh, I get it," Stubb joined in the laughter.

"I gotta guess that all these environmental laws have killed off more endangered species than Noah's flood," Sam added. "So, Festor, you might wanna give your client a call and see that they do a 'house cleaning,' just as a sort of prophylactic."

"Prophylactic?" Stubb blurted as if he'd heard it wrong.

"Yeah, you know, Festor," Sam said, trying not to sound too patronizing, "If there's gonna be a screwin', you wanna make sure somebody's wearing a rubber."

It was over Stubb's head, but he didn't want to appear stupid, so he said, "Oh, right. Sam, can you put together some sort of package that makes all this not a big deal?"

"Sure. It'll look like almost any official government information: fat, expensive and totally useless. Will that do it?"

"Get it to my office by Monday if you can."

"Got it," Sam confirmed then folded the red cell phone.

Over the years Stubb had worked with all kinds of people, but none were as smart as Sam Kiel. Even though he often found himself feeling that a lot of Sam's stuff went right over his head, Stubb knew smart when he saw it.

He was in the connections business. People led to people which led to money. The Calvin Richter connection was just one example. Stubb remembered that Calvin led to Sam, who knew about the government agency compliance stuff, a complete blind spot to him, and that made Magne possible...all links in the long chain of tasks and assignments that paid in the end. Stubb felt particularly lucky.

The surprise in the whole deal, though, was Magne. Usually the principal Pooh Pah, the money mark, the host was a passive player. But there were a lot of politics in this deal and Magne was the man who opened the important doors. Stubb was impressed and by his way of thinking, there must have been a whole closet full of skeletons that was fuel for all the fires that were burning under bureaucratic bottoms from Austin to D.C.

Stubb liked to think of himself as the master of schemes, but he'd not toiled in the fertile fields of public money. The basic method of bought loyalties, so common in the corporate world, was no surprise to him when he saw it working in the political realm. But it was the scale of it that brought tears of admiration and envy to his eyes.

In a lingering high school civics class naiveté, Stubb initially had some difficulty comprehending the way the game worked. He had thought that giving money to public officials for favors was called bribery and that it was how things were done in third world countries. He was both amazed and amused that in the U.S., the practice was virtually the same. It was simply refined by the use of language.

Magne had no such misunderstanding. It took a bit of thinking, but Stubb understood eventually.

At the state level, the regulating agencies all had to submit their budgets to a Legislative Budget Board made up of key state legislators. In meetings held long before any bills could even be submitted, these power brokers held complete sway over bureaucratic life and death: funding.

This was the wellspring of the chips they traded for votes from their lesser brethren once the session started in January. What they traded for was determined by whom they owed for what, the primary forces being individual and corporate donors. It was by this indirect tether that a private rancher from the backwaters of the state could yank an appointed department director right down to the ground by cell phone remote control. And the directors knew it.

On the federal level it was a similar game, but the variety of ways to access congressmen and senators was as broad as the canopy of their family trees. The House Majority Whip's brother was a lobbyist that anyone from a Saudi prince to a Texas rancher could hire. Monde was a partner with his brother in a custodial service business that somehow managed to land fat contracts with most all of the local government offices. Still another congressman has a ghost-written book published and every copy is sold to a wealthy friend. And so the money flowed. Brothers, sisters, wives, cousins, friends--the net was fine and far flung. A contract here and another there, and next thing you knew, a tax law loophole relevant to one company in the country or special funding for a naval station in Iowa magically appears in the small print of mind-numbing minutiae, 300 pages deep into a new law.

But the gorging didn't stop there. Even the congressional staffers learned a few tricks. Monde's chief of staff was the County Sheriff's son Mario. A plum job for the kid, a favor owed to Magne. Mario's girlfriend would get the occasional government-funded contract to write a history of, say, railroad ties, which would never see the light of day.

And so it went all across the governments, hundreds of iterations and combinations, billions of dollars. Stubb realized the vast largess of tax and borrowed money being siphoned off hourly made his schemes paltry imitations, barely single digit fractions of the daily interest on the debt incurred on the purloined money alone. He was filled with awe. It was the perfect scam. Nobody would blow the whistle because everybody was getting fat.

The more he thought of it, the more he realized that Magne was the true master and why it was certain that the deal was going to pay, big time.

Chapter 32

JASON WALKED DOWN the dock, lost in thought.

"So, where exactly are you headed?" Jack's voice suddenly interrupted him. He stopped, momentarily disoriented, then realized he'd walked right past Jack's sailboat.

"Oh, sorry, I must have been dreaming," Jason explained as he stepped off the dock onto the Beneteau and through the transom. Jack was sitting in the cockpit, Coors Light in hand, leaning against the forward bulkhead, legs stretched out on a cushion that ran the length of the starboard-side bench. "You know, brother, this is your natural element."

"Try as I do, I can't seem to tire of it," Jack agreed, smiling broadly. "Looks like you could use a little R&R."

"It's been a pretty tough week, all right, and its only Thursday. Got any more of those shiny metal things?"

"Down below in the fridge, it's just left and back a bit."

"Got it," as Jason descended into the galley to retrieve a can of beer. Moses, in his cubby, looked up sleepily then dropped his head and pulled a paw over his ear.

"So, what's the 'tough week' thing all about? I thought Mayberry was an island of calm in the great stormy seas," Jack inquired.

"Well, mostly it is, but remember when you went with me to look at that john boat the other day?"

"That missing fisherman deal?"

"Yeah, well, when I got inside the office the guy's wife was waiting for me. It was pretty tough. She was all broken up," Jason said somberly.

"What's the latest on it anyway?"

"Absolutely nada. No word, no sign, nothing."

"Isn't this a county matter, you know, something the Sheriff investigates?"

"That's the thing, Jack, I can't get anybody interested in this case."

"Case, you call it now…"

"Yeah, I guess I do. I keep thinking there's something not right with this whole thing."

"So how long does someone have to be missing before the law gets interested?"

"I guess we're going to find out. As of now, I've called the Coast Guard and the Sheriff's Office. The Coast Guard did do a search but found nothing. The Sheriff's Office hasn't even sent out a deputy and I can't get the Sheriff to return my calls. But eventually, you'd think somebody would have to do something."

"You'd think."

Jason was now sitting stretched out on the port-side bench and both he and Jack sat silently watching the last rays of the sunset reddening the high, wispy clouds. As the light dimmed, the opposite side of the marina, the outline of the sheds and the mesquite trees standing behind them made a charcoal gray silhouette that blocked any view to the horizon. The warm moist air of the afternoon quickly gave way to coolness.

"Well," Jason said after a long while, "your brother may have gotten himself into a little trouble and you ought to be the first to know."

"Oh yeah? You're the straightest son of a bitch I know. So what'd you do, tear off a mattress tag?"

"Almost. I called up Doug at the *Valley Morning Star* this afternoon, when I couldn't get any response from that goddamn sheriff."

"Pentagon papers," Jack joked.

"Not quite, but let's just say someone has sprung a leak. Unfortunately, it's gonna be pretty damned obvious who."

"So the spy is coming in from the cold," Jack said. "Speaking of which, let's get down to the warm, Jason, and I'll heat up some chili and flour tortillas."

"Man, that does sound pretty good," he said as he rose to follow Jack down the companionway into the salon of the sailboat. Jack moved to the galley and Jason sat at the dining table and picked up a magazine and began browsing through it. Moses awoke and bowed his back in a long, luxurious stretch. "How long are you going to hang out around here?"

"Not very," Jack responded as he started the butane stove. "I've got about everything done and most of my supplies. I'm just going to check over the engine tomorrow, change the oil, check the belts, you know, that sort of thing, and if all's well, I ought to be underway sometime this weekend."

Jason reached over to the navigation table and picked up a chart of the western Gulf of Mexico. "Looks like you've decided on going north, anyway," he said following the dotted lines and circles drawn in pencil.

"Galveston first, I think. It'll give me a shakedown leg where I can work out any kinks in the rigging and engine. It's just across the bay to Kemah if I need anything fixed."

"Good thinking. That chili is starting to smell pretty good."

"Won't be long."

"I really can't get this Paredes case out of my head," Jason interjected.

"Paredes?"

"Yeah, that's the name of the guy who's missing, Octavio Paredes."

"You're kidding."

"What about it?" Jason asked surprised.

"I met a lady last week named Paredes and I think she said her husband's name was Octavio."

"Was her name Anajita?"

"Anahida, yeah, that's right."

"How'd you meet her?"

"She came to the house real early on the day of that garage sale I had. She was the one who bought all my stuff."

"No kidding?" Jason said, enthralled by the coincidence.

"Yeah, she had a kid named Octavio too. She called him Ocky, for short."

"This is weird," Jason commented, "What day was that?"

"Last Saturday."

"Why, that was the same day her husband went missing."

"Wow."

"No, really, that was the morning that he was supposed to come back and didn't."

"So he was out fishing early in the morning?"

"Actually, she said he went out the evening before and planned on fishing all night."

"So he was out there when the norther blew in," Jack said.

"Yeah, he had to be."

"Do you think that maybe that had anything to do with his being missing?"

"I mean, it's possible. The way the fishing tackle was rigged and all, it does look like he was there then suddenly he wasn't. And then the boat drifted downwind to the island. I've thought about that."

"Those first blasts of wind that come on the leading edge of the norther can be pretty stiff. That could have somehow caused him to fall out of the boat," Jack speculated.

"That would be one good explanation," Jason agreed, then after a pause added, "except for one thing."

"What's that."

"Well, say he slipped or fell, he'd have to have hit his head or something or else he'd just gotten back into the boat."

"Yeah, so?" Jack asked.

"Where's the body?"

Chapter 33

"PINCHE GRINGO," bellowed Sheriff Antonio Morales when his eyes read the header on a page two story in the *Valley Morning Star*. "The Sheriff's Office has done nothing on the case," the article read. He was furious. He didn't have time to chase down every stupid fisherman out on a three-day drunk, but now the paper made him look bad. It was that damned toy cop at Port Mansfield getting him back, he knew. He wasn't halfway through the story when his phone rang.

"Hola, si," the sheriff answered abruptly.

"Sheriff Morales?" a female voice asked.

"Yes, this is the sheriff."

"I am Pat Wilson, Mr. Magne's assistant. Mr. Magne wondered if you would have the time to come see him this afternoon at one-thirty."

"Yes, yes of course; I would be very happy to see Mr. Magne today. Please tell him I'll be there."

"Thank you, Sheriff," she said as she hung up.

"Pinche gringo," Morales exclaimed. Now what, he wondered. The only time he'd ever see Magne was just before an election, when he'd call on the wealthiest man in the county for a campaign contribution and his blessing. No one was going to be elected in Willacy County without that. He speed-dialed his office. "Veronica."

"Yes, sheriff," his secretary answered on the private line.

"Oye, tell the judge I'm not gonna make it for lunch, mi hijita."

"He's going to be mad, Sheriff," she said, warning.

"Si, pues, I've got to go see Señor Magne. He called me."

"Oh, ok." She understood. "I'll call the judge and let him know."

"Gracias, mi hijita," he said as he hung up. Veronica was not his daughter but he thought of all his staff as his children. He saw his role as a sort of father figure over the people of the county, if only one of lesser rank. The County Judge was the *Patron, lo mero mero*, he knew. The judge had the power over local government much as a feudal king over his vassals. It was one of the anachronisms of the Rio Grande Valley. The calendars all showed 2001, but in some ways it was still 1501.

He had time to drive over to Port Mansfield first, just in case this summons to the Magne Ranch was related to the missing fisherman. The newspaper article did say that the boat was found on the island, just across from the Magne Ranch.

In half an hour he pulled up to the Port Office and went in.

"Sheriff," Jason greeted him as he entered.

"Grider," he said in an irritated tone. "I want to talk to you about the missing fisherman."

"Let's take a walk," Jason suggested, coming around the counter and heading for the door. The sheriff followed.

"I don't 'preciate you making me look bad in the paper, Grider," the sheriff began almost immediately after they were outside.

"I don't know what you mean, Sheriff," Jason acted surprised.

"You talkin' to that reporter. It makes me look bad."

"She called me," he insisted. "All I did was answer her questions. I didn't say anything about you."

"You know what I mean," the sheriff said impatiently.

"I really don't. If you've got a problem with the paper, take it up with them. All I do is answer questions," Jason lied.

The sheriff wasn't happy with what he was hearing but he had nowhere else to go with it. After a few minutes of walking they were standing next to the found john boat.

"This the boat?" the sheriff asked.

"Yes. We found it stranded on the back of the island, about four miles south of the old Magne landing."

"Don't look like no foul play to me," the sheriff observed, standing on the dock and looking into the boat.

"Hard to tell, Sheriff; we don't have any way to do any kinds of tests here."

"Not every loose boat is a murder, Grider," the sheriff admonished him.

"No, and I'm not sure this one is that either."

"So why all this stuff with the newspaper?" the sheriff asked aggressively, turning to face Jason.

"All I know is that a man is missing nearly a week now and what looks like his boat turns up empty. It seems to me that at least we have a missing person case, Sheriff, and there's a wife and kid that wants to know what happened to him," Jason answered back equally aggressively.

The sheriff looked at Jason for a while, as if sizing him up in some way, then said, "So what do you want me to do?"

"I'd think you'd get one of your investigators over here to see what this is all about."

The sheriff stood glaring at the boat, clearly trying to stifle his rising temper at being addressed in what he felt was disrespectful for his office. His face reddened. He turned to walk away, back up the dock, toward the Port Office. "I don't like this," he said. Jason watched him as he walked to his car, swung open the door angrily, got in and sped away, spewing gravel under his spinning wheels.

The sheriff was hitting nearly eighty miles an hour on the

road back to Raymondville before he realized he was speeding. He slowed down to sixty, trying to calm himself. He felt like a kid who'd been caught in a lie. He was embarrassed and he didn't like the feel of it. "Pinche gringo!" he yelled out loud.

When he reached Highway 77, he turned north for the fifteen mile drive to the main gate of the Magne Ranch.

He thought about how the people of the Rio Grande Valley were used to the model of the hacienda, where a benevolent lord cared for his people and they rewarded him with their loyalty and hard work. It was a way of life that was resistant to change and in many ways, had not changed. The region had for most of history been a land under occupation. The Spaniards, the French, the Texicans, the Confederates and now the Americans--each adding a new twist on the culture. To many of the poor it seemed as if the "outsiders" were merely a parade of different players who would come and go, but the hacienda remained. There was resentment for those who tried to change it and these were nearly always the late comers.

Sheriff Morales had grown up an American, attending the Raymondville schools, which taught American ways. But when he got home in the afternoons after school, the language of the house was Spanish and all the celebrations from birthdays, to Quinceaneras, to Christmas were as they always had been. Just about everyone was Hispanic, so there was no sense of minority, as his cousins who had moved north often complained about. The Valley was still home, our land.

It distressed him to see that his children, one generation later, were different. They spoke to him in English now, and preferred the ways they learned on television and in the magazines. The old ways were fading. He feared that in another generation, more would be lost and eventually all.

The sheriff drove up to the main gate of the Magne Ranch and a gatekeeper came out of the guardhouse.

"Hola, Sheriff," the gatekeeper greeted him.

"Hola."

Opening the gate, the gatekeeper instructed, "You are to go up to *Casa Blanca*, Sheriff."

The sheriff nodded and waved as he began the eight mile drive into the ranch. He began to rehearse a greeting as he drove along the narrow crushed caliche road that wound through the occasional stands of oaks. He cleared his throat and straightened himself up in his car seat. As he approached the sprawling two story Spanish style mansion, his pulse quickened and he felt a slight nausea of nervousness.

He was met by a ranch hand immediately as he drove up to the front steps. He was accompanied up to the front veranda and into the main hall--a three story tall entry room paneled with dark woods capped by a coffered ceiling. The marble floor flowed in all directions, disappearing around turns and behind doorways. In the middle of the hall floor was a mosaic medallion with the cipher of an enormous "M." Flanking the sweeping marble staircase were two huge newel posts, with a differently posed carved falcon perched on each.

It was the first time he'd been inside *Casa Blanca*. In the few times he'd been to see him, Mr. Magne had been in an office about a mile down the road among the barns and workshops.

"Sheriff," he heard Magne call out in an enthusiastic tone. The sheriff turned just in time to see Magne come out of a side room, a library it looked like, and then walk right up to him to give him an *abrazo*, the traditional Mexican hug of greeting friends.

"Mr. Magne," Sheriff Morales greeted him warmly.

"Thanks so much for coming to see me, Sheriff, how long has it been?" Magne asked.

"Two years?" Morales guessed, knowing that it was exactly that because that was when he last ran for re-election.

"That long?" Magne said in feigned amazement. "Come in to the library, Sheriff."

"Thank you, sir," Morales said, following Magne.

"Have you had lunch, Sheriff?" Magne asked in invitation.

"Yes, sir, thank you, I have," Morales lied. He was much too nervous to eat with Mr. Magne.

"Then how about something to drink?" he asked perfunctorily as he went straight to the sideboard and pulled the top off a crystal decanter. "Wild Turkey? Isn't that your drink, Sheriff?"

"Well, yes sir, it is, but I am on duty…"

"Nonsense," Magne said, handing him a glass of whisky.

The sheriff took it politely, switching his hat from his right hand so he could hold the drink. "Thank you, sir," he said.

"Come sit down here with me, Sheriff, and tell me about your kids. What are they up to?" Magne directed him to two large leather winged-back chairs that were arranged by a tall window that overlooked the front of the house. Morales sat down, then straightened himself up as he twisted his body to more directly face Magne.

"Mario, as you know," Morales began, "is still in Washington working for the Congressman Monde. He likes it very much, and I appreciate you helping him to get that job, Mr. Magne."

"That was nothing, Sheriff. Mario is a bright boy. He deserves all the credit for that. And your daughter?"

"Marisa? She's still studying at the Veterinary School in College Station. She's got another two years."

"And I hope you told her that we're going to need her here on the ranch when she graduates. She's a wonderful girl."

"I'll tell her, of course, sir. She's like her mother. She has a mind of her own."

"Modern women, eh Sheriff?" Magne said, smiling as he lifted his glass in an impromptu toast.

"Yes, sir," Morales said softly. There was an awkward pause.

"Well, Sheriff, thanks for coming out here. I wanted to talk to you about something. I need your help."

"Whatever I can do for you, Mr. Magne."

"In a month or so I'm going to host a pretty big to do for some big wigs from out east and we're going to need some help ferrying these folks into the ranch and seeing they are all taken care of. Some of these folks are pretty famous and we're going to need some extra security."

"We can help there, sir."

"Great. I was hoping you could try to keep those nosy press people away from the gate, you know, a sort of zone of privacy, so folks can get in without feeling like their going to be pounced on by the paparazzi."

"Paparazzi?"

"You know, the sleazy press photographers--tabloids."

Morales only had a faint idea what he was talking about, but he thought he had the general picture. "Yes, sir," he said.

"And of course, I'll take care of any overtime costs the sheriff's office might have because of all this."

"I wouldn't hear of it, Mr. Magne. For all you do for the county, it is the least we can do. Security is our job and you are an important citizen, sir."

"Thanks, Sheriff, I appreciate it. We're not settled on final dates yet, but I'll give you some notice once the plans firm up. One thing, though," Magne said suddenly very serious, "this has to kept real quiet. Word gets out before and we'll be swamped with gawkers."

"No problem, sir. You can count on it being kept private."

"You're terrific, Sheriff," Magne said, rising to his feet in a clear signal the visit was ending. Magne stepped over to his desk and picked up an envelope and handed it to Morales.

"What's this, Mr. Magne?" Morales asked, taking it.

"Let's just say it's an early contribution to the next campaign," he said, winking. "We need to keep good men in office," he added as he put his arm around Morales's shoulder and walked him to the door of the library.

"Many thanks, Mr. Magne."

As they passed into the great entry hall and towards the front door, Magne added, "Sheriff, I was disturbed to see an article in the paper this morning. Something about a missing fisherman."

"Yes sir, I know all about it."

"The article suggests that the boat was found just east of the ranch and it makes me worry that law enforcement folks will be crawling all over my land looking for this fellow. What's going on with that?"

"Well sir, the investigation is really not completed yet. We don't know what happened to the man, maybe nothing."

"Could you do me a special favor, Tony?" Magne asked, pulling him closer. "Before anybody comes on Magne property, will you call me in advance and tell me?"

"Yes, sir, of course," Morales said emphatically.

"I'd really like you to see if you can keep anything like that from happening, Tony. I'll send some ranch hands out to scour the shore of the Laguna. If we find something, we'll call you, ok?"

"That's good enough for me, Mr. Magne. I'll see nobody bothers you."

"Thanks, Sheriff, I knew I could count on you." Magne took Morales' hand and shook it firmly, showing him out the front door. Magne counted one more item off his mental list. Calls he'd made earlier in the day would handle this matter from another direction.

Morales felt a cool flush of relief as he descended the stairs of the front verandah to his car below. He turned to wave at his host as he was getting into his car, but Magne had already gone back inside. Morales started the drive back to the main highway when he came upon a herd of some strange looking antelopes. He stopped to let them file across the road. He remembered the envelope Magne had given him and took it from his back pocket. He opened it to find a deck of hundreds. There were fifty of them.

As he started down the road again, he smiled. The day had turned out much better than he'd expected. All was good with Magne, his position couldn't be more secure, and he had a down payment for the new Honda 50 boat motor he'd had his eye on.

The only little irritant was that son of a bitch toy cop, Grider. He needed to be taught a lesson. He needed to learn a little respect. That wouldn't be too hard to arrange. One thing was for sure, the missing fisherman matter was buried. In a week no one would much care, in two, hardly anybody would even remember.

As he sped south on Highway 77, Morales had an overwhelmingly good feeling. The hacienda was alive and well.

Chapter 34

CINDY LEANED ACROSS Secretary of the Interior Bill Rode's desk and plucked up the yellow-covered U.S. Department of Fish & Wildlife Report entitled, "*Impact of Gas Drilling in the Upper Laguna Madre of Texas.*"

"This the one, Mr. Secretary?" she asked.

"Let me see," he said tilting up his glasses to use his bifocals. "The one by USFWL's Jack Grider, yeah, that's it. Take a look at that and give me a one-page memo on it tomorrow, will you, Cindy?"

"Tomorrow is Saturday, sir. Monday ok?"

"Monday's fine."

"Have you already read it, sir?"

"Yeah," he replied, "I need the memo for the packet to send over to Congressman Monde's office."

The intercom clicked. "Mr. Secretary, Director Coyne on the line, sir."

"Thank you, Lizzie, put him through. ...Rick!"

"How are you, Bill?" Coyne asked.

"Great, Rick, thanks. Rick, I was calling you about that gas drilling program being proposed by the Magne Ranch down in South Texas; are you familiar with that?"

"Well, yes, Bill, I had some fellow in here the other day from Congressman Monde's office talking to my staff about it."

"Same deal working over here. I'm just looking over all the materials that have come our way and, far as I can tell, this all needs to go through you over at Fish & Wildlife."

"I think that's right, Bill. As far as the Federal government is concerned on this thing, this is really an impact issue, particularly regarding endangered species, and of course, their habitat."

"That's what I thought. Hey, I've got an impact report over here, done by one of your folks, a Jack Grider, is that the last one done on this? Is this the current situation?"

"That's the latest, Bill. I think it's less than a year old."

"Well, that's certainly fresh enough. Have you seen it?"

"Oh, probably, but it's been a while. I don't remember anything standing out particularly, else I guess I'd remember it."

"I read it this afternoon. Essentially, it pretty much gives a green light to drilling in the Laguna Madre. No negative environmental impacts. Does that square with you?"

"Yes, that's right. I remember now. I guess that's why it slipped out of mind. Nothing very exciting."

"Well, Rick, I guess that about wraps it up. We're going to put together a packet for the Congressman for Monday. He asked us to and we've got to accommodate him, you know how that goes. But we're not giving any opinions out. That's your neck of the woods."

"We're doing the same thing here. Sort of a comfort thing. Monde just wants some reassurance that the project won't hit a snag."

"Think with me on this, so this goes without a hitch," Rode asked, "what else is the Congressman going to want to get his ducks all in a row?"

"Well, I think as far as we're concerned, he's all set. Outside of us, well, there's Texas state requirements, which is up to them, and then there is local support. He's going to have to get the locals down there behind him. That's also off our radar. No, I think this is it."

"When are you sending your stuff over to him?" Rode asked.

"We're actually done except for one last trailing detail I've got a staff member chasing down. We found some reference in the files to a document we don't seem to have. Something about an easement, power lines, I guess, dated back twenty some odd years. I can't imagine it has much to do with any of this, though. We're not going to hold up for it, so we're sending out ours on Monday."

"Great. Thanks for the update, Rick. By the way, are you going to be in town for the weekend?"

"I thought we'd stay close in, maybe take a drive down to Annapolis."

"Enjoy it," Rode said.

Rode put down the receiver and called to his legislative aide, "Cindy, your memo, and this mother is outta here first thing, got that?"

"Yes, sir, Mr. Secretary. I'll put it all together and get it over to the Congressman's office by lunchtime Monday."

"Thanks." Rode sat in his desk chair, propped his feet up on the desk and stretched to relieve a bit of tiredness. It had been a long week, made more tense than usual by the need to service one of the key votes on the Appropriations Committee. That was his job and he was good at it.

He thought about how Monde certainly had worked all the angles on this issue. He was a pro. No holes for things to fall through and dogged pursuit of what he wanted. Smooth as silk in getting it all moving in his direction. He was a man you wanted on your side, that's for sure, he thought.

He knew what the drilling meant, hundreds of millions for the Magnes, but what he didn't know, and it was killing him to know, was what Monde was getting out of this, and how.

Chapter 35

THE CLOCK ON THE Port Mansfield Port Office wall read four fifteen. The mayor had already arrived and was sitting in the conference room, waiting for the aldermen and the Special Meeting due to begin fifteen minutes later. The conference table was set at the far end of the room. Historical scene photos lined the institutional green walls. On the right side wall was a photograph of Congressman Monde, posing with the mayor and the aldermen. At the end of the room, opposite the conference table, there were extra chairs which had very little wear on them. A lone ceiling fan turned lazily, groaning an undulating hum, and casting a circling shadow on the suspended ceiling panels.

"Jason!" the mayor called through the open door.

"Yes sir, Mr. Mayor," he answered, sticking his head inside the room.

"Got a minute?"

"Sure. What's up?"

"Tell me what you know about the missing fisherman, what's his name?"

"Paredes. Octavio Paredes."

"Right. What's the latest on that?"

"All we have is a loose john boat, Mayor, and a fellow who was supposed to be out fishing and hasn't turned up home. That's really all we know."

"So you're not even sure he's not just taken off somewhere, then?"

"No, we aren't, but I have my suspicions about this."

"Suspicions?" the mayor asked warily. "What suspicions?"

"Well, it just seems odd to me, the details and all. I just have this feeling that there's more to this than meets the eye."

"Wasn't it the night of the norther that he disappeared?"

"Yes, sir, sometime between sundown Friday and sunrise Saturday."

"Doesn't it seem to you that this old fellow might have just fallen off or had a heart attack or, hell, just ran off from that fat wife of his."

"I don't think that's it," Jason said.

"Well, I don't think we ought to be spending any time on this, Jason. I mean, this isn't really our area of responsibility. Anything outside the limits of this town belongs to the county. I want you to leave this thing with the Sheriff's Office, you got that?"

"I think…"

"That's final, Jason. The matter belongs to the Sheriff. Let him handle it from here on out," the mayor said in the tone of a direct military order, the kind he had been used to giving before he retired from the Army, a full bird colonel. Jason stood silently looking at the mayor, not sure what to say next. He was so angry he had to check himself. Just as he was about to speak, three Aldermen entered the conference room. Jason passed them on his way out, fuming.

At four thirty-five the mayor called the Special Meeting to order.

"The Special Meeting, Friday, November 9, 2001, of the Port Mansfield Port Authority is called to order," the mayor said to an empty meeting room, except for the three aldermen, Phyllis, who was to take minutes, and himself. "Gentlemen, since this is a Special Meeting, we won't have any reading of the minutes of the last Regular Meeting. That'll be done at the next one. This meeting's agenda is only one item: *'Discussion and possible action regarding certain exploration opportunities in the Laguna Madre.'*

"I think we need to do the Pledge, Mayor," Phyllis interrupted.

"Yes, fine," he agreed, and all stood for a recitation of the Pledge of Allegiance, led by the mayor. Then they sat back down.

"Phyllis, you're going to need to show everyone present except Alderman Wilson," the mayor instructed. "Kevin," he explained, "is visiting his daughter in San Antonio."

"She have that baby, yet?" Alderman Fuentes asked.

"Due tomorrow, is the word," the mayor reported.

"So ole Kevin's about to be a granddad, then."

"And he's not taking it well, either," Alderman Franklin interjected. "Says there's no way he's old enough to be a grandfather."

"I hear that," Alderman Spears laughed.

"Turning back to business," the mayor admonished good naturedly, "We're here to consider a resolution of support for gas exploration activities in the Laguna, gentlemen. As you know, McAllen over in Hidalgo County has been collecting royalties on gas leases on city property that someone had the foresight to buy many years ago. I don't mind telling you, they're sitting pretty now from those fat monthly checks coming in from the gas companies. We may have the opportunity to do the same thing."

"Mr. Mayor," Alderman Franklin interrupted, "but I had always heard that those gas fields don't reach over to the coast."

"That's been the conventional wisdom, Vern. There's been a few dry holes sunk, down the coast from us, sure, but north of us, nearer to Kingsville, there have been some finds."

"So we don't know how far south those run, then?" the alderman asked.

"No, no we don't. That's what this is all about. Finding out," the mayor explained.

"But what's all that going to cost and how would we pay for that kind of a speculation?" Alderman Spears asked.

"That's what I've got to report this evening," the mayor replied. "I've met with some geologists and engineers working with the Magne Ranch and they felt that if gas were found on the Magne lands just north of us, there would be a pretty good chance that the gas field might extend to our port district lands that abut the ranch."

"That's pretty exciting," interjected Alderman Franklin.

"I'll say," agreed Spears, "so what are the chances that the Magnes are going to find gas?"

"That's the news we've been waiting for," the mayor said, now leaning forward as if he could barely contain himself. "There was a test done, and Wednesday it was confirmed."

"What was confirmed?" Franklin asked.

"They've found gas," the mayor blurted.

"For sure?" Spears nearly yelled.

"For sure!" the mayor confirmed. Suddenly the aldermen were standing and talking over one another. Phyllis, unaccustomed to any kind of liveliness in the Port Office, was wide eyed and agape. Javier Fuentes alone, sat with his fingers intertwined in a double fist on his lap. It was several minutes before the frenzy of excitement began to settle down and the mayor and aldermen took their seats again.

"What exactly is it that you want us to do, Mayor?" Spears asked.

"Well, the first thing is to get this out on the table to see what you all think of it. And if the board is in favor, to do some things that would allow us to benefit from a gas find on district land."

"Well, I think it is the best news since indoor plumbing," Franklin said enthusiastically.

"Me too," Spears agreed. "I say we go for it."

At this moment the mayor looked to Alderman Fuentes and said, "You're awful quiet over there, Javier. What are your thoughts on it?"

Alderman Fuentes turned his head to face the mayor and sat thoughtfully for a few seconds before he began.

"Naturally, it would be good news if the district could get a steady flow of funds from something like this. There's a lot of good things we could do with it. The west docks need repair and we still don't have streetlights on the road out to that section of new houses to the south. We need to think about putting in a clinic here for minor medical emergencies…" He paused to think some more. "So long as we don't take a risk," he continued, "and find ourselves in a financial bind if nothing materializes."

"That's good advice, Javier. I couldn't agree more," the mayor replied. "What I had in mind was this. Say, we let the Magnes take all the risks bringing the first well in. Then and only then, when that proves out, we move ahead on a well of our own. What do you men think of that?"

"That seems prudent to me, Mayor," Franklin said as Spears nodded in agreement. "Have you talked to Kevin about this yet?"

"Yeah, and he's on board," the mayor replied.

"What exactly do we have to do now?" Franklin asked. "And how much is it going to cost?"

"Right now," the mayor explained, "all we have to do is pass a resolution supporting Magne's request for permission to drill."

"That's it?" Spear said, surprised.

"That's it. And of course, we want to use our influence and support to help get this approved up through channels. Mostly, though, we just need to show our strong support, and make sure everyone in town is singing the same tune," the mayor continued.

"Do you need a motion?" Franklin offered, chortling.

"And a second?" Spears immediately jumped in.

"Hold on, hold on," the mayor laughed. "We've got to do this by Robert's Rules, gentlemen."

"Mr. Mayor," Fuentes interjected.

"Yes, Javier."

"What about this drilling? Is this sort of thing going to be any threat to the Laguna?"

The aldermen looked at Fuentes, then each other, then to the mayor.

"Threat? What do you mean by 'threat'?" the mayor asked.

"You know, environmental threat. Will it hurt the shrimp spawning, or will it kill off the fish or crabs? Things like that."

"Oh, Javier, I'm sure that is not going to be a problem…" the mayor started.

"Well, mayor," Fuentes interrupted, "we do have to think about our local businesses, especially the sport fishers, the shrimpers…"

"Javier, Javier," the mayor interrupted back. "Relax. I am sure there's no way the federal government would let somebody foul up the Laguna. You know how strict they are about that. But if you're interested in local business, can you imagine the economic impact of the people working on those wells for our town? We'll have stores, and your little restaurant will have to expand for all the new customers. Imagine the jobs! More money locally will mean more houses, more investment…this could put us on the map."

"Oh, I understand that, Mayor. Don't get me wrong. I'm all for improving life in Port Mansfield. I just want to make sure we're doing this right and that we don't end up hurting ourselves."

"For Christ's sake, Javier," Franklin exploded. "This is a goddamn pot of gold for this town. You're not gonna turn tree-hugger on us now, are you?"

"It's good for everybody," Spears intervened more calmly. "That medical clinic you've been asking for these last few years could become a reality, Javier. Think of it!"

"I'm with you all the way on that, Javier," the mayor joined in. "Naturally we need to be careful. But what I need from you right now is approval of a resolution--there's one in your packet in front of you--that declares our support for drilling in the Laguna. It's going to be up to the Magne folks to make the argument to the powers up the line. And, Javier, there's no way anything we do here is going convince the feds to allow anything that will end up polluting the Laguna."

"Of course not," Spears agreed.

"So, what's it going to be, gentlemen?" the mayor asked finally.

"I move that the resolution be approved," Franklin declared.

"Second," Spears said enthusiastically.

"All in favor?" the mayor called the vote.

"Aye," intoned the two aldermen, who then joined the mayor in looking to Fuentes.

After a few seconds, Fuentes reluctantly joined. "Aye."

"Then it is unanimous!" declared the Mayor. "Today is the dawn of a new era for Port Mansfield," he said grandly.

"Let's hope," Fuentes said cautiously.

"Amen to that, brother," Spears added.

"Now what say we head over to Javier's place to celebrate," the mayor proposed. "And I'm buying!"

Chapter 36

MAGNE WAS ROLLING the neck of the Dom Perignon between his palms, making a swishing sound in the ice bucket. He stared up at the portrait of his grandfather, John Magne II, over the fireplace mantle. He had been a stern and severe man, Magne recalled, and even in his portrait, he seemed to scowl disapprovingly down at him.

Tonight, though, Magne was sure he would be smiling at his grandson. "*Forward, by all means,*" Magne repeated his grandfather's motto to himself out loud. The wheels were in motion to secure the Magne Ranch for generations to come and he had done it. Magne imagined that if his grandfather were alive today, he would have taken the same course. Times were different, but the threats against the family were not.

In the early days, when Magne's great-grandfather bought the first strip of land that was the beginning of the Magne holdings, the threats were cattle rustlers from Mexico and rattlesnakes. He was in the first wave of northeastern carpetbaggers who discovered the Rio Grande Valley after the Civil War. Under the authority of Reconstruction, he and others like him mastered the practice of "land distribution," taking from the Spanish Land Grant holders and distributing to the new Americans.

Such was the cycle of land ownership. The Spaniards arrived first, to take the land from the Coahuiltecans, the Mexicans drove off the Spaniards, the Texicans then overthrew the Mexicans, and now the Unionists had their way with the Texan-Confederates. Everyone had a complaint. It just didn't much matter. Land slipped from weak hands to stronger ones. To Magne, it was the natural order of things.

His great-grandfather may have started the Magne Ranch, but it was his grandfather who accumulated the nearly one-million acres into the dynasty that it is today. He had been relentless in his acquisition of surrounding parcels. In some cases, he patiently waited for heirs to thin out family resolve for their lands and bought them off one by one. The depression and the drought in the 1880s had forced many others to sell out just to raise enough money to survive, and he took every advantage.

The story that most amused him was his grandfather's purchase of 4,431 acres for $8.31 of back taxes. The silly owners didn't understand the new American laws installed after the Treaty of Guadalupe Hidalgo, which converted the northern Mexican lands to the U.S. A few months later his grandfather bought another 5,000 acres for $15 in delinquent taxes. It was Magne family lore that he had then complained about having to pay double in only a single month. But the real lesson, learned to good advantage for generations yet to be, was that no amount of luck was as good as a judge on the payroll.

But there were some landowners who were, as his grandfather would say, "just too damned stubborn to understand." He saw the eventual ownership of all the surrounding lands a Magne Manifest Destiny and those that didn't cooperate at first would have to at last. And for some it *was* the last thing they ever did.

"I don't want to own all the land," his grandfather was reported to have said. "Just all the land next to mine."

There had been stories that managed to survive over the years that cast an aura of invincibility upon the Magnes and the ranch, stories of reluctant sellers who disappeared or turned up dead, clusters of "unfortunate accidents" that suddenly left families without a single male to run their ranches, and other more exotic tales.

But none more mysterious or more powerful in effect than what had come to be memorialized in a local *corrido*, a "ballad," called *La Noche del Sal del Rey*.

The story was told of a family that held ten thousand acres of land on the Southern extent of the present day Magne holdings, and whose land was nearly surrounded by Magne purchases, refused Magne's grandfather's repeated demands.

The Santander family hacienda was an original Spanish Land Grant and included the *Salina de los Reyneros*, *Sal del Rey*, for short. It was so named for a salt lake that supplied virtually all of northern Mexico with the salt used for preserving meat. It was for that reason critical and valuable and why the family had been able to hold on to their land while others had not. *Sal de Rey* had once been of the vast lands of the King of Spain. "The Salt of the King."

Something extraordinary happened on Halloween Night, 1898, at the *Hacienda Sal del Rey*. It was a date well remembered, because it was also the exact day that John Magne III, the first one that is, was born. No one was sure exactly what, but one local *curandera*, a "witch" or "seer," said that she had been told by an apparition, a fifteen year old boy, that the devil himself had appeared and so terrified the inhabitants of *Sal del Rey* that they were turned instantly to stone, frozen in their terror at the exact instant of their deaths.

Official reports were almost as bizarre. On the next day, November 1, an itinerant priest, an Oblate Father who worked a circuit ministry from Brownsville, arrived at the hacienda just before dark but found the place completely abandoned. He reported that he found not even the usual barnyard fowl which were nearly always milling in the courtyard. He searched every room, and it was as if all of the people had simply disappeared in the middle of ordinary routine. Tortillas were stacked on the stone surface of the kitchen worktable as they would if the cook had just been busy patting the *masa* between her hands. The fires had gone cold, but cauldrons of *frijoles* sat on the grill, a thin crust of dried and hardened lard covering the soup. Candles were burnt down to their bowls. Beds still unmade, as if hastily emptied.

The *curandera*'s story seemed to be contradicted by the priest's report, as no one was to be found in the hacienda, as was corroborated by the sheriff, who investigated the incident. No witness ever came forward. The matter became part of the local lore as the years passed without any further clues as to what happened to the people of *La Hacienda Sal del Rey.*

The Santander family who owned the hacienda and who lived in Monterrey, some three hundred miles south, had more than suspected that Magne had been at the center of the mystery and didn't at all believe in ghosts. They were sure Magne had murdered all the inhabitants of their hacienda and they were infuriated when Texas law enforcement officials refused to arrest him.

One of their own lost was Maria Paredes Santander, only twenty-four at the time. Her seven year old daughter, Juanita, who, on the day before, had left for Monterrey to spend the holidays with the family, was devastated when she was told the news. It was a grudge inflamed by the family's hate for the Magnes that she would carry for the rest of her eighty-four years.

The very least of their vengeance was the vow never to sell their lands to the Magnes; a promise they thought they had kept, until fifteen years later, after the incident at the lake.

Chapter 37

IN THE SUMMER OF 1912 a ten year draught had tightened its choke hold on the parched South Texas ranchlands. The last of the *resacas* and *palanganas* had dried up and the land was strewn with the rotting carcasses of cattle, deer and other wild animals. As the ponds grew smaller and smaller, the few remaining alligators would snatch anything that came near the muddy water's edge. It was a grand struggle for survival that showed in the faces of the worn and weary inhabitants trying to scratch some semblance of life from drying wells and withering gardens.

The draught had turned most of the familiar roads that ran from north Texas to the Valley into beds of soft sand, which made the going easier on the seats of the wagon passengers, but hard and slow for the mules, requiring more frequent stops to rest them. For the first time in anyone's memory, even the salt lake began to recede.

It was after dark on an evening in late October that a wagon bearing travelers in route from San Antonio to Brownsville came upon the dilapidated Santander *Hacienda Sal del Rey* and decided to camp there for the night. All day they could feel the oppressively mounting heat and humidity and the disappearance of any relieving breeze. The mules were edgy and cantankerous. As evening fell, they began to see the first signs of the norther threatening from behind them. By the time they made the hacienda, the first distant rumbling could be heard. A blue norther was coming and they needed shelter from the storm that would soon be upon them.

Among the travelers that night was a Sister Barbe Voissement, who recorded in her journal the following:

> *31st October, 1912*
>
> *Have arrived at an abandoned farm house and its dependencies, some fifty miles north of Brownsville. It is an aged but substantial place, as far as I have seen from the fire we have made in the courtyard. It is absolute blackness beyond the cast of the fire's light. The bone-jarring ride was much alleviated as we had left behind the rocky roadway that led from San Antonio, now nearly a week ago, and have now sand to ride on. The climate is hot and sultry and it is impossible to fend off the flies, as there is no air to help. I have taken to covering my head with my veil, better to suffer the heat than the maddening insects.*
>
> *A storm has been chasing us much of the day, promising the relief of some rain and perhaps cooler air. The driver has called us to dinner, which I fear will be more the same faire of bean paste on flattened corn mash bread and some salted bacon. More on the terrain in tomorrow's journal entry.*
>
> *The journal occasionally skipped days, but never was there more than one entry per day until this one.*
>
> *I am barely able to write this. We have in the last hours fled from place of the last journal entry. We are at this moment huddled together in the largest room in a ranch belonging to a kind family that has taken us in. The fire blazing in the hearth is some comfort from what we have witnessed this night.*
>
> *Here is what transpired. We had each found a place*

to lay out our bedrolls after dinner, in a room on the second floor of the farm house we had come upon earlier. It was at midnight when the storm began to arrive. Bright, silent flashes of lightning stirred me from an uneasy sleep. The air was yet dead still and even the cicadas seemed chastened and had surrendered to an eerie silence. I tried to sleep but was taken by the shadows that danced on the wall across the room each time lightning flashed outside. It was on one such flash that I thought I had seen the silhouette of someone, then several. My heart leapt at the surprise of it and wondered if the driver had gone out to steady the mules.

Abandoning all hope of sleep, I decided to take up a post in a north facing window opening that overlooked what, in the occasional lightning, appeared to be some sort of a lake, to watch the storm come in. The air was electric and tasted of acid. The thunder grew louder and closer. Out of sight in the distance, the sound of trees being whipped and flailed made the hair on the back of my neck stand on end. A low moaning, in irregular undulations, slowly rose in pitch until it was the wail of banshees. The sound raced toward me and I held my breath in terror. Then, a great gust of wind rammed the house in a horrendous scream, and I was knocked off the sill and onto my back on the floor of the room as the remnants of old curtains flew over me like a white gossamer pennant. The slamming and crashing shutters reverberated through the house, waking all who were yet sleeping. I rose to my feet and looked outside just as a bolt of lightning struck not two hundred yards away.

Suddenly, in a long series of flashes, I could see them emerging from the lake.

When the darkness again enveloped, I was left, rubbing my eyes, not certain of what I had just seen. Another flash of lightning revealed that indeed there were several *figures appearing to be marching out of the lake, the nearest standing on the shore of it, followed by a line of others leading back into the water, ever deeper, until the last one was merely a head above the surface. And clearly I could see that they were made of a white stone.*

I gasped in horror, for what beings of this world would be so engaged on so foul and dark a night in so remote a place?

I was shocked senseless by a shriek coming from behind me. Without my realizing it, the rest of our traveling group had gathered behind me and had witnessed the same vision. The driver had become so disturbed that he demanded that we leave immediately, and within minutes all had thrown together what could be quickly collected, the mules hastily harnessed, the wagon attached and we fled.

After many hours, we came upon this ranch where we are now sheltered by the grace of God, as the rain had become so torrential and the blustery winds so miserable that we would have collapsed had we not found it, and certainly would not have, but for the faint pin of light we saw coming through the sheets of rain.

In the safety of this haven, we have told our story to the family that has taken us in, but I fear I shall not speak of it again. For I am not even now sure that what I have seen was more than the child of terror and would dismiss it entirely were it not that six other souls swore they too saw it.

The Night of the Sal del Rey was deeply imbedded in the mystique of the Magne Ranch. The 1912 event was investigated by authorities of the time, but on that night the norther brought some fifteen inches of rain that fell across the region, and when the Sheriff arrived at the hacienda two days later, the lake had been completely refilled. There was no sign of any "statues rising from the lake," as had been alleged. The matter was written off as yet another fanciful tale encouraged by local healers and seers.

The Santanders abided by their vow never to sell to the Magnes, but with Pancho Villa organizing an army in the north and the Zapatistas raiding in the south, Mexico sank into revolution, with the Santanders on the wrong side of it. That, and the growing availability of ice, made salt irrelevant; the bad memories and ethereal tales made the hacienda a burden. It was in 1913 that the Sal del Rey land finally sold to an agent, who as it turned out, was working secretly for the Magnes. When Juanita Santander discovered what had transpired, she flew into a rage and had to be hospitalized. It was said she never fully recovered her sanity.

Magne's grandfather had prevailed as he swore he would.

But the Sal del Rey would not so easily release its grip on local imaginations, nor would it pass so quickly to the footnotes of Magne dynasty history.

In the summer of the following year, 1914, the first son of John Magne II, who was born on that infamous night in 1898, was cavorting with friends at the Sal del Rey, and on a dare from one, jumped from an old ramp into the lake, struck something that broke his neck and he drowned. The density of the water being so great, his body floated lifelessly on the top of the salt water as if it were lying on a sheet of ice.

The sudden and untimely death of the scion of a wealthy landowner made the event news, but it was what floated up next to him that made the story extraordinary.

Chapter 38

WHAT YOUNG JOHN MAGNE had struck and had apparently broken off, was a salt encrusted head.

Further investigation revealed that it had come from a body, long submerged, chain wrapped around its ankles and completely encased in white salt. But most disturbing was there were some twenty others, including men, women and five children. The missing residents of the *Hacienda Sal del Rey* had at last been found. What was never determined was how they had gotten there.

His grandfather's reaction to the news of his son's death was said to have been more of anger than sorrow. Magne today couldn't believe that, for he couldn't imagine surviving the loss of one if his sons. But he did know that ten months later, his father was born and was given the name of his dead brother, John Magne III. It was as if a mistake had been corrected, that death was not powerful enough to reign over the Magnes. Not Death and certainly not any man.

It was this conviction of just due, destiny and certainty that was at the core of John Magne IV's confidence that his plan for the salvation of the Magne Ranch would succeed. The positive gas well test on Wednesday, the word Thursday from Stubb that the investment bankers were ready to go, word from Monde that the feds were set, and now the call from the mayor half an hour ago that the aldermen had passed the resolution of support, all marching as God intended. Forward to Magne Manifest Destiny, he mused to himself, a warm flush of well-being washing over him.

When Gabriela came into the library, she could see her husband was light as a feather.

"Honestly, John Magne, your eyes are the color of a clear blue lake and you're the handsomest man in Texas."

"And you're the most beautiful woman," he said gallantly, handing her a flute of Champagne. They both laughed. "You know, Gabriela, we ought to take a trip somewhere, somewhere special, to celebrate."

"Where exactly do you have in mind, Mr. Magne?" she asked.

"Well, where exactly do billionaires go for vacations?" he asked playfully.

"Now, don't take it from me," Gabriela said playfully, "but I think billionaires are on vacation all the time, wherever they are."

"That, Mrs. John Magne IV, is why I like you so much," he said, raising his flute in toast. She clinked hers to his and they drained their glasses.

Gabriela walked across the room to a window overlooking the meadow and the oaks and said, "Look at this. Where on earth would be better than this? It's my home," she said, "I won't leave it again."

There was an earnestness about her, Magne thought; she was so much stronger than Francie was. John Magne couldn't believe how lucky he was.

Chapter 39

"I'VE HAD IT!" Jason bellowed as he swung down the companionway into the salon of Jack's sailboat.

"Well, hello to you too," Jack said, smiling as he looked up from his charts. Moses, at first startled, yawned and stretched his paws out in front, arching his back, then curled up again on the bookshelf behind Jack.

"I mean it, Jack, I've had it with this goddamn town," he said, slumping into the seat opposite his brother.

"What's it this time?"

"I've been waved off that missing fisherman case, by the mayor, no less."

"So are you mad because you think there's something going on there or because you're bored and this is the first thing to come around that is a little interesting?"

"Don't make fun, Jack, seriously; I'm pissed."

Jack stared at his brother for a moment, realizing that he wasn't reading the whole story. "How about a beer?" he offered.

"Coors?"

Jack walked over to the refrigerator in the galley. "You're a good man, Jason," he said, tossing him the can.

"You don't have this in a bottle?"

"Sailboat, glass, waste…"

"Ok, ok, I get it. It doesn't matter if I am a good man, Jack.

It seems the world is dominated by expedience. Good man, bad man, it doesn't matter, it's all about getting along, that's all."

"Expedience! Wow. You've been taking the *Reader's Digest*, haven't you?" Jack joked.

"You know what I'm talking about. Joan told me about your canning at Fish & Wildlife."

"That garrulous bitch," Jack declared, feigning hurt.

"Garrulous! Crap, you've been stealing my *Reader's Digests*!"

"She doesn't know what she's talking about," Jack protested.

"So what was the story with all that? You didn't tell me everything the other night."

"I got tired of it."

"Bullshit, Jack. What's the whole story? Between you and me."

Jack popped open his can of beer, took a long draught. He rolled his eyes closed and said, "You know the first sip of a cold beer is as close as you can come to a French kiss, alone that is." He looked across the table to his brother, who shot back a look he knew well enough. "Ok, I'll tell you, but it's going to sound whiny and I am tired of being whiny."

"There you go, whining," Jason teased him.

Jack smiled back, looking down. "So," he began, "I get this assignment to do a quick memo on the impact of drilling in the Laguna Madre…"

"Who?"

"Who what?"

"Who assigned it?"

"Bardino, the chief of the Weslaco office, he assigns this memo. Now you and I know that the Army Corp of Engineers is strict as hell about even dredging, so I figure there would be a ton of work done on this already. So I get into the agency stacks, at least the online index, and don't find anything. I Google it and all I find are pieces from the Sierra Club, some letters to the

Corpus Christi *Caller Times*, but no scientific nor government references."

"You say it like it is unusual or something."

"Well, it is a bit, but anyway, I figure it's the Rio Grande Valley--far from D.C. and California, hell, maybe it's under the radar."

"That's true. I don't think anybody east, say, of New Orleans, even knows this isn't Mexico."

"Sad, but not actually true, brother," Jack corrects him, "It's a far smaller world than you'd think. But, anyway, I call the Corps and they say they haven't done anything on it, but they did direct me to an index at the Department of the Interior."

"And…"

"And, nothing. There are references to things, but when I went to bring them up they were all dead ends. You know, those 'page cannot be displayed' screens you get when the link goes nowhere."

"You mean on the web."

"Yeah. So to make a long story short, I remind myself that this is just a memo and no one tells me who it's aimed at, so I get into my old books and some studies done in other coastal bay areas and do some interpolation. Grasses, silting and sludge, water temperature changes due to discharge, all the stuff you get when you drill holes."

"So what was the bottom line?" Jason asked, urging him to get to the point.

"Bottom line was that drilling was problematic. It was going to hurt the ecology of the Laguna and that, at the very least, there needed to be some formal impact studies before it went forward."

"Then what?"

"Well, then I submitted it to Bardino, he thanked me, and that was that."

"So, what did you want, a pat on the ass?"

"That's not the whole story."

"No?"

"About a month later I get this call from a Congressman's office in D.C., asking me if I have any copies of my report, either paper or on my computer. I get curious and ask why, and the guy on the phone says that they just needed all the copies they could get their hands on immediately for some sort of meeting the next day."

"That's weird."

"That's what I thought, but I did have five copies and so I Fed-Ex'd them over to this guy. I asked him if he wanted an electronic copy, but he said the printed ones would do. He hangs up and that's the last I hear of him."

"So what does all that mean?"

"The next Monday I come into the office and find that I have a new computer on my desk. I go to Bardino to find out what's going on and he says that all the computers in the office were upgraded."

"And were they?"

"Sure enough, every computer in the place was a new Dell."

"And that's good news, right?"

"That's the point. It's too good."

"I don't get it."

"You know how hard it is to get a whole office full of new computers in an exile office like Weslaco? There are still phones in the place with pulse dialing!"

"You're just paranoid, Jack," Jason said, dismissing his brother's long story.

"Yeah? A few weeks later I'm clicking through my directory, cleaning out my files, and realize that my memo on Laguna Madre is not there."

"Are you sure?"

"I ran searches through the whole damned computer and

couldn't find a thing. It was gone."

"You sure you didn't erase it somehow?"

"I'm too lazy to do things by accident. It takes a real effort for me," Jack retorted.

"So you think that the file was erased when the computers were replaced?"

"I don't know how else to explain it. Only innocent reason is the contractor who had to transfer the data from the old computers to the new ones somehow dropped it in the cracks."

"Well, that's more likely, isn't it?"

"Ah, probabilities. It's all probabilities."

"But that's not what you think, I take it," Jason said.

"It is certainly possible that the department decided to get us all new computers. It's possible that the contractor hired to install the new ones and transfer the files dropped some. It's even possible that your brother is suffering from delusions and paranoia. In fact, I was beginning to think that was exactly the situation."

"So how'd all this lead to you're getting canned?" Jason asked.

"I don't like the word 'canned,' Jason. I prefer to think of it as a simultaneous realization by Bardino and myself that my ass would be better placed somewhere else."

"Yes, that's much better. So how'd all this lead to you're getting canned?"

"About a month later I am waiting in Bardino's office for a meeting we were supposed to have just after lunch. He was late and I was just tapping my toes, waiting, when I noticed my report sitting on his desk. You couldn't miss it. I put yellow covers on all mine. Well, I picked it up, idly fanning the pages, admiring my work, really thinking of other things, when I had this feeling come over me. The report seemed different somehow, the way the thing was laid out, the typeface even. I always use Times New Roman and the report copy I was reading was something else, more like a courier. I indent the beginnings to each of my paragraphs, but the report was not indented. It had double spacing for new paragraphs instead."

"You're kidding, right?" Jason asked incredulously. "You mean you even know the difference between one typeface and another?"

"Never underestimate the impact of boredom on obsessive compulsive perfectionism," Jack replied. "Anyway, so I start reading the Executive Summary, and guess what, it's not my conclusion."

"What do you mean, 'not your conclusion'?"

"I mean the conclusion of the report was different from the one I wrote."

"Is that normal?" Jason asked, wondering if the reports were refined as they moved up the channel.

"It's not only abnormal, it's unethical. But, you're distracting me. So, about that time Bardino comes back from lunch for our meeting and finds me reading the report."

"How'd he act?" Jason asked.

"He looked at me, then the report, took off his jacket, put it on the hook and sat down at his desk.

"So I ask, 'What's this?' holding the report out to him.

"'What do you mean? It's your report,' Bardino tells me.

"'This isn't my report, Gene. This has been changed,' I said.

"'Really?' he said, but clearly acting surprised, 'Must've had some editing done for you at the Department.'

"'Editing,' I said, probably too loud, 'this is an outright lie!'

"'Now, Jack,' Bardino tried to calm me down, but I was too mad to see straight. He said, 'You know that all our work is subject to review up the ladder…' and he went on with this incredible bullshit about team playing, collaboration and an all out brain dump from his last junior executive seminar in 'leadership.' I couldn't believe what I was hearing, Jason. I mean Gene Bardino has always been a straight-up kind of guy. Then this."

"So then what?"

"Finally, Gene gave me this puppy-dog face and pleaded with me. 'Please, Jack…' he said over and over as I lit into him. Turns out his office door was still open and when he realized there were ears perking up in the outer office, he turned suddenly hard-nosed."

"'Jack,' he said to me, 'if you can't cooperate with the agency then maybe you ought to think about doing something else.'"

"Uh-oh," Jason said, knowing his brother well enough to understand that giving him an ultimatum was like trying to hatch a live hand grenade by sitting on it.

"So that's when I gave my eloquent retirement speech."

"Which was what exactly?"

"'Stuff it!' I think, or far more colorful words to that effect," Jack said leaning back on the settee cushion.

"Lovely, and I suppose you don't want to show me the gold watch."

"I would, but it may take a proctologist."

"Never mind, then. Well, at least I can say one thing for you, brother," Jason said.

"I'm tall?"

"You have a way of making me feel much better, seeing how your life is so much more screwed up than mine."

"I consider it a calling," Jack said profoundly. He loved his brother. He would do anything to make him feel better.

"But it actually is whining," Jason joked.

"So, tell me," Jack asked; "exactly why would the mayor want you to drop that fisherman case do you think?"

"Says it's not our jurisdiction."

"And of course, it isn't, is it?"

"No, it isn't, but the fact is, if I don't work the case, nobody will."

"What about the sheriff?"

"He's playing opossum. If it doesn't have a donor or another politician involved, he's not interested."

"Ah, public service…" Jack mused out loud as he made his way to the galley for another beer. "Ready?" he asked Jason with the can already in the air.

"I can't explain it, Jack, but I get this feeling there's something going on here."

"Like what?"

"I can't put my finger on it, but it just seems strange to me that the mayor would care anything about what I do. He never has."

"So why the sudden interest, then?"

"Beats me. All I know is that the Sheriff drives all the way out here to complain to me about the article that ran on Paredes, says I make him look bad, then later on the same day the mayor tells me to cool it. Makes me think somebody got to him. But why?"

"This is very, very interesting," Jack played, stroking his chin between his thumb and forefinger, "Paranoia is indeed genetic."

Jason laughed at his brother's imitation of Freud. "So, when are you taking off?"

"I think I'll leave out of here day after tomorrow."

"Sunday! You'll miss the games!"

"Yeah, but I want to try to make it to Aransas Pass by dark. Besides, Moses here hates violent sports," he said stroking the cat.

"That makes sense. I wish you weren't single handing it. Makes me nervous."

"Whaddaya mean, single handing it? I've got Moses!" Jack covered the cat's ears with his fingers, "And don't go saying disparaging things, we're trying to build Moses' self-esteem. He's first mate."

"Seriously, Jack."

"So, why don't you come with me?"

"It makes me even more nervous to be with you out there," Jason kidded.

"Seriously, why don't you tell the mayor and the rest of these pointy heads you've had it, and quit."

"That's more like you, Jack, than me. Always was. You've always been the guy who could change on a dime. Not me. I like it here, the small town, familiar faces, the routine. Makes me comfortable. And the case, well, I'm still going to be poking around, whatever they say. I'm sort of curious that way." Jason paused and just looked at his brother. "Don't go falling off out there."

"No big deal. I'm careful."

"Yeah, but unlucky."

"Don't believe in luck," Jack said.

"Listen, I'm going to take off," Jason said, standing and making his way to the companionway. "Friday night. Single. Big city. Hot chicks."

"Laundry, again, huh?"

"I've been wearing my underwear inside out for three days."

"We know," Jack joked.

"Hey, something you said earlier…" Jason began.

"Yeah?"

"About the Laguna and drilling."

"What about it," Jack asked.

"Well, funny thing. The Board of Aldermen met tonight and the meeting was about exploring the idea of gas wells in the Laguna," Jason said seriously.

"What did they say about it?"

"I didn't stay, but I think they were going to pass a resolution supporting it."

"Really," Jack intoned, curious and surprised, "I wonder what that's all about?"

"Who knows," Jason called back as he stepped onto the dock.

The sound of Jason's steps on the dock faded away, leaving Jack deep in thought. One part of him wondered what was going on. The louder part declared that he didn't really give a damn. Everywhere he turned there was someone trying to screw someone else. He was sick and tired of it. He was leaving.

Jack had finally come to the end of this rope and it was a bitter end.

Chapter 40

ANAJITA PAREDES PULLED her car to the shoulder of the road and turned off the engine. She was only halfway back, but her tears blinded her. The words still stung.

"Why have you come here?" Octavio's daughter had demanded, shouting through the latched screen door. "You are not welcome here!"

"Ophelia, I've come for your help in finding your father," Anajita pleaded.

"Negra, when you took him, we lost him already, twenty years ago!" Ophelia screamed. "You do not belong here. Go back to where you came from!"

"Ophelia!" an admonishing male voice called out from inside the house.

"Callate!" she turned and yelled. Turning back to Anajita, "Now you don't come back here. I don't care what happened to that baboso. He's not my father anymore!" She slammed the inner door in Anajita's face.

Anajita stood there for several minutes, stunned and hurt, before she slowly turned and walked back to her car, hoping against hope that the door would open and a voice would call her back.

It was a half hour drive from Raymondville to Port Mansfield, but it would take more than her lifetime to bridge the gap.

There had been powerful resentment when she married Octavio. None of his family came to the wedding, and on the only occasion when they were forced together, an aunt's funeral, they were colder than the corpse to her. It wasn't an unfamiliar feeling to Anajita. She knew it well growing up in Houston. There were parts of town where blacks were not welcome, and so she was not surprised when she found similar attitudes in the Valley. But the vehemence of it among the Paredes family surprised and disappointed her. She knew better than to expect different, and she was angry with herself for doing so.

She felt completely alone. She thought it was the price of venturing beyond convention. This was the impact point between what ought to be and what was. She felt like such a fool.

A red Jeep passing her, headed to Port Mansfield, brought her back to the present. She sighed, then started the car and pulled back onto the road.

When she turned into her driveway she was surprised to see the red Jeep parked in front of her house and two women standing at her front door.

"Yes? May ah help you?" she said tentatively as she walked toward them.

"Mrs. Paredes?" the older woman asked.

"Yes, ahm Anahida Paredes," she replied, feeling an overwhelming panic come over her at the arrival of strangers who could bring nothing but the worst of news.

"I am Sophie Poole and this is my daughter Angela," the older woman said.

"Yes?" Anajita replied carefully.

"I am an old friend of Octavio's, we went to school together as children, and we've come to see what's going on with his disappearance."

Anajita was suddenly overcome, and again the tears welled up in her eyes and she began to sob uncontrollably. Sophie immediately took her in her arms, in part to support her, as she looked as if she might collapse, and in part to comfort her…to comfort herself. She helped Anajita into the house as Angela opened the unlocked door.

Sophie sat Anajita in a chair in the kitchen then began searching the cabinets for a glass, filled it with water from the tap and gave it to her.

"Mizz Poole, did you say?" Anajita managed to say.

"Yes, but please call me Sophie," she replied.

"Ah don't believe ah eva heard 'Tavio speak of you."

"Oh, it was a long time ago. I suppose he's forgotten all about it."

"You's a beautiful woman. Ah don't imagine he'd forget such a beautiful woman."

Sophie laughed suddenly, "Oh, maybe once, but I'm day old bread now!"

Anajita smiled. She instantly liked Sophie, but she was on guard. It was a posture that had served her well through life. "Just why are you here, Sophie is it?"

"Sophie, yes. Anajita…is it alright if I call you Anajita?"

"Anahida," she replied, "it's Anahida, if you please."

"Anahida," Sophie repeated. "Anahida, Angela and I saw the report in the *Valley Morning Star* about Octavio's disappearance, and we've come to see what the situation is. Has anybody got any idea where he is?"

"No, ma'am," she spoke up quickly, "an ahs been tryin' and tryin' to get some help on finding him, but nobody seems to care nothin' on it but me."

"And what are the police doing about it?"

"Police. Well, we jus' have this one nice boy who says he's tryin' to find out, and he's been real helpful, but that's all."

"And the sheriff?"

"Ain't seen no sheriff. Ah don' think they's much interested," she said looking down, cocking her head slightly, then looking to the right, clearly fighting back tears.

"Anahida," Sophie said looking straight into her eyes, "Where do you think Octavio's gone? Honestly."

Anajita's first impulse was anger at the question, but then she checked herself. She didn't know this woman, but she was the first person other than Jason to show any interest in Octavio's disappearance, and whatever the reasons she may have, good or not, it was help, and help is what Anajita needed more than anything else. She looked at Sophie and said, "Ah have a bad feelin' 'bout this, a bad feelin'."

"Why is that?"

"Jus' ain't natural. 'Tavio, he's gone fishin' every Friday night since ah known him. He ain't no fool, and he ain't unlucky. The police, they act like he jus' up and ran off or something. That's not him. 'Tavio loves me," she said, again tearing up, "an' ahs loves him. 'Tain't no way he runs off and leaves me. No, Sophie, ah has a bad feelin' 'bout this."

"Tell exactly what you know, Anahida," Sophie said seriously, as Angela drew closer. "Tell us when it was the last time you saw Octavio and every detail you can remember. Tell us where he usually went when he was fishing, how he went, who went with him, everything you can remember."

Anajita wondered why this woman, who she had never met before, nor ever heard of, would suddenly show up at her house and probe so many questions about her husband. But she was in no position to be choosy. So she began to lay out all the facts as she knew them: that Octavio had a boat that he would take out, nearly always alone, and that, as best as she could tell, he would go north up the Laguna Madre where he had some favorite spots that he kept secret from his friends. He would fish all night and usually be back to the house by mid-morning, say nine or ten o'clock. He'd fix himself breakfast and take a nap on the couch, where she'd find him when she came in from work on Saturday afternoon.

She explained that a boat had been found drifting in the

Laguna and that she had been asked to identify it, which she did as best she could, not being absolutely sure, since she had never been much into Octavio's fishing.

Sophie and Angela listened intently to every word, occasionally asking a probing question, eventually realizing that Anajita knew very little at all about what had become of Octavio. Both felt the prospects were bleak.

"Anahida," Sophie asked carefully, "do you know of anyone who would want to hurt Octavio, for any reason?"

Anajita looked at her in surprise. "Hurt Octavio, why no. There ain't a soul in the world who'd want to hurt that man. He is the kindest, sweetest man ah eva known."

Sophie knew that was true. She sat quietly for a while, thinking what else to ask. "Anahida…Angela and I want you to know that if you need anything, anything at all, you're to let us know. I want you to call me if you need me or if you hear anything." She handed Anajita a card. "This has my number on it. You call anytime, do you understand? Anytime at all."

Anajita looked at Sophie, then put her arms around her neck. "Thank you so much for comin' out here to see me. Ah do so 'ppreciate it."

As they drove away from the house, Angela said to her mother, "I don't think she has a clue about any of this, do you?"

"No, I don't think she does, but I think we can help her," she paused, "and you know, I think she can help us too." They both stared ahead for a few moments.

"Take me over to the marina for a minute, will you, Mom?"

Chapter 41

THE BREEZE WAS LIGHT, bringing a relieving coolness without dissipating the comfortable warmth of the afternoon sunlight. It was just over a month from the winter solstice, so the sun swung low across the horizon, greatly reducing its intensity. But these were the lower latitudes and winter never got much more than an occasional nod, when low-slung running clouds would claim the skies for only a day or two at a time. The marina was quiet but for the gentle ripples and wavelets that tickled the pilings and the hull.

Jack sat on the bow of the sailboat, absorbed in the untangling of the anchor rode. Moses was curled up, dozing on a sail bag nearby. Jack watched him for awhile and thought it curious how Moses would cover his eyes with a paw while he slept.

Jack was suddenly aware that the sun was blocked, a shadow spread across the furled jib in front of him and he turned and found the sun eclipsed by a backlit face and a corona of golden hair. He squinted to adjust his eyes to the light and could see a lanky legged apparition in mid-thigh, cut khaki shorts and a white camisole.

"Remember me?" a female voice sang, a voice he recognized.

He hooded his brow with his rust stained right hand. He recognized her face immediately and he felt a surge of energy.

"The teacher," he said quickly. "You came to my house for the garage sale."

"Yep, Angela, that's me, and you're…" she said cheerfully.

"Jack. Hi, what brings you out here?"

"My mom. She came to visit a friend and I tagged along," she explained. "I was just sightseeing down along the marina and I thought that was you. And then I saw your cat, so I knew it was. This your boat?"

"My home, now," he said.

"'*Wist*,'" she read aloud off the port quarter. "What kind of name is that?"

He unfolded his legs and raised himself up, wiping his hands on a rag. "I sort of made it up."

"It sounds like a card game."

"No, that's whist with an 'h.' Want something to drink?" Jack offered.

"Sure. So why not something like 'Miss Behavin' or 'Minnow'?" she asked.

"Been done to death. Come aboard," Jack invited, walking aft to the cockpit. "This way," he added.

"Thanks," she said as he extended his hand and pulled her across the foot of distance between the dock and the gunwale of the boat. "This is pretty nice."

"I like it. A Dr. Pepper all right?"

"Diet?"

"Sure," he said reaching into a cooler on the portside cockpit seat.

"So, what's with the name?" she asked again, taking the can of soda.

"It's a long story, but basically, *wist* is an archaic word, probably spelled with a 'y' for the 'i' and an 'e' on the end, meaning 'a plot of land needed to sustain a community,' but it is also related to *wit*, and of course, it's the root for *wistful*."

"Sounds like you've got a lot going on there."

"It took me a while to figure it out."

"Interesting," she said, sitting across from him in the cockpit and looking up at the rigging. "You sound like you think a lot."

Jack was taken aback by the forwardness of the comment and by the quickness of the insight.

"My brother says I think too much."

"Hmm," she said as she sipped from the can. She leaned back against the coaming, spreading her elbows behind her and crossing her legs, like a man would, ankle on knee. Moses came up and sat beside her, pleading for some attention. Angela gently kneaded his ears. "This all looks pretty complicated," she observed. "Are you a good sailor?"

"Pretty good, I think, but you never really learn all there is to know about sailing."

"Or anything else, really," she added.

While her face was turned, looking towards the bow, Jack furtively studied her. She was Nordic looking but lithe, almost lanky, making her face seem small and childlike, and her skin was a bronze color. When she turned her face back towards him, in the instant before he averted his gaze, he saw her eyes were an emerald green. He felt anxious, nervous.

She noticed Jack's discomfort and smiled. It was an effect she often had on men. "So did you ever get rid of all your junk?"

"That same day."

"Now I see why you were unloading," she said. "Are you going somewhere?"

"Tomorrow. I'm headed north, along the coast. Aransas first, then maybe Galveston. I don't know."

"Just going to head out and see what happens, huh?"

"Basically."

"So, what do you do that you can just take off like that?" she asked.

"At the moment, nothing."

"What about before?" she asked.

"I worked for the government for a while."

"You're not one of those men who says he's a special agent for the CIA, are you?" she smirked.

"No, nothing as exciting as that. I was a marine biologist for U.S. Fish & Wildlife."

"You look too young to be retired. What are you, mid-forties?"

"Forty-three."

"I guess you could have gotten your twenty year watch, then."

"No, I quit."

"Quit! I didn't think anybody quit a federal government job," she said.

"Happens," he explained. "What about you?" he asked.

"Oh, I'm just visiting my mom for a while. I'm on a sabbatical."

"Sabbatical," he echoed, surprised. "So you're an academic?"

"Paleontology. I work at M.I.T."

"Wow," Jack said, genuinely impressed. "I don't know how I got the idea you were a teacher."

"Well, I teach too, a lecturer. I'm not tenured or anything."

"And are you from Boston?"

"No, actually, I was born in Port Isabel. Grew up there, well, at least until I was twelve. Then my mom sent me to Cranbrook, that's a boarding school in Michigan. I only came back for summers back then and only visit a few times a year now. And what about you. Where are you from?"

"I grew up in Harlingen," Jack explained. "But my family had always been in Brownsville."

"Funny how thirty miles is the same as a thousand."

"How do you mean?"

"Well, we grew up about the same time in about the same

place, maybe thirty miles between towns, and we never met."

"That's true. It seems that small towns have a way of turning in on themselves. I guess there's a reason they're provincial," he said.

"So where'd you go to school?"

"I'm an Aggie."

"Oh, groan," she giggled.

"All right, enough with the wise cracks," he pretended to admonish her.

"I suppose you were a bio major, then."

"Right. But then in '95 I got my masters at Harvard."

"You're kidding," she said, suddenly sitting upright. "Harvard! We weren't three miles apart back then. Talk about a small world."

"Well, mostly I was down at Woods Hole, though, near the Cape."

"Still," she said.

"Who knows, maybe we passed on the T one time or other back then and didn't even know it," he said.

She looked directly at Jack when she said, "I think I'd have remembered."

Jack looked down with an embarrassed smile.

"I mean," she continued, smiling, "you have the kind of looks that make a gal want to hug her purse."

Jack laughed. "You know, I did see you one of those times, come to think of it. Were you fond of wearing shorts, crew socks and pushing a grocery basket down Mass. Ave?"

"Sundays, for church," Angela replied.

Jack studied her during a pause in the banter. "I kind of feel guilty about you coming all the way out to the house and not getting to buy any of my junk. How long's it been since you've had a bowl of chili?"

"I don't eat meat."

"Never?"

"Never," she said definitely.

"This is South Texas. How do you eat at all, then?"

"It's a challenge, but I manage. Sometimes I forage in the vegetable fields, mostly at dusk."

"I'd say you're going to get shot doing that, but you're too skinny a target."

"Unfortunately," she laughed, "from the side, too."

There was a way that Angela moved her head, her whole body, when she talked that riveted Jack's attention. Her laugh was light and airy and she was witty. These were his secondary impressions that came with her conversation. His first and dominant one had all to do with her body. She seemed to him like a gazelle.

"I can't stay anyway," she said finally. "My mom's going to want to get back to Port Isabel before dark and she's my ride. Maybe another time."

"That's too bad," he said half to himself, genuinely disappointed.

"I wish I could. Hey, good luck on your passage to Galveston, Jack," she said. "Who knows? All these chance meetings, I might run into you again, sometime."

"You never know."

She surprised him by extending her hand, and when he took it, he felt her grip linger a bit. "Hope so," she said. She climbed back onto the dock, waved and walked away.

Jack turned to see Moses sitting on the companionway hatch, staring at Angela as she walked away.

"Whoa, there cowboy," he said, "I can't stand much competition. Any more of that and I'll have you converted into a sports model." Moses answered in his high and guttural trill, that sounded more like rolled Rs, then he dashed below.

Chapter 42

"WHAT IS SHE DOING HERE?" Ophelia asked angrily, leaning into her husband's ear as they sat in the third pew from the front. As long as they had been attending nine o'clock Sunday Mass at St. Anthony's, she had never seen Anajita there, not since the day she married Ophelia's father.

Anajita sat in the back pew, on the aisle, just in front of the Confessional. She looked straight ahead, back straight, head high. She never met Ophelia's glare.

Twenty-one years ago she had stood at the front of the church, exchanging promises with Octavio. He was fifty-five, she had just turned twenty-five. It didn't matter to her that the church was empty, with fewer than ten people there. She was pregnant, scared and Octavio was kind and loving. His wife had died the year before of cancer. He was used to being married and it was natural for him to want to marry again as soon as possible. His life only worked in the context of a marriage.

It was fate. Anajita, Ann Tolley, as she was known then, fled Houston on a late night bus, running from her boyfriend. He wouldn't take the news that she was carrying his child well. He'd demand that she get an abortion, and if she didn't, he'd beat her until she lost it. That was the color of her life: abusive men, drugs, numbing poverty. But from the moment she realized she was pregnant, something changed in her. Suddenly, it was as if a light was switched on and the darkness of her life was pushed away. And what she saw disgusted her. Deep inside her now, for the very first time in her life, was something of value, something worth surviving for. That's when she decided she had to escape.

She packed a small bag with all her possessions, took what little money she had and bought a ticket to carry her as far away as she could go. The man at the bus station window gave her four towns that she could afford a ticket to, one in each direction of the compass rose. She picked south; she didn't know why. The town was Raymondville, Texas.

Six hours later, when the bus pulled away into the darkness, she stared after it until its taillights disappeared. She had arrived, and she spent the first night on a bench under a lone incandescent light bulb, a tattered valise guarded next to her.

The next morning her life began again. She took a dishwashing job at The Mecca and in a few weeks she was promoted to waitress. Octavio became a regular, always sitting at her table for his breakfast. He was the first person to call her "Anajita," she remembered, Little Ana. Soon everyone else was using the nickname. He was the gentlest man she had ever known, always polite, always considerate. She was delighted when he first asked her out. It didn't bother her that he was much older. Younger men had treated her like dirt. Octavio treated her with respect.

She wasn't sure why she said yes when he asked her to marry him after only three months. It seemed the natural thing to do. And she had been glad of it ever since. It didn't seem to bother him that she was black, although there were plenty of disapproving stares when the word got out he'd taken her as his wife.

When the baby came, he took it as his own son. He gave him his own name. Octavio was the kind of father she had never known. He cheerfully provided all his hard work could manage, and when that was not enough, Anajita pitched in by waitressing for a while, then buying and selling other people's junk. "Turnin' trash to treasure," she often boasted. She had become very good at it.

Their lives had settled into a quiet, gentle rhythm that melded seamlessly into the comfortable climate of the South Texas coast, where extremes were rare and remarkable and the warm humid air felt just about the same as a loose T- shirt. Life ebbed and flowed like the tides in the Laguna, steady and predictable. Finally, order and peace had come to her life. And she was grateful for everyday of it.

"Go in peace to serve the Lord," the priest said to the congregation as the Mass ended. She rose, turned and walked out the door into the sunlight. She had gone to ask God to bring Octavio back to her. She pleaded and bargained and wept a little. But she had done all the praying she was going to. God had His assignment. Now she had hers.

Chapter 43

"YOU'RE NOT GOING TO make Aransas Pass by sunset, brother," Jason warned Jack.

"Close enough, though. I'll see the lights and my chartplotter will guide me through the Aransas Pass jetties. The night sailing isn't the problem, Jason, it's not sleeping. This is going to be only one day. I'll be plenty alert to make it. I just don't want to have to heave-to out there in the dark with all the ship traffic around and all those rigs sticking out of the water. I'll never really sleep."

"You're the expert," Jason allowed cautiously. "Just be careful, goddamn it. Going it alone like this worries me."

"Not to worry. I've done this lots of times. Besides, I've got Moses here as my first mate," Jack said, stroking the kitten's nape.

"I'd feel better if he was 'Noah'." Jason looked down then added sheepishly, "I'm going to miss you, Jack."

"Oh, don't go getting all maudlin on me, for christssake, I'm only going to Galveston, not Pitcairn's Island."

"I know, I know. It's just that it seems like you're really leaving, like you are going away for good."

"It's just another starting all over again. I've done that often enough. It feels like the end of something. But it's really the beginning of something else. I'm actually pretty excited about it, to tell the truth."

"Have you checked the weather?"

"Yep. There isn't another front expected until tomorrow afternoon sometime, so it'll be clear sailing 'til I get in at Aransas Pass. I've even got a pretty good southeast wind, so I'll have the wind on my quarter the whole way. An easy run."

"And you've got the diesel tank topped off?"

"Yes, Mother, I've got the fuel tank full, enough for thirty-five hours of motoring. I'll keep you up to date on my progress, Jason, so don't worry and relay it all to Joan, will you? I don't want her to be worrying either."

"I will."

"Hey, Jason," Jack said as if suddenly remembering something, "that alderman meeting you mentioned the other night. Did they vote to support drilling or against it?"

"For it, why?"

"No reason, just curious. Now make yourself useful and untie that bow line from the piling and throw it to me."

In a few moments Jason was staring at the stern of *Wist* as it pulled away from its berth in the marina and motored for the channel that ran eight miles to the Gulf of Mexico. Jack waved back to him from the helm.

Jason partly wished his brother wasn't going, and partly wished that he was going with him.

Jack was unequivocal. He felt the overwhelming urge to flee.

Chapter 44

WALTER PRESTON WALKED into John Magne's office with a determined gait, took Magne's hand firmly and shook it. He had steeled himself for this "first thing Monday morning" meeting and his body language was in synchrony. Magne could read it too and returned equal confidence and authority when he directed the president of the Raymondville National Bank to sit in the chair directly across from his own, the massive desk marking the boundary between them.

Just before Preston began to speak, Magne's intercom carried Pat Wilson's voice announcing a call from Congressman Monde. Magne pressed the speakerphone button instead of picking up the receiver.

"Good morning, Congressman," he boomed cheerily.

"Good morning, John," Monde responded in kind. "I called to confirm that we just received all the paperwork from the Department of the Interior and U.S. Fish & Wildlife. All the reports are favorable and this afternoon the Army Corp of Engineers will be giving their 'ok' on the project. John, you are all set to go. Congratulations."

"Thanks, Lencho, I couldn't have gotten this done without your help. You and your staff have been absolutely terrific," Magne complimented.

"It is our pleasure to be of service to one of our most important constituents, John. I personally appreciate all you've done for the people of the district."

"Thanks, Lencho. I hope I get to see you again real soon. Take care and thanks for the good news." Magne reached over and pushed the speakerphone button off then looked up to Preston, and with a smile across his face asked, "Now, Walter, what can I do for you?"

Preston knew a power play when he saw it and Magne was masterful, he had to admit. He paused to gather his momentum again.

"Mr. Magne, the board has asked me to discuss with you our delinquent notes. There is a real problem that our examiners are going to classify these loans next month if they aren't brought current."

"You know, Preston," Magne said with dripping sarcasm, "it's always interesting to me how all those years of our doing business with you folks seems to disappear whenever you have to give a little. I mean, how many years has the Magne Ranch been making deposits in that bank of yours? What, thirty, forty? And you've taken those funds and loaned them out and made millions. Never a complaint then, huh? Then we get a little late on a few million bucks and you people go nuts. Frankly, it's starting to piss me off."

"It's close to ten million, sir. You have to understand, Mr. Magne, it isn't just the bank. We have to comply with all sorts of federal regulations or our charter can get into trouble."

"Is that all? Is that the matter in all this? Because, if it is, I can make a few calls to a few friends in D.C. and I can make it all go away," Magne said sternly.

"I appreciate that you are well thought of in political circles, Mr. Magne, but it is also a matter of good banking. We can't have a few notes that take so much of our capital, running a year delinquent without some sort of assurances. We have a duty to our depositors. Our stockholders won't approve."

"Your stockholders!" Magne exploded in laughter. "What a load of bullshit! I know who your stockholders are--a bunch of small town operators, what, a few lawyers, some store owners, a couple of insurance salesmen? Give me a break. They couldn't afford to buy the polish on my boots, much less pretend to have the stuff to walk in them. Why don't you bring all your stockholders in here and I'll teach them a thing or two about banking," Magne yelled.

"Mr. Magne, we have been very patient. My instructions are very clear. I am to inform you that you must either bring the notes current or assign a specific collateral and we'll write a new note to give you some more time to service it. It could get you another six months."

Magne looked across the desk with a glare that could bore a hole through Preston's head. He was furious. But he also knew he had to contain the problem. A stain on the Magne credit just when it was about to be put under the microscope of a public offering would be disastrous. It angered him that this small town banker had him in a corner. If he could have, he would have come across the desk and choked the life out of his pointy head right then. He wanted to tell him that in less than two months he was going to have enough cash to pay off those goddamn notes, buy the whole bank, and stick it so far up his ass that his face would take ATM cards. But he sat motionless, trying to calm himself. His lawyers warned him that he couldn't discuss the initial public offering, the IPO, with anyone without risking all kinds of Security and Exchange Commission problems, much bigger problems.

"Preston," he said finally, in a soft but confident voice, "what exactly are you asking for?"

"Mr. Magne, we suggest that you renew the notes into one consolidated note with a due date in six months. We would add funds enough to allow you to pay off your accumulated interest, which would satisfy the examiners. But you would have to pledge a specific collateral."

"What collateral?"

"Land," Preston said succinctly. "We would like you to pledge at least twenty thousand acres."

Magne showed Preston an impassive, stony face but smiled to himself. What an idiot this fellow was, he thought. He was in a position to demand much more, but all he wanted was a signed piece of paper, a piece of paper that would be totally irrelevant in a few months. Magne saw Preston as a desperate, scared jackrabbit. He was out of his league.

He thought for a moment just how far to push back on the issue and concluded that it was actually unimportant. He'd won. He'd have his revenge in due course. He'd get the IPO funded, pay off the note, then he'd buy the bank from the piddling stockholders and fire Walter Preston in such a way as he'd never work in banking again. He dared to offend the Magne Ranch. And he'd pay.

The working capital loan problem was solved.

Chapter 45

FESTOR STUBB SPEED-DIALED his cell phone.

"Richter, here."

"Hi, Calvin. It's Festor. I'm just calling to see if you got Sam's papers for your bankers up there."

"I got them just a few minutes ago. There's a lot of generic crap, but there are three signed letters on official letterhead that do the trick, so I think we're done with the state approvals. What's the word on the feds?"

"I just got a call from Magne's office. They'll have that to you in tomorrow's Fed Ex. You'll be getting two directly from D.C., so keep an eye open."

"Great, Festor. I think this wraps it up. We're done."

"So, when do you think we're going to see the schedule for bringing this thing out?"

"We're about a month away, two at the most. They're going to want to pick a good window, you know, so we don't have a lot of competition for buyers. A slow week is best. Then, you have to avoid a profit-taking period…IPO's don't do as well in the middle of one of those. But, I feel pretty sure we're funded in sixty days, outside."

"That would be great, Calvin, just plain great."

"You don't have to tell me. I'm already Porsche shopping!"

"You've earned it."

Stubb folded his cell phone and turned to his melamine marker board. He checked off another line. Porsche, indeed, he thought. That was just like those wannabe types. It was all about looking good--appearances. Stubb scoffed. Sure he'd be put down for a few shares of the IPO. It would look good. But he took his share in fees, always did. It was never the deal. He put together a ton of them. A few actually made money by accident, but the odds had to let that happen. He was in the fluff and excitement business, another way of saying the fools and greed business.

At the funding he'd be issued checks, via a handful of different entities, totaling over one million dollars. And he'd pay taxes on next to none of it. It was a matter of pride for him. Being able to take from the rich and give to himself was science. Being able to get away with it and not even pay income taxes; that was art.

Every Monday morning it was like a ritual. He'd make his tour of branch post offices all over Houston to pick up his checks from the dozen or so post office boxes that were the only physical address his panoply of enterprises had. Deals were paying off like slot machines, only he was the house.

The Magne deal, though, was on a scale that dwarfed the others. There weren't that many fat, ripe plums to pick out there. So he had to take most of his harvest from the lesser folks, smaller perhaps in wealth but still vast in greed and pride.

Oddly, he'd found that Magne confirmed a long held suspicion that the bigger the mark the easier. It was simple to understand. The bigger the ego, the greater the greed and more inflated the arrogance, in geometric proportion.

Stubb traded in hubris and sold myths, two sides of the same coin. He used to think he maneuvered under a cloak, the fog of ignorance, but he learned that he did much better among the educated, for they were smart enough to create their own rationalizations for ruses he proposed. And their imaginations were often bigger than his and their needs more profound.

For now, all he had to do was wait. All the work was assigned, the wheels were turning, and others were carrying the virus. In the meantime, there were others that needed his attentions.

He leaned back in his leather chair, feet elevated to his desktop and stared out the window where a perfect spider web had just ensnared a hapless moth. He watched it struggle to free itself, all the while becoming further entangled. The web vibrated with the desperate exertions.

At the center, the spider awakened.

Chapter 46

THE PORT MANSFIELD JETTY passed behind *Wist* and Jack planned to continue east, farther into the Gulf for about thirty miles before turning north. This would clear the main fairway where the big ships traveled, and beyond most of the oil well platforms. By dark he wanted to be closer in, where he could use the land lights as a guide. He knew that some of the older platforms weren't lit and a night time collision could be fatal. He expected to make Port Aransas later that Sunday evening, in about fifteen hours.

But when he reached the point to turn, the winds would have been dead on his stern if he did, which made for slow going and a precarious watch against an accidental gybe. That was more tension than he was in the mood for, so he pointed more easterly, to keep the wind on his starboard quarter. It was a quiet and more relaxing point of sail. The boat moving with the wind had a breezeless quality about it, and the waves at barely a foot, were of no consequence.

The breeze built throughout the day, and he was making nearly eight knots at times. The speed was exhilarating. He set the autopilot to steer and went below to do chores and see after Moses. He busied himself in that mindless, happy work of cleaning and organizing. It gave him a sense of order and control he could not feel on land.

The vastness of the Gulf of Mexico and the smallness of a boat tended to focus the sailor on little things in a finite world, totally reliant upon himself, unbothered by humans. Jack felt the power of it. There were no other authorities at sea. Even the power of the United States of America ended at twelve miles. There were no phones, no postman, no intrusions. It was as much or as little as one made of it.

By middle afternoon he grew more comfortable with his place in the emptiness of the gulf and his climbing up the companionway to the cockpit for a look around became less frequent. He tore open a package of cat food for Moses, who adapted surprisingly quickly to the continuous motion of the boat. Jack fixed himself a sandwich and opened a beer then sat at the table in the salon, idly browsing through a magazine. After a while, he put his head back on the cushion to rest his eyes.

He began to dream. He was again at the Target, where he first met Angela. Then he saw her again in his house that morning, just over a week ago. He dreamt that she had come with him on the boat and that he kissed her softly on the lips and that she pressed back, her mouth hot and moist. He felt her tickle his ear with her nose, then whisper, "Jack, wake up, Jack."

Then he awoke.

Moses had come and sat on his shoulder and was nestled in the crook of his neck, his ear next to Jack's. Jack lay there motionless, listening to the water moving against the hull. He was suddenly aware that he was in total darkness. He jolted upright. How long had he been asleep? What time was it?

His legs were still asleep and he stumbled as he bolted for the companionway. He climbed the steps and swung around facing the bow. It was pitch-black darkness, and it frightened him that he had been sailing full speed into the unknown. The adrenaline was surging as he realized that his navigation lights were off. The darkness not only cloaked the world around him, but no one else could see him either. He dashed below to the nav. station and flicked on the salon lights so he could read the labels on the other switches. He turned on the running lights only, as he was under sail.

He came back up the companionway, blinded by the salon lights, and went immediately to the helm to check the chartplotter. At least it would show if he was near any drilling rigs. He quickly found the cursor that marked his position on the chart, and to his horror, immediately in front of it he could see a marker of some kind. He squinted and frantically zoomed the image larger with the control keys. It was an abandoned rig.ABoard. Instantly he tried to turn the wheel to starboard, but it wouldn't follow. The autopilot was still engaged. He fumbled for the button to turn it off then swung the wheel to full starboard. The wind came around from the quarter to the beam, pushing the boat into a deep heel. Jack looked down at the chartplotter and could see the cursor pointing barely right of the object. He looked up and to his left in the darkness and saw the slightest glint of reflected light from his red port running light. In seconds there were reflections of the brighter white light on his stern. Suddenly he was aware of looming gargantuan legs that made the abandoned platform appear like a giant black sea monster, standing ankle deep in the ocean. It towered above his fifty-five foot mast by at least three times. Jack's heart pounded so hard it hurt and then his knees grew wobbly, and he was forced to sit down.

Chapter 47

JACK LISTENED TO THE pounding in his ears and the sound of his rapid breathing. He watched the marker for the monster offshore rig pass slowly behind the cursor on the chartplotter. He then looked ahead on the chart for more obstacles. He was beyond the last of them. Somehow, he had managed to miss all the others.

When he recovered his composure, he realized that he was far offshore. He had slept for nearly four hours, and during that time had traveled more than twenty-five miles. He was more than forty miles into the Gulf.

The next fact was obvious. There was no point in making for Port Aransas now. The very gauntlet he wanted to avoid in the dark now lay squarely between his present position and the port. It was more logical to continue northeast to Galveston. He looked to the companionway where he saw Moses sitting on its top step, staring at him.

"Don't look at me like that," he complained.

As he had begun to do in the last week, the cat rolled Rs in a trilling sound when Jack spoke directly to him, as if he were answering. Sometimes it was a simple trill, other times it had syllables.

"Good point," Jack replied. "Setting the radar alarm would have been a better idea, in retrospect." The cat looked around the cockpit, but had yet to venture out of the cabin since the boat left the dock. "Not ready to come out here, yet, I see," Jack observed. "No hurry. I guess I'll take all the watches until you are." Moses raised an eyebrow impassively.

Jack did not re-engage the autopilot for a while. He needed the feel of the wheel and that sense of control of the boat, at least until he calmed down. As his eyes adjusted to the darkness, he could see the faintest change of green-gray fuzz where he imagined the horizon to be. Gradually, the rhythmic undulations of the boat and the soothing sound of water swishing by returned his calm. After an hour or two, he re-engaged the autopilot and went below to make some coffee.

Gliding through the inky black waters of the Gulf on a starless night had its tensions. There was a feeling of utter helplessness, as if the boat was suspended in time. Jack had known the feeling before. To sail on blindly was the consummate act of faith. Faith that what lie floating out there was so far dispersed and so unlikely on a particular course as to be mathematically irrelevant.

Mathematically irrelevant. These were cold, lifeless words. They were fine when describing the unlikelihood of the space shuttle colliding with space junk or a meteorite. They even made sense in calculations of probability in Black Jack, or calculating life expectancy in actuary. But when the consequence was struggling for your life to the deck of a fatally gouged boat, far at sea, mathematics seemed to offer little comfort.

And so it was, at first. But eventually, as in life itself, one learned to accept the nature of things. Jack gradually tired of worrying about it, and each passing uneventful hour seemed to add credence to the argument for pressing on. Eventually, the thought was displaced with other business. But it was never fully resolved for him.

He sat on the starboard side cockpit bench, listening to the occasional whine of the autopilot, as it intermittently adjusted to maintain course. At first he wondered if his eyes were so adjusted to the dark that he now could see through it, but then he realized that the eastern sky was turning from charcoal gray to purple. In minutes it grew lighter and wider until the ocean took on a soft pastel gray color, then teal. The air began to feel different. Relief came over Jack, a relief of tensions he forgot he had. Every muscle relaxed, and he was suddenly sleepy again.

He went below to make another cup of strong coffee and found Moses curled up on the settee, nestled among some pillows. "Now you have the right idea," he said. Moses looked up through sleepy eyes and yawned.

The coffee and the risen sun revived him. The easting curve of the Texas coast and a fortunate slight shift in the winds made it possible for him to adjust his course more directly for Galveston. He was still a good two days away and the issue of sleep had to be addressed.

His options were to go "space shuttle," sail day and night, and play the odds, which many around-the-world solo sailors have done, or to heave-to while he slept, taking at least his motion out of the collision equation. Option two made sense at night, given the inherent disadvantage of darkness, the threat of floating obstacles, and the natural tendency to sleep then. But the boat was easier to avoid in daylight, making sense that one could sleep more safely then. Option one was also more efficient. He'd make Galveston sooner.

He applied his quantitative mind to the problem and determined that the odds were essentially equal. He laid out the problem to Moses, feeling only a little silly speaking out loud to the cat. Talking to yourself is one of the true luxuries of being at sea, Jack allowed.

He pretended to hear an answer. "So what's that you say? What's the hurry? What's the point of efficiency when there's no use for the saved time?"

Moses trilled as if to say, "Oh, cut the crap."

It was a hard urge to contain, this drive for efficiency. In his car, on an airplane, even in a sailboat, where "fast" wasn't much more than a human sprint, he found himself constantly calculating when he'd make a waypoint or a destination. It was as if he was in a constant race. The fact that he lived most of his life in this endless process of measurement meant that a great deal of it was mired in disappointment.

A whole lot of it was stuck in unresolved calculations. The need to make the right decision, most often led to none. It was why Jason accused him of being too analytical, of thinking too much.

Jack had always advised his brother that the benefit of so much thinking was that more bad outcomes could be averted. Jason had always countered that the thing that eventually gets any of us is the thing we never thought of. Jack's answer was that it only proved that he ought to be thinking of even more things.

By noon he was still undecided whether to heave-to and sleep, or sail on. He put off the choice until after lunch. Moses had at last ventured out into the cockpit, though the fifteen degree heel made his slant on the deck comical. Jack worried a bit that he might get too confident, not understanding the risks, and fall overboard, so he kept a wary eye on him. A man overboard was hard to find. A cat would be impossible.

In the mid afternoon Jack ran the diesel for a few hours to charge the batteries. Moses didn't much care for the noise, nor did he, but the autopilot needed juice and so would the navigation lights after dark.

To the northwest, Jack began to make out what looked like the curved blue-gray shape of distant mountains. It was as if he was finally in sight of land. But he knew the Texas coast was flat as a pancake. What he saw had to be the leading edge of an advancing front.

In the short time he'd been at sea, he had forgotten that

he planned to weather it, secured at the dock in Port Aransas. In his calculation for efficiency, he forgot to factor in the storm.

Chapter 48

IT WOULD BE HOURS before Jack would have to deal with the front, but he tidied up the sheets and halyards and planned how he'd reduce sail as its passage became imminent. Down below he secured the odd items, and he thought through the procedure he'd follow for locking the hatches and otherwise weathering the gusty front arrival. He made himself something to eat and sat at the salon table to start a novel. Reading was his favorite way to pass the long hours at sea, but wary of his last lapse, he set an alarm for five o'clock, and eventually nodded off to sleep.

    Jack dreamt of the night his mother attacked his father with a fork. He was too young to recall much more than the image of his father grabbing her wrist and her struggle to free herself. It was at dinner. She was screaming at his father, but even then Jack knew that a fork was not an earnest weapon, more an implement of frustration. What provoked the fight, he did not remember. Verbal conflicts were frequent, but the physical confrontation was new and frightening. He did remember Joan and Jason crying. He did not remember crying himself.

    In the dream there was a small brass bell, etched with red and green stars and the words "Merry Xmas," a gift from a couple who were friends of his parents. Somehow he remembered that they had said it was to sound the end of round for their fights.

Jack realized from those words and the nature of the gift, that others thought his parents fought too much. Up till then he thought that such behavior was just how married people acted. Normal, perhaps, but it upset him terribly.

Jack would often run out of the house into the night to escape the anger and invective, his skin stinging and his stomach aching at times from it. At seventeen, his running took him off to college and he never looked back.

Joan had said that the constant stress of conflict in their childhood made all three of the Grider children averse to confrontations. Jack could see the pattern of it in his own life. He couldn't stand people who argued and he rarely argued himself. He had changed majors in college from the Business degree his father favored because the whole context of competition bothered him. When he took his first real job as a programmer in a small company, it was to set clear boundaries between him and the outer world. He could work mostly alone, on simple computer problems.

But his fellow workers were attracted to his gentle personality, and when the company got into financial trouble, he was the leader pushed to the front. He loved the work and the people he worked with, but he eventually sold out to the bigger competitor because the constant pressure they applied triggered ancient anxieties.

He chose his latest career as a marine biologist because it was most like those quiet and independent days when he was programming. Marine biology in a government setting was as close to a neutral environment as he could find.

That is, until that damned report. For even though he valued peace more than any other thing, there was an underlying sense of justice in him, of right and wrong that could not condone what was done. True to form, rather than stand and protest, he ran. He ran for peace.

The buzzer had barely started when it woke him. Once

back on deck, he surveyed the northern horizon and saw the front was approaching about on schedule. The wind had waned considerably, and the sailboat was making only three and a half knots. Jack knew it was wiser to reduce sail early than fight too much, too late. The winds would quickly shift from southeast to north and could build quickly into gale force. Jack furled the genoa to about the size of a stay sail and double secured the furling line. Then he furled the main into the mast about a third the length of the sail's foot. He wondered if he ought to furl them completely, but thought that too conservative.

With the winds would come a cold driving rain, so he went below to get a slicker and to check on Moses, who had taken up residence in a tight cubby as if he had some sense of what was coming.

Back on deck, Jack tacked the boat through the wind to starboard, to avoid having to gibe, then watched as the storm approached on his starboard bow. After a time, the waves grew sloppier, causing the boat to bob uncomfortably, and with little wind to fill the sails, the genoa sheets went slack and the boom swung confusedly.

Jack felt a growing excitement as the steel gray frontal cloud pulled over him like a thick blanket, blotting out the setting sun. The underside of the clouds began to bubble and petrify, looking like cauliflower. The water took on an eerie opaque green, made more intensely so by a darkening sky rising from the horizon. In the distance Jack could make out a line of color change on the water, and above it, a gradual fading of the horizon line; as it drew closer he could see white caps on slate colored waves.

Then, suddenly, the air went perfectly still, the sails sagged, and the boat coasted to a near stop.

There, not more than a few hundred yards away, he could see the rains racing towards him over angrier seas. He turned the helm to take the boat dead into the coming blast, but there wasn't enough speed for the rudder to have any effect. The boat stalled and began to turn broadside to the coming front. Jack dashed to the winches to further reduce the mainsail, but it was too late.

The first cold blast caught the boat on the beam and the wind screamed through the rigging. The boat heeled deep to port. Jack could see it all happening in slow motion. He grabbed hold of a winch on the cabin top as the port gunwale dipped into the water, and with his right hand, struggled to clip his harness tether into anything, but he couldn't find a good hook and slid down the heeled over deck toward the water. He landed on the lifelines that now ran horizontal below the water's surface, acting like a net and stopping him from going any farther.

Jack could see the boom sticking down and the sail cupping the water. He knew he had to release the mainsheet so the boom could swing loose and the sail could empty of seawater when the boat tried to right itself. If he didn't, the boat could turtle.

Hand over hand he fought the waves and gravity as he pulled himself up the deck toward the cabin top, which was now like a wall. He found the rope clutch that held the mainsheet taunt, and after a struggle with it, got it to release. Suddenly the boat began to right itself, lifting from the sea, but at the same instant the sudden righting lurch caused him to fall backwards, head over heels into the water. If he were to fall overboard now, the righted boat would quickly sail away from him and he would be lost.

As he slid into the water, the cold of it shocked him, taking his breath away, but he felt a rope slip past his leg. Instinctively he surged for it, plunging himself deeper into the water. He felt it running by the tips of his fingers but he couldn't seem to grasp it. The boat was now sailing, and he was desperate to catch the rope. It was his last chance.

Exhaustion began to reason with him. He ought to stop and rest. He ought to give up the pain and the struggle. If he would just relax and surrender, the whole desperation of it would be

quieted. All the pain and sorrows and disappointments of his life could be finally ended. He could at last have the peace that he had always hungered for.
    Eternally.

Chapter 49

JACK WAS SUSPENDED in the water both in thought and person for a time that he could not, as a human, measure. He was suddenly completely calm and all fear left him.

He saw an image of his fifth birthday. He wore crisply pressed gray shorts and matching shirt with red buttons. His hair was blonde and he had a broad smile. He was blindfolded and swinging a piñata stick at a papier-mâché donkey. His mother wore a flower printed dress with padded shoulders and was young and smiling, while his father was working the rope that zoomed the piñata up and down, laughing and urging Jack on. Jason and Joan were jumping and clapping their hands in delight.

Jack tore off his blindfold and wound up, pulling the stick all the way back, and in slow motion, the stick came around him and struck the donkey square on the side, candy exploding out, spreading through the air like the foam blown from the top of the wind driven waves.

His right hand closed around the line and it jerked him violently. Holding as tight as he could, his fingers and palm burned as the rope slipped through, and stopped only when he came to a knot tied on the end. His body plowed the water behind the boat, and he choked on the spray, but letting go was certain death. Struggling, he brought his other hand around to the rope and tried to pull himself along toward the stern of the boat.

Exhaustion and aching arms forced him to pause to regain some strength. Painfully and slowly, he continued to pull himself toward the boat. After what seemed like hours he was in reach of the scoop shaped stern, but he was too weak to pull himself up the one foot of height from the waterline to the first platform.

His hands were beginning to fail their grip and he felt himself slipping away. Then in one last surge of effort, he released his right hand and followed the rope down to his thigh, pulled his right foot up to the rope and wrapped two turns around his foot. He quickly straightened his leg, transferring all his weight to his foot just as his left hand gave way from the strain. The rope crushed down on his arch and he cried out in pain. But he could not let go.

After a moment's rest, he pulled again with his hands, freed his foot and then repositioned it in a similar loop, but farther up the rope toward the stern. He repeated this procedure until stretching one last time brought him within reach of the boarding ladder that was folded up and held by a bungee cord. He gave it a desperate jerk and it fell into the water beside him. He took hold of the bottom rung and let go of the rope.

He tried to climb the ladder onto the stern, but he felt his knee begin to shudder in the strain. Another desperate pull and he was standing on the bottom rung, three steps up and he was back in the cockpit. He collapsed on the sole and laid there, oblivious to the dime sized rain drops pelting his face. Warmth flushed through his body as he lay there, panting from exhaustion.

The squall line passed, and the wind became a brisk blow from the north, steady at about twenty knots. It took him ten minutes before he could gather the strength to stand and begin tacking the boat to starboard so he could re-set the autopilot for a close reach to Galveston.

He looked around the deck and saw that for all the commotion, nothing was ruined. But he realized the companionway had been open to the heavy rains and waves and, as he expected, he found water all over the cabin sole. A check of the bilge showed there wasn't more water than the bilge pump was handling on its own, though. He took some towels and began to dry things up, wringing the excess water into the galley sink.

Suddenly, he realized that Moses was nowhere in sight. He went immediately to the cubby where he usually curled up. Only the blanket was there. He went about the cabin, calling his name. He began an intensive search from the forward head to the rear stateroom, continually pleading his name.

After a quarter hour, he sat down at the salon table, not understanding what he was feeling. A pain in the pit of his stomach, distantly familiar, immobilized him. A stray cat lost at sea, he chastised himself, what does it matter? It's just an animal, for godssake.

He was lucky to have survived himself. He shook off his moodiness and went to the galley to make himself some coffee. Just the mechanics of starting up the burner and readying the pot seemed to bring him a little comfort. Routine was a tonic.

It was growing chilly and he was still in wet clothes, so while the water was heating, he changed into sweat pants and a fleece pullover. He pulled on warm woolen socks. The dry, warm clothes made him feel instantly better.

He decided to make himself a sandwich with ham and some Swiss cheese. He had some shredded lettuce and added some relish. As he always did, he cut the sandwich into two rectangles, then took them on a paper plate, with a beer, to the salon table.

The sandwich was good, and he was taking his second bite when he found himself suddenly overwhelmed with a profound sadness. Tears welled in his eyes, and he winced in a pain he did not expect or understand.

And like a child, he wept.

Chapter 50

JACK WAS TOO TIRED to think. Any further debate about sailing or heaving-to was beyond his caring. He was at least four hours sailing from any offshore rig, so he set the autopilot for a course that would give the rigs a wide berth, set an alarm for three hours and slept in the forward stateroom.

When he awoke his muscles were sore and stiff. He pulled on a thick, thigh length coat and shuffled to the cockpit to check his progress on the chartplotter. The night air was cold and crystalline. The Milky Way poured across a diamond-studded canopy that was so bright the sea took on a magical aura that defied darkness, but was not quite light. The occasional foam on the large, undulating swells took on iridescence.

Jack felt like he was traveling through deep space, and he was filled with the wonder of it. He thought of all the sailors who spent such nights over the millennia under these same stars. What the first sailor saw was what Jack saw. He felt a kinship and was struck by the timelessness of space and brief second that was one life in it.

And yet, how we toiled and struggled in the minute slices of it, Jack thought. His mind inventoried the parade of crises in his life and how they seemed to raise their ugly heads every five years or so. One by one, he tried to re-create the feelings he had at the time. And one by one, he recalled how he somehow survived each one.

Under the same stars he stared up into this night, were other eyes, millions of them, staring up and wishing, or wondering, or pleading. Each soul in his hour of crisis. Alone. But in fact, none of them mattered for anything, in the grand scale of things, he thought.

The world could be a cruel place. Hours ago the sea tried to take him. It didn't care about his existence, his suffering. It was the sea, and men died in the sea. It wasn't important. The struggle was his own personal event and he was alone in it. Whether he chose to live or to die was irrelevant. The cold sea breeze sent a shudder through him.

Death could not be outrun. There was little point in trying. Life could be made miserable, lived with a constant wary eye cast over one's shoulder. Yet, this was exactly how he had lived his life. When confronted by an obstacle, he did the rational thing. He went around it. When threatened, he fled.

In the context of certain death, it seemed useless to butt heads against rocks and other hard places. The point of it all was to get through it with as little damage and discomfort as possible. It was a matter of efficiency.

As the sailboat glided silently through the inky black waters of the Gulf of Mexico, Jack could find little warmth in his thoughts. His argument for his insignificance did not stay the feelings of emptiness and longing that gnawed at him from within his chest.

The sound of air gushing startled him and he looked left to see a glint of light reflecting from the wet back of a dolphin, breaching and diving off the starboard side coaming. It was running with the boat, and each time its head rose from the water, its eye seemed to stare at Jack. Jack could clearly see the line of its mouth, seeming to be smiling, as dolphins always do.

These were creatures that seemed happy with their lives. It occurred to him that he had rarely seen a lone one.

Jack's thoughts drifted to Angela. Her smile and the lilt of her laugh lingered in his head. He didn't really know her, yet he felt drawn to her. At that moment he felt a hunger for her company. He yearned for the feel of her holding him. A deep feeling of loneliness washed over him as he watched the dolphin swim into the darkness.

In his mind's eye, as if seen from the heavens, he saw himself below, just as he had observed other people he didn't know, going about the execution of their little lives. He saw his little boat, bobbing on the vast ocean that covered a blue marble, suspended in the eternal emptiness of space, getting smaller and smaller until he could see only the faint outline of the boat. Gradually that reduced to a mere mark, then it was lost on the surface of the planet.

Then the truth of it dawned on him. He had very nearly died yesterday. Somehow the fact of it didn't capture the essence of it. He would be dead, and though it didn't matter at all to the universe, he was suddenly aware that it mattered to him. And it made him sad that it might not matter to anyone else.

He was yanked back to the present by a sound he did not expect.

Chapter 51

JACK TURNED HIS HEAD to listen again. In the starlight he thought he saw something but he couldn't be sure. He squinted to focus his eyes on the companionway.

He heard it again.

His eyes followed the sound and he flicked on the compass light, pouring a soft yellow glow across the cockpit sole and painted out swatches of sepia and gray and two yellow buttons of light.

"Moses!" Jack exploded.

"Wow," the trilling sounded like.

Jack jumped to his feet and dashed across the cockpit and swept the kitten up into his arms. Jack was full of surprise and delight, but more than that he realized he loved the cat.

It seemed impossible, but he did.

Chapter 52

"U.S. FISH & WILDLIFE, may I help you?" the voice answered.

"Jack Grider, please, Amesha Spentas calling."

"I am sorry, Mr. Grider is no longer with us."

"Oh," she said, "well, do you know how I can contact him?"

"I am afraid I don't."

"Could you tell me who is the ranking officer in your office, operator?"

"Why, yes, that would be Mr. Gene Bardino."

"Could you connect me to him, please?"

"Yes, one moment."

"Bardino, here," a strong male voice answered.

"Mr. Bardino, I am Amesha Spentas with Fenre Pease Investment Banking, New York, and I wonder if you could help me find a Mr. Jack Grider, who I had thought was employed by you."

"Ms. Spentas, did you say?"

"Yes, that's right."

"Well, Jack Grider is no longer with U.S. Fish & Wildlife, Ms. Spentas, and I don't really know how you can contact him. Could I help you with something?"

"Perhaps you can, Mr. Bardino. I was interested in speaking

with Mr. Grider about his impact brief on the Laguna Madre. Are you familiar with it?"

"Impact brief, hmm, Laguna Madre," he seemed to be saying to himself as he thought. "No, I can't say I recall anything like that."

"I see," she said. "Is there anyone in your office that might have more information on it?"

"I can't say that I know who. We are involved in so many projects, you know. It's hard to say," he stalled.

"Well, then, thanks very much, Mr. Bardino." She hung up. A bureaucrat who didn't know about a government report that was supposed to have come from one of his staff was not a rarity. Admitting it was. She smiled to herself.

Bardino stared at his desk for a while with an uneasy feeling. He dialed the phone.

"Mario?" he asked.

"Speaking," Congressman Monde's chief of staff answered.

"Gene Bardino, calling from Weslaco. U.S. Fish."

"Gene! How you doing?"

"I'm not sure. I just got a call from some lady from a bank. Fenre Pease, I think she said. She was looking for Jack Grider."

"And…"

"Grider. You know, the guy who wrote that Laguna report on the gas drilling."

"The Magne's project?"

"She was looking to talk to him about the impact report. I thought I ought to give you a heads-up on it," Bardino explained.

"Not to worry, Gene. It's just routine due diligence. Listen, if she calls back, just play dumb. We'll handle it from here. Thanks for calling." Mario put the phone down and squinted at the calendar across from his desk. He wondered where the congressman was scheduled to be.

He pulled on his sports coat and headed for the door, calling over his shoulder, "Myra, I'm going up to the floor. If the congressman calls, tell him I'm looking for him."

Chapter 53

"HEY, MARIO," CONGRESSMAN Monde called across the hallway as he came out of the House Chamber.

"Congressman. I need to talk to you about something that happened today," Mario said nervously.

"What's up?"

"I'm not sure. The U.S. Fish & Wildlife office in Weslaco, Bardino, got a call today from some banker looking for Jack Grider."

"What's that have to do with anything?"

"She was asking about the impact report."

"What do you suppose she wants with that?"

"I don't know, but I don't like it."

"Probably nothing to worry about, Mario. Let's just keep an ear to the rail and see if she shows up again."

"Right."

"Just one thing, where is this fellow, Grider, anyway?"

"I don't know. He quit over a month ago. Want me to check around?"

"It might be a good idea. We don't want the banker talking to him, that's for sure."

"I'll see what I can find out," Mario said.

Chapter 54

BY MID AFTERNOON Wednesday, Jack sailed through the Bolivar Roads, between the Bolivar Peninsula and Galveston Island. He swung to port to enter Galveston Channel, heading to the marina near the old town Galveston itself. Moses was alert and sitting on the cabin top, just forward of the companionway's sliding hatch, like a seasoned sailor on his watch. Jack felt a mixture of relief and regret as he maneuvered *Wist* into a slip. He was ready for a real shower and a bed that stayed still. But as soon as he had secured the dock lines, he made straight for the marina office and a phone.

"Hello?" a female voice answered.

"Hi, this is Jack Grider, and I am calling for Angela Poole. Is this her residence?" Jack asked. It was his third try of Pooles through directory assistance.

"Yes, this is Sophie Poole. Angela's my daughter. One moment please while I get her."

He could hear her put the phone down, but little else. It was not like him to call someone he barely knew, but he had decided to call Angela yesterday. He was having second thoughts as he waited and considered hanging up.

"Hello?"

"Angela?"

"Yes?"

"Jack. Jack Grider."

"Well, what took you so long?" she laughed.

"I didn't know your phone number," he explained.

"So, how'd you find it?"

"How many Pooles do you think there are in the Rio Grande Valley?"

"Good point. Where are you?"

"Galveston."

"So you made it."

"Guess I did."

The conversation stalled.

"So, what do you want?" she asked.

He didn't know quite how else to put it, and he was afraid it would sound close to idiotic but he tried anyway. "I was wondering if you might ever come up to Galveston."

"Why?" she asked, feigning cluelessness and enjoying making him feel as awkward as possible.

"Well, to see Moses, for one thing, and maybe me, for another," he joked.

"Hmm," she paused. "Well I guess I would like to see that cat again," she played along.

"What about this weekend?"

"I'll have to ask my mother if I can go," Angela teased.

"Let me talk to her. I'll convince her," Jack teased back.

"Ok," she said simply then made sounds of handing the phone off.

"Wait! I was ..." Jack panicked.

"Hello?" Sophie answered.

"Oh, hello, Ms. Poole," Jack said as calmly as he could, then realizing his voice had changed to himself at sixteen years old.

"What is it that you want with Angela," she said in a voice that suggested she was simple and hard of hearing.

"Well, uh," Jack stammered, completely nonplused by the sudden turn of the call. He heard female laughter on the phone. Both of them were enjoying the squirming.

"I can see where your daughter gets her, uh, personality, Ms. Poole," he finally said.

"Here's Angela again," Sophie said, laughing.

"My mother said I could go," Angela said like a teenager.

"You enjoyed that, didn't you?" Jack admonished her.

"It's Port Isabel," she said. "We have to do whatever we can."

"So are you going to come up or not?"

"Well," Angela seemed to demur. "I don't know."

"What's the worst that can happen?" he asked, as if beginning an argument based on calculations.

"That's an interesting way to look at things. So, if the worst is tolerable, less than worst is better?"

"Before too long, *terrible* can begin to look like only *just awful*," Jack explained.

"Do you get many dates thinking like this?" she asked.

"Is this a date?"

"You tell me," she answered.

"Can we just call it a 'visit'?"

"A visit. Well, that's different. Sure, ok, I'll come up. But I have a confession," she explained. "I've been promising a college classmate of mine, she runs the Moody Gardens up there, that I'd come and see her, so I've got to let her know and check if this weekend is good for her too."

"Not a problem," Jack said, "whatever it takes."

"What's your cell number," she asked.

"Don't have one."

"You don't have a cell phone?" Angela asked incredulously.

"Never saw the point."

"You're kidding."

"Mostly, any call to me is to either give me bad news or sell me something. I can't see paying fifty dollars a month to make sure I don't miss any of that."

"You are an interesting case, Jack Grider. So how do I reach you?"

"If you've got to, call the marina, I'll give you the number. Just leave a message. They'll let me know."

"Ok, I can be there by three in the afternoon if I leave at nine, right?"

"That's about right, six hours, I think."

"Where am I going?"

"When you get onto the island, head to the north end, but on the bay side, by the docks. It's called the Galveston Yacht Marina. I'm in Slip 36. You can ask at the front office if you have any trouble."

She repeated his instructions as if she were writing it down, getting the marina's phone number too. "Ok," she said, "I should show up between three and four, then."

"That's really great," he said in his sincerest tone, thinking he wished he had rehearsed it.

"We'll see," she said, teasing him, then added, "If you don't hear from me, it means I'm coming."

"Thanks. I'm looking forward to seeing you, Angela."

"Me too," she said more seriously.

When she put the phone on the hook, she turned to her mother with a wide smile.

"That him?" Sophie asked.

"Yep."

"On schedule, then."

"Well, so far, so good. It's a long way from a sure thing, though."

"Oh, I have confidence in you, hon. I'd say he doesn't have a chance in hell."

"I'll do what I can," she said modestly, although they both knew her record.

"How long will you be gone?" Sophie asked.

"As long as it takes, I guess."

It wasn't something Jack had felt since high school, the time Alicia Perez had said yes when he asked her to the prom. He felt a little embarrassed; after all, he was a grown man. But he felt excited too, a reaction he couldn't remember having for a long while.

Jack called his brother to tell him he had arrived safely.

He had two days to wash off dirt and salt that gathered on the passage from Port Mansfield. Tomorrow he'd start below, organizing and cleaning. He was curious to find the niche that Moses had been hiding in. He'd work his way out the companionway, then across the deck and cockpit. He wanted to get *Wist* gleaming. He couldn't help remembering a like project on his father's car, when he got it to take out Alicia way back then.

As he walked back to the slip, he thought how unlike him it was to do what he was doing. He would never admit it to anyone, but he was a little afraid of women. He never felt completely comfortable with them, so he would put on a face that wasn't really his, like holding a fake smile for a long time. After a while, it hurt. He preferred not to have to work that hard.

But somehow, this was different. He didn't know why or how. It just was.

Chapter 55

"JOHN, THIS IS LENCHO. I hope I'm not interrupting anything this late at night."

"Never, Lencho; it's always great to hear from you," John Magne said, then covered the mouthpiece and whispered to his wife across the game table, "It's Lencho Monde."

"Listen, I wouldn't bother you at night, but I think it would be a good idea if we could visit a little, face to face, you know."

"Sure, what did you have in mind?" Magne said cautiously, sensing the trepidation in Monde's voice.

"I've got to be in Austin tomorrow. I wonder if I could meet you at the airport, the new one on the south side, I'm flying commercial, say three o'clock in Continental's Presidents Club? I'll buy you a beer."

"That'll be fine, Lencho. What's this all about, anyway?"

"Oh, nothing all that major, John. I just need to talk to you."

"Tomorrow, then," Magne signed off.

"What was that all about," Gabriela asked, seeing the serious look on her husband's face.

"Dunno. Lencho wants to see me tomorrow in Austin. Obviously didn't feel comfortable talking on the phone."

"I'm sure it's just another hit for campaign money, John. Primaries are next year again."

"Already? Christ."

"That's going to be interesting," Gabriela said raising her eyebrows. "Have you decided what way you're going to go?"

"Not yet. Lencho has come through for us, Gabriela, every time. And he gets stuff done."

"Yes, but last summer you were worried that he was wearing out."

"And he is, and we have to think about who we want up there to replace him. I'm just not sure who it is this time around. He might have another lap in him."

"What have you told Marco?"

"To be patient. His time is coming."

"Is that working?"

"What's he going to do? He may be a state senator, but he's basically a school supplies salesman. If it wasn't for those consulting contracts we've arranged through the lobbyists, he'd be eating out of trash cans, for godssake. He'll do what he's told."

"Do you suppose Lencho's gotten wind of it?" Gabriela asked.

"Who knows. It's Washington. The walls have ears," he said. "And you know what? Who cares. He can't complain. He knows what side his bread is buttered on. Once upon a time he was a state legislator, just like Marco, and now he's had his turn at the big trough. He can't be a pig about it."

"Well, I guess there's no need to decide now, is there?"

"Nah. Let's get this gas deal done, relax and enjoy it a while, then we can think about all that."

Chapter 56

"GOOD OF YOU TO come up to meet me, John. I know how busy you are," Monde said as they found a quiet corner in the President's Club at the far end of the Austin airport--never a problem on a Thursday.

"What's so important that you didn't want to talk about it on the phone," Magne asked directly.

Monde could feel the edge in Magne's voice.

"There's this fellow, Jack Grider, who wrote the impact report on the drilling project," Monde began, "and yesterday, somebody working for your investment bank was nosing around for him."

"So what's the problem?" Magne asked.

"She can't be allowed to find him," Monde said succinctly.

Magne narrowed his eyes and looked straight into Monde's. The eyes said it all, Magne knew. "I thought we had all that worked out."

"I found out that Grider discovered the revised version and blew a gasket," Monde explained.

"When did this all happen?"

"About a month ago," Monde replied.

"And so, what did he do about it?"

"He quit."

"That's it? He quit?" Magne was incredulous. "Sure someone along the line didn't pay him off?"

"Never got the chance. He just took off."

"That's sort of odd, isn't it? I mean, you'd think he'd have either made a bigger stink or just put his head down and kept his job."

"You'd think."

"So, where is this guy?" Magne asked.

"Not sure. But I thought you ought to have some of your friends look into it. I don't have to tell you that he's a loose end we really don't need."

"Loose end or loose cannon?" Magne leaned back in his upholstered chair and stared out onto the runway below, then the tree line in the distance. "Leave it to me, Lencho," Magne sighed. "Now, are there any other wrinkles in this thing?"

"No, John, we're all set. I already started moving things up the line to Fenre Pease. I've got some friends at corporate who owe me some favors. We'll see that this energetic staffer gets more to keep her busy…on other matters."

"Good."

"And the project is all 'go' from Washington's standpoint, so I don't think you need to worry about this. Let's just take care of this Grider fellow to be completely safe."

"That better be the last screw up, Lencho. I'm getting tired of cleaning up after…"

"Now, John," Monde interrupted him, "don't go getting all excited about any of this. I'm not trying to ring an alarm. I'm just dotting the Is, here. It's taking care of detail. That's why I get stuff done."

"You're right. I'm sorry," Magne apologized. "I just need this to go smoothly, Lencho."

"As smooth as silk, John. That's a promise."

Monde dashed off to catch the direct flight back to D.C., leaving Magne nursing his single malt, gazing out the window. Just another small hump in the road, he thought, confident but irritated. Another piss ant bureaucrat with hurt feelings. It was incredible how some people could screw up his life. Magne resented it. He had no time or patience for them.

He dropped a five dollar bill on the table for a tip and went out to short term parking. He could be home by sunset if he left before the traffic started.

On the way back he would think about what to do with Jack Grider, and how.

Chapter 57

SATURDAYS MEANT LOTS of weekenders messing about on their boats, and Jack enjoyed the sounds of them working on this and that. There was the occasional friendly wave or nod between them and the understanding this was principally "alone" time. The typical autumn cloud cover offered some shade, but Jack worked up a serious sweat polishing out the few rust spots on the stainless steel stern rails. At noon, he began to look at his watch more frequently. He felt anxious.

At two o'clock he headed to the marina showers to get cleaned up. He didn't want to greet Angela smelling of sweat and solvents. He found himself hurrying.

The minute hand swept past the twelve and Jack looked out the companionway, down the dock. It was three o'clock. That's when he expected Angela. He ducked back down into the salon and paged absentmindedly through a sailing magazine. Moses was asleep on the navigation station table.

At four o'clock Jack began to feel irritated. He was himself punctual and didn't like tardiness in others. Perhaps she had car trouble, he thought, or a flat. She couldn't easily call. Maybe he ought to check for messages at the marina office. He'd give her another quarter hour.

The marina office clock read four-thirty when Jack walked in and inquired about any messages. There were none, and he was becoming worried. He walked up to the parking lot and looked around, although he didn't know for what.

He walked back to the boat slip and went below for a beer. As if on cue, the gushing sound of the pulled pop top was followed by the clean, clear soprano tone.

"Hey sailor!" she called from the cockpit.

"Angela?" his heart jumped.

"Expecting someone else?" she said, smiling.

"I was worried something happened to you?"

"Me? I just took the long way around. Sorry I'm late."

"Come on down for a beer," he invited her.

"Don't mind if I do, bartender," she responded.

She stepped down the companionway into the salon and surveyed the room. Moses immediately sat up and came to her.

"Nice digs," she said, "and I see the cat has decided to keep you."

"Nice digs," Jack echoed. "You *are* an academic." Jack took the seat opposite her in the booth. "So how was the drive?"

"Long. I shouldn't have come in the Jeep. I still can't hear anything."

"Oh, yeah, the red Jeep."

"My mom's. She's more the four-wheeler type than I am."

"Somehow I find that hard to believe."

"So," she asked, "how was *your* trip up? See anything interesting?"

"It was fine, I guess, not much to see from there to here. I was just glad to get in and have a chance to sleep for eight uninterrupted."

"Eight! Wow. I wish I could sleep eight hours straight. "I'm lucky to manage six," she said, "and I have to be dead drunk to do that."

"Hard to imagine you being the type to get drunk."

"Why's that?"

"Well, you being vegetarian and all, I'd bet you are real health conscious."

"Vegan. I'm a vegan, not a vegetarian."

"Excuse me, *vegan*," he corrected himself.

"And vegans aren't necessarily health conscious, unless you mean health conscious for the animals they don't eat. Veganism is more a lifestyle, really. It's about a consideration of the impact of our choices on the lives of other living things. Not using other animals is just one aspect of it. So that's why I only drink alcohol that is made from non-animal parts and I don't drink stuff that has animal names or images on the label."

Jack looked at her then squinted doubtfully. She laughed out loud. "I didn't know there was alcohol made from animal parts," he said.

"And thank god for that," she said, holding up her beer bottle for a toast.

"It's pretty unusual to find a Texan who doesn't eat meat," Jack observed.

"It's a big state, there, pard'ner," she joked.

"You don't really live here anyway, do you?" Jack asked.

"I grew up in Port Isabel, but I've lived out East since I graduated college, so no, not really, but I do consider myself to be a Texas girl. It's got an exotic air about it, at least in New England."

"So what exactly is it you do there?" he asked.

"Dating."

"Dating?" he asked confused.

"Dating," she re-affirmed. "Carbon dating. Bones mostly."

"Bones?"

"Bones. Tell me, Jack Grider, is this conversational style of yours a celebration of an economy of words, or are you essentially dazzled beyond speech by me?"

"Both," Jack replied smiling.

"Both?" she reposted.

The sun had set and the light was waning when they headed up the dock to the town to find a restaurant. Moses stayed back to guard *Wist* and his can of chopped tuna.

Chapter 58

JASON HAD COME to expect her everyday at nine o'clock in the morning. Whether he was just starting the day shift or ending the night one, there she would be, standing at the counter at the Port Office, her purse resting on the counter before her.

"Any word?" Anajita Paredes would consistently ask.

"No ma'am," Jason would have to consistently reply. She would ask what was being done to find her husband and each time Jason would have go through the routine that rang hollow even to him. They were still on the case. There was nothing to report.

And she would shake her head and announce that she would be back the next day and continue to come back until somebody took notice. Then she would storm out the door, leaving it to bang on the door stop.

With the mayor calling him off the case and the Sheriff's Department uninterested, there was in fact no one looking for Octavio Paredes. Officially. But Jason was taking his bay boat out more often lately and cruising up and down the edges of the Laguna, running north.

Except for the work begun near the Magne Landing, it was a world that belonged to long legged white egrets, blue herons, white pelicans and the occasional roseate spoonbill.

"Good morning, Mayor," Jason said as the door of the office swung open.

"What's new?" the mayor asked.

"Nothing much. Quite a few boats headed out for the bay today."

"Thank goodness for weekends and South Texas weather," the mayor said.

"Yep, looks like it's going to be a pretty nice day for fishing *and* business."

"Even better for sailing," the mayor said. "Hey, Jason, that big sailboat that was in the marina last week..."

"The Beneteau?"

"A forty-footer, where is it?"

"It left out last Sunday. That's my brother's boat."

"No kidding? Nice boat. Where was he headed?"

"Galveston," Jason replied, "I heard from him on Wednesday, I think it was."

"He made it ok?"

"Yep, seems so," Jason confirmed.

"Where's he off to from there?"

"I don't really know. I don't think he knows. Believe he said he'll probably hang out in Galveston for a while, though," Jason explained.

"Must be nice, eh? I've always wanted to just take off like that, gunkholing from town to town. Man, that would be so great. Listen," the mayor said, changing the subject to business, "we're going to be hosting a public hearing on the Laguna gas drilling project the Magnes are working on. Looks like its going to be held here at the Port Office. We'll need to plan for it."

"When's that, Mayor?"

"Friday."

"A week from today; *that* Friday?" Jason asked incredulously.

"Yes, this one," the mayor confirmed.

"You know that it's the day after Thanksgiving."

"Yeah, I know. Congressman Monde wants to officiate the

thing while he's back in the district for the holiday. It shouldn't be such a big to do, press-wise at least, with everybody out for the long weekend. I don't know how many locals will be much interested in it, but they tell me to expect some out-of-towners, tree huggers, you know what I mean."

"Well, I'll think about how we are going to arrange the conference room for it and all that."

"Great," the mayor approved.

Chapter 59

OF THE FEW TABLES available on a Saturday night at Jean Laffite's, Angela selected a booth near the back of the restaurant. The warm sepia lighting gave her skin an amber color that made her green eyes glow like emeralds. There was a lightness in her laugh that made him feel like staring, no, gawking at her, and he made himself look away when she caught him.

Angela smiled at Jack's attention, and it didn't make her feel uncomfortable, as such usually would. As the hours passed, the conversation wandered over a surprising array of subjects. She thought him funny, but there was a tinge of sadness about him. His humor was sometimes slightly dark. But she knew she liked him.

"How long did it take for you to sail up to Galveston?" she asked.

"Almost three days," he replied.

"What do you think about out there all that time?"

"Lots of things. Then sometimes nothing, just sort of like gazing. The hours pass, sometimes quickly, sometimes on the back of a paraplegic snail."

"Pelagic snail, you mean," she corrected, laughing.

"Both," he replied.

She burst into song, "Para-pa-legic pelagic, parle' vous?"

Jack laughed.

"But really, what *do* you think about?" she probed, turning serious.

"Life, I guess," he said cryptically, then after a pause continued. "When you start out, you think about sailing the boat. You deal with the details and you get absorbed by the newness of being at sea. It's very exciting at the start. "Then, as time passes, you settle into the rhythm of it. The sea is in charge. All I can do is work with what it gives me. It lays out the full context. I'm just a rider on it. The vastness of the open sea has a way of making you feel your smallness. And, if there is any illusion left by dark, the utter aloneness of it all, the helplessness of it grows as the night takes over. But conquering the fear, that's a real high. Then, if it's a clear night, you've never seen so many stars. It's like the sky was painted with shiny white pearls."

"It sounds beautiful," she said.

"There is a beauty about it, there's no doubt, but it is also frightening sometimes. It's then that I remember my life and think about what things I've done and haven't done. Regrets, I guess you'd call them. It sounds like it can be depressing, but actually, it isn't. I do inventories about how I feel about things, what I want to do next. In a few hours, I start talking to myself out loud. It sounds nuts, but it feels really good, you know?"

Angela followed every word.

Jack continued, "I think I can sort things out more clearly when I hear the arguments with my own ears. Silly, but it works better for me, anyway."

"And what arguments are those?" she asked.

"Varies. I guess I wonder if I've made the right choices. I even wonder if there *were* any choices. I think we have an illusion of choices sometimes. I mean, I remember my senior year homeroom teacher at my high school. In the fall we'd have to sell tickets for a raffle. Catholic School. Need I explain?" he asked.

"No, go on."

"So each Monday he'd challenge us to go out and sell more

tickets than the other classes. It was a sort of competition. He'd say each time that this was a democracy and that we could make a choice. Then he'd give us the choices: We could sell twenty tickets each by Friday or we could sell twenty-five."

"A Hobson's Choice," Angela said.

"Exactly. No real choice at all. When you look at our lives, don't you find that we are all stuck in our context? Aren't we really just choosing among no real choices?"

Angela studied Jack's earnest face. He was a serious, shy, and interesting man, she thought.

"I'm not so sure," Angela said. "I think we do have choices. I think the fact is that we choose mostly not to make them. We narrow our options as a sort of strategy for avoiding the hard ones."

There was a strength about her that attracted Jack. She was unlike any women he had known. She was smart, definite, but didn't take herself too seriously. Yet, she had something to say and wasn't afraid to say it.

"For some people," Jack said, "it's different. They are special. They are that five percent that get it."

"Why five percent?" Angela asked curiously.

"I think that was God's real penalty for Eden. It wasn't mortality. Hell, if you're serious about religion, death is curtain number three and behind it is the big prize. No, I think that the penalty was that God fixed it so that maybe five percent of the human race has any idea what's going on. And the other ninety-five percent rely on them for everything. And here's the punch line. He won't tell us which the five percent are. And we can't tell geniuses from idiots."

Angela laughed. "So are you in the five percent or not?"

"If I am, we're in huge trouble," he said in mocked seriousness. "But I think you are."

"I don't know if I am or not, but I can fake it," she said.

"Sincerely?" he asked.

"Yes, I can fake that too," she laughed.

Jack was disappointed and yet relieved when Angela left him at the marina parking lot to stay with her friend, the director of the Moody gardens. He didn't get her name.

They agreed to meet at noon, Sunday, the next day, to go for sail on Galveston Bay.

"Hi, Mom," Angela spoke into her cell phone, "I made it all right."

"Where are you staying?"

"The Galvez," she said. "I told him I was staying with a friend."

"And how did it go today?"

"Good. We're making friends. I think he likes me, well, at least he likes looking at me," Angela said with a chuckle. "He invited me to go sailing tomorrow. That's a good sign, I think."

"Be careful, Angela," Sophie warned.

"No need to worry, Mom. He's a good guy. A little confused, maybe, but basically a good guy."

"Well, just remember what it is you're doing, girl."

"Focus, I know."

"Call me tomorrow?" asked Sophie.

"I promise."

Chapter 60

THE CLOUD COVER HAD cleared by noon and down the dock came Angela, with the sun, Jack thought.

"Hi, sailor!" she called out and waved as she approached.

"Hi back. Ready to go?"

"Ready and rarin'," Angela replied. "I brought some Subways and Dr. Peppers."

"Excellent," he said, helping her on to the boat. She fell forward and he caught her in his arms. She was firm and soft at the same time, he realized. She felt good.

"What do I have to do?" she asked.

"Have you ever sailed before?"

"On a boat?" she asked, suddenly realizing the stupidity of it, and smiling with a blush.

Jack laughed. "Then, your job will be to sit here in the cockpit and yell for help when I fall overboard," he advised her.

"Are there any, like, special words for that, like 'Man Overboard!'" she shouted out. A man on a boat four slips down looked up from his chores, but Jack waved him off.

"That would probably do just fine. You have great lungs," he said.

"My mother's very proud," she teased.

Jack started the diesel, freed the warps, and pulled away from the dock. *Wist* glided across the rippling waters, past the other boats, the docks, and finally past the channel markers into Bolivar Roads, headed for Galveston Bay.

"What do I do if I get seasick," Angela asked.

"Well, there are certain rules of etiquette for that, actually," Jack answered seriously.

"Yes?"

"First and foremost you want to do all your throwing up on the leeside of the stern."

"And second?" she asked.

"Keep it to yourself."

Jack unfurled the mainsail, then the genoa, and brought the boat around to a beam reach. The sails filled with a snap and the boat heeled fifteen degrees, sending Angela flying across the cockpit into Jack's arms as the boat leaned and surged forward.

"Hold on there," Jack called out, all smiles.

"For dear life!" she called back.

The boat speed grew to a bit over seven knots. The sound of water rushing replaced the engine noise, as he shut off the diesel.

"This is wonderful!" Angela suddenly blurted out, overwhelmed with the feeling of it. Jack had seen it before in some passengers. It was new and exciting, almost to the point of an unrestrained joy. He knew the feeling, but the intensity of it in a newbie was something special, and he enjoyed it all over again vicariously.

"Look!" she cried out when she spotted a pod of dolphins rolling nearby. Jack veered the boat closer to them and they began to run along side the port quarter. Angela leaned over and seemed to yearn to touch one of them. When the larger one rolled on its side and stared up into her eyes, she suddenly tensed her grip on the railings and gawked. When he had swum on, Angela turned her face to Jack, and he saw it was full of an almost religious amazement. She seemed speechless. Then she smiled appreciatively.

Angela was full of questions. And Jack began to explain the parts and functions of the sailboat. He took the boat into some tacks, working the genoa sheets from side to side, showing her each of the steps. Then he let her try.

He brought the nose of the boat through the wind and yelled for her to pull in the sheet to secure the genoa. She struggled awkwardly with the slack line and finally got it around the winch and, with Jack's help, tailed it.

He handed her a winch handle and ordered, "Now grind that winch!"

Angela looked at him with a feigned indignity, "There better not be a coma in that, mister!"

"That, my dear, would be up to you," he replied sharply with a laugh.

Angela looked down and began turning the winch to tighten the genoa sheet. The sail flattened, and the boat began to pull ahead.

"You know," she said with a broad smile of satisfaction painted across her face, "I could get used to this!"

Jack smiled at her and looked ahead.

They traversed the bay toward Kemah. Jack engaged the autopilot and they broke out the sandwiches. The boat had settled into a comfortable groove and the two of them ate and chatted as W*ist* sailed on its own.

"I can't get over those dolphins," Angela said. "Don't you get the feeling that they're intelligent, almost like humans?"

"I do," Jack said. "I get the feeling every time I see them. I've been out and had them actually showing off. Jumping straight up, facing the boat. You just know they are performing. And they seem to care for one another. I guess in some ways they are actually better than some of us. Hell, maybe *they* are the five percent!"

Angela studied Jack as he spoke. She began to see the introspective side of him more clearly. He didn't seem shy, as she had thought, but insular. It was more a choice than a condition. It seemed to be a defense. A gentle soul in a harsh world, perhaps.

After more than four hours, Jack maneuvered the sailboat back into its slip at the marina and secured the warps to the dock cleats. Moses felt bold enough to peek out of the companionway and Angela reached over and picked him up and cradled him in her arms, gently stroking the white fur under his chin. Moses curled his head back in appreciative encouragement and purred.

Jack stared on feeling jealous. You dog, he thought.

"Beer?" he asked.

"Got any red wine?"

"I've got a Pinot," Jack suggested.

"Perfect."

Jack went below to retrieve two wine glasses and the bottle. He looked and found a corkscrew and brought all the equipment up to the cockpit.

"I'm always screwing up the cork with these rudimentary corkscrews," he confessed as he peeled away the foil around the top.

"Here let me do it," Angela said with authority, taking the bottle and corkscrew from Jack without hesitation. She put the bottle on the bench between her bare legs and worked in the corkscrew, then in one swift movement, "Pop!"

"I like the way you handle that," Jack complimented.

"I waitressed in college," she explained. She poured both glasses and handed one to Jack, who was sitting on the cockpit bench across from her. "Here's to the five percent!" she toasted.

"Long may they wave," Jack replied and touched glasses.

"I enjoyed our dinner last night, Jack," Angela said. "I've thought a lot about what you said about choices, about our not having any real ones."

"Me too," he said. "I say we have no real choices, but then there are times when I can't seem to choose. It's like I am hung on the horns of a dilemma and the gap between points seems an ocean wide."

"Exactly. If it all doesn't matter," Angela posed the question as she leaned back on the coaming, resting on her elbows, and crossing her outstretched legs at the ankles, "then why is choosing so hard?"

"That's the mystery, really," Jack said pensively. "It's the cynic in me, I guess. And it is in a death struggle with the altar boy."

"Who's winning?"

Jack looked at her and smiled. Then he shrugged.

Angela was struck with how handsome Jack was. She hadn't noticed it as much before, but there was something about his boyish grin, his tussled hair, and the way he held himself. She was feeling something unexpected. She felt a little aroused. The wine, the salt air, the day on the water, the exhilaration of sailing, all these were working on her, she sensed.

Jack stared across to her. He could see she was thinking hard about something, perhaps another comment about choices. She looked into his eyes as if she was constructing the words for a question.

"Jack," she said after a few moments, "I think I better go."

"Go?" Jack blurted in surprise.

Angela smiled and said, "There's that economy of words again."

"I'm sorry, no, don't go. Stay. We'll have dinner," he was desperate to persuade her. She could hear it in his voice.

"I can't. I promised my friend to have dinner with her tonight."

"Invite me!" he chirped, "I'll even buy."

"That's sweet, but it's going to be just us girls tonight," she said. "I'll be back tomorrow. Promise."

Jack could see that she saw he was disappointed, but he was too proud to plead any further. "Tomorrow, then," he acquiesced.

Angela stood up as Jack did and they were face to face. Jack could feel her warm breath on his face. He could see deep into her eyes.

Angela looked down suddenly, then turned and climbed back on to the dock. "It was lovely, Jack, honestly," she said.

"Breakfast, say at nine?" Jack proposed hopefully.

Angela smiled and tilted her head in that way that she did. "All right."

Jack watched her as she walked back up the dock and out of sight. Moses turned his head up to look at Jack. Jack was sure he saw a look of disgust just before the cat turned and walked back down into the cabin.

Chapter 61

JACK WAS DREAMING OF Angela when Moses woke him sometime after two A.M.. He was trilling oddly and Jack noticed he was fixated, ears alert, on the canvas covered companionway. When he felt the boat give, and tilt toward the dock, he knew that someone had stepped into the cockpit from the dock.

"Angela?" he called out, his heart rate suddenly surging with excitement.

The canvas cover was pulled back, and in the dark all Jack could see is a dark form coming down the steps into the salon.

"Angela," he repeated. Moses dashed away through the doorway to the forward stateroom.

"Angela, huh," a twangy male voice repeated, as another figure came down the companionway steps behind him.

"You Jack Grider?"

"Who is that?" Jack demanded, sitting up, trying to see.

"Depends, are you Grider?"

"Yes, I'm Grider, who the hell are you?"

"Now, Ed," he seemed to be saying to the other figure, "isn't it just awful how rude people are becoming, I mean, the language!" he protested sarcastically.

Jack reached back to turn on a light.

"Now, now, don't be doing that," the first figure said, grabbing Jack's wrist. "Why don't we just keep this real friendly."

"I don't know who you are, but I want you off my boat right now!" Jack demanded.

"Why can't we jus' git along," the voice said, mimicking. "Besides, I'm here to give you some good news, Mr. Grider, really, really good news."

Jack felt the sting of an adrenaline rush and sensed immediately that he was in an exposed position. His mind ran wildly in an assessment of his options. He had no good ones. He thought his best strategy was to remain quiet.

"You see, Ed, here, has come all the way out from Houston tonight to discuss your future. Isn't that right, Ed? The thing is, Ed just isn't much for words. I'd have to say that Ed--well, Ed is more a man of action, if you get my drift."

Jack tried to make out the man's features in the dim light.

"I'm just gonna help translate for ole' Ed, here. That's my job, sort of like an interpreter," the voice said in a matter of fact manner.

Jack could see the second figure was bigger than the first, as it moved quickly towards him. Jack felt a sharp blow to the left side of his face that stunned him and left him seeing stars. "What the fuh...," Jack cried out.

"Well you see, what Ed was trying to say with that was he's awful worried about your health, Jack. He says you're just not taking care of yourself."

"If it's money you want," Jack pleaded, wincing from the pain, "I don't have much but my wallet's on the table behind you; take it, but leave me alone."

"You know, you were right all along, Ed. Right, again, gall darn it," the voice said to the second man. "He doesn't understand at all. Good thing you brought me along. What's that you want to say, Ed?" he asked as if he was hearing a voice that Jack wasn't.

Jack threw up his arms to block the second assault, but it only made the man strike more furiously. Jack felt himself briefly losing consciousness on the third blow.

"Oh, *that*," the voice said. "Why didn't you say so?" he asked sarcastically. "Ed says that you need a lot of fresh sea air, for your condition, that is. He thinks you ought to take a nice long sail in this great big boat of yours as soon as possible. When would that be, Ed?" he asked out loud.

Jack winced and covered his head at what he expected next. He felt a single blow to the top of his head. He was suddenly dizzy, and his ears rang.

"Gee, Ed says you need to leave yesterday and that he's very disappointed you're already running late, aren't you Ed?"

The man speaking drew closer to Jack's ear and in a stage whisper said, "I don't want Ed to hear this, Jack, but I'm thinking he might not be real happy to see you again. He's like that, you know, sort of, what's the word, ah, petulant. That's it, he's petulant. And there seems to be a whole lot of important people, a whole lot, who are worried about you, Jack. Must've been something you said, I guess, or," he paused for effect, "something you wrote, maybe?

"Here's my advice to you, Jack. I suggest that before the sun rises you ought to get this boat of yours underway, headed for the Caribbean, or the Atlantic, or, hell, even the Pacific. Anywhere far away from here. Do you understand?" He slammed his elbow into Jack's side, "I said, do you understand?"

"Yes, yes," Jack pleaded, "I understand."

"Good, good," the man said in an appreciative tone, patting Jack's shoulder, then straightening up. "Well, Ed, do you have anything else for ole' Jack here?" Jack covered his head. "No? Fine."

"Jack," he said his name in a sing song, "Ed seems to be all talked out. Me too," he said now turning to Ed with a sigh, "this is just too much work." The man called "Ed" went up the companionway, and the first man followed him then paused on the first step and turned back to Jack. "Oh, Jack, Ed and I don't want to hear that you've been talking to some fancy tree-huggin'

New York lawyers about birds and fish and shit. Ever. And we don't want to see you back in Texas for a year, got that? We'll be watching and, you know Ed, when he has something to say, well, you just can't shut him up," the man said in a hoarse laugh. "Remember! Sunrise," he said, then, "See ya!"

Jack laid shivering with terror. Every sense was heightened as he froze, wondering what was going to happen next. He could feel the warm ooze of blood running down his cheek and he could taste iron in his mouth. Who were these men, he wondered. What did they want? "Birds and fish and shit….New York lawyers," what were they talking about?

He replayed the words over and over in his head: "important people, something you said, birds and fish…" then it struck him like a lightning bolt, "something you wrote."

Jack struggled to his feet, wiping his face with his T-shirt sleeve. He needed to call Angela, but how? He didn't have her cell phone number, and it was the middle of the night. He'd never find her in time. He sat down at the nav. station, switched on a map light, took out a piece of paper and wrote her a note. He stuffed it into an envelope and wrote on the outside, "Hold for Angela." He stopped before he wrote her surname. What if they found this at the marina office door first? He had to protect her. He wrote below it, "from Jack." He ran up the dock and stuck the letter in the office mailbox and pulled up the flag.

Thirty minutes later, Jack motored *Wist* out of the marina and ran for the open sea.

Chapter 62

THE LEAD ATTORNEY ON the Magne Project IPO stood up at the head of the conference room table and called the other attorneys to order to get started.

"Good Monday morning, everyone," he cheerily greeted the group, drawing a chorus of groans. "This is the first review of the documents on the Magne IPO. I'd like to try to get this meeting done by noon, so let's go around the room and get a report on each of the sections, beginning with the auditor's opinion. Clark?"

"Amberson has signed off on it. In short, it's done and ready to send to the printer."

Each in turn, the lawyers made their reports, coming eventually to the section on environmental compliance.

"Amesha?" the lead attorney cued her.

"I have received documents from the Department of the Interior, U.S. Fish & Wildlife, the Army Corp of Engineers, other materials for Texas Parks and Wildlife and other state agencies. All permitting appears to be proceeding and is either granted or will be granted within a month," she reported. "The only exception to the list is an easement that is referred to in certain documents at U.S. Fish & Wildlife, but they are unable to produce it. My conversations with officials in Washington indicate that it is not relevant to this matter and that they do not intend to pursue any further search for it."

"Would you say you'll be clear in two weeks then, Amesha?"

"From what I am being told, yes," she responded.

"You sound tenuous," the lead attorney commented.

"I have to rely upon the representations given me, and I can't be sure they will meet their schedules, that's all."

"You are aware that this is a pet project of Congressman Monde of Texas?" he suggested.

"Yes, I am," she acknowledged, "and I do understand that his position has a determining influence over what gets done in D.C."

"Well, then, I think we can assume that you'll have everything when promised. I want you done by the end of next week. That goes for all of you, by the way." The lead attorney then quickly moved on to the next report.

When the meeting was breaking up, the lead attorney came across the room to Amesha Spentas.

"Amesha, you don't need to be so uptight about getting your stuff from the agencies. I've got it on good authority that this is being fast-tracked and that Monde is all over these department chiefs like sand on a beach."

"Well, that's the influence you get when you're on the House Appropriations Committee. I get it, Phil. But you know there's an election coming up next year…"

"Oh, sure. The re-election rate on Congressmen is, what, 98%? Like he's going anywhere. But, seriously, Amesha, you need to get onboard with this thing. People are watching. It's ok to be dotting the Is, but don't get caught dragging your feet on this."

"Just doing my job, Phil," she said, then added, "but my mama didn't raise no fool."

"Just a heads up, that's all. Anyway, I'm pretty sure that Monde will be around awhile."

"That's not what I hear," Amesha said coyly.

"What exactly do you mean?" he asked urgently. He knew the firm was dealing with several issues that made Monde's support important.

"Nothing official, and don't quote me, but I heard there's stuff on the winds about him not running for re-election," she said in a confidential tone.

"But why?"

"Don't know, but you know there are four minority party members who've decided to retire, and two Senators. Guess it's not as much fun when you're not in charge of the Franking privileges."

"You're kidding," he said incredulously.

"Phil, look who you're talking to. When did you ever hear me kid about anything?"

Amesha Spentas--the "Queen of Darkness," she was called around the office. He was convinced she was a lesbian, wound up so tight that the key broke off in the winder. She probably slept exactly as she came to work, the pulled-back hair, large rimmed glasses, dark pin-striped suit, and clunky shoes.

She was hired only a month ago, out of the blue. He knew the type: female, black, Harvard Law…must have been cutting her teeth in the non-profit sector…, he thought, the curse of Affirmative Action.

He thought about the impact of her news. If Monde was not going to be a player in the next three years, several of his clients would love to know it, and it would look very good for the firm, for him, if he provided the insight. "Thanks," he said as he made a bee line for his boss's office.

Chapter 63

ANGELA PARKED HER JEEP in the marina lot and bounded playfully down the steps to the docks, toward Slip 36. From a distance she thought she saw the slip empty and walked the whole way to confirm it. She stood for a moment in confusion, wondering if she was on the right dock. Perhaps she was one off. She turned and surveyed the marina, looking for *Wist*, or at least Jack.

She walked up to the marina office and went in.

"Have you seen Jack Grider? His boat was in Slip 36," she asked the girl at the desk.

"Are you Angela?" she asked.

"Yes," she replied, surprised and hopeful.

"Mr. Grider left this for you," she said, handing Angela the envelope.

"Where's Jack?" she asked before she opened it.

"He's gone, ma'am. He left that envelope there with two hundreds clipped to it, for slip rent, in our mail box last night sometime. I guess he moved on," she explained.

Angela walked out of the office and crossed the boardwalk to the railing that overlooked the marina. She opened the letter and read it.

"Angela," it read, "Getting to know you has meant the world to me. I hope to see you again one day. I have to go. I am sorry. Jack."

She looked out toward the open bay and gazed at the glittering morning sunrays dancing on the ripples of the water. "Oh, Jack," she sighed.

As her Jeep crossed the causeway back to the mainland, Angela dialed her cell phone.

"Hello?" Sophie answered.

"He's gone, Mom."

"Angela?"

"He's gone."

"Who's gone?"

"Jack Grider. I went to the marina this morning and he just up and left."

"Why? What happened?" Sophie asked in surprise.

"I guess it just got too intense for him, hell, I don't know."

"Damn!" Sophie blurted.

"I know, I blew it."

"Oh, Angela, I'm sure you did the best you could, honey."

"Well, it wasn't good enough. Now he's flown the coop. What are we going to do now?"

"Oh, we'll think of something. Don't go losing heart, dear. Your ole mom may be rickety of limb, but she ain't but solid of frame," Sophie tried to reassure her daughter. "You just get back down here as fast as you can. We've got work to do."

"What's happening?" Angela asked.

"They've called a public hearing for next Friday."

"Damn!"

Chapter 64

"HEY, FESTOR!" CALVIN Richter hailed Stubb on his cell phone.

"You're sounding pretty chipper, there, Calvin, what's up?" Stubb asked.

"Just heard from my inside man over at legal. We've got us the golden goose, my friend."

"Man that's good to hear. So what's the schedule?"

"Well here's the plan, according to him. They've got all the due diligence done and expect to have all the documents ready a week from this coming Friday, let's see, that would make it the thirtieth, yeah, November 30."

"Any wrinkles?" Stubb asked.

"None reported. I've got to tell you, Festor, this is the fastest-tracked son of a bitch I've ever seen. Somebody up there has some real juice, that's for sure."

"Nice to be on the power side for once, eh, Calvin?"

"It sure takes the pressure off."

"Well, don't relax too soon, buster. I'm always gun-shy until the money's in the bank," Stubb said.

"I hear ya, but I wouldn't put much worry into this one, man. Trust me, there's too much Fenre Pease money in it to stop now. They don't go this far unless it's going all the way," Richter assured him.

"Well, that's good to know."

"Just wanted to report in. Talk to you next week." Richter hung up.

Stubb turned to his melamine board and circled the November 30 date. He decided to run the rest of the traps and dialed Sam Kiel.

"Hello?" Sam answered, opening the red cell phone.

"Sam?"

"Yes?"

"This is Festor. There's lots of wind noise. I can hardly hear you."

"Oh, hi, Festor, hold on, let me pull over. I'm on the highway."

"That's better. I just got a good report from Calvin. Looks like the thing is going to fund in December after all."

"Wow. It's hard to believe this is finally going to happen."

"What's the latest on your end?" Stubb asked.

"Just got word. There's a public hearing on the environmental issues scheduled for this coming Friday in Port Mansfield."

"*This* Friday?"

"No kidding," Sam confirmed.

"Those crafty SOBs. I gotta tell you; my respect for these political types is growing by the day. Now that's moxie, calling a public hearing on the day after Thanksgiving. Hell, it's a wonder the electricity will be working with all the linemen watching football!" Stubb said.

"And think of this. What do you think the Sierra Club types are likely to find when they try to fly in from California to testify?"

"What do you mean?" Stubb asked, puzzled.

"Try it. Go online and try to find a flight to the Valley on Friday before five o'clock."

"Hold on," Stubb said as he turned to his computer and brought up Travelocity.com and searched for flights. "My god!"

he exclaimed. Then he tried Continental Airlines. Again, nothing. Then Southwest Airlines. Nothing. "Every damned flight is booked solid."

"I think you can count on a quiet meeting, what do you think?" Sam assured him.

"You're a goddam genius, Sam, how'd you do it?"

"Not so hard, really. There's a lot of help with all the travelers for the Thanksgiving Day weekend and for the rest, well, lets just say there's going to be a lot of no-shows."

Stubb laughed out loud. "So anything special that needs to be done on our end?"

"Not really. I'll keep on eye on it. You take it easy and enjoy the long weekend," Sam said. "Oh, by the way, I'm going to be out of the country for a long holiday weekend myself, and won't be back until later next week, so don't freak out if you can't reach me. I'll report back when I return."

"Well, you've earned it, Sam. Enjoy!"

Stubb had one more call.

"Mr. Magne," he said.

"Yes, Festor," John Magne replied.

"I just wanted to report that our man at Fenre Pease called and said they are going to be ready on November 30. Looks like we'll fund in early December. I thought you'd want to know."

"Thanks, Festor, this is great news. Everything else is on track too."

"You mean the hearing on Friday?" Stubb prompted him.

"Why, yes, how'd you know about that?"

"I'm nothing if not diligent, Mr. Magne. My team has been working on making sure it is, let's just say, as quiet as possible."

"How's that?" Magne asked curiously.

Stubb explained the airline scheme Sam had set up.

Magne laughed as he listened to it.

"Well, Festor, it looks like all the long hard work is about to pay off for all of us," Magne said with a tinge of relief in his voice.

"Yes, sir. You know what they say: 'To the victor go the spoils.'"

"Indeed, Festor, just as God intended." Magne agreed.

Stubb folded down his phone and leaned back in his chair. He stared at his calendar by the TV. It was a grand vista of the mountains around Geneva, Switzerland. He always loved the calendars Credit Suisse sent him each year. He was looking forward to his next trip there. It would be very soon.

Chapter 65

THE ICE PACK HAD done about as much as it was going to, Jack could see. There was a nasty gash over his left eye. Ed must have been wearing a ring, he figured. The puffiness under his eye was not getting any worse, but he was going to have a real shiner.

It looked to Jack that Moses had been as traumatized as he had by the whole affair, but he was at least out in the salon again, sitting in his usual cubby. The adrenaline had finally subsided enough for him to think, though his hands still shook. It was all such a shock to him. He couldn't remember the last time he was in any kind of a fight. As a kid he had always avoided them, even with Jason.

Not that this was so much a fight as it was just a beating, Jack thought. As the fear subsided he sensed a rising anger to replace it. He was angry with himself for not striking back. But he couldn't, he told himself. His was the most prudent way to handle it.

Yet no amount of argument assuaged his sense of humiliation. He was angry enough to kill them both. These feelings surprised him. He rarely let himself get upset about much of anything. What was the point?

By now he was well off shore, heading northeast to the Louisiana border. Not knowing who the thugs were or who sent them, he had no way of knowing how serious their threat was. But he wasn't taking any chances. He would decide where to go next when he was out of Texas waters. In the meantime, he needed more supplies than he had for any extended passage.

He wondered if Angela had gotten his note. Over and over he replayed in his mind the words he wrote, and then thought how he could have done it better. Most important, he had to keep Angela out of this. He didn't want her getting hurt.

Jack disengaged the autopilot and took the helm. He was edgy and needed to be occupied with something, anything, to quiet his mind. But he played and re-played last night in the dark. His hands began to tremble again. His cheek ached.

After hours of this his mind began to tire of the iterations and intermixed in them were flashes of Angela smiling at the dolphins. He heard her laughter, the sweet sound of her voice. And as the hours passed his thoughts went mainly to her and he felt himself calming. By evening, his pain was gone.

Jack looked over his shoulder at the spokes of yellow and rose that radiated from the last of the setting sun. It was a sunset he thought he'd watch with Angela this night. Instead, he wondered if he'd ever see her again.

As the day wore on, Jack began to wonder how the thugs had found him in Galveston. Very few people knew where he'd gone and these men knew exactly where he was, down to the slip. How could they have known?

He didn't want to think of the possibilities, but his mind ground on against all efforts to resist it. And his disciplined, scientific mind was drawing one simple Venn diagram. The only persons who could expose his location were the unique subset of all who knew where he was.

It was a very short list, and it saddened him profoundly that Angela was at the top of it.

It was the problem of knowing, he thought. From knowing came wanting and from wanting, want. Before he knew Angela he never suffered from the want of her.

Now he wasn't sure who or what she was. Too many coincidences. Had she sent the men that night? Or was she merely the Judas?

"What do I do now, Moses?" he asked out loud.

Chapter 66

PEDRO REMEMBERED HIS boss telling him that the contract said the waterline had to be laid and operating by December 31, and the County was paying top dollar for the expedited schedule. The primaries were coming soon and the local County Commissioner, who was up for re-election, liked the idea of dedicating the new park just before Election Day.

The soft sand and clay on the Laguna-fronting land just north of Port Mansfield and just short of the ranch country was easy enough going. Even though it was the Tuesday before Thanksgiving, and they had more than a month to finish, he had to agree that it made sense to start a week earlier than planned. Christmas was coming and it would be hard to get the workers out once the *pachanga*s and *posadas* began.

At noon, Pedro pulled the fuel cut-off on the diesel engine and climbed down from the trencher to have lunch. The rest of the workers were already sitting in the crew-cab of the pick-up. They should have dug more than the four hundred feet before noon, but the trough cost them at least an hour.

The plan called for a straight run from the caliche roadbed to the new concrete pavilion on the edge of the Laguna, but there was an old water trough directly in the way. Pedro suggested they run the trench to miss it, but the foreman told Pedro to follow the dotted line on the printed plan. The men didn't want to move the concrete tub. It was heavy. But they respected old Pedro, the father figure of the group, and agreed to push it to one side if they could take an extra half hour for lunch.

As Pedro walked towards the pick-up to get his lunch bag, he stepped over the rill of trench sand and caught his foot on a snagged loop of grass. Before he could catch himself, he fell face forward into the 2' wide, 4' deep trench. Laughter erupted from the crew eating lunch in the truck, but then the three of them ran up to the trench to help Pedro out.

"What are you doin', old man?" one called out, teasing. "You trying to crawl into your grave?" The others laughed at the joke. Pedro wasn't hurt. He began trying to stand up when he saw something odd in the wall of the trench to his right. He drew closer to inspect it and used his fingers to dust it off.

"Hey, look here," he called out. "I think I found a ring."

"That's coming from your ears, Pedro," a crewmember said, laughing.

"No, really," he said. He began to use his fingers to try to dig the ring free. He pulled on it but it was stuck in the sand and clay. "Hey, give me that shovel," he ordered, and one of the men complied as they all gathered around to watch the amateur archeologist. Pedro took the shovel and carefully plied it behind the ring, using the handle as a fulcrum to pull it free.

"Dios, mios!" shouted one of the men suddenly.

"What?" Pedro said looking up, weary of the ribbing.

"Look!" he called out in shock, pointing into the trench.

The ring was freed from the dirt and with it the decomposing hand that wore it.

Chapter 67

WEDNESDAY MORNING, THE sheriff walked through the door of the Port Office with a bit more than his usual swagger.

"Where's Grider?" he asked Phyllis, who looked up at him through coke bottle lenses.

"Pardon?" she said.

"Grider, where is he?"

Jason, hearing his name from the back office, came out to see the sheriff standing at the counter.

"Sheriff? You looking for me?" Jason asked.

The sheriff pulled out a plastic zip lock baggy and dropped it on the counter. Jason looked down and saw it was a dirty gold ring. Confused and curious, he picked it up and studied the ring through the plastic film.

"I hear you might have somebody who could identify this," the sheriff said.

"Where did you find it?"

"In a trench at the new park Commissioner Ordan is putting in."

Jason's head jerked up, "Buried?"

"About three feet deep," the sheriff elaborated.

"So what's the big deal about a ring?" Jason asked.

"It's more about what was with it," the sheriff said, then added, "We're gonna need some DNA."

Jason drove up to Anajita Paredes' house on the western edge of the small town. She met him as he reached the front screen door. Through it he could see in her face a look of dread. Without a word she pushed the door out to let him in.

"Mrs. Paredes," Jason said quietly, "I need you to tell me if you've seen this before," then Jason handed her the ring. Her eyes followed it from his fingers to her palm, where it rested as her head hung down over it in deep study. Jason felt time stand still as he stared at the ring in her brown, worn hand.

A glint of light caught the flight of it as a tear fell from her cheek and struck the ring. Suddenly, her knees seemed to weaken, and Jason reached out to steady her, but she pushed him off and wobbled to a wooden straight back chair next to a table in her kitchen. She sat with her feet together, shoulders slumped, quietly sobbing.

"This here ring," she said, "I gave to 'Tavio on the day we was married." She looked up into Jason's face with a look of pleading that there was nothing more for him to tell her. She clung to the last fraying threads of hope as she searched his eyes for the truth she did not want. But found it.

"Where is he?" she said.

"The body is at the coroner's, ma'am. We're going to need Mr. Paredes' dentist's name and some hair from his brush," he said as delicately as he could manage, "to make sure, you understand."

Anajita already knew. From the day she slipped the ring on Octavio's finger twenty years ago, he had never once taken it off.

Chapter 68

IT WAS THE DAY BEFORE Thanksgiving and Cindy was too absorbed in the report she was keying for Secretary of the Interior Rode to pay much attention when she heard the fax machine starting up in the outer office. She had a deadline for next Monday morning and wanted all her work done so she could enjoy the long weekend at her in-laws where she and her husband had their traditional Thanksgiving Day dinner. Her husband was used to these late sessions by now, she knew, but she still felt guilty about it.

Then she recalled that she was expecting a copy she would need for the report, but thought she remembered being told it would be hand delivered. She figured Records decided to call it quits for the holiday too. Just as well, she thought. She could use a caffeine bump, so she went to the outer office to get a cup of coffee and the page off the fax machine.

She was blowing the hot off the top of the cup as she read the cover page.

"Document Number USDI 81-4356," she read. That sounded oddly familiar, but not what she had ordered from Records. She turned the page and read on.

It wasn't at all what she was expecting. "Goddamnit," she heard herself saying out loud as she walked briskly to the phone on her desk and dialed the Records Department.

"Hello?"

"Is this Records?" Cindy asked, impatient with the informality.

"Yes, but we're closed. Is that you Cindy?" a familiar voice asked.

"Doriel?" Cindy speculated.

"Yes, it's me; what's the matter?"

"This doc you faxed me, this is not what I asked for. I wanted the copy of the Resolution, remember?"

"Yeah, Alice is walking it over to you," Doriel replied.

"Oh," Cindy said, momentarily confused "Then what's this fax?"

"What fax?"

"Didn't you just send me a fax?"

"Not me, honey."

Cindy was interrupted by a tapping on the glass door to her office, which then opened. It was Alice. She waved a folder in the air, seeing that Cindy was on the phone, and Cindy motioned her to put it on the corner of her desk.

"Never mind, Alice is here," Cindy said, hanging up. "Thanks, Alice, Happy Thanksgiving!" she called out as the door closed. Cindy reached over and picked up the folder with the copy of the resolution and headed back to her computer in the workroom, sat down and began to key.

Something was distracting her, though. She stopped and walked back to the fax machine and picked up the document again, reading on.

Stamped across the top right margin was the document number and a Bates number. She read further on and an alarm went off in her head. "Whoa!" she said.

Cindy immediately picked up her cell phone and hit speed dial button one.

"Hello," a male voice answered.

"Secretary Rode?" she said. "Sir, I hate to bother you at home, but there's something here I think you need to see immediately."

Chapter 69

"YEAH, JASON, IT'S for sure. It's Octavio Paredes, all right," his friend at the Coroner's Office reported. "It was open and shut. The dental records were an exact match. We're not even going to send in the DNA."

"Well, I think we were all expecting that. What was the cause of death?"

"Homicide by gunshot wound to the chest," he said, "and it was a pretty clear shot through the heart."

"So, now we have a murder on our hands," Jason sighed.

"'Fraid so."

"What else do you know?" Jason asked.

"We've got the slug, but it's an odd caliber, nothing I've ever seen before. The Medical Examier has already sent it to Austin by Fed Ex. No telling how long that will take."

"Did the sheriff get all this already?"

"Yeah. He was in here about an hour ago. I think he was headed to inform the next of kin."

"Thanks," Jason said, feeling strange about expressing any kind of gratitude for the news. He didn't like the idea of the sheriff calling on Mrs. Paredes, but he was also relieved. He didn't want to have to repeat the experience he had with her the day before.

Tomorrow was Thanksgiving Day and he tried to imagine

what it would be like to have a stranger arrive at his door to report that Joan or Jack was dead. It made him shudder to think of it. He hurried to erase the thought. Then he wondered why he hadn't heard from Jack. It had been more than a week.

    He had a bad feeling.

Chapter 70

"CONGRESSMAN, THIS IS Bill Rode," Monde thought he heard over the din of noise then suddenly rose as the Aggies scored a touchdown on the Longhorns.

"Bill?" he shouted into the mouthpiece. "Hold on, let me get to where it's a little quieter," Monde said as he stepped outside the family room of his home overlooking Corpus Christi Bay. "Sorry, go ahead."

"Congressman, I've had a heck of a time tracking you down. Your chief, Mario, told me you had gone back to your district for Thanksgiving. I apologize for intruding, sir."

"Not a problem, Bill, we're just watching the game. My side's getting creamed anyway, I could use a little distraction."

"You might not want this one, sir," Rode said ominously.

"What's up?"

"Do you recall my referring to an easement document that we couldn't locate? It had to do with the Magne project."

"Vaguely, but I don't recall that you thought it a big deal," Monde remembered.

"Well, it's turned up and I hate to tell you this sir, but it's a Conservation Easement granted by the Mr. John Magne III, in 1981."

"What's the big deal?" Monde asked, knowing full well what the big deal was but hoping that Rode did not.

"I need to get you a copy of this so you can see it, but essentially, it grants to U.S. Department of the Interior a full and absolute easement for wildlife conservation over most all of the Magne Ranch. Essentially, we have complete control over any kind of project that would in any way affect the ecosystem there," Rode explained.

"Does it specify exactly what part?"

"Let me see," Rode paused as he read the document, "yes, well, it looks like it covers the entire Laguna Madre and twenty miles inland."

"Christ, that's nearly all the way to the highway!" Monde blurted.

"I don't know the land well enough to say," Rode replied.

"What's the term of it?" Monde asked hopefully.

"Perpetuity," Rode replied.

"Damn!" Monde blurted unintentionally, then recovered himself. "I don't think I've heard anything about this before, have you?"

"I've only been on the job for a year, Congressman, so, no, I haven't."

"Well, how do we even know this thing is authentic?" Monde tried to minimize it.

"I'd have to say it looks pretty authentic. I can have the Bates numbers and document number checked for duplicates, but if there are no other documents with these numbers, it would be difficult to challenge them."

"Still and all, Bill," Monde tried to pressure Rode, "I'm not sure the easement applies, do you?"

"Sir, as you know, we are bound by statute to enforce these easements as part of our charter for the Department of the Interior."

"Unless…" Monde interjected.

"Unless," Rode added, "Congress acts specifically to abandon the easement."

"Now, Bill, I don't think we need to go to all that trouble. Even if this thing turns out to be real, you have the authority to grant a variance, don't you?"

Rode paused and realized that he was at last delivered to one of the moments he had long agonized over before agreeing to take the president's appointment to the secretary post. It was classic, he thought. The Perfect Storm of factors: a powerful member of the committee that had oversight and budgetary control over his department, a powerful and wealthy fellow Texan donor to the president's campaign, and the momentum of a movement well underway with hundreds of millions at stake.

The Congressman was exposed and vulnerable, the political capital on the table was huge and the favors payable would be worth millions and millions of dollars. It was a political dream come true…or nightmare, depending on what he was made of.

Chapter 71

"I'VE GOT IT, MOM," Jason called out as he picked up the phone in the family room.

"Jason?" It was Jack.

"Where the hell have you been?" Jason heard himself shouting and realized what he'd bottled up.

"Listen, Jason," Jack said earnestly, "I don't want to tell you too much on this line. You ought to be careful too."

Jason could hear the stress in his brother's voice. "What's going on, Jack?" he asked in a lowered voice, worried.

"I don't know who set it up, but I got jumped late Sunday night in Galveston."

"What?"

"Yeah, my face is a little messed up, but otherwise, I think I'm ok," Jack reassured him. "I don't want you telling any of this to Mom, do you hear me?"

"Ok, ok, don't worry. What happened?"

"Some thugs came on the boat at the marina. I was trapped. They worked me over pretty good."

"Was it a robbery?" Jason asked.

"No, these guys weren't thieves. They were sent to warn me."

"Warn you!" Jason exclaimed. "About what?"

"I put two and two together and I'm pretty sure it's on

that report I told you about. Somebody doesn't want me talking about it."

"I thought you said it was changed and all the copies were gone?"

"All but one."

"Where is it?"

"In my head."

"Jesus," Jason blurted.

"It's a good time for praying, brother; I can tell you that," Jack said.

"So what are you going to do?"

"I'm going to get out of Dodge for awhile, that's for sure. Who knows what they'll do if they get nervous. So I figured I'd head for the Caribbean for awhile."

"Who's behind all this, Jack, do you know?"

"I'm not sure, but it has to be somebody who knew I was in Galveston. How else could they have found me?"

"Who knew, then?"

"I've thought about it hard in the last day or so and it's a pretty short list. There were the marina folks--but they would be a needle in a haystack--Joan, you and one other person."

"Who?"

"I'd rather not say on the phone."

"Anybody I know."

"No, I don't think so. It's been a real kick in the gut," Jack said.

"Jack, they found Octavio Paredes's body."

"Oh, no," Jack lamented, thinking of Anajita.

"He was shot."

"Shot! Oh my God. Where'd they find him?"

"Just north of town, buried under a water trough."

"So it turns out you were right to be suspicious, Jason."

"Here's one time I didn't want to be right, Jack."

"Who's suspected? Any ideas?"

"The forensics work isn't completed yet. I'm waiting for that before jumping to any conclusions. Right now it's an open question."

"This is getting curiouser and curiouser."

"By the way, the mayor's got a public hearing scheduled down at the Port Offices tomorrow. It's on that Laguna drilling issue."

Jack went totally silent.

"Jack? Are you still there?" Jason panicked.

"I'm here," Jack said succinctly, preoccupied with some intensive calculating.

"Jack, can you tell me where you are?" Jason asked.

"Can't tell you, brother, but I want you to put Mom on so I can wish her a happy Thanksgiving, and you need to back me up when I tell her I'm skiing in Steamboat, got that?"

"Yeah, sure, but what are you going to do?"

"What I always do," Jack said solemnly.

"Take care of yourself, be careful, Jack," Jason pleaded.

"Don't worry about me; now put Mom on."

"Hold it, Jack. Come to think of it, there is another person who knew you were in Galveston. Damnedest thing. Monday I got asked where you had taken the boat to and I didn't know any better, so I told him."

"Who?"

"The mayor, but surely…"

"I think I better hang up now. Quick, put Mom on," Jack said suddenly.

When he finished the call, Jack pulled open the bi-fold telephone booth door, but remained seated, bathed in a yellow cone of the only light on the dock. He figured he must have looked a little like a Rodin sculpture in an Edward Hopper watercolor. But his weak effort at humoring himself fell flat and hollow. He had never felt so alone.

His mind began its incessant re-calculating. A public hearing on an environmental issue meant someone somewhere was trying to get a permit. Anyone wanting to drill would need one. You'd need land for that, or at least leases. The big owners of the nearby Laguna Madre wetlands were the U.S. government and the Magne Ranch people. The mayor ram-rodded the resolution for support of the Laguna drilling through the board of aldermen. He wouldn't have any incentive to do that for the government. They wouldn't need him either. He is connected to the Magne Ranch people in a sycophantic sort of way.

Now, he thought, what is the one thing that could screw up this grand plan? A negative environmental report. That's why his report was changed, he suddenly realized. It was the last obstacle.

"I am the last obstacle!"

And finally, *the mayor knew he was in Galveston.*

This was a logical explanation, Jack thought, though not proved.

It could be as easily true that Angela is working for the Magnes, or both she and the mayor are. He couldn't be sure. He just couldn't be sure.

Jack left the phone booth and started back down the dock toward *Wist*. There was something bothering him, something that did not fit in his calculus, but what was it?

Chapter 72

JACK JOINED THE SHORTEST line and stirred impatiently. It had come to him in the night, just hours ago.

Octavio Paredes.

Murdered.

Buried just outside the Magne Ranch.

If these were connected he was in much more danger than he'd imagined. But worse, he had called her name out and the thugs heard it. "Angela." If she wasn't in with them, they might be looking for her next, and the thing that frightened him was that the extent they would go to had a name: Octavio Paredes.

If, if, if. He had to make a choice.

Jack dashed up to the Continental Airlines counter and threw his driver's license on the counter.

"I need to get to Harlingen, Texas as soon as possible," he said urgently.

The airline customer service agent keyed into her terminal. Paused. Keyed again. Paused again. Then keyed a third time. "I'm sorry, sir, we can get you to Houston, but all the flights to Harlingen are oversold for today."

"How about Brownsville or McAllen? Any city in the Rio Grande Valley," Jack insisted.

"I've checked. There's nothing until tomorrow."

"That's too late. I need to get there today, before two o'clock. How about stand-by?"

"I have to say, it doesn't look too promising, sir."

"Look, get me to Houston, and get me on the stand-by list from Houston to Harlingen."

"We can't do that from here, sir. You'll have to get on the list at the gate in Houston."

"Fine, get me to Houston and I'll take it from there."

The clerk picked up Jack's driver's license and began to enter his information for the flight.

"Hm," she said pausing, "that's odd. Sir," she mused, "you didn't say you already had a reservation from Houston to Harlingen."

"What?" Jack asked, confused by the question.

"I have here a reservation for a Jack Grider going to Harlingen from Houston at 11 A.M. today. Is that you?"

Jack stared at her in total bewilderment. He had made no reservations. He hadn't even decided to go back until two hours ago.

"Mr. Grider?" the clerk asked impatiently.

"Uh, yes," Jack blurted. "Yes, that's me."

Running for the gate, Jack wondered what was going on, but his adrenaline pump choked when he read the gate marquee.

"Delayed," it taunted him.

Whatever was going on, it didn't look like it was going to make much difference.

Chapter 73

THE MAYOR LOOKED nervously out the window from the Port Office conference room. The hearing was scheduled to start at three o'clock, but at a quarter to, the congressman had not arrived.

It was the Friday after Thanksgiving and not even the aldermen would commit enthusiastically to attending. It was their duty to show support, he thought, but even he would rather be watching the football game.

"Jason, have you heard anything?" the mayor asked.

"No sir, but I'm sure he'll be here pretty soon."

The mayor looked around the room and saw that all the chairs but one were empty. In the center of the front row sat a black woman, purse held on her lap, looking straight forward. The mayor turned to see what she was looking at but could see only the flag standing to the right of the head table. The mayor walked over to Jason, who was standing near the door, and leaned into his ear.

"What's she doing here?" he asked.

"Mrs. Paredes? I really don't know," Jason answered.

"That the fisherman's wife?"

"Yes, sir, it is."

"I can't see what any of this has to do with her," he thought out loud to Jason, who shrugged at the comment.

The sound of a vehicle driving up to the building sent the mayor dashing to the window again, only to find a red Jeep and two women walking toward the door. He looked up the road for any sign of the congressman.

Sophie and Angela walked into the conference room and were greeted by Jason, who explained that anyone wishing to testify during the hearing needed to fill out a card with name and address. Sophie and Angela each complied and sat in the second row, behind Anajita. Sophie patted her on the shoulder and Anajita, without looking back, touched the hand with her own.

A young woman entered the conference room but stopped Jason's instructions, saying she wouldn't testify. She was there from the *Valley Morning Star*, the Harlingen newspaper.

The sweep of the second hand slowly ascended to exactly three o'clock and drifted past. Jason checked his wristwatch. The mayor looked at his, then out the window. He was like a grim and fidgety sentinel there, Jason thought.

A van and two older cars pulled up to the building together and unloaded. Two men, three women and half a dozen children, aged six to fifteen, filed shyly into the conference room and stood at the back. Jason invited them to sit and they took their places in the last row. None wanted to fill out cards. Jason didn't recognize any of them.

Just afterward, a stream of local townspeople, whom he did know, began to trickle in, some taking cards, others not. By three fifteen, when two Aldermen arrived, there were no seats available and Jason had to bring more chairs and place them at the front of the room, where the mayor would sit. Among the last to arrive was Ocky, Anajita's and Octavio's son. He stood in a back corner of the room.

Jason was surprised to see as many people as this for a public hearing during a holiday weekend, or any other time, for that matter. Port Mansfield was not a hotbed of political sentiment.

He wasn't sure why they were there now and hadn't heard anyone talking about the hearing during the week.

The mayor suddenly seemed to brighten up and dashed out of the conference room and to the front door of the Port Office as a Suburban drove up and screeched to a stop by the steps. Out jumped Congressman Monde, two other men, and a woman carrying a stenographer's machine in one hand and what looked like a tape recorder in the other. Monde straightened his tie as he shook hands with the greatly relieved mayor while the others dashed past them and to the front of the conference room to set up.

"I'm sorry we're late, Mayor," Monde apologized calmly, and to Jason it seemed insincere.

"No problem," the mayor assuaged him, "but we ought to go in and try to get started as soon as we can."

The instant Monde strode into the conference room and saw so many chairs filled and people standing at the back of the room, his posture straightened and his body stiffened. A broad smile drew across his face and he metamorphosed into a completely different persona. He began grabbing hands to shake them and patting people on their shoulders, speaking in a booming voice, occasionally appearing to wave to someone across the room.

As is the nature of people in the Rio Grande Valley, they all nodded and smiled politely, a few of the men offering an *abrazo*. Monde worked his way to the front of the room and took a chair in the center of the table that separated the head of the room from the attendees. He leaned over and spoke softly to the stenographer, who nodded to some question. Then he looked down at a folder of papers she had put there for him, paging through, then arranging some around the table in front of him. When he seemed ready, he motioned with his fingers for the mayor to join him.

"What's all this?" Monde whispered into the mayor's ear.

"I dunno," the mayor said. "I guess folks are curious about the project. Probably just here to find out what happens next, stuff like that," he speculated, unsure himself.

"Any out-of-towners?" Monde asked as he surveyed the room.

"Maybe a few from down the Valley."

"Seems odd, Mayor," Monde said, straightening up and looking out into the audience as he smoothed his tie. He looked at the clock. It was three thirty. He nodded to the stenographer and rose.

"Bienvenidos!" he opened.

"English!" called out a Hispanic accented voice from the back of the room.

"Welcome!" Monde corrected himself, smiling. "Welcome to this public hearing on exploration in the Laguna Madre. I'm Congressman Lencho Monde and I'll be conducting the hearing today. Let me first say thank you all for attending to discuss this important topic today. As you know, your public servants rely on the advice and input from citizens like yourselves in the deliberations we undertake on your behalf. You should feel free to testify today as you see fit. All I ask is that you fill in a card so that we can have your name spelled correctly for the record that Alma here will be taking down on her recorder. Please speak clearly so she can get every word right."

"Joining me today are Dr. Alvin McGee, from the Army Corp of Engineers, and Gene Bardino, who runs the Weslaco office for the U.S. Fish & Wildlife Department. These gentlemen are here to answer any questions you may have about the topic today. And I might know a little bit too," he added, hoping to lighten the mood some.

Monde motioned to Jason, who stood at the back of the room, near the door, to bring up any cards that had been filled out.

Monde took the first one and read the name, "Sophie L.

Poole." He looked out into the audience and saw her stand. "Please come forward to the microphone, Mrs. Poole."

Sophie moved sideways, past Angela, then to the aisle and walked to the microphone, a folded piece of paper in her hand.

"That's *Mizz* Poole, Congressman," she corrected, and immediately began, "I've come today…"

"Excuse me, Ms. Poole," Monde interrupted her as he looked up to the mayor. "Mayor, could we get this mike turned on?"

Jason reached over and flipped the switch to the amplifier. Sophie tapped the mike and it registered in the speakers.

"Go ahead, Ms. Poole," Monde invited her.

"Thank you, Congressman," she began again. "I've come to testify against any drilling in the Laguna Madre." Sophie began to lay out an argument that explained the negative impact of drilling upon the grasses in the delicate Laguna Madre ecosystem. "No grasses, no shrimp…simple as that…and that means thousands of shrimpers and their families paying the price. But we humans are the least of the victims of this terrible idea. To literally thousands of species of flora and fauna, this is their entire world and more than half of the marine species in the Gulf rely on the Laguna Madre.

"Finally," she began to summarize, "I would like to know from the two gentlemen sitting with you there, Congressmen, what their response is to my warning."

Monde turned to one then the other of the two men. "Dr. McGee? Would you like to comment on the lady's testimony?"

"I would be happy to, Congressman," McGee started. "First, let me assure you that we and others have done exhaustive environmental impact studies of various kinds on the Laguna Madre ecosystem, and to a large extent, much of what the lady testified as a concern is accurate. However, that said, we believe the negative impacts are exaggerated as to scope and scale. While there may be small and temporary disruptions of the ecosystem, they are quite limited, with no long term deleterious effects. And, very importantly, any of these limited losses are more than offset by the benefits derived from the project."

"May I ask Dr. McGee a question?" Sophie asked Congressman Monde.

"Of course," he replied.

"Dr. McGee, you say that all the reports on the environmental impact of drilling say the threat is minor?"

"No, ma'am," McGee corrected her, "I'm saying all the *official* studies done by government agencies and others done by authentic and qualified academic and scientific institutions do. I'll admit there are some others that are done by special interest groups that do not agree, but in all fairness, they are proponents for particular agendas and are not objective. We do not consider those reliable."

"So, what you are saying is that you consider only the reports that agree with your position?" asked Sophie, turning aggressive.

"No, that's not what I said," McGee responded testily. "What I said was that our conclusions are based upon official and properly qualified findings."

"Double talk," Sophie said angrily.

Monde injected himself to provide a cooling down for the both of them. "Now, let's try to keep this civil. Is that all, Ms. Poole?"

"No Congressman; I have a question for Mr. Bardino."

Bardino sat up straight in his chair and looked at her.

"Mr. Bardino," she began, "wasn't it your office that issued the latest impact report on this issue?"

"I can't be sure it is the 'latest', ma'am," Bardino dodged.

"Well, you will agree that there was a report issued from your office in the last six months, won't you?" she pressed.

Bardino seemed to be thinking, and after a few seconds admitted, "Yes, I think that's right."

Monde was irritated by Bardino's tone and bureaucratic dodging. "Is that it, Ms. Poole?" he interjected.

"No, Congressman, I still have one more question for Mr. Bardino."

"There are others who deserve their turn, Ms. Poole," Monde admonished her.

"Just this one last question, Congressman," she pressed.

"Very well," he acquiesced.

"Mr. Bardino," Sophie asked, "this last report you refer to, did it in fact say that the impact of the drilling project upon the ecosystems of the Laguna Madre was minor?"

"Not in those words, exactly," he responded.

"In what words then," Sophie insisted. "Why don't you read us the words?"

Gene Bardino looked over to the congressman with a question on his face, "Would that be all right, Congressman?"

"Ms. Poole," Monde sighed, "is this really necessary? There are many other people here today who are due a chance to testify…"

"Let her talk," a voice called out from the back of the room. Other voices joined in a mumbled agreement.

"Fine, go ahead, then," Monde proceeded to assuage the crowd.

Bardino shifted in his chair, then reached into his black briefcase and brought out a yellow covered report. "I have it right here," he said.

"Read the conclusion," Sophie demanded.

Bardino opened the booklet and turned a few pages to the "Executive Summary." He cleared his throat, then began to read:

"In conclusion, there is no credible evidence that the drilling project as described will have any intermediate or long term negative effects upon the ecosystems of the Laguna Madre area proximate to or distant from the subject site."

Bardino looked up at Sophie as he heard the stenographer keying in the last of his words, and was surprised to see her smiling.

"Thank you, Mr. Bardino," she said, and sat down. Sophie put on the best face she could, but she knew she hadn't shaken him and nearly all her cards were played. As she walked back to her seat, she met Angela's eyes. Angela could see the deep disappointment in her mother's face and patted her knee when she had sat down next to her.

Monde looked down at the next card and read, "Candelario Gomez."

An elderly man rose to his feet, crossing his arms awkwardly, and asked if it was all right for his son to speak for him. Another voice called out, "And me, too."

Monde sensed that many wanted the young man to speak in their stead and asked if any of the others who turned in cards agreed, some did. A young man of about twenty years old came forward to the microphone then took out a sheet of paper and unfolded it.

"My name is Juan Gomez and my father and I, and many of the others here, take our living from the Laguna. We trap crabs and collect bait," he explained, "and also work as guides for the sports fishermen who come here."

"Very well, Juan," Monde encouraged him, "proceed."

The young man held up the sheet so it faced the congressman. "It says on this paper that drilling in the Laguna is going to kill the grasses and that when they are gone, our fishing will go too. Is that true, sir?" he asked sincerely.

"Let me see that, son," Monde said, beckoning him to bring the paper forward.

"No, read it, Juan, the part that's marked," Sophie stood up and demanded.

Juan looked at her, then the congressman. Monde nodded and Juan looked down at the paper and began to read.

"In conclusion," he carefully pronounced each word, "there is overwhelming evidence that the drilling project as described will have inter, inter," Juan struggled with the word.

"Intermediate," a strong male voice boomed from the back of the room, and continued, "Intermediate and long term negative effects upon the ecosystems of the Laguna Madre area proximate to and distant from the subject site."

Angela bolted upright and spun in her chair with a gasp, "Jack!" The room began to stir in confusion.

Jack Grider walked briskly up to the mike and stood next to the young man. "Good job," he said to him, "I ought to know. I wrote it."

"You are out of order, sir," Monde bellowed indignantly.

"I am here to testify," Jack said.

Bardino lunged over to Monde and demanded, "He didn't fill in a card! It's too late!" Then he looked at Jack and found Jack's glare boring a hole through his head.

Monde struggled to regain control and pushed Bardino aside, then demanded, "Who are you, sir?"

"I'm Jack Grider," he said, "the man who wrote the impact report."

Monde suddenly realized the situation. Somehow he had to manage a soft landing. A camera flash dazed him for an instant, reminding him that the newspaper reporter was witnessing the entire event, and to his left, the stenographer and a tape recorder were memorializing whatever she missed.

His keen political instincts kicked in.

"Mr. Grider, yes, yes," he said as he gathered himself for his next tactical assault. "We appreciate your being here today for this hearing." Monde then looked over and past Jack and spoke to the crowd. "We are glad to have anyone who can help cast light on decisions before us," he said, dismissing Bardino's objection. But then he turned to his right and said, "Mr. Bardino, is Mr. Grider still employed by U.S. Fish & Wildlife?"

"Ah, no," Bardino answered, unsure of what Monde was doing.

"And when did he separate from public service?" Monde asked, leading.

"Why, Grider was terminated almost two months ago," Bardino answered.

"Terminated, did you say?" Monde further led him along.

"Yes, Jack Grider was fired for dishonesty."

Jack was shocked to hear what Bardino was saying.

"What exactly do you mean by 'dishonesty'?" Monde asked.

Bardino was in his groove now, fully in tune with Monde. "Well, Congressman, as you know, I cannot disclose personnel matters to the public."

"But you did say he was fired for 'dishonesty,' is that right?" Monde intentionally repeated for full effect. "Isn't that covered by privacy?"

"No," Bardino explained, "that's public record. It's the details that we cannot discuss."

"You're a Goddamn liar!" Jack bellowed.

"Am I?" Bardino yelled back, rising as if to challenge Jack physically.

Monde pushed Bardino back down into his chair. "Gentlemen, gentlemen!" he called out, "Order!"

"That's a lie, Monde," Jack said strongly.

"Grider," Bardino declared, "you had your chance to protest the charges. You had your due process. You didn't take it!"

"I don't know what you're talking about," Jack yelled back, feeling confused by the accusation. Then he remembered the letters from USFWL and how he threw them away unopened. He thought them unimportant. He was done with them. He didn't want to play any of their games anymore.

"Mr. Grider," Monde said, interrupting his thoughts, "are you still insisting on testifying?"

Jack's head was swimming. He realized that they wouldn't make this easy, that they were playing hardball now and he might be far out of his league. He wondered why he thought he could beat them. How could he? It was the entire U.S. government. It was power and money and influence beyond any resources he could ever assemble in three lifetimes. He could feel Bardino's invective cutting through him, laughing at him, snuffing out the last of his waning hope.

Then in the din of noise and confusion that tangled his mind in flashing and convoluting images and conflicting memories, he heard a soft voice calling, "Jack. Jack, wake up." He swung around to his right and there, not six feet away, was Angela. Their eyes locked. Suddenly he felt a jolt of electrical energy surge through him, as if a beam of atomic particles flowed between them. He gasped, and for a frozen instant in time, the whole world around him went silent. He felt a warmth wash over him and he was at once calm and serene, and he saw light flowing from her face to him. She smiled and he felt at total peace.

"Mr. Grider!" a voice boomed, intruding from another world. He turned and looked at Monde. "Do you want to testify?"

Jack looked at him and calmly said, "Yes, Congressman, I do."

"What the young fellow was reading, I wrote. That's the true executive summary from my report. The one Bardino has is a fraud."

"That's a serious accusation, Mr. Grider," Monde intoned grimly. "Can you prove that?"

"How can I prove it? You'll have to take my word," Jack said firmly.

"Well, sir, can you produce the original of this alleged version of the report at least?" Monde challenged him.

Jack stood silent. He knew he had no such original or copy. They were all gone, discarded, like so much of the rest of his life.

"I repeat, sir, can you produce that alleged original report?"

After a tortured pause Jack replied, "No, I can't."

The room buzzed with talk among members of the audience, and Bardino leaned back in his chair, put his hands in his pockets, stretched his legs, crossed his ankles and smiled superiorly into Jack's face.

"Ah can," came a clear and definite voice from the front row. The room went completely silent as Anajita Paredes rose to her feet. She raised a yellow booklet into the air above her and everyone's eyes were drawn up to it.

"And you are...?" Monde began to ask.

"Anahida Paredes," she said proudly and boldly. "Ah bought this here report with a whole lot of other personal stuff from Mr. Jack Grider, stuff he was throwin' out. He didn't even know ah had it." She then opened the booklet to the "Executive Summary" and stepped forward to pass it before Monde and the other men and the stenographer. Monde moved to take it, but she pulled it back from him. "Not so fast, honey. They's some real folk I wanna see this furst." She then turned to the audience, and many gathered close to inspect it.

It was just as Jack had said. The reporter climbed over every person between her and Anajita and nearly fell to the floor just in front of her. "There now, chald," Anajita said, pulling her to her feet. "Here," she said handing the booklet to the reporter, "now go do your duty."

Jack was dumbfounded and the only thing that closed his gaping mouth was the feel of Angela's lips collecting his into a warm, soft kiss.

The room exploded in cheers and applause, while Monde and his group quickly wound their way through the crowd to the door and fled to the Suburban.

The newspaper reporter ran for her car, screaming into her cell phone something she had always wanted to say, "Doug! Honest to God, hold the presses!"

Chapter 74

OCKY TURNED TO HIS mother. "Mom, who was that tall skinny woman you were talking to at the hearing?"

"Why, that was Angela Poole, hon, why do you ask?"

"Well, I was curious. I'd seen her before."

"Ah knows you did, Ocky," Anajita told him.

"She's that woman with that red Jeep I liked so much, isn't she?"

"Yes, she has that red Jeep, all right."

"Well, then, she's the lady who bought all those papers we got from that Mr. Grider."

"That's right, hon, she is."

"Well, I don't understand something," Ocky said, scratching his head.

"What's that?"

"How did you end up with that yellow booklet, then. I know I remember her giving me fifty dollars for the whole box and that booklet was in it, I am sure of it."

Anajita smiled at her son. "Well, Ocky, honey, let's just say that sometimes even the angels need a little help."

Chapter 75

THE SHERIFF WAS SURPRISED when his secretary told him it was DPS Crime Lab on the line. The Medical Examiner only Fed-Ex'd the slug out Wednesday. There was no way there could be a report already. It must have been lost in shipment.

"Sheriff Morales," he answered in his best and most officious tone.

"Sheriff, this is Morgan Cade with the Crime Lab here in Austin."

"What's the problem, Mr. Cade?" the sheriff rushed him to the point.

"Problem? Oh, no Sheriff, no problem. I was just calling to give you the results of the ballistics test on the specimen we received this morning. In fact, they all ought to be this easy."

"What do you have?"

"Well, Sheriff, you must be just plain lucky. The specimen is a .43 caliber bullet and it was fired by a Merkel 543," Cade said cheerfully.

"A what?" the sheriff asked bewildered.

"Merkel 543, the 1924 model, actually."

"What the hell is a Merkel and how could you know all that?"

"It couldn't be an odder slug, Sheriff. It's an antique and there aren't many of them."

"I don't see how that is any help," the sheriff complained. "I mean, who the hell around here would have anything like that?"

"That's the thing," Cade began, "there's only the one."

"Great," the sheriff sighed, "a needle in a haystack."

"Sheriff?" Cade asked in a didactic tone, "have you ever spent much time up around New Braunfels?"

"What? No, I can't say that I have?"

"Figures."

"What do you mean, 'figures'?" the sheriff began to become irritated.

"No offense, Sheriff, but if you had you'd know about Germans."

"Germans?"

"They are a whole different breed of people."

"Cade, or whoever the hell you are, I don't have time for this bullshit. What the hell does any of this have to do with the ballistics report?" the sheriff boomed.

"I'll tell you. The Merkel Firearms Company has been building rifles in Stuttgart, Germany since about 1895. They make a very fine rifle, let me tell you."

Sheriff Morales sighed quietly. There was no stopping an *Anglo* lab geek when he launched into a history lesson. He decided it would all go faster if he just listened.

"Very fine rifle. And something else Germans are real serious about, and that's record keeping. These folks are so proud of their rifles that they have kept test slugs from every rifle they ever made, clear back to 1898, and about ten years ago they photographed all those test slugs and put them on computer. Then Interpol connected that all up to the web and, well, we have access to all their records now too."

"Mr. Cade, I'm not sure what all this history lesson has to do with us here," the sheriff interjected.

"I'm sorry, Sheriff, what I'm trying to tell you is that they know who bought the rifle."

Marcie was startled when she saw the sheriff abruptly jump to his feet, looking as if he'd seen a ghost. She quickly rose from her secretarial desk and ran into his office, thinking he was having a heart attack. "Sheriff, are you all right?"

"I'm not sure," he said, obviously dazed. "Marcie, call over to Judge Morello's office. Tell him I'm coming over, and tell him it's Goddamn important," he yelled as he headed out the door.

Chapter 76

"WHAT THE HELL IS going on with the state permit?" Magne began the instant Festor Stubb answered his cell phone.

"Mr. Magne?" Stubb asked, confused.

"You know Goddamn well who it is. I just by accident ran into Gary Grosse, the executive director at Texas Parks & Wildlife, and he had some interesting advice for me. You know what that was?" Magne asked sarcastically.

"No sir, I'm not sure what you're talking about."

"I'll tell you what I'm talking about. He said that, just because the feds hold public hearings on the project doesn't mean we don't have to get state approval and hold separate hearings. You were supposed to take care of all the state permitting for the drilling project and the one most important state agency in the deal tells me we haven't even applied yet."

"No, Mr. Magne, there must be some kind of mistake. I've had someone on that and they even sent the needed papers up to Fenre Pease in New York," Stubb explained.

"Then why does the head of Texas Parks think we haven't?"

"I can't understand it, sir, but I am sure it is wrong. Let me find out and I'll report right back to you."

"You sure better do something, and fast, Goddamn it," Magne bellowed and hung up.

Stubb's hands were shaking as he tapped out Sam Kiel's phone number and listened to the ring tone. It was a hell of a way to start a Monday, he thought. When he got no answer, he cursed that he had apparently misdialed the number. He hung up and more carefully dialed. It rang. Still no answer and no message taking service. Then he remembered that Sam was taking an extended weekend.

He wondered what Magne was talking about. He picked up the *Houston Chronicle* page he had folded to show the article on the public hearing in Port Mansfield. There in the picture that accompanied the story, standing in the crowd, but unidentified in the caption, was Sam Kiel, proof that Sam was on the job. He dialed the number again. Still no answer.

Chapter 77

SOPHIE POOLE HATED technology. Anything that needed a one hundred page manual or a tab for "Help" was just too complicated to bother with. What ever was wrong with just buttons, she would complain.

But she had promises to keep. Anajita had brought over an old roll-paper fax she had bought on one of the many garage sales she hijacked, and Angela changed the settings so that there would be no return address or phone number information on any fax page. So Sophie's job was reduced to essentially dialing the number and feeding in the picture. It was same picture she used in the Historical Society's November newsletter. And the same one she submitted to the *Morning Star* for the feature story in the Sunday paper on the historical museum project.

"A thousand words," she said to herself as she watched the photograph crawl through the machine.

She hated technology, all right, but there were some things she hated more.

It was late Monday afternoon in Port Isabel when she got it out.

Chapter 78

MONDE STORMED PAST Cindy and right into Secretary Rode's office.

"Congressman!" Rode said, surprised, suddenly seeing him in his office, especially on the Monday morning after Thanksgiving.

"We've got to talk. Right now," Monde said urgently.

"It's ok, Cindy," Rode reassured his assistant who followed Monde in. "Close the door."

Monde sat in the first chair he came to and faced Rode.

"Look, Bill, you've got to put this Magne conservation easement to bed. The hearing fiasco has got the press all heated up, and we just don't need any extra problems right now," Monde said earnestly.

"I'm not so sure I can do that, Congressman," Rode replied.

"Oh, you *can* do it, Bill, we know that and you *will* do it," Monde ordered him.

"Yes, Congressman, technically I *can* do it but I've got the *Washington Post* breathing down my neck now. They picked up on that story. Hell, it made the wires. It's all over the country."

"That guy Grider is a hack!" Monde exploded. One of your departments canned him, for Godssake. It's just sour grapes."

"We're looking into it, I promise you that, but it isn't as

clear as you make it sound. I've got the FBI looking into it."

"The FBI! Are you frigging nuts?" Monde leapt to his feet and stood over Rode. "Let's get this clear, Rode. You call them off or else! You don't know what you're fooling with here," he shouted.

Rode looked sternly up into Monde's face and intoned in a calm and serious voice, "Congressman, I think I do. My advice to you, sir," he said, "is that you might want to start looking for an exit from this matter."

Monde straightened up as if he'd been struck on the nose with a rolled up newspaper. He didn't like what he heard, but worse, he didn't like what it meant.

Congressman Lencho Monde sat behind his desk, looking out over the mall from the window in the capitol building. The low, gray clouds and the falling snow drew a dim curtain over the distant Lincoln Memorial and gradually blotted out the top of the Washington Monument, eventually the buildings became mere shadows in the white-out of the advancing blizzard. The world looked cold and forbidding, and it felt like it was closing in on him.

The conservation easement Rode's people found would kill any chance of Magne's drilling wells in the Laguna, without Rode's granting a variance, and Rode was playing hardball. Monde was angry that he was in this position. Rode, that son of a bitch, probably had it all along, Monde thought.

He was cornered. If he didn't deliver for Magne, it would be the end of his political support. But if he did, and the FBI were to confirm Jack Grider's claim that the report was a fraud, Bardino would cop a deal and turn state's evidence, and the trail could lead right up to his office. He could be in serious trouble with the House Ethics Committee, or worse. Either way, he was finished. It was the crossroads of his career. He saw himself, though, as more in the crosshairs of it.

Monde's mind drifted back to his childhood. He saw his

mother's bloody hands, cut by the cotton bolls. Then he saw her nursing her aching back harvesting lettuce. She died young. Simply worn out. At every point in his life when he could not see how he could go on, he remembered her admonition to him, "Lencho, never give up!" She never gave up.

Monde rose to his feet and walked briskly to the empty outer office with a new determination. He would survive, he declared to himself. All he needed to do was pick the course that was in his best interest, no matter what, and never give up. He would have to see to his own first. And the strongest choice, both in money and political force, was John Magne. That was the best way to go and that was what he'd do. He grabbed his coat, headed back to Rode's office. He'd make a deal at any cost.

A clicking sound and a red light on the fax machine began to blink, and slowly a page crawled out and fell into the tray. Monde looked at it from across the desk and squinted. He came quickly around and picked it up to look at it more closely. It was a photograph. John Magne smiling broadly, his arm wrapped around Marco Luz, both hamming it up for the camera. Across the bottom was printed:

"Just thought you ought to know what John Magne is planning for your future."

Monde looked to see if there was a cover sheet and finding none, studied the top and bottom margins of the fax to see the sender's information. Blank. Someone, somewhere out there, was sending him a message. He studied the picture. And he thought, then he put down his coat and sat down.

His mind again drifted back to his childhood. He remembered sleeping with his little brother on the canvas cot by the window. South Texas nights in summer were hot and the breeze was the only thing that made sleeping possible. Every morning, he would be stirred to waking by the cackling, taunting laughter of the Chachalacas. It always made him smile to hear them calling back and forth from the trees. Roosters that could fly, he thought of them.

He wished he could hear them tonight.

Chapter 79

AMESHA SPENTAS WAS TEN minutes early for her Tuesday morning appointment with the lead attorney at Fenre Pease on the Magne I.P.O. and was surprised that his secretary showed her in the moment she arrived.

"Amesha," he greeted her.

"Good morning, Mr. Casady."

"Have a seat. You seemed disturbed when you called yesterday afternoon. What's the problem?" he asked.

"It's the Magne IPO, sir. I am beginning to get some bad vibes."

"'Bad vibes'," he echoed. "Have you gone sixties on us? You're a bit young for that, you know," he joked.

"Well, first it was that missing document, that 'easement' that was missing from the Department of the Interior. It didn't feel right; I mean, the government losing documents?"

"Believe me, Amesha, it's not unusual."

"Perhaps, but then there was this," she said as she handed him a copy of a newspaper account of the Port Mansfield hearing.

He skimmed it quickly. "Hmm. And so what was the determination on this disgruntled employee? Anything to his claim?"

"There may well be. The major papers are now starting to pick up on it."

"Well, Amesha, you know there's going to be the usual opposition on these environmentally sensitive projects. Happens all the time. It doesn't mean that the government won't ignore them or work out some benign mitigation."

"Normally, sir," she said carefully, "I would agree with you. These issues in themselves may not be an impediment to the project going forward. But there is one more I found today."

"Another? What?" he asked.

"Do you recall my report at our working group on this, when I said that I had received all the state paperwork and proofs of approvals?"

"Yes, last week or so, wasn't it?"

"Well, when I ran the due diligence on them I got an odd response from the Texas Department of Fish & Wildlife."

"What was that?"

"They had issued no permit. Furthermore, they had never even received an application for the Magne project. Sir, I was given incorrect information."

"Who was responsible for that?" he asked.

"Well, sir, my contact was through Calvin Richter."

"Now, let me get this straight. Are you telling me that you were given papers confirming the state processes were successfully completed and that these were incorrect?"

"I say 'incorrect', sir, but in my opinion, I think they were fraudulent."

"That's pretty strong language, Amesha," he said.

"Yes, sir, and I don't use it loosely. I think Mr. Richter, or whoever was his source on this, may have been trying to put something over us."

"But, Amesha, that just doesn't make any sense. Richter would know that this would be discovered and that it would be his head if he was negligent, or worse. There is no way to fake the permitting. The state would never let the project start. Why in God's name would Richter or anyone supporting the project be a part of that?"

"You make a good point, sir, I don't know."

The lead attorney thought quietly for a moment. This offering would mean millions to Fenre Pease and neither he nor any of the other year-end bonus recipients would want the deal lost, especially due to some silly technicality.

"Amesha," he said at last, "if you have to, I want you to get on a plane and go down to Texas and get to the bottom of this. But keep it to yourself. If this is some sort of mix-up, we don't want the firm embarrassed by an over-reaction. But if it is more serious than that, something we can't fix quickly, then I need to know this as soon as possible. We're just about to put this out on the market, for God's sake," he said nervously.

"I can be in Austin tomorrow," she said as she rose to go back to her office.

"Oh," the attorney interjected, "I heard a rumor around the office that Congressman Monde might not be running for re-election. Have you heard anything like that?"

"Yes, sir, I have," she replied confidently.

The attorney looked pensive, but then said, "I want to know what you know as soon as you know it, you hear?"

"Yes, sir," she said, going out the door. Amesha did what she could to suppress her urge to skip down the hall, but when she closed the door to her office behind her, she couldn't help but dance.

She knew all she needed to know.

She knew she would take off early today, and take tomorrow off too, maybe take in a matinee on Broadway or head over to the Guggenheim. She earned it. She also knew she'd be giving her two weeks notice on Friday.

She knew she wasn't flying to Texas.

And she knew the Magne IPO was DOA.

Chapter 80

SHERIFF MORALES TOOK a deep breath and steeled himself for what he had to do next. He dialed John Magne's cell phone number that he had gotten from Magne's executive secretary, Pat.

"Mr. Magne," the Sheriff began.

"Who is this?" Magne asked sternly.

"Sheriff Morales, sir."

"Morales? How'd you get this number?"

"Your secretary, sir. It's very important."

"Listen, Morales, I'm in Austin right now, and I have to go into a meeting, couldn't this wait until day after tomorrow when I get back?" Magne said testily.

"If you say so, sir," the sheriff said, surprised by his own authoritative tone and amazingly good luck. "You won't be back sooner then?"

"No, can't possibly. Call me day after tomorrow," Magne said quickly, and instantly hung up.

The sheriff dialed the County Judge's office.

"Judge," the sheriff reported, "looks like he'll be off the ranch tomorrow. That's going to be our best day, I think."

"Good. Now Sheriff, I want you to call up DPS and get some troopers to accompany your deputies into the ranch, just in case there's any trouble. A show of force will keep things peaceful."

"Yes, sir," the sheriff said tentatively.

"Listen, Morales, I know you're nervous about dealing the Magnes, but you have got to remember who the hell you work for. No one's above the law. You've got probable cause; Judge Helms has given you the search warrant. You have no choice but to go in there and look for that rifle."

"Yes, sir," Morales replied, sounding like a scolded child.

The echo of it replayed in his ears after the county judge had hung up. He was afraid, all right, but not in the way the judge thought. Elections were around the corner. He had come to rely upon the favors and political support Magne money bought. He was addicted, and he wasn't sure how he'd survive the withdrawal.

He suddenly had a thought. Maybe there was a way to cover all bases. He dialed Jason Grider at the Port Mansfield Port Office.

"Grider," he said, "we're going to serve a search warrant on the Magne Ranch tomorrow, want to come along?"

"The Magne Ranch? Why?" Jason asked, both curious and careful.

"Ballistics," the sheriff replied. "The rifle slug matches a gun registered to John Magne."

"You're kidding me," Jason blurted in shock. "Magne?"

"'Fraid so. So are you in or not?"

"In. When and where do we hook up?" Jason asked.

The sheriff put the phone down and smiled. He knew that the mayor and Magne were tight and that the word would get to him through Grider. Later, the sheriff would be able to remind Magne that he had given him a head's up. He'd owe him.

Jason put the phone down and stared at it, still trying to reconcile what he had just heard. Magne? Was it possible? Why would someone as rich and powerful as John Magne use his own rifle to shoot someone so innocuous and insignificant as Octavio Paredes? It just didn't make sense. At least not yet.

The wind was whipping up in the marina and the sound of a halyard slapping a sailboat mast suddenly triggered a memory. It was the night that Octavio disappeared. Jason was on the porch looking across the Laguna. A norther was approaching. It had just turned dark. That's when he had heard it. The muffled popping sound. My god, he thought, that was the rifle shot!

His thoughts were interrupted.

"Jason," the mayor called out as he came into the Port Office. "How're things going?"

"Ok, Mayor," he replied.

"Anything new?" the mayor asked as he always did.

"No, sir," Jason lied. "Not really."

Chapter 81

MONDE ROSE FROM HIS desk when the man and woman came through his door. He was effusive in attention and invited them to sit down, being sure to seat them so they had the best view out the window to the mall and the monuments beyond.

"Congressman Monde, I am FBI Special Agent Conrad Cole and this is my partner Agent Maureen Spikes. Thanks for taking time from your busy calendar to see us today on such short notice."

"It's my pleasure to be of service to you in any way I can, always," he said cheerily. "What can I do for you?"

"We are investigating allegations that a report issued by the Weslaco, Texas office of U.S. Fish & Wildlife may have been tampered with. Are you familiar with this matter sir?" Cole asked.

"As you know, Mr. Cole, I was present at the public hearing in Port Mansfield when these allegations were raised. I was back home for the Thanksgiving Day holiday, and thought I could save some of our people from having to give up their holiday with their families, so I volunteered to run over there and preside."

"I see," Cole intoned. "What can you tell us about this claim?"

"Well, I am just as surprised as anyone else about this thing. I don't really know much about the goings on in every government agency office in my district. I just can't," Monde said, carefully choosing his words, "I can't say that I really know any of the folks involved in this, to tell you the truth. So, I'd have to say that I don't really know much that would be of help to you."

"So you were unfamiliar with the report before the hearing?" Cole probed.

"Oh, I think I knew there was an impact report, but I can't say that I actually ever saw it before then."

"This man, Eugene Bardino, are you acquainted with him?"

"He's the fellow who was at the hearing for U.S. Parks & Wildlife, isn't he?" Monde asked.

"Yes, sir, he was. According to the transcript, he was seated next to you."

"Yes, I remember. No, I can't say that I know him, other than officially, that is."

"This Mr. Jack Grider. Did you know him?"

"No, I never met him, at least not before the hearing when he testified."

Cole looked down at a notebook in his hand and read briefly.

"John Magne," Cole began. "We understand that you and Mr. Magne are closely associated."

"Associated? Well, he is one of my constituents, you know. A strong supporter of mine. One of a many, actually. We've had dinner a few times I guess, but 'associated'? That might be an exaggeration," Monde tiptoed.

"So you wouldn't describe your relationship with Mr. Magne as anything but as constituent, is that right?"

"Well, yes, that's essentially right. I am friendly with many of my constituents, Mr. Cole. I tend to be familiar with them. It's part of the job."

"I understand," Cole said. He turned to his partner and asked her if she had any questions.

"Are you familiar with the firm of Stembark Engineering of Dallas, Texas, Congressman?" she asked.

Monde leaned back and tapped his fingertips, as if making a tent of them helped him think. "Let me see," he said, looking up at the ceiling. He scoured his brain, trying to remember if any of the Stembark principals were listed as campaign donors or event sponsors. He was pretty sure their only connection to him was the "no-show" job they provided for Monde's younger brother. Surely Cole couldn't know that. Even if he did, there was no law against a congressman's brother having a job.

"Sounds familiar," he said at last, "but I am not exactly sure how."

"But you have no dealings with the firm yourself, then," agent Spikes probed.

"Me, directly? No," Monde said, pursing his lips.

Cole rose and thanked Monde and both agents left.

Monde stared at the door as it closed. "Caca doodle doo," he muttered to himself, and it was getting deep fast.

Maureen Spikes didn't turn her head as she walked with Conrad Cole through the hall leading out of the capitol, but asked in a matter of fact monotone, "So, Connie, what do you think?"

"Well, agent Spikes," he said, drawing in a deep breath, "I'd be more interested in hearing a woman's intuition on the matter."

"Isn't that gender biased?" she asked drolly.

"Depends," he replied.

"Depends on what?" she asked.

"Depends on if you're right. In which case it'll be skill."

"Hmm," she said. "Well, I'd have to say he's lying, then."

"You're right," he said, "and you know how I know that?"

"Men's intuition?" she suggested.

"No, but close. Men's imperative," he answered.

"Men's imperative? What's that?" she asked, curious.

"It's why we have a democracy," he said vaguely.

"I don't get it," she confessed.

"Mostly, men in power are sure that whatever it is that they are doing is for the good of everyone else. So anything they do to advance that is justified. Including creating their own versions of the truth," Cole explained.

"How's that different for women," Spikes challenged him.

Cole pulled up and stopped and without turning his head from his gaze upon the distant Washington Monument, said, "It isn't."

Chapter 82

JUNIOR MAGNE KNEW HIS father didn't approve of his hard drinking on the weekends and insisted that weekdays he wasn't to have his first beer before noon. But these were extenuating circumstances, he thought. It was Wednesday, "Hump Day." His father was out of town, and driving the ranch roads was sometimes boring, and boring could make him pretty thirsty. So, just today, he thought, he'd bend the rule a little and have a couple at ten and go easy in the evening, to sort of even things out.

By eleven he had also taken more than a few shots from the bottle of Cuervo Gold he kept in his truckbed tool box. He sat in his pick-up, looking west and listening to a Randy Travis tune on his CD player, enjoying the growing alcohol buzz. With a squint he could see what looked like the beginnings of a cloud coming toward him, but he soon realized it was a rising cloud of dust.

Sheriff Morales drove the lead car, followed by two other Sheriff Office cruisers and two Texas DPS cars. Jason rode with the sheriff. The advantage of surprise was hard to achieve with an eight mile private road to run between the highway and the Magne's main ranch house, so he pushed the accelerator down and drove for it as fast as he safely could over the caliche road.

Junior started his truck and drove toward the dust cloud,

and within minutes realized it was a line of cars headed for *Casa Blanca*. He sped up, coming from the opposite direction. He wondered if something had happened to his father.

When he had made it to the house, he found the five law enforcement vehicles parked in the circular drive at the foot of the main stairs to the front porch. It looked like half a dozen or so officers were standing and talking to one another. Three others were ascending the stairs to the front door.

Junior left his truck running and ran up the porch.

"What's going on, Sheriff?" he asked, worried.

"Junior," the sheriff said, "we have a search warrant for the ranch," as he handed the folded document to him.

"A search warrant!" Junior blurted in surprise. "What for?"

"We have a signed warrant from a judge, Junior, that's all we have to tell you," the sheriff said.

"Well, you can't come onto our property. My father will have all you fired!" Junior was yelling now.

One of the DPS officers stepped forward and got between Junior and the sheriff. "Do you have some identification, sir?" he asked.

"Identification!" Junior glowered at him. "Tell him, Sheriff. Tell this sonofabitch who I am."

The DPS trooper didn't change the tone or cadence of his voice at all when he asked again, "Sir, please show me some identification."

Junior was livid and the surge of anger was unimpeded by the restraint of sobriety. He turned and began to walk to his pick-up to get his cell phone. As he did, the DPS officer saw a gun rack through the windshield of Junior's truck. "Stop!" the officer called out.

"Stop, my ass," Junior called back over his shoulder.

The officer began to run at Junior, but Junior was far enough ahead that when he broke into a run for his pick-up all he had to do was jump into the seat and put it in gear to escape. Realizing he couldn't catch him, the officer turned and ran for his car, and Jason and the other officers followed suit.

Junior wasn't sure what he was running from but he floored the pick-up and tried to shake the pursuers by winding through the maze of narrow roads that wound through the oak wood.

When he seemed to have lost them, he pulled up and went for his cell phone. He dialed his father's cell.

Chapter 83

STUBB WAS EXPECTING something different from what he found at 4200 Smith School Road in Austin. Instead of a government offices complex, he had to follow a long winding blacktop road that led from the street, across a field and up to the edge of a wooded ravine. Texas Parks & Wildlife Department was housed in a concrete, sixties looking institutional building in as much of a rural setting as could be managed on the southern boundary of sprawling Austin, Texas.

He had driven the three hours from Houston and timed it to arrive a half hour early. He couldn't sleep the night before anyway. He sat waiting in his car in the parking lot across the driveway from the entrance.

The meeting was a waste of time, he thought, but holding a client's hand as he led him to slaughter was just part of the job. He actually enjoyed it. It never failed that as the deal heated up and was nearing the close, the clients would often be overwhelmed with their own greed and it took on the flavor of impatience, sometimes paranoia, like Magne this time.

It was like a lot of times before, Stubb told himself, but why did this time feel so uncomfortable? He wished that Sam would call. The fact that the hearing turned into a zoo wasn't Sam's fault or very surprising. You never knew what those crazy Goddamn tree-huggers would do. Those "aginers" would try to outlaw polio vaccine if they could. The main thing was that the hearing was done. Now all he had to do was herd the cattle into the pen.

A black Hummer rounded the turn at the far end of the building and headed towards the entrance. This *had* to be Magne, Stubb thought. It pulled up the curb in front of the main entrance and Magne got out. Stubb was already walking across the parking lot toward him.

"Mr. Magne," he called out.

Magne was pulling out a brief case and turned and glanced at Stubb. He made no greeting. I guess the honeymoon is over, Stubb thought.

"Stubb," he said absent-mindedly. "Come on, let's get it." Magne walked briskly into the lobby. On the left was a counter manned by a uniformed TPW officer. Magne said curtly, "Tell Grosse that John Magne is here," and continued walking through the lobby, headed for the stairs.

The officer was taken by surprise but thought he'd better call up to the Executive Director's office before he offended someone important, and his instructions confirmed his judgment.

Magne, with Stubb in tow, climbed the stairs and made a bee-line for Gary Grosse's office.

"Good morning, Mr. Magne," Grosse announced cheerfully, coming out of his office to intercept him. "Let's go to the conference room," and he led the two through his office to a room with a long table.

"Now what's all this crap about permits, Gary?" Magne drove straight to the point.

"If you're talking about your gas drilling project, we haven't issued one," Grosse replied succinctly.

"And why not?" Magne said in a loud, irritated voice.

"Well, sir, for one thing, you haven't applied for one," Grosse replied.

"That's impossible," Stubb blurted.

"Are we talking about the same thing?" Grosse questioned, sensing that the amount of certainty on his visitor's part might suggest a misunderstanding.

"The gas drilling project on the Magne Ranch," Magne exploded impatiently.

"On the edge of the Laguna Madre," Grosse tried to confirm.

"Yes, yes, that one," Magne said.

"Well, I'm telling you, we don't have an application for any drilling project from you or any of your people, Mr. Magne."

Magne turned abruptly to Stubb. "What the hell is this?" he demanded.

"I don't understand," Stubb stammered. "I know for a fact that one of our contractors, Sam Kiel, collected up all the paperwork and sent it all to Fenre Pease in New York and they confirmed receiving it."

"Sam Kiel, you say," Grosse said, turning to pick up his phone. "Marcy, will you get me Eva in Permitting? I need her to come up here right away."

The room was awkwardly quiet as they waited the three minutes for Eva to make it to Grosse's office.

"Yes, sir," she said, walking into the conference room.

"Eva," Grosse asked her, "does the name Sam Kiel mean anything to you?"

"Sam Kiel?" she echoed. "What would this be about?"

"This is Mr. John Magne," Grosse said, nodding to Magne. She nodded back. "He and his assistant here are sure that permit application was made for gas drilling near Port Mansfield, on the Laguna Madre, by a Sam Kiel. Does that ring a bell with you?"

She paused to think but quickly replied, "No sir, I can't say I remember anyone by that name."

"You are sure?" Grosse said to confirm it.

"Yes, sir, pretty sure."

"Thanks, Eva. That's all," Grosse dismissed her and turned back to Magne and Stubb as Eva left the room.

Gross could see that Magne's face was a study in angry bewilderment, and Stubb just looked down at his hands.

"Oh, Mr. Grosse," a voice came from the door. Eva was leaning back into the room. "I just remembered. There was someone inquiring about permitting requirements for something on the Laguna Madre about three months ago. I don't remember the name though."

"What became of it?" Grosse asked.

"Well, we supplied all the forms and instructions. I think I even provided some sample applications and permits that were requested. But that's the last I heard of it."

"Thanks, Eva."

Grosse looked back across the table to Magne. "Mr. Magne, now you know what I know."

"This is ridiculous," Magne said weakly.

Stubb did not know what to say except that he'd get to the bottom of this right away. Then he rallied.

"Mr. Grosse," Stubb asked, "what can we do right now to get this permitting underway?"

Grosse was surprised by the sudden change in the direction of the meeting. "Now? Well, you can go on down to see Eva and she can walk you through the whole process."

"How long do you think this will take?" Stubb asked energetically.

"The application? Well, if you have the impact study done and the engineering reports, I think you could get the paperwork processed in a few weeks. Then you'll need a public hearing, and…"

Magne's cell phone rang.

"Hello," Magne answered.

"Dad!" Junior shouted.

"Junior?"

"Dad, the sheriff's here at the ranch with a search warrant!"

"Hello? Junior? You're breaking up. Can you hear me?"

Magne could only make out a few of the words--"ranch," "search,"--the rest was garbled. He'd have to call Junior back when he was outside the concrete walls of the building or nearer to a cell tower.

Grosse was finishing his explanation to Stubb and offered to take him downstairs personally to get things rolling.

Stubb turned to Magne, "Mr. Magne, I don't know what the story is on this but I suggest we worry about that later, after we get this work done. Leave it to me and I'll go downstairs with Mr. Grosse right now and work this out."

"This is your screw-up, Stubb," Magne growled. "You better make it good."

"Don't worry," Stubb said positively, "I'll handle it from here. And I'll square all this with the people in New York."

Magne shook Grosse's hand and thanked him for any help he could provide, and Grosse realized he could seize on an excellent opportunity to ingratiate himself to one of the state's most powerful figures. Grosse knew he was good at his job. His ex-wife called him the Prince of the Sycophants, but he wasn't familiar with Greek mythology. Anyway, today he would build capital.

On the drive back to Houston, Stubb still nursed the hope that this was all a simple mistake. Maybe Sam had worked through another agency for the permit and that *other* agency was the right one. Magne was no expert and he was given to flights of frenzy as the project neared funding, like lots of other clients before him. Stubb knew nothing about permitting and had relied entirely on Sam to fill in that blind spot. He just needed Sam to explain things.

But now he realized that he had put himself on the line to save the project. He didn't like being so much out in the open. It made him squeamish. He preferred the shadows, the deep background. Anonymity was his favorite color.

He called Calvin Richter.

Richter heard his cell phone vibrate and flipped open the phone to see who was calling. When he saw it was Stubb, he excused himself from the department meeting and stepped out into the hallway.

"What's up, Fes?" Richter answered.

"Hi, Calvin. Listen, do you have a phone number for Sam?"

"No, I don't think I've ever had one, come to think of it," Richter replied, "what's the problem?"

"Man, I *really* need to make contact, and the number I have isn't getting answered."

"Wish I could help."

"Well, don't you two have friends in common? Maybe I can track Sam down that way," Stubb probed.

"Can't say I know any of Sam's friends," Richter said.

"Really," Stubb said, surprised. "I thought you two were old friends."

"Sam and me? No, I didn't even know Sam until that fender bender at the mall. And Sam introduced me to you, remember? At the Renaissance Hotel. That party. I thought *you two* were old friends."

"Calvin, I hadn't even heard of Sam Kiel until that night. You introduced Sam to me," Stubb said, confused.

There was a long pause between them.

"Fes," Richter finally said, "what's going on here?"

"I don't know, Calvin," Stubb said, feeling a sudden sinking feeling, "but I'm beginning to think that Samantha Kiel isn't exactly who we think she is."

Chapter 84

"CAN YOU HEAR ME Dad? Damn!" Junior looked at the screen on his phone. The battery was dead. He decided to sneak back to *Casa Blanca* and wait for his father. He could see the center tower in the distance, craning above the trees.

As he started down a back road to the main house, the line of police cars dashed by on a crossroad.

"That's him!" the trailing vehicle's driver shouted to his partner. The DPS officer then radioed to the other cars and they stopped. Cut off from the main house, Junior headed for the barn complex, the cars in close pursuit.

As he rounded a turn, Junior headed for the mechanic's shop and drove into the open garage door. He grabbed his rifle, jumped from the cab and climbed up a ladder to the loft and took a position at the window facing front, just as the police cars pulled up outside.

"He's in the upper window," a DPS trooper warned the others, "and he's armed!" The officers piled out of their cars and took cover behind a long, metal above-ground tank, drawing their pistols. Jason peered over the top carefully.

Junior was feeling half sober now, adrenaline competing with the alcohol, but he was confused and his heart was racing. He peered over the window sill and could see the officers crouched behind the butane tank. Dumb shits, he said to himself, one shot and they'd be blown to pieces.

"Junior!" the sheriff called out, "throw out the rifle and come out with your hands high in the air."

"What do you want?" Junior responded.

"The rifle. We want the rifle first and then we want you to come out!" the sheriff demanded.

"Get off our land," Junior called back.

"Magne!" yelled the DPS trooper, "you toss out that rifle and surrender or we're going to come in after you."

"Screw you," Junior called back and fired blindly out the window.

The officers dropped behind the tank for cover.

Jason heard a voice, he was sure it was one of the DPS troopers to his left, "Frank?" Then an eerie silence. "Damn, he's been hit!" the voice cried out.

Jason crawled around to the right end of the tank and could see the barn at an angle. Out of the corner of his eye he thought he saw movement toward the back of the barn.

Junior cocked his head at the sound of movement behind him, but he could see nothing. Someone was coming up the ladder. He turned and pointed the rifle toward the ladder.

"Junior?"

"Clint?"

"Yeah. What the hell's going on?"

"Were you down there?" Junior asked confused to see his brother.

"I was in the tractor barn and heard a commotion and come in the back door."

"Goddamn Sheriff is out there!" Junior said, wild eyed.

"What for?"

"They've come for me."

"You? Why you?" Clinton didn't understand; Junior wasn't making any sense.

"I'm not going with them, Clint, I'm not!"

"Calm down, brother. This is getting blown way out of

proportion. Let's just go down and see what they want," Clinton tried to reason.

"No way. I say we wait for Dad," Junior countered.

"He's in Austin, Junior. He won't be here anytime soon. We need to deal with the sheriff now, before somebody gets hurt." Clinton moved closer to his brother, to try to calm him, and to get closer to the rifle.

"When Dad comes, he'll get all this straightened out. We just have to wait for Dad," Junior argued.

"Junior. Dad's not coming. We have to work this out right now. Give me the rifle."

Junior pulled back, holding the rifle close to his chest with his arms crossed over it. "No!" he insisted.

"Give me the gun, Goddamn it, Junior," Clinton demanded and lunged at his brother to pull the rifle away from him. They struggled.

"There, in the window!" the sheriff alerted the officers.

Crack!

Suddenly Junior felt Clinton's pull on the rifle go limp and he saw in his brother's eyes a startled look. Then Clint let go and fell backward, off the loft and into the bed of the pick-up below.

"No!" Junior cried out. He threw the rifle down and dashed down the ladder to his brother. Clinton lay awkwardly and perfectly still, staring with glassy eyes, the look of surprise still on his face.

The officers stormed the garage and surrounded the pick-up. The sheriff climbed onto the truckbed and pulled Junior's hands behind him and locked him in hand-cuffs. Junior was crying out loud now. "Clint!" he called and called again.

A DPS trooper pulled Junior off the pick-up and dragged him to the ground. "You son of a bitch, you have the right to remain silent," he screamed.

Jason jumped up on the truckbed and put his forefinger on Clinton's jugular and felt for a pulse.

"I'll call EMS," a deputy volunteered.

"Tell them to hurry for the trooper," Jason said solemnly, sliding his fingers over Clinton's eyelids, "this fellow's not going to need them."

"Neither will the trooper," the deputy said.

The DPS trooper holding Junior left him to the sheriff and ran back to his partner lying behind the tank.

One of the deputies climbed up to the loft, found the rifle and brought it back down.

"Let me see that," the sheriff said, taking the rifle and studying the script on the barrel. It read *Merkel*. He compared the serial number with the email printout from the crime lab. A match. "It's the murder weapon," he said.

Chapter 85

BANG.

Monde jumped out of his desk chair, startled by the loudness of it. Mario Morales tripped, and would have fallen on his face if he hadn't extended his arms and slapped his hands against Congressman Monde's office door, but he never lost his stride after he dashed half way across the capitol building, up three flights of stairs and into Monde's office.

"My god," he gasped, trying to catch his breath.

"What is it, Mario?" Monde yelled, infected by Mario's excitement.

"Magne," he said, gulping for air, "my father…killed."

"Your father's been killed?" Monde repeated in horror.

"No," Mario tried again, "My father called me…Magne has been killed."

"What? How?" Monde blurted incoherently.

"DPS officers…shot him."

"Shot! Oh my god," Monde said, suddenly needing to sit down. Mario sank into the chair across the desk.

"What happened? What did your dad tell you?" Monde demanded details.

"My father took some of his deputies and some DPS officers to Magne's ranch to execute a search warrant…"

"A search warrant! Why?"

"Let me finish," Mario insisted. "They were investigating a rifle that was used in a murder. It was registered to John Magne, so they went to see if they could find it or find out what happened to it."

"But why did they shoot Magne?"

"I'm coming to that. They get to the ranch house and Magne's son, I think they call him Junior, well, he resists them and takes off. They chase him and corner him and there's a shoot out. One of the troopers hit the Magne boy and killed him."

"So it wasn't the elder John Magne they shot. It was his son," Monde tried to verify.

"Yeah, the one named Clinton, I think."

"Not the junior?"

"No, the other boy."

"That's Clinton, all right. Oh, my god. I can't believe it. Where was Magne, senior?"

"Don't know, but he wasn't there."

"This is unbelievable. You're sure you have this right, now, Mario…"

"My dad's the sheriff. He was there. It's right."

"So what did they do with Junior?"

"He's arrested for the murder of some fisherman and a DPS officer."

"Fisherman, fisherman…wasn't that woman at the hearing, the one who suddenly had Grider's original report, wasn't she the one whose husband's body was found last week?" Monde asked, putting the pieces together.

"Anajita Paredes. Yeah, it was her husband, Octavio, that Magne supposedly killed."

Monde's brain spun like a dervish. He could see exactly where this was going. It was going to look for all the world that Magne tried to silence the opposition by killing it off, gangland style. The D.A. would be all over this now. The FBI would be swarming. The press would have a field day. FOX, CNN, you name it, would be scratching each other's eyes out to land the story. An old fashioned cock fight.

The Magne ship was going down and so was everybody on it. Everybody, that is, except Lencho Monde.

"Mario," Monde reached across the desk and took Mario by the collar and dragged him up close to his face and said in a tone of earnest and specific instruction, "listen to me. I don't care who calls about Magne, this shooting, the drilling project, the report, I don't care what, you are to tell them one thing and one thing only. We know nothing about any of it. Do you hear me? Nothing. The Magnes are just constituents. Got that?"

"Yes, sir."

"Now go to your office and call the Defense Department. I want to be on an Air Force plane before the cock crows tomorrow morning."

"Going where, Congressman?" Mario asked, perplexed.

"I don't care. Anywhere, Taiwan, Korea, Japan, the Philippines. It doesn't matter. Just far away, out of touch and for at least a couple of weeks," he said in a rapid staccato delivery. "I think it's time I reviewed the troops, don't you?"

Chapter 86

STUBB DROPPED THE phone when it suddenly started buzzing. He was a nervous wreck. Finally, Sam was calling in.

"Fes?" he heard Calvin Richter say so weakly he could hardly hear him.

"Calvin? Is that you?" Stubb asked.

"Yes. It's me, Calvin," he said in an odd, feeble way.

"What's wrong with you?"

"Me? I'm sick. I've been throwing up," he explained.

"What, did you get food poisoning?" Stubb asked.

There was a hoarse laugh, almost demented, then coughing and wheezing. "I just got a call from Casady."

"Casady?"

"He's the lead attorney on the Magne IPO. I guess I should say *was* the lead attorney."

"What do you mean *was*?"

"Goddamnit, Fes, they've called it off," Richter said, sobbing.

"Calvin, what are you talking about? What do you mean they called it off? What does that mean?" Stubb's heart was pumping double speed now.

"Fenre Pease is pulling it off the table. They're not going to issue. It's over."

"What?!" Stubb felt his pores stinging. "What the hell happened?"

"Everything. It's just all screwed. That impact report turned out to be bogus, the FBI is crawling all over it, they're talking to Stembark, Spentas has found a conservation easement, I hear the SEC is going to investigate, Monde's bailed out, and now this Magne murder…"

"Did you say *murder*? Calvin, did you say murder?" Stubb jolted upright.

"Yeah, they've arrested one of Magne's kids, the one called Junior. They say he killed somebody opposing the permit, or something, you haven't heard about it? Shit, it's all over the news!"

Stubb suddenly felt like his vision was tunneling. He could see a dark cone around his center field of vision. He was breathing hard now. He laid the phone down, hanging up.

A panic began to wash over him. He sat rod straight in the chair and stared with big eyes directly ahead of him, seeing nothing but a kaleidoscope of images and colors. He thought he might pass out.

He didn't know how long he had been sitting there, but suddenly he was aware that he was awake. He reached over and turned on his desk light, then stared at the Magne Project board above his desk. He didn't have time to think about this now. He needed to act.

He stood and wiped the eraser across the melamine board as if he were trying to rub the white out of it. He collected up his files and began feeding them into the shredder, choking it. He ran to the kitchen and got a black lawn bag. Back in his office he began to dump every file he had into the trash bag, shaking pages out of binders, tearing at paper clipped packets. He was working feverishly now. He didn't know how close they were. He didn't know if they were gathering outside in the yard now or if they were climbing into vans at their offices, but he knew they were coming.

He dragged two full bags out to his car and dumped them

in the trunk. He ran back into his bedroom and began throwing clothes into a large valise. He scraped the toiletries off the bathroom counter into another carry-on bag, and dragged everything into his office. He found his passport, then opened the wall safe and unloaded every bit of cash and his Rolex into a briefcase.

He stood in the center of the office, surveying the room, looking for anything he might have missed. His adrenaline was pumping through his veins like a torrent through a fire hose. He had to go. Now!

Stubb loaded all his bags and baggage into his car's back seat and climbed into the driver's seat. Maybe he ought not open the garage door until he took a look first, he thought. He climbed back out of the car and ran into the kitchen to peer out the window to the front yard.

Clear.

Back to the car he ran, jumped in, pushed the remote to open the garage door and backed out fast, screeched to a stop, changed gears and peeled away from the house. He couldn't stop looking at his rear view mirror. Every flashing light--white, red, yellow--spooked him. He didn't start breathing normally until he was on the expressway.

"Damn, damn, damn," he cursed out loud, strangling the steering wheel.

He began replaying that night in his head. They had been practically done planting *Repete*. It had all gone like clockwork, that is, until they were interrupted.

It was so ingenious, so simple, so elegant, he said to himself. *Repete* was merely a breadboard of common Radio Shack parts that anyone could buy. A few microphones to listen, a processor to interpret the sounds and calculate the "right" sound waves, and a few speakers to broadcast those waves, all in a plastic black box. And the knot that tied all these strings together was any electrical engineering graduate student with a load of school debt, a dash of discretion and unfettered by absolutes.

Stubb and Junior had waited until an hour before dusk Friday evening and snuck out to the test site at Magne's Landing to plant *Repete* at about five feet below the surface. It was hard physical work for a corpulent, balding accountant, Stubb complained, but it insured a glowing report from the geologists who are due on site the next Monday.

Repete's job was to sing harmony. When the sonar test unit sent down sound waves in search of layers and pockets indicative of gas, it listened for that certain sound, those particular sound wave echoes that were the signature. Stubb liked to call those sent down sounds *Pete*. When his little black box heard those waves, it broadcast out the signature echo. *Pete* then *Repete*.

Above ground, the engineers' sonar unit would read "bingo"!

So frigging simple.

Neither of them had noticed him, they had been too busy, so Stubb didn't know how long he had been there, sitting in his fishing boat, not a hundred yards away. When Stubb first got a glimpse of him, it was a shock. Who was he working for? How much did he see? Stubb told Junior to bring him some binoculars, but all he had was the scope on his old hunting rifle. Junior went back to the shack to collect some shovels while Stubb peered through the narrow cone of dim light, trying to focus on the fisherman's face, but it was getting too dark, too fast.

He knew that in a few minutes he'd be practically invisible. Stubb could only make out a silhouette, but even that was becoming fuzzy. He had to act before it was too late. He slipped his forefinger onto the trigger, set the cross-hairs in the middle of the fuzzy form, then squeezed.

Pop. That was the only sound. Stubb looked through the scope and saw only the outline of the boat. In two seconds Stubb had made the mental calculation. Nobody was worth risking his million dollars for.

"What were you shooting at?" Junior asked, running toward him.

"Just some old bird, I guess," Stubb answered coolly.

"Damn, Festor, you can't shoot birds out here. Hell, they're nearly all protected. What're you trying to do, get us arrested?" Junior chided him.

"Don't worry, I didn't hit anything to speak of."

He took his handkerchief and wiped the stock and trigger down before he handed the rifle back to Junior. He told Junior to go on home. He'd finish up. After Junior had gone, he took a shovel and waded out to the boat and found the old man floating face down in the water. It was a little, skinny old man. He had little trouble pulling the body along the shallow water to a knoll a couple of miles south, then loaded him on his back and carried him inland a few hundred yards to a water trough. Even in the soft sand, it took him over an hour to dig a hole at an angle, under the trough, dump the body in, then cover it over.

On the way back to the Landing, the norther blew in and by the time he made it to where the boat had been, the wind had carried it out into the deeper water, too deep for Stubb to retrieve it.

He wasted no time jumping into his car and putting as many miles as he could between himself and that place. He drove straight back to Houston.

Now he was headed south, eventually; but Mexico was closer, traveling due west to Laredo. He wouldn't stop until he made the border. Then he'd catch the first plane he could to Argentina.

It was the race of his life.

Eventually, Junior was going to talk, not that anyone would believe a spoiled lying drunk. There were no witnesses. No one knew that they were together that night. Even Magne was sure he'd gone back to Houston. He was careful not to leave any trail, not even credit card charges. But there wasn't any point in hanging around for the fall out. He'd come back in a year or so, when things had cooled down.

For a fleeting instant, Stubb wondered who that man in the boat was, then thought it really didn't much matter now, did it?

Chapter 87

"SOPHIE?"

"Yes, dear, is that you Amesha, honey?"

"Guilty as charged," she said. "Just checking in. Did you get the fax off?"

"Sure did, much as I hate working these damned machines," Sophie complained.

"You done good, Sophie. Hey, when do I get to talk to that daughter of yours? She's not answering her cell."

"It's going to be a while, Amesha. She's gone off to New Orleans with that Grider fellow. They went to go get his sailboat."

"Really," Amesha said as if she had just discovered a juicy secret. "Doesn't she know the deed is done?"

"Yes, but it's looking like *the dude* isn't quite yet."

Amesha laughed out loud at the words coming from that woman's mouth. "Shame on you, Sophie," she teased.

"Oh, once upon a time, honey…," she said.

"So is this anything serious?" Amesha asked.

"I don't know, but I'm finding big feathers all over the place down here."

"Molting?"

"Starting to look like it to me."

"Wow," this *is* serious.

"Amesha, I think we might have to get used to a new way of things," Sophie began slowly.

"What do you mean?"

"Angela. I think we ought to let her go."

"Oh, Sophie, it isn't up to us. There's no way Angela will drop out of the movement. After all these years. All these projects we've worked together? So many innocents being tortured and killed everyday, no way she'll give it up. No way."

"Amesha, honey," Sophie could hear the rising concern in Amesha's voice, "You, me and Angela, we're always going to be committed to animals. They are our lives. But it's a long war and not all of us can be soldiers in it for life. Some of us are going to move on. I think Angela is there. I think, for all she's done for the movement, for us, we owe it to her to let her go."

There was a long silent pause on the other end of the line. Amesha was stunned, but as she thought, she recognized that yearning in her own life, that want of a loving relationship with another person, the kind you could lose yourself in. She understood completely what Sophie was saying, and she loved Angela as a sister. She wouldn't stand in the way of her happiness.

"I'm going to miss her terribly," she said finally, tearing up.

"I know, honey, I know. But you do understand why you can't contact her. There are too many crossing trails," Sophie pleaded.

"Of course," Amesha said in resignation, "But maybe, someday…" she said hopefully.

"Maybe someday," Sophie repeated, knowing it could never be.

Sophie put down the phone. From her little house in Port Isabel on Huisache Street, she could see through the back window the old Magne Mansion that was now to be the new historical museum. It was a fitting analog, she thought. The big, strong, once beautiful mansion and the little cottage. The powerful and the meek.

For all its grandness, the mansion was a decayed icon of a time and life withering away. Now, she, the simple girl grown old, would come into the stewardship of the grand old house to make it new again. Her eyes rested on the middle window on the third floor. It was there that they would meet and make passionate love so many years ago.

The third John Magne was the only truly good man of the Magne brood, she thought. He was handsome and strong and they shared a love of all things natural. She never knew what excuses he made to be at the Port Isabel house while the rest of his family stayed on the ranch, but they were splendid times, she reminisced, feeling a certain warmth as she did. Her favorite of these were the autumn days they spent exploring the Laguna and collecting specimens. This time of the year always reminded her of those wonderful days. They learned about every species of bird in the region and knew details of the delicate ecosystem that not even experts knew. They also learned to love one another.

When she became pregnant with Angela, he was delighted and provided for every need, even the expensive private schools up north. Angela was twenty-one when he died in 1981, but she never knew John Magne III was her father.

Sophie turned from the window and sat in the leather chair that faced the hearth. She stared at the painting hanging over the mantle. It was an original Audubon that John had given her on one of their "anniversaries." She always treasured it. To the right of it was a square of wallpaper that was lighter than that surrounding it. She had forgotten. She rose and walked to the table next to the fax machine. The page was where she left it.

It was an official looking document, even stamped with registration numbers and bore an engraved seal of the government on the top of it. She gingerly turned it over and placed it on the glass, then laid the matting, followed by the backboards. Carefully, she pushed down the little metal teeth that held the board in. She then re-hung the frame on the nail in the vacant space.

"A Grant of an Easement for Conservation," she read aloud.

It was John's last gift, a gesture of incalculable meaning to her. In his last months of life, when it became clear that the cancer treatments weren't going to work, he asked her what was the one thing he could do for her. She said that more than anything else in the world, she wanted to preserve the beauty they had so lovingly enjoyed those many years together.

Tears welled up in her sea blue eyes, then escaped to run down her cheeks.

She thought of Angela and her new found love and it brought a smile to her, a familiar joy, long past but never forgotten.

"One day, John" she said weeping softly, "one day."

Chapter 88

"I'VE GOT TO ADMIT," Angela said as she sat on the salon settee tickling Moses' twitching ears and watching Jack flipping pancakes, "you do have your pluses."

"And this is one of them?" he complained, wondering what soy milk batter was going to taste like.

"Well, we've got to start modestly," she laughed. "You are quite a project, Jack Grider."

He smiled at the truth of the statement and for the gratitude of circumstance. He didn't remember ever being as happy as he was with Angela, and at the core of it was how he was beginning to feel about himself. It all began with her.

"Who'd have ever thought," she said idly, as if her words rode on the back of a breaching dolphin, that then slipped silently back below the surface.

"What?" Jack said.

"You know…how things have turned out," she said.

"It is pretty amazing, when you think about it," he agreed. "I mean, what were the chances that we two particularly would end up on the same aisle of the same Target in the same town and at the very same time?" he marveled. "And then you showing up at my house for the garage sale," he added, "you know how close we came to never meeting?"

"Oh, I don't know," Angela disagreed, "I think Fate has a

way of seeing things turn out as they should." She wouldn't add for Jack to hear that it was especially true when Fate's name was *Angela*. "Take Moses, here," she added. "You two were meant to find each other." Of course, neither she nor Moses would ever let on how Angela had rescued the kitten from the Animal Shelter the week before and followed Jack to the Target and planted the basket next to Jack's Jeep that day. It was the first test and Jack passed it with flying colors.

"But take that impact report," Jack argued. "One last copy in the world and it survives to show up at the very last possible moment in that public hearing. I mean, you've got to wonder why Anahida wouldn't have tossed that with all the other scrap she took that day."

"It is a lucky thing, all right," Angela said, smiling at the whole idea of chance at the hands of purpose. When Sophie, Amesha and she had started their plan, they knew that a Jack Grider had written an impact report. It was a public document. It was just a hunch that she'd be able to turn him. She never dreamed that it would be he who would turn her.

"I'll say. If it weren't for Anahida, we'd be anchored next to a drilling rig and the Laguna would look like an industrial zone."

"Quite true, Mr. Grider, quite true," she agreed. "You know what Anahida told me before we left?"

"No, what?"

"She said she's thinking of running for Monde's congressional seat."

"Now that's a wow," Jack yelled in approval.

Angela went up through the companionway and stretched out on the portside cockpit bench. *Wist* was anchored in a cove in the Laguna Madre just north of Port Mansfield. It was December and the sun set early. Soon she would need a jacket as the cool evening breeze won out over the last of the warming sun rays. She held up her wine glass and let the light play through it.

She saw a world washed in a crimson filter, dark and eerie, but as the sun began its swan song and slipped behind far distant thunderheads, it seemed to toss up handfuls of gold and orange and red, then wash them across the aquamarine sky. It was a Maxfield Parrish fantasy. She was dazzled by it and lost interest in the prism the wine made.

"Jack," she called out, "quick, come see this!"

Jack bounded up the steps to the cockpit and gasped at the sight of it. They sat nestled together until the last of the darkening hues turned to charcoal and then they listened to the music of the Laguna at night.

"This is so beautiful," Angela whispered, "I don't think I could ever give it up."

"Don't," Jack said.

"Easier said than done," she sighed.

"Angela, if there's one thing I've learned from you it is that we can be the heroes of our own lives."

"Well, sir, you are quite the Pip," she teased.

At that Jack reached down to Angela's woven-straw bag and pulled out her cell phone. Angela suddenly froze and held her breath.

"My god," Jack said, "it's even *RED*! Talk about 'A' types," he said.

"Give it to me, Jack," she said suddenly urgent, stretching to take it from him.

Jack held it away from her reach briefly then let her take it. "Angela," he said, "this is your tether to that other world. Let it go."

Angela took the phone and reached to put it back into her bag, stopping midway. She looked into Jack's eyes. She wondered what he meant by that, and for a long moment she tried to read him. She saw something in his eyes she had not noticed before, and she knew this was the only man she wanted to spend the rest of her life with.

Angela handed the phone back to Jack and, after a tentative pause, nodded.

Jack took it and stood up next to the helm, pulled his arm all the way back, and in slow motion, like swinging at the piñata, the arm came around him and he threw the red phone deep into the distant darkness.

"Adios, 'Sam'…and good riddance," Angela said softly, then pulled Jack down and wound herself around him. "I love you, Jack. I want to marry you, but there's so much you don't know about me."

"And so much you don't know about me," Jack said. "What if we live the rest of our lives in the future, Angela? I've already done the past once. That's enough."

Angela nodded.

"Are you going to save me, Jack?" she asked.

"God does work in mysterious ways," Jack said quietly.

The world began to disappear in a long, warm and delicate kiss.

Angela moved her lips against Jack's ear.

"Sometimes, Jack," she whispered, "it's the angels."

Chapter 89

GABRIELA WAS SURPRISED to see the ceiling lights of the library turned off and the book-lined walls darkened. When she looked in, the only light came from a green-glass shaded lamp on the desk. In the cone of light it cast, she found John Magne sitting at the desk, hunched forward, hands cradling a snifter filled with Glenfiddich, staring, confused, at the pistol on the worn leather desk blotter.

"John?" she asked. "What are you doing?" He didn't answer. So she asked again.

"What the hell do you think I'm doing?" he said in a slurring, hoarse and gruff voice, saturated with alcohol. "I'm watching four generations, four generations," he bellowed, "of sweat and blood," he paused to get his breath, "evaporate to nothing."

"Oh, John," she said, trying to console him, "it isn't your fault." There was a hollow quality to her words that surprised even her. "You need something to eat. I've fixed you your favorite."

"You? Where's Mica?" he asked weakly.

"I've sent them all home for the weekend. It's just you and me tonight."

"I've lost it all, Gabriela. All of it." He looked up at her and spoke in a little boy's plaintive cry, "They took my boys, Gabriela, my *boys*!" He was weeping now. "They've broken the ranch. It's broken. It's ruined," he said in a rising rage, heaving the crystal snifter across the room, where it shattered into slivers against the wall. "It isn't fair," Magne mumbled weakly, from the depths of sadness. "It wasn't supposed to be like this."

Gabriela walked slowly around the desk and stood behind his right shoulder and leaned over him, nuzzling her face in the rough of his unshaven cheek. Magne's eyes closed and breathed in deep the lilac scent of Gabriela's perfume. Slowly, he moved his hand across the desk and took the pistol in his turned down right palm and dragged it toward him. As he slipped his index finger on to the trigger, he felt Gabriela's gloved hand cover his. He relaxed at the smooth touch of it.

"Now, John," she whispered softly into his ear, as she carefully lifted his hand, pulling it up, her fingers deftly moving around his to the pistol. He was too broken to resist. She drew up his hand until his forearm rested on its elbow. He felt her finger caress his index finger, and gave way when she gently twisted the pistol.

Gabriela lowered her head behind his chair then pushed John Magne's finger against the trigger.

His head exploded and the blood sprayed the glass doors on the bookcase to the rear and left of his chair.

An eerie blue haze hung in the leaden air of the library, as Gabriela carefully laid John Magne's hand back on his desk, the pistol still firm in his grip. She walked around the right side, away from the blood, careful not to leave any trace she was there. She went to the laundry room and removed all her clothing and her gloves and put them into the clothes washer, adding soap and bleach. She walked naked through the darkened house, up the stairs to the bedroom, and directly into the shower.

She stood in the marble walled chamber and stared at the gilded handle. Tears ran from her brown eyes into the corners of her mouth. They tasted of salt.

Gabriel de Santander turned the spigot then raised her face

into the warm wet stream of cleansing waters. She saw again the plea in Mama 'Nita's eyes, her grandmother, when they used to sit on the verandah of the old Santander family hacienda in La Villa de Santiago, just outside Monterrey, Mexico. Long after everyone else had wearied of her incessant retelling of the story of how her mother was killed by the Magnes at the *Hacienda Sal del Rey*, Gabriel would listen, holding her grandmother's hand and comforting her.

Mama 'Nita's full name was Juanita Paredes Santander, and on the day she died, Gabriel heard her asking God why He had been so cruel. The tears still lingered on her death gaze when the question why there was no justice expelled with her last breath.

Gabriel bowed her head and let the shower spray wash over her like baptismal waters. And made the sign of the cross, then whispered softly.

"*Por fin, la justicia.*"

For more about Laguna and the author,
visit www.putegnat.com